MIND SPLIT
Ross Richdale

The bees that attack a group of students at a graduation party are far from ordinary. Every student is stung once in the neck, except Madison who is stung twice and collapses.

When she wakes up she finds she is in a new strange place called Buckoway but still remembers Earth. Her friends have no memories of home. Buckoway is a strange hybrid of modern and old civilizations. There is electricity but no motor vehicles, aircraft or firearms. It is as if something wanted to recreate a simple society but with modern health and living facilities With wagonmasters, Hamish and Sean she sets out to find the reason she has been transferred to this new world.

Madison awakes from her next sleep to find herself back on Earth and again with her friends. They, however, have no memory of this Buckoway. Madison realizes there are two versions of her friends. She alone seems to travel back and forth between her two existences whenever she awakens.

One of the weagonmasters' jobs is to bring in the bodies of newcomers from a strange boat called *Gentle Lady*. Hamish does not know where the boat comes from or who operates it. The newcomers are taken in the wagons back to Buckoway where they are awakened and join their society. No newcomers know they were originally from Earth. With help from the Earth and Buckoway versions of Kirsty, Madison attempts to find the reason for this strange situation.

PURRBOOKS

National Library of New Zealand Cataloguing-in-Publication Data

Richdale, Ross, 1941-
Mind split / Ross Richdale.
Previously pub.: 2001 (e-book).
ISBN 978-1-877438-24-0 (pbk.)
I. Title.
NZ823.3—dc 22

Purrbooks
Palmerston North
New Zealand

Cover design by Ross Richdale

CHAPTER ONE

The dark sky turned pale in the east and the all night party entered a quiet stage as the graduates drank their full, participated in other ways to celebrate and returned to gather on the patio. Twenty or more were awake and talking quietly when the attack came.

Bees descended in a swarm and engulfed everyone. It was a planned attack, premeditated and ruthless. Screams and waving arms failed to dissuade the creatures. Sobs and groans followed as shocked bodies were pierced with violent stings. It was over within moments after everyone there was stung ... once in the neck. Nobody was excluded and not one person received more than one sting. That may have been the intention but even the best-made plans of whatever it was that organized the assault could not have anticipated one slight imperfection.

Madison Evans stood on her wobbly legs when the attack came, felt the agonizing pierce of her skin on the side of her neck and flung her hand up to ward off the insect. She stepped forward but her weak right leg crumpled and she crashed against one of the other girls who was sitting on the carpet beside her. Just as a bee headed for this girl's neck, Madison bumped it aside and the sting pierced her own ankle.

Her reaction was one of surprise and relief. For the first time since the car accident six weeks earlier she felt pain in her leg. It wasn't the piercing sting still throbbing in her neck but a low prick. She never really had time to absorb the news for her body reacted again. Her friends around began to spin, a sort of purple cloud hovered before her eyes and she grabbed a supporting arm of her friend, Kirsty.

"Two of the bastards stung me and I don't feel too good..." She collapsed on the floor.

"Madison," Kirsty screamed. "Oh my God. Help me someone. Madison's collapsed."

But no help arrived. Everyone seemed to be in a drunken state and wandered around crashing into each other. Most of the girls were crying in pain while the boys bravely attempted to show male fortitude by squinting back tears and holding their wounded arms. Haunted cries rung throughout the patio as everyone held their necks in a futile attempt to stop the pain.

And it did stop and for everyone, it was at exactly the same time. As the swarm flew off in a cloud, the victims' necks stopped throbbing and became just a tender spot. It was as if an anaesthetic had kicked in ... and it had.

Except for Madison lying unconscious on the floor they all stopped and began speaking at once. Kirsty's screams pierced their minds and they turned to gaze at the girl on the floor.

Norris Moore ignored the girl he'd been chatting with and tore across the room.

"She's having a fit," he cried as he bent down beside her. "She'll come through it. It's happened several times since the accident."

"It's not," Kirsty gasped. "Look at her. She's like a ghost and isn't moving."

"She's been stung too," Norris said. He grabbed Madison's wrist and frowned.

"Well?" someone else muttered.

"There's no pulse," Norris gasped. "No ... wait a minute. It's very faint but ... Hell could someone call for help?"

"I've already done it," one girl replied.

*

The two air force officers ignored the *No Admittance to Operating Theatre Wing* and turned to the stern nurse who intercepted them.

"This is a restricted area," the nurse said in an icy voice. "The security guard should not have let you in. Please leave at once."

One officer spoke. "Colonel Brad Davis," he retorted and flashed an identity card. "We believe a young woman was sting earlier by ... err... bees and is being operated on. It is imperative that we speak to the surgeon before he proceeds with any corrective surgery."

"It is an emergency operation. I cannot..."

"You will, madam," Davis cut in. "Not only is this young woman's life threatened but there are far more serious consequences to consider. I have a code red security order directly from Washington."

The nurse held the cold gaze, nodded and took a cellphone from her pocket. "Is Doctor Joel Mitchell still in the theatre with Miss Evans?" she asked. She listened and nodded "I see ... two air force officers are here and wish to speak to Doctor Mitchell immediately... Yes I know that. Apparently... " Her voice continued in a hushed but authoritative tone. Principal Nurse Zanna Perez was the second highest staff member on duty that morning and except for Mitchell himself, her word was law.

*

Mitchell, still dressed in his green surgical gown, waved at two chairs in his office and sat in the third.

"This time it was different, Brad," he said.

"How!"

"Every victim except my patient fitted in the same category as the other cases reported, that is a male or female between the ages of eighteen and twenty seven who was stung in the neck. They suffered initial pain and had following drowsiness symptoms but should recover within a few hours."

"But this girl?"

"She was stung twice," the surgeon said.

"Circumstances?" Davis retorted.

"Madison Evans was involved in a car accident several weeks ago. Her spine was bruised and she has only recently been able to walk. Her right leg is still weak and she requires a crutch to help her..."

"Go on," Davis cut in.

"We believe that when she was stung on the neck, she toppled sideways, her weak leg couldn't support her and she fell against a female colleague who was about to be stung."

Davis nodded.

"Her leg hit the other girl's face and the sting was injected into the calf of her leg rather than her friend's neck. This second injection caused her body to react violently and almost killed her."

"Why?"

"There are two possibilities. One, the double dosage poisoned her system or there was a reaction with the chemicals already in her body."

"She'd been taking drugs?"

The surgeon glanced up. "Not in the way you think. She had a moderate quantity of alcohol in her bloodstream but there were no other drugs except one, a subscription drug used to relieve the ongoing pain in her damaged leg. It is basically a morphine substitute that... "

"Okay, but what did you find?"

"You were right," Mitchell whispered and took a small phial from his gown pocket. "The sting is an artificial metallic device, not an insect sting at all. I glanced at it under our electronic microscope and it appears to be an instrument a hundred times smaller than anything we use at the present time is. In size it's as big as a comma one would write in a sentence.

Even at that minute size if it had travelled to my patent's heart it would have proved fatal."

"Why?"

"The electrical charge the instrument discharges would have stopped her heart beating. It would have been as if she had touched a live twenty thousand volt power line."

"You only got one device," the second officer asked.

"Yes. As usual the one in her neck had already reached her brain by the time she arrived here. An operation there would have been too difficult to perform." The doctor looked up. "I am not about to kill any of my patients to provide you with the injected device."

"So we got lucky? " Davis grunted as he reached for the phial.

"I believe so."

"Will the girl recover?"

"Yes. Like everyone else who has been attacked, she will be suffering no long term consequences."

"Except for having some goddamn monitoring device embedded in her brain," Davis whispered. He stood up and reached out for the surgeon's hand.

"This is classified information, Doctor Mitchell," he said. "The girl suffered from a reaction after being stung from a particularly nasty strain of Asian bee. Understand?"

Mitchell nodded.

"She is reacting to antibiotics and should be able to return to her normal life..."

"The media will be curious as to why every patent was only stung once and always in the neck?"

"I'll get a botanist to make up a story," Davis said. "Something about this particular type of bee being able to smell if a victim has already been stung."

"So we've proved your theory that it is not a natural sting but what of the carrier. Was it a real bee?"

"We doubt it, Doctor. We believe it is a flying drone, artificially made and pre-programmed to attack highly educated young people."

Mitchell frowned. "How can you be so precise?"

"Nothing goes beyond these walls," Davis cautioned.

"I realize that and have already signed your secrecy documents."

"Very well," the colonel replied. "As far as we a can ascertain there have been forty seven attacks over the last four years. Every one has been in similar circumstances with a gathering of educated young people being attacked. These range from a private girl's high school in New Zealand to a

6

university in Scotland, two universities in Canada, one in Brazil and others throughout the world. To date, sixty percent of the victims are female but last night's attack was almost exactly fifty-fifty male and female." The Colonel sighed. "That is really all we know. That microscopic implant you found in the girl's leg is the first one that has not become imbedded inside a victim's brain."

"And what is the scenario, Colonel Davis?"

"We are being observed by an alien species. For what reason we have no idea. The victims are like birds with a radio-tracking device clipped on their leg. The victim carries on with his or her ordinary life without realizing every movement, every heartbeat, perhaps even their conversations are being monitored and transmitted to, we know not where."

"A radio transmitter?"

"Crudely put," Davis replied. "I would imagine the technology used would make our monitoring devices appear as effective as the flags the Admiralty used on their sailing ships in the civil war." The air force officer stepped towards the door. "Thank you, Doctor Mitchell. I shall forward you a report on the device you cut from the girl's leg."

"Subject to the usual censorship, I gather."

"Of course," Davis whispered and walked out.

*

"And how are you, Madison?" Doctor Mitchell knew his patient from her previous operations and his voice showed warmth often missing from a doctor's beside manner.

"That second sting in my leg, doctor. I felt it."

Joel Mitchell frowned. "Are you sure? Sometimes you can get those ghost sensations I told you about."

Madison shook her head. "It wasn't as painful as the sting on my neck but I definitely felt it."

"I see. Do you feel anything in your right leg now?"

"I'm not sure. Everything else is sort of numbed. I haven't really thought about it until now."

"Okay, we'll do our little test then."

The doctor took out a needle and lifted the sheet so Madison's leg was exposed. He dabbed a swab in cleaning alcohol and rubbed the top of her leg. Madison jumped.

"It feels cold," she said. "Did you prick me?"

Joel frowned. "I never got that far," he said. "You say you felt the fluid?"

7

"Sort of. I can't recall any touch but it definitely felt cold."

"And this," the doctor said.

Madison frowned in disappointment. "I felt nothing."

Joel smiled. "Good. I didn't do anything."

"So you still don't believe me when I ... oh hell you just pricked me above the knee didn't you?" Madison wriggled up into a sitting position and stared at the doctor. "The sheet's cold. I can feel it with both my feet. Both my feet Doctor Mitchell ... Oh my God!"

"What is it Madison?"

"My whole leg is aching. My right leg is aching."

The doctor frowned and examined the leg. The section where he had cut into the vein and extracted the slither of metal was bandaged but, otherwise, the leg appeared no different than before with pallid skin and loose unused muscle.

"But, why the returned sensations?" he muttered to himself

Every test he made showed a positive reaction. It was as if feeling had returned to Madison's whole leg from her heel and toes right up to her upper leg.

"Would like to attempt to stand?" he asked. "I can give you a hand."

Madison nodded. She slowly swung herself around on the bed and let her feet touch the floor. At this stage she normally used a crutch to assist her as she placed her left foot out, balanced and brought her right foot forward. Now if she could do this without a crutch!

In a burst of confidence she swung out, her left leg hit the carpet and crumbled. She crashed on the floor with a thump.

"Hell, that hurt," she grumbled and accepted the doctor's hand.

He steadied rather than pulled her and she hopped up onto her good leg. This time she placed her right leg firmly down before she shifted her weight onto it. Again it crumbled but the doctor anticipated the action and caught her.

"Well, that part is normal," he said.

"What do you mean? It was awful," Madison snapped.

"But normal for someone attempting to use a leg that's been out of action for six weeks. You can't expect to suddenly walk out the door."

"But I can feel the carpet. The initial pain has gone. It feels normal, Doctor."

"So you'll soon be able to use it to walk normally, Madison. I don't know why but feeling has returned to your leg. Now you have to teach your body to handle your new improved condition."

"But I will be able to walk properly, Doctor Mitchell?"

Joel smiled. "After your accident I only gave you a thirty percent chance of ever stepping out of a wheelchair. You achieved that three weeks ago and now..."

"How long, Doctor?"

"To be frank, I have no idea, Madison. There may be a relapse and you'll lose your feeling again. I do know that that sting had something to do with your recovery, but whether it was a trigger that set your body working again or something in the chemical composition of the fluid injected into you, I'm not sure." "

"Like snake venom being used in some medicines?"

"Something like that," the doctor said. "Let's get you back into bed, shall we? You can try walking again tomorrow."

Madison nodded. "Thank you," she whispered.

"Oh yes," Mitchell said. "There's a young guy called Norris and your friend Kirsty in the waiting room who want to visit. I can send them away if you wish."

Madison grinned. "I'll see them," she said. "Were they stung, too?"

"I believe so. Everyone with you last night except the girl you bumped out of the way, were stung."

Madison laughed. "It's a wonder it wasn't Kirsty. I reckon she has a charmed life."

"I'll tell them they can come in ten minutes," the doctor said. "The nurse will give you a little freshen up first." He gave Madison's hand a tiny squeeze and walked out.

*

The microsurgery that Joel Mitchell used to find and extract the foreign substance in Madison's leg had been recorded and stored on the computer. The doctor would normally just file it away for future reference but the present situation made him curious. After he left his patient he walked back into the operating theatre.

"I just want to review the operation," he said to Principal Nurse Zanna. "Is the disk available?"

"It's on Miss Evan's computer file," she said. "If you wish, I can gave it transferred to your computer."

"No, I'll just check it here, thanks. There's one small point I wish to review."

He ran the file through to the section where they found the foreign slither. He increased magnification until the metal appeared the size of a needlepoint and slowed the speed down. As a pair or tweezers touched the metal it twitched almost as if it was alive. The tweezers caught it and the object disappeared from sight as blood flooded by.

Mitchell typed in a code to remove the blood's colouring from the view and replayed the scene again. This time the blood appeared like water and he could see the slither caught between the tweezers points. Just as it was lifted out, a minute yellow bubble floated out the side and dissolved in the bloodstream.

Mitchell grunted and replayed the section with increased magnification and at a slower speed. This time he noticed a minute panel slide aside and three honey type bubbles came out. The panel closed and the tweezers covered the whole object.

"Nurse," Mitchell called out. "Did we take any samples of our patient's blood?"

"The usual ones. Doctor but why do you ask?"

"Did we take one after I removed the sting?"

The nurse frowned. "You never asked for one, Doctor Mitchell. Her pulse was in the normal range so I didn't think it was necessary."

"That's quite right," Mitchell replied. "However, I would like another blood sample taken. Can you get one for me, please?"

"Me?" Nurse Perez replied.

"Yes, you nurse and right away."

"Of course, doctor." The principal nurse swung her chin up and strutted out of the room as if it was below her dignity to do such a routine procedure.

*

By late afternoon the blood test results were back. As well as the usual anaesthetics and the painkiller drug in Madison's bloodstream there was a low radiation count. This was about equivalent to the dosage a person would receive in a tooth x-ray so would not harm the patient. Of more interest, though, was an unknown substance present that fitted in with nothing he had seen in human blood before.

"So our invader has a benevolent streak," Joel muttered He glanced up at a wall chart, found an emergency telephone number and reached for the telephone.

"Hello, State Poisons Centre?" he asked and gave his name. "I have a blood sample that contains a chemical unknown to us here. Could you test it for me, please? ... Yes... It is actually. My patient had a toxic reaction after being stung by those exotic bees we've had reported in the area. We need to know what this substance is. ... Yes, I'll have it couriered to you straight away... Thank you."

He sat in his chair and thought about the events of the day. Two things about Madison Events' condition were unusual. He still did not know the reason why the feeling returned so suddenly to her damaged leg nor did he really know why she had reacted to the so-called sting in the first place. Perhaps the second one had flooded her body with this unknown substance or it could have been a reaction to the painkillers already in her bloodstream. He grimaced and switched his attention to another document that had sat in the emergency file all day. He doubted if he'd be home before midnight. No wonder his wife had threatened to leave him on more than one occasion.

*

CHAPTER TWO

Madison heard a rhythmic squeak and felt the bed shuddering while she was still half asleep. She opened her eyes and saw white canvas flapping above her. Now why would she be under canvas in the hospital? She frowned and did what she always did over the last few weeks, which was to rub the toes of her right foot together. My God, she did have feeling in her toes. Further more there was no pain in her body at all. She remembered the bee stings and her attempt at walking the previous day, or was it the same day? It was still daylight outside. She went to move her arm and found them restrained by a loose fitting strap over a course blanket.

Now what?

She wriggled both arms out of the restraints.

Oh hell! Everything was different. She was in a moving object that was squeaking and rattling. She was dressed differently, too. Anger rose in her throat. How dare anyone change her clothes when she was asleep! She glanced at her arms and saw a grey woollen sweater. She undid the remaining straps around her arms, body and legs, sat up and looked further. She was on a stretcher and found she wore a blue tweed skirt, white socks and quite solid looking shoes; perhaps they could even be called boots.

"What's happened?" she called but nobody replied.

Anger turned to apprehension as she attempted to make sense of what was happening. There was a clunk as the thing they were in swayed.

"Get a grip on yourself, Girl," she muttered to herself. "Be rational!"

Okay she was in some sort of wagon; it was travelling too slowly to be the back of a truck. Her head almost touched the canvas covering above and the floor was a couple of metres below her. Across from her was another stretcher and someone was in it. Oh hell, the person didn't move. Was it a corpse?

The stretcher was a bunk with a third person or body below it. Of course, she was on a top bunk so there must be someone below her.

Apprehension turned to fear as Madison flopped back against a soft pillow. What now?

12

She decided to get down off the stretcher but remembered her attempt at walking earlier. "Is anybody here awake?" she called, this time in a whisper.

Again there was no reply.

Okay there was no help forthcoming so was up to her. With great care, she slid off the stretcher so her good leg touched the floor below first. She swung down and placed her right leg beside her strong one. It felt fine. She shifted her weight onto her weak leg. There was no pain, it never crumbled and took the weight of her body with ease.

Okay, that was great. Madison was so relieved that it wasn't until she stood up and gripped a bunk pole to steady herself in the swaying wagon that she noticed the other stretchers.

There were eight, stacked two high and two along on each side of a narrow gap.

Beneath her own stretcher a blonde head was tucked up. She reached forward and pulled the blanket aside and gasped in relief. It was Kirsty. On the left bunk were Yasmin and one of the other girls from the party. She swung around and stepped towards the back.

The rear stretchers all held her friends; Norris was on a top bunk and beneath him a stretcher was filled with luggage. The last bunk contained Wade and one of the other boys at their graduation party. She knew everyone in the wagon!

But initial relief turned to despair. Everyone lay still like the corpses that she had thought of earlier. She swallowed her fear and reached out to touch Kirsty's cheek. It was warm! Further examination showed that all her friends had tanned skin and warm bodies. The girls were all dressed in similar clothes as her own while the boys wore course looking work pants that appeared quaintly old-fashioned. She checked Kirsty's neck for a pulse. Yes, it was faint but there. However, no shaking or talking with the girl woke her. She moved over to Norris and checked him. He also had a faint pulse but didn't wake up. They were all in some sort of coma.

Madison frowned. There was no sting on anybody's neck. She reached up and felt her own but found no tender swelling. Trembling now in conflicting emotions she lifted her right leg and stared at it. There was no sting or any bandage from the operation. It also looked tanned and as healthy as her left leg. She sucked on her lower lip in nervousness, grabbed a bunk frame and lifted her left leg. Oh hell, her bad leg held her weight with ease.

There was nothing wrong with it!

She stood in the swaying wagon and again collected her thoughts. She was with her friends who were asleep but appeared to be in as good health as herself. Now she could check that. Yasmin had an appendix scar that always annoyed her as she reckoned she couldn't wear a bikini because it showed. Madison bent down beside the sleeping girl and discovered something else. She could bend down with ease, again there was no pain what-so-ever in her legs and her knee joint had become quite flexible.

She lifted the girl's sweater and the blouse beneath. Her friend's tummy was slim and tanned. She looked closer. She had no scar, not even a faint line. Oh hell, what was happening?

Madison froze! Her family had never been religious and the thought of an afterlife had never entered her mind. But perhaps this was it; the bee stings had killed her friends and herself and they were in heaven or the other place. She gulped and thought of the previous evening. One of the boys had almost persuaded her to get into bed with him. It was a little hazy. After all she had been half drunk but she was sure she had dissuaded the guy.

Oh damn! It fitted in ... no pain ... perfect health ... Yasmin's old scar gone.

"I don't like this," Madison cried and without really thinking, stepped forward, moved the canvas flap aside and looked outside.

Two men sat in front and above her. She was staring out between their legs at a line of beasts pulling their wagon. They were solid brown creatures with massive horns and steam snorting from their noses. The wagon was travelling along a dirt road and the grass at the edge appeared white with frost.

"Get up there!" a voice boomed above her. "We have to get through this mud before the real Muds get yah!"

Madison gulped. The voice was in English but had a heavy accent as if the owner came from England... or was it Scotland?

"Slow and steady," the second man said. "Don't let the oxen stop or we'll sink down to our axles."

"The newcomers are too heavy," the first man replied. "I told 'em that eight in a wagon was too many."

"I'll get out if that'll help" Madison said without thinking.

*

The reaction was unexpected. Both men physically jumped in fright, swore and swung around.

A man with a wild ginger beard and blue piercing eyes stared at her. He appeared almost terrified.

"You're alive?" he stammered. "But that's impossible!"

14

"And why shouldn't I be?" Madison asked.

"There's been no final charge. Without a final charge you are cannot be alive."

"Like my friends?" Madison asked.

"You're talking just like an ordinary person?" The second man with black beard and brown eyes also appeared nervous.

"And why not?"

Both men stared at each other then back at her.

"And you remember things like your name?" Gingerbeard asked.

"Of course. I'm Madison Evans and these are my friends, Kirsty, Norris and..."

"You're right," Blackbeard said after she had finished. "Just as it is written on the inventory."

"So why are we being held as prisoners in this funny wagon?" Madison asked.

Gingerbeard suddenly laughed. "This is one for the books aye, Sean?" he said.

"You could say that?" Sean, the black bearded guy replied. "I reckon we keep mum on this though, Hamish?"

Were they Scottish or Irish names? Madison couldn't quite remember but the pair seemed uncomfortable and still nervous so she decided to take the initiative.

"I'll say nothing if you don't want me to," she said. "Of course you'll both need to agree that it's our secret, won't you?"

Hamish stared back at her and broke into a grin. "Aye Lassie, I see you have gumption. What did you say your name was?"

"Madison."

"Well Madison. Everything is not quite right, is that a correct statement?"

"It is!" Madison opened her mouth but clamped it shut again. Perhaps some things were best left unasked.

"You were going to ask a question, Madison?" Hamish said.

"Yeah, dozens of them."

"For sure," Sean said. "If you're patient, though, there are a few things we need to ask you ... no offence mind you."

Madison grinned. "None taken," she whispered. The two guys looked fierce but she could sense that they were quite friendly. Caution though was still necessary.

"Okay Lassie, could you check on your friends and see if of them are alive... I mean ... have woken up."

Madison noted Sean's change of terminology and said, "They're all in a deep sleep or coma. I'm the only one awake or would you say alive?"

"Deep sleep would be a good description," Hamish said in a soft voice. "Do they look well cared for?"

"Yes," Madison said. "The straps are to stop them falling out of their bunks and not a restraint to stop them from escaping, aren't they?"

"Right again, Madison," Hamish said. "So you're the only one awake?"

"I said that."

"Good. Now if you can wriggle up here between us we'll see what we can do to help each other. We can't stop until our oxen get us through this mud patch. It's been raining for two weeks now but I guess that's better than the snow had last month."

*

Madison would never have managed the climb with her weak leg but even with the swaying wagon she swung herself up with ease. Hamish grabbed under her arm and she was lifted up and plunked on a wooden seat between the men.

"Like your clothes, Madison?" Hamish said. "You need warm clothes in these conditions."

Madison stared out. As well as the frosty grass a thick fog hung around the hills above them. They were in a valley of course grass and tussock and it was so cold her breath puffed out when she spoke.

"My clothes are great." She shivered. "It's cold out here, though."

"Are you hungry or thirsty Lassie?" Sean asked.

My God, she was! "I am a little."

Sean produced a woven basket from a leather pouch beside him and handed it to her. "Help yourself and perhaps you could pour us both a drink. You'll find some mugs there."

Madison found a thermos that steamed when she unscrewed the top.

"Only tea, Lassie," Hamish said. "If we'd known we were going to share we'd have got coffee. Milk's added I'm afraid and there's sugar in that wee bag."

Madison found the sugar and a couple of teaspoons. She managed to fill two mugs with tea and handed them to the men. Next she spied a larger brown bag and took out a pile of thick sandwiches.

"Ham and pickle," Sean said. "I hope you eat meat."

Madison laughed. "Yeah, I do," she said. "I don't think Yasmin does, though."

"Fair enough," Hamish said. "Everyone for their own poison, I say." He laughed at his own joke and turned his attention back to the oxen he was driving.

The hot sweet tea and ham sandwiches warmed Madison and she accepted a second sandwich before she sat back and began to think about what was happening.

For perhaps ten minutes the two men concentrated on urging the oxen forward. They were in a sea of mud and the narrow wagon wheels barely moved. Finally, though, they were pulled though to a section of gravel and Hamish called a halt. He turned and grinned at Madison.

"We were going to stop for our lunch, anyway," he said. "A bit of company from a bonnie lass won't do us any harm, now will it?"

"And a few answers," Madison said.

"Aye, a few answers there be." Hamish smiled. "Don't worry, Madison. I'm sure your friends and yourself will find most of us agreeable chaps."

*

The sun had appeared and they sat on a sunny outcrop. The oxen had also sat down and appeared to be contentedly chewing their cuds. Madison's questions came thick and fast and the answers were equally candid. Some things were wrong, though. Hamish and Sean had no idea about her home or the hospital. In fact the pair appeared quite perplexed whenever she mentioned her life.

"So you remember everything about yourself," Hamish said.

"Yes."

"So what do you know about the city and the orphanage?" Sean asked.

"I know of no orphanage and what city do you mean? I come from Sacramento in California, if that means anything to you."

Hamish stared at Sean again. "Madison has genuine memories not implanted ones," he said.

"What do you mean?"

"We don't know," Sean said. "We have never met anyone with a past before, that's all."

Madison frowned. "Can you explain yourself, Sean?"

"Only if we remember our pact, Madison. We must keep everything we say between the three of us. You cannot even discuss it with your friends when they wake up."

"Why not?"

"It's like a rebirth," Hamish said in a serious voice. "Do you know about babies?"

"Of course," Madison said.

"Have you had one?" Sean asked. Madison glowered but relaxed when the intense eyes staring at her showed nothing except empathy.

"Not yet," she said. "One day perhaps."

"But you could ... I mean you can give birth if you wish?"

Madison nodded. "What has this got to do with me now?" she asked.

"Everyone except you it seems and that includes us, have no memories of our past life. We only remember being in a crowded city and being brought up in orphanages of children our own age."

Madison stared. "How awful," she whispered.

"Oh they are not bad memories," Hamish said. "In fact they are gentle and warm, if that's the word. We remember fun things at school, having Christmas, going on holidays and playing with friends. Sean and I remember each other as children. Our memories comfort us."

"So I am dead?" Madison said.

Hamish smiled in almost a sad way. "No Madison, You are very much alive... We all are."

"But my leg is better." Madison told the pair about her accident and how she still had trouble walking.

"I don't know what a car is," Hamish said. "I certainly know what can happen in an accident, though. "

"So why am I in perfect health, then?"

"I don't know," Sean said. "We all began like that. However, I do know that if you were in an accident now and received the wound you speak of, Madison, your paralysed leg would stay that way. There are no miracles here, just ordinary humans who get ill, have problems and accidents the same as you did."

"But where am I?"

"The land through which we are travelling is the outer land of a town called Buckoway."

"But where is it? Am I in Scotland or America?"

"I'm sorry, Madison," Hamish whispered. "I've never heard of either of those places."

18

The two men couldn't really offer any more of an explanation but they did tell her what would happen to her friends.

"When we arrive at Buckoway, you'll all be taken to the Buckoway Castle. I guess it is a little like the hospital you talked about. Your friends will be put in a bed by a machine and charged up," Hamish said.

"Charged up? What's that?"

"It's like a bolt of lightning. It's called ... you know the thing that runs the lights at night."

"Electricity?"

"That's it. They clamp these things on their head and this electricity passes through their mind and body. They wake up a little like you just did."

"Except they won't know who they were," Sean added.

"What will they know?" Madison asked.

"They'll know you and each other but think you all came from the same orphanage in the city. If any of them had diseases or were ill in their first life, it will have gone."

"I saw Yasmin," Madison said. "A scar she had across her tummy is gone." She frowned. "What do you mean by first life?"

"Nobody talks about it but we think we have all lived somewhere else before," Sean said. "We have never met anyone like you who woke up early but many of us have flashes of memory, especially if something unexpected happens."

"Yeah, one lad called Carl burnt himself in a house fire and he could remember the same thing happening to him before," Hamish said. "The referees took him back to the Castle and he forgot everything again."

"Referees. Who are they?"

"The people in charge. Anyone can be a referee if enough people vote for them. Didn't you have them where you were?"

"I guess. We call them politicians or judges. There are the police of course."

"We have border guards," Sean said. "The referees are more important than the guards. All the guards do is give us tickets if our wagon is overloaded or our oxen aren't being looked after."

Madison laughed. "That sounds like our police."

Hamish frowned. "Now, Madison I think we have to very careful when we reach Buckoway Castle. If you a go inside the castle with your friends you could lose all your past memories like Carl did."

Madison paled. "Of course. So what should I do?"

Hamish grinned. "We'll change our inventory to show only seven arriving so all you need to do is wait around until they come out

"So I can still be with my friends?" she added.

"Oh yes. Once out of the reception centre at the castle you can meet up with them in the courtyard and do whatever you like. You'll all have places booked for you in the dormitories. People come and go there all the time. Newcomers just mix in with everyone else."

"Sounds okay," Madison said. "Will I see you guys again?"

"Whenever you like," Sean said. "We make this trip quite often but whenever we're in town you can see us. We'll give you our addresses."

*

When the wagon headed off again Madison sat between them on the wagon driver's seat. Two hours slipped by and their dirt road turned into gravel. They passed other wagons and a coach pulled by two horses. Several pedestrians who walked along the roadside waved at them.

"One more hour," Hamish said. "Twenty minutes if we had horses."

"Oh I don't mind," Madison murmured.

Actually she was feeling quite sleepy. Her head slipped sideways and she shut her eyes.

*

CHAPTER THREE

"Hi Madison. Supper's ready. I thought you'd never wake up."

Madison opened her eyes and jumped in fright. Principal Nurse Zanna Perez stood by the hospital bed with a tray of hot food in her hand.

Madison realized she was back in her hospital bed!

She swallowed and just stared at the nurse. What was happening? She wriggled herself up into a sitting position. "My friends," she said. "Are my friends safe?"

"Which ones Madison?" the nurse said. "There were four or five here earlier. You are certainly a popular young lady."

"All of them," Madison said. "I know it sounds stupid but I must know."

Zanna Perez frowned. "You think they may be affected by the bee stings?"

Madison flushed. "Something like that."

Zanna studied her patient. "Do you have any contact numbers, Madison?" she asked.

"Norris and Kirsty share an apartment with me. You can find them at my address. I have the cellphonenumbers of the others."

"You want me to contact everyone that was stung?"

Madison sighed. "No, how stupid of me. I had a funny dream that's all, almost a premonition that ... oh it doesn't matter."

"That can happen," the nurse said in a soft voice. "Look, I'll call your apartment and check. You have your breakfast before it gets cold."

"Thanks," Madison replied. She watched the nurse walk out and thought back. Every detail of her ride in the wagon was vivid in her mind. She could even feel the crisp air and hear the men's broad accent. They sounded Scottish but had never heard of Scotland or America for that matter. She reached for a piece of toast and crunched on it. My God, she still had the taste of the ham sandwich in her mouth.

"Madison, are you okay?"

A concerned blonde girl stood beside the bed with a bunch of carnations in her hand,

Madison's eyes lit up. "Kirsty." she said. "I'm so glad to see you. How do you feel?"

"Me, I'm okay. Why? You seem so serious."

"What about your sting?"

Kirsty shrugged. "There's a tiny lump and white spot just like the one on your neck. All the bruising has gone. I feel great, actually. That persistent cough and sore throat I had for weeks has gone. But you never answered my question."

"You, Norris and the others were in this weird dream I had. It was so real, I thought you may have been hurt or something."

"No, we're all fine. You're the only one who reacted so badly."

"That's fine then. I thought you might have all vanished."

Kirsty placed the carnations in a vase and sat on Madison's bed. "Tell me all about it," she said.

Madison shrugged. "No, it's just silly."

"Madison!"

"Well okay, but don't tell the others. I can almost hear Norris sniggering and you know how nervy Yasmin gets."

"It's a deal."

Madison had known Kirsty since high school days and they often traded intimate details about their lives together. She knew that if her friend agreed to keep something between them confidential it would go no further. As she finished her toast she told Kirsty everything.

"And I just lay in a stretcher like a waxwork dummy?" Kirsty said after Madison had finished.

"No. You were warm like a person in a coma. Hamish said you all needed an electrical charge to wake you up."

"Like that thing you see on those medical shows to get a heart beating again?"

"I guess, but here's one other strange thing."

"What?"

"This toast had peanut butter on it."

"So?"

"I still have a taste of ham in my mouth from the sandwich I ate in my dream."

Kirsty reached out and took Madison's hand. "You are the most practical person I know Madison. What do you really think is going on?"

"That's the trouble, I have no idea. This has never happened to me before."

"Well, nothing evil was intended was it?"

"What do you mean?"

"You're here talking to me. If you had died like you thought may have happened or were whisked away into a parallel universe you wouldn't have come back, now would you?"

"Oh Kirsty," Madison said with a laugh. "You do watch too many of those fantasy shows."

Kirsty shrugged. "Well, look after my alternative self next time you visit, won't you?"

"You think I may go back?"

"Isn't that a logical conclusion?"

"Nothing about this is logical, Kirsty. Nothing."

"But we were attacked by those strange bees. Everyone except you and Leona received just one sting in exactly the same place on the neck. This could just be the next piece of the puzzle."

"But you say nothing to the others. Remember our pact?"

"I won't." Kirsty said. "I will do a bit of research though. You've got me curious."

Madison lay on her bed well after Kirsty had left and tried to make sense of everything but the more she thought the sillier it all seemed. She shrugged and settled down. Without realizing it, her eyes grew heavy and shut.

*

"You'll be able to see Buckoway from the next summit." Hamish's voice cut through her mind and she jerked awake.

She was back on the wagon seated between the two men!

In some ways Buckoway reminded Madison of a fortified castle from the Middle Ages for the entire town was surrounded by a stone wall and a gigantic castle sat on the only hilltop. Outside the town were fields of grass and other crops. There were barns and sheds but appeared to be no farmhouses. If it was an attempt to copy an old town, though, it had gone sadly amiss. Sure, the wall was constructed of stone but they looked crisp and new. The castle was too boxy looking with a three-story cube at each end filled with narrow windows. The middle section was more authentic with two floors and a steep roof like a university administration block.

"Is the wall built to keep citizens in or undesirables out?" Madison asked without attempting to remove the disdain from her tone.

"Keep the undesirables out. The gate is shut at nightfall. We tried to negotiate friendship treaties with them but their morality is different than ours," Hamish said. "After our initial settlers were wiped out we had to fortify ourselves."

"Against whom?"

"The Muds," Sean replied.

Madison frowned. Hamish had muttered something about them when she had first woken up.

"Who are they?"

"Our scientists think they are what humans developed from hundreds of years ago."

"Do they talk?"

"Oh yes," Hamish said. "It is a basic oral language. Many of us have learned it but we have not managed to teach many of them to understand English."

Madison raised her eyebrows. "So we speak English?" she asked.

Hamish frowned. "Some people call our language Buckoway after the town but the proper word is English. Why does the word interest you?"

"No reason. I just wondered where you got the name from."

"It has always been so," Sean said as if that was a satisfactory answer.

Madison shrugged. "So where are these Muds now?"

"They have villages dotted around but many lead a nomadic life and follow the beasts." Hamish noticed Madison's curious gaze. "They're vast herds of ox like creatures that the Muds use for just about everything. You know, food, clothing and so forth. We are starting to trade with them a little to improve their lives otherwise we tend to ignore each other."

"So why the fortifications?"

"For some unknown reason their various tribes join together every few years and go on a rampage. Thousands of them attacked our original village without warning and slaughtered nearly all the citizens. Since then they have been attacked twice but our walls protected us. Only those caught outside were killed." Hamish waved his hand out. "They destroyed all our crops and killed our farm animals. That's why the gates are closed at night and farm workers live inside the walls."

"So why stay here?" Madison said. "Surely you could all go back to your city and leave the Muds alone."

Hamish glanced at Sean. "Your questions are searching, Madison. We've asked each other the same thing when we've been out on the road together. We don't believe there is a city so there is nowhere else for us to go."

Madison sighed. "Can you answer one last question, then?"

Sean nodded. "What is it, Madison?"

"I woke up in this wagon. Where did you pick my friends and myself up from?"

24

"About an hour's journey back from that muddy section is a tunnel that goes under the range of hills. On the other side there is a river, a few buildings and a jetty where we met the barge. The twenty-two newcomers were unloaded straight onto three wagons. The other two wagons are probably already in Buckoway. We broke a wheel rim and were held up a day."

Madison nodded. "That is probably everyone from our graduation party," she said. "Where does the barge come from?"

"Up river somewhere." Hamish said. "Oxen like our ones pull the empty barge back upriver."

"But you don't know?"

"No. The guys in the castle tell us how many newcomers there are and when the barge will be there. After we take our load to the castle we are paid a hundred crowns per wagon load," Hamish said. "It's quite high pay but there is always the risk that we'll be attacked by Muds during the journey. Luckily, that hasn't happened yet."

"We'd better go," Sean said. "If we're too late they'll deduct a penalty fee."

*

When they reached the gateway under an archway in the wall a guard stopped them and examined their invoices now with Madison's name crossed out so only seven newcomers were registered. He glanced at her still sitting on the driver's seat but merely nodded and waved them through. Once inside, Madison found other strange items. It was as if history was muddled up. The streets were paved and electric light poles were everywhere but there were no motor vehicles. Horses with riders, stagecoaches and oxen wagons competed for space with pedestrians.

Most of the women were dressed in tartan skirts like herself while the men wore the quaint looking trousers that Norris had on. Hairstyles though were quite modern. At one point a platoon of guards marched by.

"The changing of the guard," Sean said. "It happens every six hours."

Madison stared. The guards were like her two companions, large men with bushy beards. What was unexpected, though, was that they were armed with and swords. Madison glanced up at the wall they were travelling beside. Towering above them she could see other guards manning the ramparts but they also only had bows and arrows or swords.

"Where are the guns and rifles?" she asked.

Hamish frowned. "I'm afraid your words are unfamiliar, Madison. What do you mean?"

Madison gasped. "So you have nothing that fires bullets to shoot at an enemy?"

"The new steel tipped arrows can go right through a man at a hundred metres," Sean said. "They're too powerful at my reckoning."

"Oh hell," Madison muttered.

"I'm sorry, Lassie," Hamish said.

"Yeah, I know you've never heard of guns. Tell me, what do you use electricity for?"

"Lights, stoves, refrigerators, microwaves, hot water and heaters in winter."

"But not for computers, videos, radios, DVDs, cellphones or ordinary telephones?"

Hamish shrugged. "I guess not."

"So someone or something decided what you should or should not have?"

"You still speak strangely Madison," Hamish said. "As long as we don't break the laws we are free to do whatever we wish. Wasn't this allowed where you come from?"

Madison smiled. "Some things were different, that's all. I didn't mean to be judgmental." She changed the topic. "Can we go over what happens at the castle again?"

"Act confident," Hamish said. "Blend with the locals until your friends come out. They'll recognize you like I said but they could be confused. Many newcomers are."

*

The courtyard inside the castle wall was really only large enough for the oxen to tow the wagon around a semi-circle in front of the austere looking castle itself. A few pedestrians wandered around and there was no sign of any guards or soldiers. The wagon stopped by the southern 'cube' and several workers came out. Madison's friends were carried inside a double door that was shut when the last stretcher went in.

"Okay, Madison. Away you go," Hamish said. "Anybody is allowed to wander around the courtyard or go into the reception area. There's a rest area there and a small waiting room." He nodded at the ornate entrance in the middle section of the tower. "We have to take the oxen back near the main town gate to the stables where they are washed down and fed. We'll be there for a couple of hours if you need us. Good luck."

"Thanks," Madison said. "I'll still contact you and tell you what happens." She bit in her lip. "That's if you're interested."

"We are," Sean said. "I have a feeling we are going to help each other again and quite soon, too."

He gave her a sort of half salute and climbed on the wagon beside Hamish. The ginger bearded man grinned and shouted an order at his team. As Madison watched the wagon rumble away under the gate archway, loneliness gripped the pit of her stomach. It was as if she was utterly alone in this strange world

"Okay," she said to herself. "Let's go."

Inside the main doors was a corridor with a reception area on the right and a row of seats to the left. A dozen or more people sat on the chairs and an extremely tall flat-chested female receptionist glanced up at her.

"Can I be of assistance, Ma'am?" she said

Madison glowered and forgot Hamish's warnings. "Are you real or a hologram?" she snapped.

The woman's reaction would have been amusing if the situation wasn't so dangerous. She gasped and held her hand to her mouth while her face drained of all colour. She replied in a high-pitched unknown language but was obviously apologizing about something.

Act confident, Hamish had said. Madison felt her own hands trembling but thought quickly.

"We speak English here," she said in feigned anger.

"Of course," the woman replied. "Your clothes made me assumed you were a newcomer, Guardian. A new group is being activated at this moment. I'll contact the director for you."

"That is not necessary." Madison frantically wondered what to say next.

"I guess you came in with the newcomers?" The woman still appeared nervous.

Madison frowned.

"I'm sorry. I didn't mean to intrude but we're so far out we haven't had a random inspection in years. Where would you like to go first, Guardian?"

Madison almost muttered that she only wanted to leave but the woman appeared ready to do anything she asked. These Guardians must weld considerable power.

"I would like to watch the final charge without any officials knowing of my presence" she said. "You are to tell nobody I'm here."

The woman almost looked relieved. "Do you wish to participate or watch from the observation deck, Guardian?"

"Observation deck," Madison said almost too quickly. "I only have time for a brief visit today..." She glanced at a wall clock if she was in a hurry.

*

A moment later, with a visitor's label pinned on her collar, Madison was escorted by a guard into an elevator, up three flights and out into a long thin room with curtains across one entire wall opposite a row of comfortable chairs. Electric lights lit the room.

"I shall leave you, Guardian," the guard said and gave a sort of head bow.

"Pull the curtains, please," Madison said and almost bit her tongue. She doubted if these Guardians would say *please*.

The guard merely nodded and without him appearing to do a thing, the curtains slid back and Madison stifled a gasp. Her seven friends were lying on the other side of a glass wall in containers that looked like plastic coffins. Above them were a battery of television monitors and other instruments. In some ways it looked like the operating room she'd been in back home. So Hamish and Sean's theory that there were no computers in Buckoway was wrong. Four people dressed in silver suits that gave them the appearance of astronauts monitored the equipment.

"Sound, Guardian?" the guard asked.

Madison nodded and foreign language voices filled the room.

"What are the procedures when I wish to leave this room?" she asked the guard.

"The usual, Guardian."

"Enlighten me, young man."

The guard blushed. "Of course. You speak your destination and the correct doors will open for you."

"In English I assume."

The guard nodded.

"Very good," Madison said in a schoolmarm tone. "You may leave now."

The guard bowed his head and left.

Madison watched, fascinated as the scientists, or whatever they were, attached helmets to each of the patients while monitors above their heads lit up. These beeped slow rhythms that sounded just like the heart monitoring equipment in a hospital TV drama.

28

Words were spoken, again in the unknown language and a sort of bang sounded. Every patient jerked and the monitors showed an increased wave patterns. Either their hearts or brain waves had been activated.

Madison sighed in relieve but gulped again as the room through the glass changed into a very ordinary looking sitting room with armchairs, sofas and a coffee table complete with a coffee percolator, mugs and two plates of sandwiches. The seven patients lay on the floor in a jumbled heap. The four scientists lifted them up and seated them on the sofa and chairs and left the room. A moment later a man and woman dressed in business clothes walked in and sat in two empty arms chairs.

"Are you ready?" the man asked in English.

"Yes," the woman replied and waved her hand.

Madison gasped when she saw Kirsty's eyes flutter and open.

*

CHAPTER FOUR

Kirsty glanced around. "I'm sorry," she said. "I must have nodded off. What were you saying?"

"Call me Milton," the man said. "Gwen, my wife and I are your hosts. It is our responsibility to introduce you to Buckoway, the new home you graduates chose to emigrate to." He glanced around at everyone who were now awake and listening to him.

"You all know each other, I gather," Gwen said.

Kirsty grinned at Norris. "Of course," she said. "But where are the others? We were told our whole section would be here."

"You should remember your journey from the city was delayed. The others arrived earlier. You'll meet them at your apartment block later this afternoon."

"Oh Kirsty." Yasmin laughed. "Can't you remember?"

Kirsty grinned. "It just slipped my mind. I thought Madison was with us, that's all."

"Don't worry about Madison," Norris said. "Knowing her, she's gone ahead to get us the best apartment rooms available." He laughed. "She's probably got jobs for us all by now, too."

Everyone laughed.

"Okay," Gwen said. "Have a coffee and relax. Bathrooms are off to your left if you'd like to freshen up. Later, we'll explain the procedures and tell you about our town. You should remember that we told you that a coach will take you to your apartments where all your documents and luggage are waiting. Tomorrow there will be an organized grand tour and you will be given a month's salary to spend how you wish. In return, you should remember you volunteered to do the border guard training."

"We realize that," someone replied.

Everyone smiled and nodded in agreement.

*

Behind the one-way mirror, Madison gulped. Her friends had almost inadvertently given her away. She studied the man called Milton. She didn't like him at all. Also there was something about the words, *you should*

30

remember. It was as if he used it to place a suggestion in her friends' minds. She had once seen a hypnotist at home control his audience in the same way.

She watched and listened as the pair talked. It could have been a talkback at university or one of those organized tourist trips. After listening for ten minutes she decided she had better leave and try to find the coach.

"I wish to leave the building and be directed to the newcomers' coach," she said.

The curtains slid across and a new door opened at the far end of the room. Madison walked in to find it was an elevator. The door slid shut and she felt herself going down. A moment later the door opened and she saw a lobby outside.

"Proceed outside and you will see the coach waiting in a parking area to your left. Thank you for visiting and have a nice day," a voice said from an unseen speaker

Madison scowled. She would have to be very careful. These aliens, or whatever they were, were too sophisticated for their own good.

She walked out into the same street as the one she'd left and laughed in delight. Not only was a coach with two horses there but also across the road the familiar wagon was parked. The oxen were all sitting down chewing their cud while Hamish and Sean stood on the footpath munching food.

"We thought we'd wait a while just in case," Hamish said. "How did it go?"

Madison shrugged. "Different. My friends are all awake and will be coming out soon. That coach is going to take them to our new apartment."

"But there were problems?" Sean asked.

"Lots," Madison admitted.

"But you don't feel you can tell us about it?" Hamish said.

"I want to but..."

"We aren't in with them, Madison," Hamish said. "We know everything isn't what it seems. That's why we really stayed. We thought you could be in trouble."

"And if I was?"

"We would have organized a rescue," Sean said. "Our own resources are not very sophisticated but we have friends to help us."

"Did you know I went home when I fell asleep on the wagon?"

"We guessed," Hamish said. "We also think you will go home every time you fall asleep."

"And come back every time I fall asleep at home."

"Possibly. We're all just guessing again."

"Psst," Sean cut in. "They're coming out."

Madison flushed. "I can't thank you enough..."

"Go Madison," Hamish said. "Act as if you expected to see them there. Okay?"

"Sure." Madison grimaced and walked out onto the road. "Hey guys," she called "Wait for me. I came to meet you."

Kirsty glanced up and dug Norris in the ribs. "Hi Madison," she yelled. "It's good to see yah."

The friends all gathered around and embraced Madison before they climbed into the coach together. To Madison it seemed so strange but the others settled down as if they'd ridden in stagecoaches all their lives. As the horses pulled the coach away she waved at the two men watching from the oxen team across the road.

*

Their journey in the coach took the eight friends through a commercial area with shops lined along both street sides like a typical small town.

"This will be so much nicer than the city," Yasmin, the quiet member of their group, said.

"Why?' Madison couldn't resist the question.

Yasmin shrugged. "I don't know. More room, our own apartment, jobs to choose from." She glanced at Madison. "Why? Are you having doubts."

"Not at all."

Except for their lack of any memory from home, her friends seemed no different. Even their mannerisms and personalities were the same.

Madison, like all her friends, gazed at the scene outside but she noticed things she thought she'd ask Hamish and Sean about when the opportunity arose. The local citizens looked normal enough with the women all in dresses or tartan skirts and the men, those old fashioned trousers. Nobody wore jeans. Hairstyles though were similar to those at home and the men appeared to be clean-shaven or bearded in about the same proportion at home. However the ages of the people were different, well actually the same. Everyone looked to be within a few years of her own age. There were no school-aged children or teenagers anywhere. She saw no elderly people but there was a high number of pregnant women or young mothers with babies in their arms.

"Look at all the babies," she said.

32

"Yeah," Kirsty said. "I can't wait."

"For what?"

"To have a baby. Isn't that what we all want?"

Madison froze. Now this was different! At home, none of her female friends had indicated any wish to have a family. Kirsty, in particular, had shown no interest in becoming a mother. She was more interested in starting her career and travelling to Europe, Japan or other exotic places. This reaction was quite old-fashioned and more like the aspirations of her grandmother's generation.

The indoctrination at the Castle made her think and the words, *you should remember.*

She noticed the others were chatting together and not listening to their conversation.

"But you said you would rather be a career woman than have a bunch of kids. You don't want children until you're at least thirty-five. You should remember that."

Kirsty stared at her and her eyes sort of glazed over. "Of course," she said. "That's right."

It seemed to work but Madison thought she'd check her theory out further. She repeated her earlier conversation about all the babies.

"Yeah," Kirsty said in an uncommitted voice.

"Wouldn't you like to have a baby?"

"Me!" Kirsty laughed. "One day when I'm thirty-five perhaps. Not now, though. No way!"

It did work! Now she'd have to make the same suggestion to all her friends, perhaps even the boys. But what other suggestions had been implanted in their minds? Perhaps she could try something else.

"Hey guys," she said so everyone could hear her. "Isn't this coach better than the old school bus we used to ride in?"

The result was spectacular. Her friends were ignorant of the word *bus*. Oh hell, this was becoming ominous.

*

The apartment block looked typical of the student halls of residence at a university. Bedrooms accommodated three or four, there was a bathroom along the corridor and a large dining room and lounge on the ground floor. It appeared, though, that they were segregated with the men directed to another building.

The coach driver brought their bags in and Madison found one with her name on it. She unzipped the side and looked at the contents. Oh damn, everything was exactly what she'd have packed at home except that there were tartan skirts instead of jeans. Even the hair shampoo and cosmetics were the brands she used at home.

The others made no comment as they unpacked luggage and placed their things in drawers and closets.

Afterwards they all went downstairs and laughed in delight when they walked in the lounge. All the girls from their graduation party except Leona were there to welcome them.

Madison tugged Kirsty's sleeve. "Do you know a girl called Leona?" she asked.

Kirsty frowned. "No. Who's she?"

"Oh just a friend from the city who thought she might like to come to Buckoway."

"You know, the name seems to be at the back of my mind. Perhaps I did meet her once."

"You could have," Madison said in a casual voice. "Anyway, isn't it great that we were all given the chance to come here together?"

"Sure is." Kirsty laughed and went to grab a can of beer.

*

If it wasn't for the thoughts swirling through her mind, Madison would have enjoyed the following few hours. All her friends were with her and the local officials were so helpful it was almost embarrassing. They met up with the boys and were given the guided tour of the town. Kirsty and the others were utterly engrossed but Madison noted that the town wasn't old. The commercial buildings were crisp and clean with modern fittings such as power points and recessed lights.

A guide told of early days when Buckoway Castle was owned by an eccentric warlord who spent his time gathering up wives and territory.

"The great old man had fifteen wives and local folklore tells us he died of a heart attack on his wedding night after marrying his sixteenth..." He continued with a sexist comment about the old guy's performance before he died.

"I think that comment is in poor taste" Madison muttered in annoyance.

The guide frowned. "You should remember..."

Oh hell. Those words again. Madison never bothered to listen to the guide's explanation.

Kirsty dug Madison in the ribs and replied. "Of course, we realize that."

Madison glowered but said no more. It was foolish to give away any hint that she wasn't influenced by the words. She was, however, determined to help her closest friends from being affected by them as well. Under a hypnotic or suggestive state they could be made to do anything.

*

The time came that evening when the Norris and Wade visited Kirsty, Yasmin and herself in a way that was surprisingly similar to times when they were together back home.

"Can I try a little experiment?" Madison asked when there was a lull in the conversation.

"What's wrong?" Norris said. "You've been so quiet and serious all evening."

"Just go along with me for a moment," Madison said.

"Why not?" Norris said.

"When I tell you, you will not be able to use your hands," she said.

"What are you talking about?" Wade grumbled.

"You should remember that you are to place your hands on your head and find you can't move them until I clap."

"Of course we realize that," Kirsty said and like robots, the four placed their hands on their heads.

"Okay, " Madison said. "Take them down."

Grinning friends found they couldn't move their hands. They tugged and bent over, pushed against furniture and fun began to turn to fear.

"Get us out of this," Norris cried. "The joke's gone too far."

Madison was going to clap and undo her suggestion but decided to go one step further. But how could she do it? If she said something like, *ignore anything said to you* there could be a problem if someone suggested something helpful. What, for example would happen if someone said, *You should remember that it is dangerous to climb on the castle wall?*

"You should remember to sit down and listen," she said.

Everyone stopped trying to pull their arms down and sat on the beds.

Madison swallowed and spoke very methodically. "You should remember that after I clap my hands you will have full and proper use of your hands again. "

"Of course we realize that," Yasmin said

God, they nearly always replied that way! Perhaps that was part of the conditioning. Madeline frowned.

"Get on with it," Norris grumbled.

"You should remember that after I clap, there is one other condition. You will never hear the words, 'You should remember.' Instead you will hear "I suggest" but it not compel you to doing anything unless you want to."

She clapped her hands. Everyone moved their hands off their head and grinned at each other.

"What were talking about?" Kirsty asked.

"I'll say it again and get you to repeat it, Kirsty."

"Sure."

"You should remember to touch your finger on your nose."

"I suggest you touch your finger on your nose." Kirsty laughed. "It doesn't make sense."

Madison sighed in relief. Not one person touched a finger on their nose. "What did you others hear?" she asked.

"Something about you suggesting we touch our nose but it wasn't like when you told us to put our hands on our heads," Yasmin said. "I just thought what a silly order it was."

"So will you have power over us?" Wade asked.

"No and neither will anyone else," Madison said. She sucked on her lip but decided not to offer an explanation.

"Thank God," Norris said with a laugh. "I'd hate you ordering me to do the dishes every night for a month."

"And come across to our rooms and make all our beds," Kirsty added with a giggle.

Everyone chuckled and the whole episode was treated as a prank. Later that evening Madison tried the words again but the others just smiled at her and laughed.

"The great magician has lost her powers," Norris said as he grabbed her in a massive hug and plunked a kiss on her cheek.

*

Madison was almost scared to go to bed that evening but realized she couldn't stay awake indefinitely. The other two were already asleep as she crawled beneath the blankets and reached for the light switch.

Three blinks later, or so it seemed, she woke up and knew she was home for she could smell the carnations Kirsty had brought her and see morning light through the hospital window. She stretched and sat up. One thing felt okay, though. It was as if she had had a full night's sleep and she was ready for another day. Perhaps her strange experience relaxed her mind like an ordinary dream.

She almost leaped out of bed but remembered her wounded leg. Her crutches were placed within reach so she used them to help herself stand up.

*

CHAPTER FIVE

"I don't think it's really us there," Madison said and sipped a glass of wine. She had been released from the hospital an hour earlier and was with Kirsty at *The Hooded Lady*, their favourite haunt even though it wasn't yet noon.

"What do you mean. Madison?"

"It's like a video being played or perhaps more like one of those interaction games. In this game I haven't got my bad leg and Yasmin's appendix scar has gone."

"But can you touch things?"

"What do you mean?"

"If you were a computer program or virtual person you wouldn't be able to touch each other or anything around, for that matter."

"Except for me being able to walk okay, everything is normal. Norris still acts the same and you do, too." Madison sighed. "It's so hard. I feel so utterly alone."

"So everyone's personally is the same?"

"Pretty much."

"And you trust me right now?"

"Of course. You know that."

"Then take my other me into your confidence. You did talk to those two guys on that bullock wagon, after all."

"They knew I woke up early. All our guys assumed I arrived from this city the same as they did. It's hard. They remember we are friends but have no knowledge of our lives here"

"Like listening to somebody on that video?"

"Exactly."

"There's one thing you mentioned that might help."

"What was that?"

"When you mentioned Leona, didn't Yasmin say she thought she remembered her."

"I guess. She may have just been trying to be polite, though. You know how Yasmin hates to hurt anybody's feelings?"

"But couldn't it be there in her mind but suppressed because that particular memory isn't needed in her new existence?"

"It could. I never thought of that."

"So do the same thing with the alternate me. Mention something that had a huge impact on me."

"Such as?"

"Mom died when I was thirteen. I remember every tiny detail and had nightmares for months. Poor Daddy was pretty cut up too but helped to get me through it all. I still think of Mom almost every day. I can tell you little things I've kept to myself for almost a decade."

"Won't it be too painful?"

Kirsty nodded. "If there is a chance that my alternate self has forgotten memories, this will be one way to find out. If it works, we can talk to the others and try to do the same for them."

" And if it doesn't?"

"I'm sure you'll be able to trust me anyway," Kirsty grinned and gulped a mouthful of wine. "Perhaps it's the evil me over there."

"No, it's not like that."

"Just joking. If that was the case you'd be pretty nasty and horrible there."

"Why?"

"Because you're such a gentle and kind person here."

"But pretty neurotic lately."

Kirsty smiled and ordered another wine for them both.

*

"Kirsty," Madison said back at Buckoway the following morning. "When we've finished filling in all these application forms and the stuff the Border Guard wants us to choose, can we have a private chat?"

"About Norris coming onto you?"

"No, I can deal with him. It's something personal."

Kirsty grinned. "What could be more personal than Norris trying to hop in your bed?"

"It's about you."

The other girl frowned. "Okay, give me a few moments with these forms and I'll be with you. What did you choose as your major skill to learn with the Border Guards?"

"Archery," Madeline said. "Who wants to go nursing or fix fences?"

"Oh Madison, fencing is sword fighting, not fixing fences."

"Whatever!"

"Oh my God, there you are all serious again. What say we stroll along to that park near the wall and we can chat without Norris or Wade butting in?"

The park followed the inside of the wall and had a pebble path that wandered through shady trees. Even though it was by the main ring road everything was quiet and peaceful. At least cursing ox wagon drivers weren't as noisy as motor vehicles! The two girls found a bench beside a small artificial lake and tossed bits of bread out for the ducks.

"Okay, fire away," Kirsty said.

"Can you remember..."

"It's not that mind bending game again?"

Madison laughed. "No, it's something real I'd like you to try to think about."

"What?"

"The lady in a pink nightie who held your hand and told you how proud she was and that it was okay to cry."

Kirsty stopped half way through throwing out another crust of bread into the water and placed a hand across her mouth. She gasped, turned and stared at Madison. "Who was the lady?"

"You tell me, Kirsty."

"But at the orphanage?"

"We were never in an orphanage, Kirsty. None of us were."

"What did she look like?"

"A lot like you, I think. She would have been in her thirties I guess. You told me she had long blonde hair that she combed in front of a wall mirror every morning."

"I told you?" Kirsty gasped.

Madison nodded. "Just yesterday."

"Oh hell." Kirsty gasped, stood up and ran away.

Madison rushed after her friend and caught up to her by a little footbridge. When Kirsty turned her face was tearstained. "It was Mom," she sobbed.

Oh my God. Madison's own lip trembled as she grabbed her friend into her arms. "It was. I had to find something in your suppressed memory to see if you really had it."

"Had what?"

"Childhood memories, Kirsty. Not implanted ones about the orphanage."

"But you said I told you."

"We always shared our innermost secrets, remember?"

"That horrible word again."

40

"Sorry. I'm just trying to say we've been friends for eight years now. We went to high school together, then university. We both graduated just last term. You teased me because I got a higher mark in applied math than you. We were always competing over our math scores."

"Yeah. You got A- and I got B+"

"Oh hell!" This time it was Madison who felt like crying.

*

"No girls," the grizzled Border Guard sergeant grumbled at the two new recruits. "You're too tense. Don't look at the arrow. Line your eye along it to focus on the target, that red and yellow circle across the field."

"Sarcastic old sod," Madison muttered but moved her bow slightly so the target came into view. She let the string go and heard a sort of whiz as the arrow shot away.

"You did it, Madison," Kirsty screamed. "You hit the target."

Madison glanced up and saw her arrow quivering on the outer section of the target. After half a dozen attempts she finally hit it.

She grinned. "Okay Kirsty. Your turn to get your one there."

The sergeant watched as the blonde girl pulled her bowstring, moved her front hand ever so slightly and let the string go. Her arrow ended up closer to the red inner circle than Madison's.

"At last," the sergeant snorted. "Now if that was a Mud you were aiming at, he'd have a sore shoulder by now. Hit the red and he'd be down for good."

"I don't want to kill anything," Madison said. "Not even an animal."

The sergeant pulled on his bushy beard and broke into a grin. "I'm pleased," he said.

"You are?"

"Aye. Most of the lads I have here are hell bent on shooting every deer or wildcat out in the grasslands. If you don't like killing, when an emergency arises you will use your talents with discretion. Now this time hit the red."

When Madison let the string go, the arrow curved up like a glowing slither in air before it dropped back and hit the outer edge of the red.

"I did it!" she gasped

The sergeant nodded at Kirsty. "Your turn, Girl."

Kirsty nodded and concentrated on the target. Her arrow whizzed through the air and hit the red just beside Madison's arrow.

"Good," the sergeant said and walked away.

"Did you hear that?" Kirsty said with a laugh. "He paid us a compliment."

*

The newcomers were in their second week of Border Guard duty. They were up at six thirty every morning, which worked out well for Madison. Whenever she woke up either in Buckoway or in Sacramento it was six-thirty in the morning, almost to the exact minute. At the camp, they worked all day and were finally allowed to return to their tent thirteen hours later. Everyone except Madison was exhausted. She returned *home* every time she fell asleep and told the Earth-bound Kirsty of her day at Buckoway. A day on Earth was followed by another sleep cycle when she woke up relaxed and ready for another day of military service. Having two Kirstys to confide in was now a strange routine.

*

Three weeks slipped by at Buckoway when another strange event took place. Every female newcomer from the graduation group on Earth started her period on the same day. For Madison, this was out of synchronization with herself on Earth by about two weeks.

"Damn nuisance," she muttered to Kirsty back home in California. "Having two a month is ridiculous."

"But it proves something we had guessed," Kirsty said.

"What?'"

"You do not physically leave here."

"So there're two of me just the same as there are two of you."

"That's right but for some reason you have only one conscious mind that is split between the two places."

"That's why my leg is perfect there."

Kirsty smiled. "But your leg is getting better here as well, isn't it?"

"Slowly," Madison admitted. "I don't need crutches now but still limp and need to rest if I try to walk too far."

"Oh there's one other thing," Kirsty said. "I've found a contact address on the internet."

"What for?"

"Your situation."

Madison sighed. "Yeah so have I, dozens of them. They range from groups who reckon the earth is still flat to ones that say the Second Coming is already here and cloned UFO's are circling our planet. They're all a bunch of nutters, lonely old men with nothing else to do in their lives."

"This one is different."

"How?"

"It's part of a government site. It's called *Our Century* and is aimed at making the twenty-first century a place of peace for our world."

"Well, they've failed miserably so far."

"Madison," Kirsty retorted. "I'm trying to help you ... all of us actually."

"Sorry. I was being cynical but after a month it seems so hopeless."

"They have an article on those bees that attacked us and want to hear from anyone who has had unusual side-effects. Now nothing could be more unusual than yours."

Madison looked interested and read the article with interest when Kirsty brought it up on her computer.

"Nothing new is included," she said with disappointment in her tone. "They still suggest it is a variety of bee that probably arrived here in a container ship."

"They're cautious, yes but I think they know more than they're letting on. What harm would come if we contact them?"

"Plenty," Madison said.

"Like what?"

"Somebody is colonizing Buckoway with humans. The wagons that Hamish and Shane are a part of, brought in another group of about sixty only last week. They're all our age, well educated and I'd swear the new ones have Canadian accents. Couldn't the very same people who are doing these abductions have this site set up to check on anybody like myself? It would be dead easy to infiltrate an official looking site like the United Nations or government site."

"So let's check anyway," Kirsty said.

She clicked on a link icon and a heading Latest *Reports* came up.

"Our one was the most recent entry when I checked few days ago." Kirsty said as the page began to load.

"But not now," Madison whispered. "Look at this. It's dated a week ago."

The Vancouver Sun in British Columbia as well as several local television stations reports that sixty-three students from the University of British Columbia were attacked by the Alpha Strain bees in a lecture theatre. The bees swarmed in through an open-air duct and stung the sixty-three students just once in the neck. The lecturer, five foreign language and ten adult students over thirty-five in the room were ignored. Apart from the initial pain from the sting, the students were unharmed and have now fully recovered from the attack.

Kirsty stared at Madison. "Your new immigrants?"

"Yes, and they're becoming more selective."

"So what do we do?"

"Don't contact anyone on this site" Madison whispered. "It is too risky."

"But we can do nothing here on our own. If we don't reply we'll get nowhere."

"No,"

"Then what?"

"I'll talk to somebody I can trust."

"Who?"

"I have an appointment with my surgeon, Doctor Joel Mitchell, this afternoon. He was quite amazed with my leg. Apparently my spine has repaired itself by regrowing cell tissue. He asked me last time if there was anything unusual I knew that I should tell him about."

"But you said nothing."

"I almost did. That was two weeks ago. Since then ... well you know everything that has happened. I'd rather talk to him than reply to an anonymous web site."

"Perhaps I could come too," Kirsty replied.

"Thanks, I'd like that."

Madison stared at Kirsty but neither of them smiled.

*

"We would like to give you a head scan as well as the one of your spine," Joel Mitchell said after his examination was almost complete.

"Just in case my nano-sized transmitter is broadcasting beyond the Milky Way?" Madison said.

The doctor stopped and studied his patient but the eyes that held his were serious. "Is there something you haven't told me, Madison?" he asked.

"It's nothing to do with my accident but there is something I've experienced since I was stung by that artificial bee. Up until now I have only confided in my closest friend. She is in the waiting room now."

"What happened, Madison?"

"It sounds impossible but I have found myself split between two places."

"Two places?"

"Yes. When I go to sleep I wake up somewhere else and I don't believe it is even on this world."

Doctor Mitchell walked behind his desk and sat down, tapped his fingers on the wooden surface and looked up. "You say you've talked to just one friend and she's here now?"

"On this side she's the only one. There are a couple of men who found me on the other side who know of my situation. Everyone who was stung is there too but they have no memories of their life here."

Doctor Mitchell held his hand up. "And your friend's name?" he asked.

"Kirsty Bell."

The doctor nodded and pressed an intercom button. "Helen, could you ask a Kirsty Bell to step into my office please. Also, please inform my other patients there has been an emergency and all appointments are delayed an hour. Please give those who can't wait a new appointment." He glanced up at Madison. "Would you object if I recorded our conversation?"

"It is confidential, Doctor Mitchell. I don't want what I'm about to say given to a third party."

"But you would talk to somebody else if we guarantee your confidentiality and security?"

Madison frowned and was glad when Kirsty stepped in the room and stood beside her. "How can you do that?"

"The Federal Secrecy Act will be invoked."

"I've never heard of it," Kirsty cut in. "How can some law stop people from talking?"

Mitchell smiled just a quiver. "Oh it can," he whispered. A buzzer sounded. "Yes, Helen."

"Colonel Brad Davis has arrived, Doctor Mitchell."

Mitchell frowned. "He can wait ten minutes. Tell him I'm in emergency surgery..."

"He won't believe me, Joel."

"Do whatever is needed Helen but keep him out for ten minutes." He glanced up at the two women. "That's the man I was talking about. He appears ruthless but has Federal Government clearance to Code Red level that is just below the level held by senators. "

"Oh hell."

"If you wish to say nothing I can let you out a back door." Joel Mitchell said. "All I can say is that if you don't talk to this man, you shouldn't talk to anybody ... in either world."

"So you believe me?" Madison whispered.

"You may have the proof were waiting for, Madison." the doctor said. He grinned when he heard a thump on the door. "Our security locks are strong. If you want to leave, tell me now and even our overbearing colonel won't know you've been here."

Madison stared at Kirsty who screwed her nose up. "No, we'll stay, Doctor Mitchell," she said.

*

"Kirsty stays or I say nothing. She is involved in this situation as much as I am." Madison was not the slightest bit intimidated by the uniformed colonel. "I am not a part of your military hierarchy so will not be ordered around."

Brad Davis glanced up at Kirsty and gave a slight shrug of his shoulders. "Very well, Miss Evans as long as Miss Bell also makes the secrecy pledge."

"I shall do that," Kirsty whispered.

The three were seated in a fifth floor office in an indiscreet building in downtown Sacramento. No signs indicated who the tenants were but once inside, marines stopped anybody without a pass from moving beyond the reception area. To Madison it was in many ways like the castle in Buckoway.

With the formalities over Madison began her story. She decided that if she was to trust the colonel she would tell him everything. He sat cross-legged and listened to the unfolding story.

"So why do you think this town of Buckoway was set up as it is, Madeline?"

"It reminds me like a museum piece rather than real life?"

"Why?"

"I think modern facilities were picked for convenience in what would otherwise be a Middle Ages village."

"Like what?" Davis asked.

"Electricity for lights, heating and cooking but there are no radios or television. There are modern buildings with elevators but no cars or aeroplanes."

"But you saw computers in that castle?"

"I know but nobody else did. When Kirsty and the others woke up the room looked like the interior of a house."

The colonel turned to the other girl. "And you have no memory of this alternate place at all, Kirsty?"

"None. I only know about myself there from Madison's descriptions."

"But the Kirsty in Buckoway has memories of here," Madison added.

"Only old ones of her childhood, not of what is happening here at the present time?" Davis asked.

Kirsty frowned. "I think I know what you mean. The other Kirsty is not picking up my thoughts or knows anything of my life after I was stung by that robotic bee."

"It appears so," Davis said.

"So how come I have a full memory of everything?" Madison asked.

The colonel looked up. "That second sting probably caused it but to be frank, we don't know why."

"Will I be in any danger?"

"Are you threatened at the moment?"

"Not at all. Except for that '*you should remember*' suggestion and the strange castle, everything appears quite free. I believe we were somehow copied with the idea of using us to help them rather than changing our present lives. We are just a donor."

Davis frowned. "Why do you say donor, Madison?"

"It's only my theory."

"But an important one. Go on, please."

"I tried to think of a comparison where I could give a part of myself to someone else. The closest analogy I can make is comparing it to donating blood. My blood would go into someone else's body and help them. It is still alive but I know nothing about it. I believe our minds and personalities have been copied, put in an empty shell and restarted. The new person is a copy of the old one in every way and from that moment on is a new person who lives and adapts to this new environment."

"Like a robot?" Kirsty said.

"No, everyone there is alive. You have the same mannerisms, way of talking and even eating habits that you have here."

"Perhaps we are going about this the wrong way," the colonel said. "What do you find that is different about your friends in this new place?"

"I told you about our health, no memories of our life here and all my females friends starting our period on the same day..."

"Which suggests you were all created at the same time."

"I noticed that any interests or hobbies we had here are forgotten. Norris is crazy about his old car here but over there he has no equivalent interest."

"What about life in general?' Davis asked.

"I think us females are there to breed," Madison said. "As well as that bit about my friends stating they wanted babies I found several other things."

"What?"

"There is no contraception at all, no pills, condoms or any other preventatives." She flushed slightly. "Oh hell, there's something else, too."

"Go on."

"Babies all have their mother's surname."

"So the men get off Scott free," Kirsty retorted.

"No. All males and females without children pay a family tax. As soon as a female becomes pregnant she stops paying and receives a benefit. No women with children are expected to work."

"Can they if they want to?" Davis asked.

"I don't think they want do work. Perhaps this is part of the *remember* programming."

"Interesting," the colonel said. "I have one last question for now."

Madison nodded.

"Can Buckoway sustain itself?"

"What do you mean?"

"You mentioned farms but is there enough locally produced food available to feed the population?"

"Oh hell," Madison whispered. "I never thought of that. There couldn't be, could there?"

"You tell me."

"The supermarkets have everything; canned and frozen food, salt, pepper, fresh vegetables and even things like bananas and coffee that couldn't be grown locally."

"So where does it come from?"

"I've no idea. It's just there. Like here, we just assume the food will be there for us to buy."

"Exactly," Davis said. "Perhaps this might be a good starting point for you when you go back. Perhaps ask Hamish and Sean." He leaned forward. "Just be discrete, Madison. Back off if people become vague or hesitant."

"You think there may be something sinister behind all of this?"

"All isn't as it appears on the surface, that's all I'm saying at the moment. With your help, we'll try to find out what's happening and, if possible, stop any more attacks by these aliens. It's like our war against terrorism, Madison. With your help we can stop it before it is too late."

*

CHAPTER SIX

Brad Davis and Joel Mitchell sat in the office after the two women had left. Davis turned to a television monitor that flickered on to show a man in a Canadian Armed Forces general's uniform.

"Was the interview of help to you General Finlay?" Joel asked.

The man on the screen nodded. "She confirms the research we've obtained from the BC University students. Our findings may be of interest to you but first a question."

"Go ahead, Sir," Colonel Davis said.

"It's really for Doctor Mitchell. What did your microsurgery labs find in that device taken from your patient's leg?"

"It is some sort of transmission device, General Finlay but we now believe we only recovered the container. The circuits inside had some sort of self-destruct mechanism that we first thought would harm our patient's heart rhythm. We now believe the actual device was in the liquid absorbed in Madison Evans' bloodstream. It was not metallic substance but bacteria that can reproduce itself in her blood stream. It has stimulated her nerve endings and her bruised spinal cords have become healthy tissue. Within a few weeks she will have no difficulty in walking at all."

The general nodded. "It is a hybrid, Doctor Mitchell, an artificial creation that the human body recognizes as a biological substance. The antibiotics created to destroy this intruder are what helped stimulate your patient's spinal cord, not the substance itself."

"Can I ask how you obtained this information, Sir?" Davis asked.

The general's eyebrows rose slightly. "A post-mortem was carried out here in Vancouver on one of the students who had a fatal seizure after being stung in the latest attack. We kept him on an artificial respirator while the tests were performed. There's more, too."

The two men in the room glanced at each other.

"Research from Great Britain has arrived at an interesting scenario. I'd like to switch you over to Professor Graham McDoyle in Cambridge, England. He can tell you everything in his own words."

The screen changed to show a middle-aged man staring at the camera. "Good evening gentlemen," he said in a British accent. "I shall get straight to the point. We believe that in every attack by these robotic insects, one victim's body is injected with a receiving transmitter possibly programmed to transmit information into the victim's subconscious brain when he or she is asleep. Everyone else has a device that only transmits information out."

"How are they different, Professor?" the general's voice said.

"We can only guess. The information sent out is possibly a recording of the victim's brain patterns and also a digital representation of their DNA. The one victim with a receiving device may well receive information that will let the alien control their thoughts and actions. They could be dormant for years and lead ordinary lives until the transmitter is activated."

"So these could be the dangerous ones?" General Finlay appeared on the screen again.

"Yes."

"And can they be traced."

Professor McDoyle nodded. "Our scientists are working on it."

"How does this fit into everything we have learned from Madison Evans?" Joel Mitchell asked.

McDoyle smiled slightly. "Our theory is that when Miss Evans was stung in the neck the device immediately began gathering and transmitting information about her DNA. A few seconds later the second sting was injected and began receiving information. However, the information being received was the same information going out being looped back. In other words, she was receiving information about herself. This is still happening. The section that works on her subconscious still operates so the transmissions only come and go when she was not using her mind for normal everyday functions."

"When she's asleep," Joel said.

"That's what we believe. We also have a theory that our alien adversaries don't know Madeline has this unique ability."

"Why?" General Finlay asked.

"What do you gentlemen do if something goes wrong in one of your highly classified experiments, say a spy satellite goes astray?"

Colonel Davis answered. "Destroy it and try again."

"Exactly. The fact that our young friend is still alive and looking very self confident and healthy means that she has not been discovered."

" ... Or that the enemy are playing a close chess game," Finlay muttered.

"There are no absolutes, I'm afraid." McDoyle replied. "I assume you have the girl monitored at all times."

"Yeah," grunted Mitchell. "It's crude by our alien's standard but I doubt if she's even noticed the new filling in one of her back teeth."

*

The *Buckoway Stables Co-operative* building was a low wooden structure beside the town wall south of the main gate. Inside, were stalls for thirty oxen and a dozen horses as well as feed storage bunkers and an access way through the centre. A massive door on the wall side stood open so the beasts could be led outside to fields of grass and oats.

It was morning and Hamish was cleaning his wagon down with a high-pressure hose. He glanced up and saw three people watching him.

"Well, hello there, Madison," he said and grinned at the other two. "What are you doing down here so early on such a grand summer's day?"

Madison held up a notice she had just ripped off the notice board outside. "We've come for the jobs," she said.

Hamish squinted at the notice. He knew what it said, of course, as he'd only written it himself the evening before.

Wanted, two strong employees to act as oxen drivers and tally clerks. Must be good with animals and numbers, able to defend themselves in the outer lands and be able to work independently. Some overnight stays outside the town walls may be necessary on longer trips.

"Well?" Madison said.

"Norris here looks a strong lad but you two lassies..." Hamish stroked his red beard. "You may find it a little hard. As much as I would like..."

"Hamish," Madison scolded. "Didn't you read that pronouncement in only last week's *Gazette* stating no discrimination by sex was allowed."

"It's dangerous out there, Lassie. How could you defend yourself against Muds if they turn up?"

Kirsty grinned and took a yellow card from her pocket. "We have all completed our military training and received a master ranking in archery. Have a look."

"All of you?" Hamish muttered. "In archery?"

"Well mine was in fencing," Norris said. "The girls are the hot shots with the bow and arrow."

"There're only two vacancies and three of you," Hamish continued. He glanced up and flushed when he noticed Sean watching them.

"We'll spilt the wages," Madison said. "Pay us each two thirds of the going rate."

"They want the jobs, Sean. Do you reckon they can handle it?" Hamish said.

"For sure, Hamish. We know Madison here is reliable and I reckon her friends are our friends. How about a wee test, though."

"Like what?" Madison asked with suspicion in her eyes.

Sean grinned. "Aye, you can see I've just hitched Doris and Daisy up to the wagon. Over in that stall there, you'll find Diane and Ducky. Now all you need to do is bring them out and hitch them up in front of the other two oxen." He grinned. "It usually takes me about five minutes."

"We'll do it," Norris retorted and, followed by the two girls, walked over to the stalls and opened the first gate.

The gigantic ox just glowered at him and stood chewing her cud. Norris grabbed a rope around the animal's neck and undid the end tied to a metal hoop.

"Come on, girl," he said and pulled the rope.

The rope went taut but nothing else happened! The ox just stamped a front foot and moved not one centimetre.

Sean grinned. "Old Ducky can get stubborn at times," he said. "Give her a sharp slap on the rump."

Norris coughed. "Slap on the rump, you say?"

"For sure. Show her whose boss."

"And if she decides to make a run for it?"

Sean shrugged.

"Come on Kirsty," Madison whispered. "Let's do it our way."

"How?" Kirsty looked decidedly nervous.

Madison tugged her friend's arm and walked across to where a pile of silage sat in a wooden trough. It was warm and stunk like half-fermented malt wine.

"Help me," she said and gathered an armful in her arms.

"Yuck," Kirsty moaned. "You could get drunk on this stuff." She did, however, grab an armful and followed her friend back to the stall.

Madison held a handful just out from Ducky's nose. "Come and get it Ducky," she coached.

The ox stepped forward and the girl stepped back. Half way across to the wagon she let Ducky curl her tongue around the silage and suck it in.

"Your turn," she said to Kirsty.

"Me!"

"You want the job, don't you?"

Kirsty coached Ducky in front of the other two oxen and Madeline grabbed the rope around its neck. The ox sort of rolled her eyes and walked into place ready to be hitched up. The last ox ambled out, had her mouthful of silage and was also hitched up.

"Ten minutes," Sean said. "Do you think these three will be an asset or liability, Hamish."

"They'll do, I reckon." Hamish chuckled. "Well, get aboard you lot. We've got a major journey today."

Madison frowned. "You mean now?"

"Why not? Didn't I just hear you asking Kirsty if she wanted the job?"

Madison laughed and grabbed her friend's hands. "Come on," she said. "We've just joined the ranks of those employed and contributing to society. I'll teach you the commands we use for the oxen."

Norris stared at her. "How do you know them?" he asked.

"Oh, I've been aboard before," Madison replied. She turned and raised her eyebrows "So have you, actually."

*

Once outside the town, Hamish turned their wagon away from the road they'd come in on and headed east towards rolling hills. The farms petered out into course grass and shrubs.

"Big game country," Hamish said to the three jammed between the drivers' seat and a wagon filled with cardboard boxes. "This is where the wild herds are. I guess they'd be a distant relation of our oxen here."

"Are they are what the Muds hunt?" Norris asked.

"Yeah. The trouble is the herds are getting smaller and Muds find it more difficult to get enough food. That's where we come in."

"How?" Madison asked.

"You'll see," Sean replied. "You will soon meet some."

"Oh hell," Kirsty whispered. "We should have brought our bow and arrows."

"No Lassie, mutual respect is more important. These are proud people with generations of traditions. Us wagonmasters have learned a little of their ways and have found it helps."

Madison frowned. "But you originally said they were like humans hundreds of years ago with grey skin and stooped shoulders."

"That's the official description, Madison. Few people at Buckoway have ever seen a Mud so the story grows."

"It helps the referees at home to keep the image of savages, alive," Sean added "For sure they are primitive people but they're as human as we are."

"Like the Australian aborigines," Madison said. She glanced at the vacant stares of her companions and laughed when she realized they had no idea what she was talking about. "It doesn't matter," she added and shrugged.

*

After almost an hour they crossed a high range of hills before the wagon came to a plain of dull brown grass that stretched out to the horizon. Closer, though, was a village.

"Oh hell," Kirsty whispered and grabbed Madison's arm.

To Madison the huts looked like round cottages made of stone with thatched roofs. They were arranged in a circle around a large round building in the centre of a dusty field. It was like a gigantic marquee with open sides and a thatched roof. Children were playing a game while several adults appeared to be sitting in chairs under a veranda that hung out from the large building.

The children glanced up, there was a scream and en-mass thirty or forty children ran towards them.

"It's called The Trading Post," Hamish said. "Would one of you hand me that yellow canvas bag under the seat, please? When they arrive, smile and say..." The strange words curled off his tongue but sounded a little like hanky and songi, songi, songi.

"What does it mean," Norris asked.

Sean laughed. "The closest we could get to *hi* and *candy* in their language. This happens every time we arrive."

Within moments chatting, shouting children surrounded the wagon. They did have grey skin but their hair was a reddish brown and their facial features were not unlike Asians on Earth.

Every child wore leather shorts but nothing else. The older girls were quite mature with bosoms that bounced as they walked.

Madison grinned and dug Norris in the ribs. "Simmer down," she whispered.

She noticed that when the wagon stopped, the older girls each placed their arms around two smaller children as if they had been assigned to look after them. The children patted the oxen and stared up at them.

"Songi, songi, songi," they shouted.

Hamish and Sean stood up and very slowly brought the yellow bag into sight. The children screamed in delight.

"You do it." Hamish said to Madison. "It'll show them you're a friend."

54

Madison and her two friends reached in the bag and pulled out handfuls of candy, each wrapped in wax paper.

"Stops them getting dirty," Sean said.

Madison stood up and the circle of chatting children stopped, silence descended on the area and the Mud girls gripped their charges tightly.

Hamish stood beside Madeline and placed a hand on her shoulder. "Madison," he called in a loud voice and whispered. "Say the words and throw the candy out. Remember little throws for the young ones."

"Hanky," Madison called. "Songi, songi, songi."

She threw her candy out over the children's heads. All hell broke loose as the children dived for the candy. Kirsty and Norris joined in and threw handful after handful out. At one point, Madison glanced down and saw large hazel coloured eyes staring up at her. The little children wanted their candy.

"Songi," Madeline laughed and dropped two handfuls over them.

The little ones laughed and rushed around picking it up.

When the bag was empty, Hamish held it up. "All gone!" he called.

The surrounding children stopped and Madison saw that all the older children gave the little ones some of their candy before everyone backed away, waved and ran, screaming back to the dusty field. "They aren't savage," she said. "Did you notice how the older girls protected the little ones?"

"These are the Sumatti," Hamish said. "They're the local tribe that we trade with. Other tribes aren't so friendly towards us."

He shouted an order and the four oxen pulled the wagon around the back of the central building. Everywhere were long tables piled with row after row of fruit, vegetables and other goods. Oranges, bananas and coconuts were on one table while another held tomatoes, cucumbers and other species unknown to Madison. Another table held what looked like spices and coffee beans all in white cloth bags the size of pillowcases.

"Our tropical food!" Kirsty gasped.

"But where does it come from?" Norris asked.

"As far as we can work out, on the other side of this plain is an ocean. Apparently, ships sail in and they trade goods, often the stuff we barter with here."

"And what do we have?" Madison asked.

"Food they want like powdered milk and cheese, medicines, tools, nails and household things such as pots and pans."

"Also clothes," Sean said. "Tartan skirts like you're wearing are in fashion. Boots and footwear are also becoming popular."

Madison noticed the adults who waited by the tables. The women were bare breasted like their children but over half of them wore tartan skirts and some had sneakers on their feet.

At the far end of the building were two empty tables.

"That's where we put our stuff," Sean said. "As well as trading with us, they trade with each other. People come in huge distances to this trading post. Some just sell basic things like skins and woven baskets while others have more sophisticated things like jewellery."

"Wander around," Hamish said. "Always smile and if there is anything you'll like, come and tell me. I'll do the bartering."

After they helped unload the supplies from the wagon and set out their tables the three friends walked around the Muds' tables. Immediately, they were followed by children who clutched their clothes or hands as they walked around. At every table, women stood patiently and gave shy smiles when they approached and looked at the goods on display.

"Madison," Kirsty screamed. "I want this. Look!"

She held up a long red and crimson wrap around skirt. She smiled at the woman at the table who gave a tiny bow as Kirsty wrapped the exquisite silk around herself.

"Like it?" she said.

"It's beautiful," Madison replied,

The woman stepped forward and tugged on Kirsty's tartan skirt then gazed into her eyes.

"Oh hell," Kirsty said, "She wants it." She undid the skirt and began to wriggle out of it.

"Kirsty," Madison cried in horror, "You can't undress here in public."

"Why not? "

Nobody took the slightest notice as she slipped out of the tartan skirt, wrapped the new silken one around her waist and stood back.

"How's that?" she said.

"Yeah why don't you swap the top half too," Norris said with a smirk over his face,

"But she's wearing nothing..."

"That's what I mean," Norris said and ducked as Madison aimed a powerful fist at his shoulder.

"Behave yourself," she hissed "Or next time we'll leave you behind to wash the shit out of the stables in Buckoway."

*

"You mean I stripped in front of everyone and paraded around in my panties," a horrified Kirsty gasped in The *Hooded Lady* back on Earth.

"Oh it wasn't too bad," Madison admitted. "We wear pretty modest underclothes over there and you didn't parade around either."

"But Norris was all eyes."

"Yeah, I think he fancies you."

"Here or there," Kirsty whispered.

"Just there," Madison replied in quite a serious voice.

"Thank goodness," Kirsty said. "Anyway, what happened at that village?"

"I bartered for a lovely necklace and earrings."

"Your skirt too?"

"No, two shovels and a spade from the wagon, actually. Hamish will take the value out of my wages. We stayed at the trading centre a couple of hours and went home loaded with oranges, bananas, spices, other food and more of the clothing. Back at Buckoway, Hamish sold the stuff to the local supermarket warehouse. I think he made quite a profit."

"So we're both enjoying life there?" Kirsty asked.

Madison smiled. "You know I think we are. You're just the same, you know, even down to your giggle. Often, I forget there are two of you." She sipped at the glass of wine in her hand. "I'm still worried, though. It's almost too peaceful at the moment, you know, like the calm before a storm."

*

CHAPTER SEVEN

It was close to midnight when the twenty-year-old Mustang headed along the highway. Madison and Norris had celebrated their success in their job applications with an evening at the theatre. Madison thought about new position as computer programmer for a local company and grinned. What a contrast it was to working with the oxen across on the other side.

"What's the grin about?" Norris asked.

"My jobs," she said.

"Jobs?"

"You know what I told you about us in the other world? Over there I drive oxen and do some quite heavy physical work. Here I sit in front of a computer screen all day pushing keyboard keys." She glanced up. "You're pretty good at handing the oxen now, you know."

"It's not me," Norris said with a stubborn streak in his voice.

Madison sucked on her lip. While Kirsty had become completely open and cheerful about her alternative self, Norris was still somewhat sceptical. Sure he believed her but didn't really grasp the idea of being there as well. Perhaps it was his male pride that let him down.

"Okay," he said. "There's a copy of me in this world of yours but I according to what you say I behave differently, don't I"

Madison pouted. "How?"

"Well I don't drive a car."

"There aren't any cars there."

"Perhaps we should think of the other ones as our twins," Norris said.

Perhaps Norris was trying to understand, after all. Of course his scenario didn't take into account that she was one person, not two. She sat back as Norris turned off the highway and headed up Cosgrove Drive, a tree line road where they lived. Their apartment was the part of a long two-storey building with an outside staircase and balcony to provide access to floor two. After her accident, their landlord had shifted them to Apartment 16 so she could have wheelchair access directly off the car lot. When Norris drove the Mustang in, neither of them took any notice of the white van parked at the end of the lot.

*

Colonel Davis peered through the semidarkness from the van and heaved. "It's them. Alert everyone."

"Yes Sir," the sergeant at the back already had earphones on. He reached up and pressed a button on the sophisticated looking radio that filled half the van, "Red Base Alpha calling all stations. Please respond with your positions"

"Red 2 is ready in Apartment 26." This was directly over Madison's apartment.

"Red 3 is on the corner of Garden and Highway Five."

"Red 4 here. We're south on Riverside Boulevard."

And so it continued with even one call in from a spy plane flying fifty thousand feet above the city.

"Satellite 4473 will be online in three minutes," another voice said.

"Good. What can you see Red 2?"

"The pair are heading for the master bedroom and ... hell colonel do you really want all the details?"

"No son," Davis muttered. "Will you be able to tell me when the girl is asleep?"

"Sure, we are recording her heartbeat now. As soon as she falls asleep the computer will alert us."

"And are you sure it'll be her and not the male?"

"It'll be her, sir."

"Good. All stations home in on Red 2's signal. We can practice our triangulation."

Another voice came on line. "North Shield Radio Telescope here, Colonel Davis. We have every radio telescope in North America and Hawaii tuned in. Every transmission made to or from your site will be intercepted."

"And blocked from going beyond the atmosphere?" the colonel whispered.

"All known frequencies will be blocked."

"Thank you. Yellow alert standby."

Davis leaned back and glanced at Doctor Mitchell sitting across from him. "Why do I get the feeling we're like children playing with fire, Joel," he asked.

"Because there are too many variables, Brad. We're assuming that the transmission coming the girl's body will fit in with our knowledge."

"I know. We've been through all that but we must try."

"Yes," the doctor said. "Even though we might kill the girl in the process."

Madison sighed and rolled over. After a frantic and exhausting bout of lovemaking it was amazing how Norris could fall asleep in seconds.

"Well here we go again," she muttered. The sensation of awaking an instant later feeling refreshed and ready to continue her other life was now routine. Not once did she awaken in the same world as the one where she went asleep. Now she always awoke in the other world at six thirty in the morning, local time.

Madison shut her eyes and drifted asleep...

*

"Red 2 here. The subject is asleep."

"Good," Davis muttered. "Switch it all on, sergeant."

*

"No!" Madison managed to scream before her heart began to race and every muscle in her body appeared to jump at once.

In seconds the girl was shaking and moaning, her arms and legs stiffened and she gave a spluttering cough. Foam formed around her mouth and her eyes rolled back beneath the lids.

Norris awoke instantly when Madison's arms hit him across the body and face. The bed's blankets disappeared and the girl's moans pierced the night air. Norris found a light switch but to see his partner was worse than just hearing her.

Her face was chalk white except where blood ran down a cut lip. Perspiration poured off her body and, even as he watched, she jerked up as if hit by lightning, flopped back and her limbs went taut.

"Madison!" Norris screamed.

The door opened and Kirsty stood there in her pyjamas. "Oh hell," she gasped. "It's some sort of fit. Make sure she doesn't swallow her tongue." She turned. "Yasmin," she screamed. "Phone emergency. Something is terribly wrong."

Norris grabbed Madison and used a hairbrush handle and forced her mouth open. Blood poured out. "She's bitten her tongue," he cried.

"Turn her over sideways," Kirsty yelled. "She'll drown in her own blood."

The three friends did what they could but Madison continued to squirm around. She gave one mighty jump, flopped back on her pillow and stopped moving.

"Madison," Norris screamed. "Madison... oh my God. Madison." He grabbed her and burst into tears.

*

"Madison," Kirsty screamed in their Buckoway apartment. "What's wrong? "

Yasmin rushed across the room and stared in horror at her friend. The girl on the bed amongst the wet sheets and strewn blankets was covered in perspiration. Her eyes were shut and skin white.

"What happened, Kirsty?"

"You know how she always wakes up at six thirty?" She nodded at the old fashioned clock on their wall.

"Yes," Yasmin gasped as she grabbed Madison's wrist and tried to find a pulse.

"Instead of waking she went into this sort of fit... Oh hell, is she okay?"

"There's no pulse," Yasmin cried. "I'll go and get a doctor," she said."

"Oh hell," Kirsty sobbed. "I think it's too late!"

*

"Red alert. Abort all transmissions. Repeat; switch the Goddamn thing down. The subject's heart has stopped."

"Mission aborted, Colonel Davis," a metallic voice responded. "Shut down was forty-seven point one three seconds after activation."

"I hope we can get to her in time, colonel," Mitchell muttered as he flung the van door open. He'd already sounded the alert and the standby medical team was running across the car lot. "If we can't don't her heart started I am going to personally lay a complaint with the White House."

"Do that," Colonel Davis snapped but he looked shaken as the monitor in their van made a monotonous hum and a white line ran flat across the screen.

*

The officer at North Shield Radio Telescope watched the instruments light up. "We have a trace," he muttered to nobody in particular. "My God, it's not going into deep space. It's as if there is a receiving satellite orbiting out there. Look, Sir!"

The general was already looking over the other man's shoulder as a yellow and white wave slid across the screen and stopped. Without warning the screen went blank and the steady pulse noise turned to static.

"Get it back!" the general snapped.

"Can't Sir. The signal has shut down. No transmissions are coming from Sacramento."

"Damn!" the general muttered. "How long did we have it for, captain?"

"Forty-seven seconds, Sir. We may have a trace. Forty-five was the absolute minimum but to be realistic two or three minutes were really required."

"Keep monitoring. Perhaps it will come back."

*

"Doctor Mitchell!" Kirsty gasped when she answered the medical team's frantic knocks. "It looks bad, doctor."

"Right," Mitchell nodded and rushed through to the bedroom. "Move aside!" he said to Norris who was holding Madison in his arms. "Sorry son. If we hurry we may be able to get her heart beating. You have to move aside."

"Of course," Norris muttered. He placed Madison's head down on the pillow and slid out of the way. "It happened so quickly," he said. "I think she woke me up... Oh hell ... can you save her doctor?"

"We'll try," Mitchell said.

He grabbed two saucer-shaped metal plates and bent over the still body. "Ready!" he said and held them against Madison's skin.

Kirsty grabbed Yasmin's hand while Norris squeezed both girls close.

There was a sort of thud and Madison's body jerked up.

"Again!" Mitchell hissed.

The second charge sent Madison's body into another spasm but this time when she flopped back her arms continued to shake. The doctor placed his stethoscope on her chest and listened. The concentrated frown changed to a smile. "Her heart has begun to beat," he said.

"Thank God," Kirsty whispered and burst into tears.

"It's steady," Mitchell said. "Her heartbeat is steady." He glanced up. "I think she will be okay."

Madison's eyes fluttered and opened. She looked up and focused on Norris's tear stained face. "I'm okay but must get back," she whispered.

Her eyes shut as she flopped back.

"Madison!" Norris screamed.

"It's okay, Norris," Mitchell said. "She's fallen asleep. This is normal sleep. Her heart beat is normal."

"It happened to her in both places, doctor," Kirsty said. "She's gone back to her other life so our alternate selves won't be worried."

Joel Mitchell stared at her. "You could be right, Kirsty. I can only hope that she has no permanent injuries."

*

The Buckoway doctor, a young man not much older than the friends, looked perplexed.

"Her heart has stopped, I'm afraid. There is nothing I can do... No, wait a minute..." He bent forward and held his hand above the patient's nose. "I was wrong. She's breathing. Her heart definitely stopped but it's started again."

"Thank God," Kirsty whispered and burst into tears.

Madison's eyes fluttered and opened. She blinked and stared around. "Oh hell, it did happen," she gasped. Her eyes caught Norris's tear stained face, switched to the two girls and finally to the doctor. "I'm in our Buckoway dorm, aren't I?"

"Yes," Kirsty whispered. "Something terrible happened but you recovered. It's a miracle."

"No ... more like Doctor Mitchell," Madison said.

"My name is Doctor Chris Burton," the stranger said.

Madison turned her eyes and smiled at the man. "I'm sorry Doctor Burton. I must have been dreaming. Of course it was you who helped."

"But I..." the doctor said.

"You helped doctor," Madison whispered. "Thank you for coming so quickly." She caught Kirsty's eyes and gave a twitch of a wink.

"Oh hell, Madison," Kirsty gasped. "It's good to have you back."

*

The guard at the air force station slid back the sliding glass and stared at the driver of the vehicle that had screeched to a stop in front of the lowered barrier.

"I've come to see Colonel Davis and I wish to see him now." The woman driver spoke quietly but there was ice on her voice.

"If you have an appointment, please give me your name and pull across to that shoulder Ma'am," the guard said.

"My name is Madison Evans. I have no appointment but tell Colonel Davis he either speaks to me immediately or to my attorney at a later date. Oh yes, also inform him I shall be in contact with CNN this afternoon unless he can give me a very good reason for his actions last night."

"You can not come in here threatening us, Madam..." The guard glared at Madison.

"You contact him, Sergeant," Madison hissed. "I would not like to be your shoes if he hears what I have to say over tonight's CNN news."

The guard hesitated. "I shall contact him Ms....err... Evans. However, I don't even know if he is on base."

"Oh he is," Madison said. "Doctor Joel Mitchell informed me he was."

The guard nodded, slid the glass window shut and reached for his phone. Madison could hear nothing but the man's expression told a lot. A moment later the window slid back and the sergeant handed her a yellow card.

"Put this so it can be seen though your front windshield, Ma'am," he said. "Proceed straight ahead to Lane 16, turn left and park in Lot 16k. A military policeman will meet you there."

"Thank you Sergeant," Madison said as her car moved forward.

Ten minutes later she was shown into Colonel Davis's office where he was standing beside his desk waiting for her.

"You made a remarkable recovery, Madison," he said. "I don't know how I can help you, though. Surely it is Doctor Mitchell you should be consulting."

"You practically murdered me with your obscene experiment, Colonel Davis. I trusted you and you treated me like guinea pig."

"Come now, Madison?"

"My heart stopped, Colonel. It stopped in both worlds. You not only almost killed me here but on the other side, too."

The colonel sat down and waved Madison into another seat. "Both worlds you say? How do you know that?"

"Kirsty and Norris told me what happened here, how my heart stopped and how Doctor Mitchell got it beating again. Now wasn't it strange that a top surgeon just happened to be outside my apartment and just happened to have all the correct equipment to restart my heart?"

"I can explain but you are still bound by that secrecy pledge you signed."

"Which doesn't give you the licence to kill, Colonel Davis. Tell me, what was in your white van you jumped out of in our parking lot?"

"Yes, I was there," Davis admitted. "We made a calculated risk and it proved successful."

"What?" Madison appeared dumbfounded. "You almost killed me, twice."

"What happened on the other side?"

"Exactly the same as here. When Doctor Mitchell started my heart here, my heart at Buckoway started, too. The doctor there can't explain why."

"So you are linked in more than just your mind," Davis said.

"I guess I am but I don't know why."

"We traced a transmission coming from your body before you had that seizure," Davis said and gave Madison an explanation of the test they'd made. "Our one mistake was to try to intercept it."

"Why did you do that?"

"We thought we might be able to contact this other world, existence or whatever it is without having to go through you."

"But they were too smart for you?"

"It appears so."

"But you said you were successful?"

"Yes, just as you dropped asleep your body transmitted and received low powered signals from above The Equator."

"Low powered?"

"Yes, that was unexpected. It didn't come from deep space, Madison but from a small satellite placed in a stationary orbit above the Equator."

"But you never knew it was there?"

"It's the size of a golf ball."

"Okay, but why did I have that seizure?"

"It's only a theory. We transmitted a jamming signal as soon as we realized you were asleep. You body apparently needs to transmit information to your otherself, I guess they're memories of the day's events. When the signal was blocked your body tried to overcome the jam by increasing power. This continued until your mind crashed like a computer on overload. Your heart followed."

"And my otherself?"

"It was probably doing the same thing. When your heart stopped we switched the jamming transmissions off. You heart began to function and a signal was sent out with the information to stimulate your heart in your otherself. You woke up there and went back to sleep so you could wake up here."

"Almost right," Madison said. "I woke up here first and somehow knew my friends in Buckoway were worried about me." She frowned. "How did you know when I fell asleep?"

"You apartment was monitored."

"Oh hell," Madison blushed. "Okay, so from now on I want to know anything you intend to do. I trusted you and told you everything I knew. Don't you think you could trust me now?"

"I was under orders, Madison."

"So were three quarters of the officers in Serbia in the 1990s, Colonel. I don't believe The Hague Tribunal accepted that as a legitimate defence."

Brad Davis smiled. "You do have an extensive knowledge for your age, Madison."

The girl shrugged. "It was one of my university papers, that's all."

"I can't tell you everything but anything directly related to your friends or yourself will be discussed with you. In return I'd like you to make another observation on the other side."

"What of?"

"See if there are any star patterns at night you can remember. It may help us trace where your planet is in relation to Earth."

"So you think it's out there somewhere, not in some parallel universe?"

"That satellite they have must send your signals somewhere. Their technology is obviously very advanced but the same laws of quantum physics apply."

"You hope," Madison whispered.

*

CHAPTER EIGHT

It was going to be a hot day. Even at quarter to seven in the morning the thermometer hovered over fifteen degrees in the Celsius scale used in Buckoway and Hamish predicted an afternoon temperature in the high twenties.

"Why were we asked to come to the stable so early?" Norris asked.

"We are taking two wagons and going to pick up twenty newcomers," Sean replied.

Madison and Norris responded in different ways.

"Newcomers?" she gasped and thought back to her arrival.

"Two wagons?" Norris asked. "So it's today?"

Hamish gazed at Madison from beneath his shaggy eyebrows but answered the other question.

"You three will be in charge of the second wagon," he said. "Do you reckon you can handle the oxen?"

"Of course," Norris said.

"It could be fun," Kirsty cut in.

Madison though appeared more serious. "Why don't you put Sean on the second wagon?" she asked.

"Aye, it's like this," Hamish said in his slow voice. "Sean and I have bought the second team and wagon from Alfred."

"Him!" snorted Kirsty. The man in question was one of the wagon masters associated with the stable. He was a bit of an old drunk who was not well liked.

"Yeah, well he decided to leave the business and has a near new wagon."

"And stroppy uncared-for for oxen," Madison added.

"But they'll improve under your care, Madison."

"My care?"

It was Norris who grinned and flung an arm around Madison's shoulders. "It was unanimous. We all want you to be our wagonmistress."

"Me!"

"If you want the position I will put you in charge of our second team," Hamish said. "It means you'll get another shilling a day for the responsibility."

"Make it four pennies each and I'll accept," Madison said, her eyes shining. Like the old money in Scotland on Earth there were twelve pennies in a shilling.

Kirsty punched Norris on the arm and laughed in delight. "I won my bet," she yelled.

"Bet?" Madison was flabbergasted. Everything was happening too quickly.

"I bet Norris a day's pay that you'd accept the job offer and split your raise between us all."

Norris chuckled. "It's one bet I don't mind losing."

"You don't?" Madison studied her friend. Only a few weeks ago she was sure he would have felt insulted at not being offered the position himself.

"As long as you don't get too bossy," Norris replied.

"Of course not but I notice those new oxen of ours are covered in mud. You'd better get a bucket of warm water and wash them down."

"Yes Ma'am!" Norris gave a mock salute and, followed by Kirsty, went to find a bucket.

"So our cargo will be unconscious like we were?" Madison said to Hamish.

"That's right. Does it worry you, Madison?"

"No. We're getting quite crowded with all the new babies and so on, that's all."

"The rumour is there won't be many more newcomers coming," Sean said. "From now on our society will continue the natural way."

Madison frowned. "What do you mean, Sean?"

"We have lots of births and very few deaths. Our oldest children are four so they are going to start building a school soon. Us old guys will grow older but by the time our time has come every age group will be represented."

"You aren't old, Sean. What's your age?"

"Forty come next month," Sean laughed. "Isn't that ancient?"

"No," Madison said. "Most people on Earth live to be eighty or older."

"They do?" Hamish cut in. "You mean at this other place you go to there are very old people?"

"There are. I have a grandmother who is eighty-one."

"Glory be," Sean said and glanced at Hamish. "There's hope for us yet isn't there old-timer?"

"Speak for yourself, Lad," Hamish retorted but winked at Madison.

Alfred in his unimaginative way had named his oxen, One, Two Three and Four but Madison and her friends changed the names to Olive, Twinkle, Thelma and Florence for the female beasts. These oxen were quite unsettled compared with the Hamish's but responded to Madison's original trick when she gave them silage to munch as they were hitched up.

"We'll lead the way," Hamish said after the two wagons were outside the town wall. "The trail isn't muddy now so ruts in the road will be the main problem. Ride the humps not the ruts. If you have a problem blow that whistle I gave you and I'll come running."

"Okay," Madison said.

"One more thing. It'll pay for one of you sit on the backboard and watch behind us."

"Why? Are you expecting trouble?"

"No more than usual. This is more isolated territory than our usual trips to The Trading Post and any Muds we may come across are not be as friendly as the ones we trade with, that's all."

"What say we swap every hour?" Kirsty said. "I'll have first turn back there."

"That's a good idea," Madison said. She grinned across at Norris as Hamish walked back to the front wagon. "Come on girls!" she yelled as the pair shook their reins. "Let's go!"

The four oxen gave a snort but responded and plodded forward. Slowly, the town walls disappeared behind them and Madison's first trip as wagonmistress had begun.

*

"Miss Evans, are you all right?"

Madison shook her head and saw the computer screen in front of her. Of course she was creating a new style sheet for a client's web page. She looked up to see David Wood, the manager beside her. Oh hell, she was back on Earth and it wasn't even a new morning.

"Yes, I'm fine David," she said and shook her head again to clear it.

"You seemed to be in sort of trance," the manager said. "Look, take an early lunch break. You've been working on that program all morning."

"If you don't mind, I think I will. I do feel a little groggy."

"Then go home, Madison. You've done most of the page. I can get one of the others to finish it."

For once, Madison didn't object. Her head felt sort of clogged up. Perhaps that ear infection she suffered from at high school had returned. As usual she took a cross-town bus home and felt quite self-conscious as she crossed their empty car lot and went inside their apartment. Nobody was home so she turned the coffee percolator on, sat on the sofa and her eyes grew heavy.

*

Kirsty was sitting beside her on the wagon.

"Thank God," the girl said. "When you fell asleep Norris didn't know what to do. We decided not to awaken you."

Madison glanced at her friend's concerned face and shook her head. Unlike a few seconds before, though, she felt refreshed. "How long was I asleep?"

"About an hour. Norris is sitting at the back now. It's okay, nothing has happened except that it's damned hot."

"Thanks," Madison said. "It's not very good for my first day as wagonmistress is it?"

"Don't worry about it. In this heat anyone could fall asleep."

"But I went back, Kirsty. This is the first time it's happened during the day."

"Would you like to tell me about it?"

"I woke up at my Earth job and..."

"I know what happened," Kirsty said when Madison had finished. "You got bored operating that computer thingie and nodded off at the same time as it happened here. You fell asleep in both places at the same time."

"I guess that could have happened," Madison said in a worried voice.

The front wagon pulled to a halt so Madison pulled their wagon in behind his and waited as Hamish walked back.

"Just ahead is where you came into our world. Madison," he said. "Remember how we were stuck in the mud?"

"Is this the place?"

"It is. Now, there're a couple of things I want to tell you."

"Go on."

"First, this dried out mud is almost as dangerous as when it's wet. There are deep ruts everywhere. You could easily break an axle if a wheel slips into one. It'll pay if someone goes on each side to guide the driver through."

"Okay, I'm wagonmistress so I'll drive."

70

"Do you want Sean to help?"

"Madison can do it," Kirsty said with a confidence Madison didn't feel.

Hamish grinned. "Okay. Once we are beyond this rough bit we turn off the trail towards those hills to your right. It looks desolate but doesn't worry. There's a gorge that we enter that leads to a dead end."

"Dead end?" Madison repeated.

"Just follow me and you'll be okay."

Madison shrugged. "Okay, Hamish. Let's go!"

*

"Right," Norris screamed. "Go right."

Madison held both reins and was too tense to even glance sideways. Her arms ached and perspiration soaked her blouse. "Okay, Twinkle and Florence." she called to the oxen on the right and twitched the right hand reins. "Pull us through."

The wagon veered right but the larger rear wheels began to wobble.

"Too far!" Kirsty's voice alerted Madison. "You're on the edge of another rut."

"Whoa!" Madison cried and pulled on the reins. The wagon stopped and the oxen stood still. Sweat ran down the animals' nostrils and saliva dripped from their mouths. She turned to her friends who walked around the wagon.

"What do you think, Kirsty?" Norris asked.

Kirsty glanced down and studied the ground that Madison couldn't see.

"What is it?" she called.

"The left wheels are okay but the right back wheel is balanced between two ruts," Kirsty said. "Go either way and it'll fall in."

"So we use the planks," Norris said.

"What planks?" Madison gasped.

"There are half a dozen on the wagon floor. You just stay there, Madison. We'll get them."

"I'm going nowhere," the driver hissed.

Kirsty and Norris hauled four solid planks from the wagon and carried them around by the wheel.

"You okay?" Norris panted as they struggled to move one heavy plank into position.

"Of course," Kirsty grunted. "You're the one walking backwards, you know."

"Just hold it while I swing around and get this end under the wheel then I'll come back and help you push it in."

"Shut up and damn well do it!" Kirsty gasped, her face contorted in exertion.

It worked. With one plank slid across in front of the two rear wheels it was easier to push the others across.

"Okay," Norris yelled at Madison. "You have one metre max then you have to stop again."

"Right!" Madison coached the oxen forward and the wheels turned. The back ones gripped the first plank and rose onto it.

"A little further," Kirsty yelled from the other side... "That's it ... Stop!"

"What now?" Madison called after she'd halted the oxen.

"We slide out the back plank and move it to the front," Norris said.

"Oh damn," Kirsty gasped but again she rose to the occasion.

They moved every plank twice while Madison edged the wagon forward. Finally Norris gave the all clear and the oxen pulled the wagon forward to a smooth section of the road.

"God, and I get four pennies a day extras for this," Kirsty gasped as she climbed up beside Madison. "Look at my hands!"

Both her hands were covered in purple blisters.

"And mine," Madison whispered. Her hands had swollen red cuts across them where the reins had cut in.

Kirsty chuckled and slid over so Norris could fit up beside her. "But we did it guys," she said. "It's just like when we hit that target with our arrows. We thought it'd be impossible but we did it."

"Yeah, I'll make you both honourable males," Norris said.

"There's no need," Madison snapped. "Who wants to be a male?"

"I've no idea," Kirsty said. "Hell, I couldn't think of anything worse than having to shave every morning."

"Or growing whiskers like Hamish." Madison laughed.

Norris grinned. "Point taken," he said. "I'm just proud of you both, that's all."

"Sure," Madison said. "We are proud of you, too, Norris. After all it was your idea to use the planks,"

"Not really," Norris admitted with a grin. "I saw Sean doing it with their wagon, that's all."

*

They moved forward and found the other wagon waiting around the next corner with Hamish and Sean sitting on the grass munching sandwiches and drinking beer.

"You knew we'd have trouble, didn't you?" Madison called down after she stopped her wagon beside them.

Hamish wiped froth off his beard. "Thought you might."

"So why didn't you come and help?" Kirsty yelled.

"You didn't need it," Sean said. "You're here aren't you?"

"And if we'd broken an axle?" Madison asked.

"You never blew your whistle," Hamish said. "I said if you did I'd come running."

"You're impossible!" Madison retorted.

"And you've proved to us that we selected well in our choice of wagonmistress. Did you know there were a dozen young lads after the job?"

"No but what would you have done if we screwed up?"

Hamish shrugged and turned to his companion. "What would we have done, Sean?"

"Now that's a tough one, Hamish after that bet and all."

"Bet, what bet?" Madison hissed.

"We bet Alfred half the cost of this wagon team that you would get to this point without breaking the wagon or loosing control of the oxen."

"Great," Norris cut in. "But how can you prove it. He'll just say you made it up?"

"See that grassy knob above that old slip up the hill opposite us?" Hamish said and pointed to a gap in the steep forested slope "Alfred and John Wilson, the stable manager been sitting up there with binoculars watching us. There should be a flag waving?"

Madison squinted in the sunlight and saw the tiny outline of two men waving a white flag from the top of the slip.

"White means they concede and we won the bet."

"Oh hell," Madison gasped then broke into a grin. "You could at least offer us a beer," she added.

"Dainty little thing ain't she, Sean?"

"For sure, Hamish. Wolf in sheep's clothing, I'd say." He grinned and took three cans of beer from his haversack.

Sean reached for a pair of binoculars in the wagon and handed it around so everyone could study the two men.

"Old Alfred doesn't look too happy," Kirsty said.

"Does he ever?" Norris said. He took the binoculars Kirsty handed him and focused on the scene. "How did they get up there, Hamish?" he asked while he still held the glasses to his eyes.

"There's a good path and steps that wind up from this road. When this road was made it was used as a lookout. There was once even a little platform there but last winter a storm carried it away."

"So who's there," Norris continued.

"Just the two. Why?"

"I can see half a dozen people. Oh hell, they look like Muds."

Hamish frowned and reached out for the binoculars. He focused on the slip and moved his head around to a section of the track visible further down the hillside.

"We have to go," he said in a brisk tone. "Just act casual but get in the wagons and move. Madison, stay right behind our wagon and Kirsty, you take your bow with you and sit at the back. Don't expose yourself. "

"Why. What's wrong?" Madison whispered.

"That hill is filled with Muds." Hamish said. "There are hundreds of them."

"What?" Norris said. "I saw only a couple."

"That's all they wanted us to see, lad. You only see the Muds if they want you to."

"And why would they do that?" Madison asked.

"They always give forewarning of their presence. If they attacked us without warning, their victory would be without honour. Likewise, if we show any sign of panic they will launch an immediate attack because we are seen as cowards."

*

Madison followed Hamish's directions and kept their wagon right behind his. The road had a dusty but firm surface so they made quite a fast pace if lumbering along behind the oxen could be called fast.

The valley appeared empty with grass and tussock stretching back from the road to the hills where shrubs turned to full forest further up the hills. The sun shone down and the only noise was from the oxen and squeaking wagon springs.

Kirsty sat at the back and peered out through a slit between the two canvas sides that she'd unrolled across the back. "Madison," she called with her voice high pitched in alarm. "They've come out behind us. Oh hell, they're everywhere."

"Can you handle both reins?" Madison asked Norris.

"Sure but why?"

Madison slid over the seat and grabbed her bow and arrow. "I think Kirsty will need help. Put the whistle in your mouth. If I tell you blow it so Hamish will know we're in trouble. Okay?"

Norris nodded. "Be careful," he whispered.

Madison nodded and made her way back to Kirsty.

"They're following us openly, Madison."

Madison moved the canvas aside ever so slightly and peeped out. Two dozen or more males were spaced across the road about fifty metres behind them in three rows. They looked like the trading post Mud except for red war paint on their faces and bare chests. Every one carried a long spear but nothing else.

"So they like chivalry do they?" Madison muttered. "Do you reckon we could hit them with our arrows, Kirsty."

"If necessary," the other girl stuttered.

"They're coming closer but we are still our range of their spears."

"But not for long"

"So we act now," Madison said. "Are you game. Kirsty?"

The other girl's face drained of all colour but she reached for an arrow to load her bow and nodded.

Madison turned. "Norris can you hear me?"

"I can, Madison."

"We are going to pull back the canvas. When you see us stand up, blow your whistle and keep blowing as loud as you can."

"But you can't..."

"Do it!" Madison snapped.

"Will do."

*

"The fools," old Alfred grunted.

"No ... tactics, Alfred," his companion said. "That girl you lost your bet about is anything but a fool. Haven't you realized that by now?"

Both men focused their binoculars on the two wagons below

The two flaps at the rear of the second wagon had just been pulled aside and two women stood in full view. They were dressed in identical dark red blouses and blue tartan skirts. Each held a massive bow and had one foot braced against the backboard for support.

The front row of Muds gave a piercing howl, raised their spears and charged. Two arrows shot out and the two middle warriors crumbled. Two more arrows found their target before the remaining Muds in the line threw their spears. These fell well short of the wagon. As the first line of Muds moved to the side the second row took their place. More arrows shot out, four warriors collapsed with arrows in their chests and again the spears fell short. Wounded warriors on the ground were ignored as the third row moved forward. Meanwhile, the two front rows regrouped at the rear.

This time the attackers showed more caution. They peeled off to each side of the road one behind the other and slowed their pace to match that of the wagon. Their spears were held low and not in a throwing position.

"Sheer numbers will get them," Albert grunted but kept his eyes glued to his binoculars.

Neither man noticed six warriors rise out of the grass behind them.

*

CHAPTER NINE

"Don't shoot!" Madison ordered.

"Why?' Kirsty gasped.

"Trust me and do exactly what I do."

Madison lowered her bow and brought her right foot back beside her other one. She stood up and placed her bow against the canvas flap on her side of the wagon.

"I hope you know what you're doing," Kirsty grunted but did the same.

They stood in full view of the attacking warriors while the wagon creaked forward.

"Norris," Madison called without moving her head. "Give two short peeps on the whistle then stop blowing."

Norris obeyed. The short peeps meant nothing but Madison reasoned that the Muds might be impressed.

They were. Every Mud warrior stopped and lowered their spears. More important, though, dozens of other warriors materialized out of the tussock on each side of the road. They stood shoulder to shoulder with spears held with the points poked into the ground and watched as the wagons passed.

"Look straight ahead," Madison whispered. "Don't copy me this time. Understand?"

"I do."

Madison swallowed back bile that had formed in her throat and took one more calculated gamble. She held her bow up with her right arm and shouted out the only word that could possibly be appropriate.

"Hanky! Hanky! Hanky!" She hoped the language at the trading post was used by these warriors and *hi, hi, hi* would be seen as a gesture of friendliness.

The warriors reacted. All except one stepped back a step and again placed their spears into the ground. The one warrior who had not moved was now abreast of the front wagon. He stood looking straight ahead as the two teams moved forward.

"Tell Norris to stop the team beside him." Madison hissed.

"I heard you," Norris replied. "Whoa girls," he shouted and the oxen halted.

*

"If I'm killed it will solve the problem of me having two lives," Madison whispered. She turned and stepped backwards down the three-step ladder at the back of the wagon. Once her feet hit the ground she swung around and found she was exactly where she wanted to be, right in front of the warrior waiting on the roadside.

He was a massive man almost two metres tall. Unlike the others he wore no war paint and his only clothes were a pair of machine made cotton shorts. His hair was cut short and he was clean-shaven. He glanced down and his eyes linked with Madison's.

"You are either very brave or very foolish, Candy Lady," he said in accented but understandable English. "I thank you for your respect of my people. Few of the newcomers care to learn our ways."

"My name is Madison," the girl said.

"And I am Thinrisodor."

"Are you Sumatti?"

"We are different arms of the same people."

"I see," Madison said. "How have we offended you?"

Thinrisodor frowned. "Your words fail me," he said.

"We did something that was bad. What was it?"

The warrior's expression turned to anger. "You come and take without regard for our kind. Ships of thunder land and humans with fawn skin build a town. More arrive and we are driven back because we happen to be here."

Ships of thunder!

Madison studied the warrior but decided not to ask him to explain. "I am not like that," she said. "I wish to help."

"Do you?" Thinrisodor said. "You may or you may not, I do not know. Your two wagons today may pass forward and return in peace, Madison but this is out of respect to you but not your kind."

"I thank you."

"Your two wagons have been marked. They will be the only ones allowed through our land after this day. When you return you must warn the other wagonmasters they are not to enter our lands."

"But why?"

"Every one who comes back in your wagon is but an empty shell who needs the power passed through them to come alive?" the warrior said.

78

"That's true."

"Except for you. You alone awoke by yourself at this very place where the mud runs deep in the rains. Why is this so?"

"I don't know," Madison said. "There are forces here that neither of us understand."

"But that makes you different. Your friend and yourself showed bravery with your bows. For that reason your wagons will be allowed to travel through Sumatti lands."

"Thank you. I am honoured by your statement."

Thinrisodor studied her with unblinking eyes before he finally nodded and stepped back. "Many warriors were killed today as were two from your town. What has happened has happened."

Madison immediately thought of Hamish and Sean in the front wagon and her chin trembled for the first time. "Two?" she whispered.

"The two on the hill watching you. They were not worthy," the warrior said. He stepped back and glanced away.

Madison walked to the front of their wagon and swung herself up beside Norris and glanced ahead. "Where's the other wagon?"

"They kept going. I think Hamish knows what he's doing."

"I'm sure he does," Without any warning, Madison began to shake and had to grip the wagon frame for support.

"You saved us, Madison," Norris said. "I'm so proud of you, you know."

Madison reached across and squeezed his arm. "Oh Norris," she whispered. "They killed Alfred and the stable manager so we aren't out of danger yet. Let's get our oxen moving before he changes his mind."

"Sure, Madison," Norris whispered. He shouted an order and the four oxen began to move forward through the twin lines of Sumatti warriors.

*

"They aren't following," Kirsty shouted from the rear. "Oh my God..."

"What is it?" Madison called back.

"They've gone. They just all turned and disappeared into the trees."

"Come up and sit with us," Madison said. "I think we all need a little mutual support at the moment."

Kirsty almost ran forward and squeezed in the space between her two friends. She grinned and squeezed Madison's arm before she tucked her skirt up under her bottom and sat down.

Norris grinned across at her. "Your shooting was pretty spot on, too, Kirsty," he said. "I reckon you both scared the hell out of those Muds."

Kirsty nodded. "When you're damn scared you don't think of any consequences," she whispered. "And when Madison jumped down in front of that big chief I just about pissed myself."

"We make a good team," Madison said.

Five minutes later they went around a corner and found the other wagon waiting. Madison pulled in beside it and glanced across at it.

Nobody was there!

"Oh hell," she muttered but her worry turned to relief when she saw the two men appear out of the bushes.

"We went back to help but weren't needed, were we?" Hamish said with a wide grin on his face.

"This was one test we didn't set up," Sean added.

"Aye, but let's go before those Muds have second thoughts about letting us go," Hamish added

"We have free passage but no other wagons will be allowed through," Madison said.

Hamish pulled on his beard and stared at her. "Tell me everything when we're safe, Madison and thank you. I reckon if it wasn't for you we'd all be lying face down on the dusty roadside by now."

The two wagons turned off the road ten minutes later and headed up a narrow trail towards the gorge Hamish had mentioned earlier. Trees grew so close they almost met above them to form a tunnel until two sheer cliffs that towered above them replaced them.

Everything became peaceful with only the creaking wheels disturbing the silence. In the second wagon the three friends were immersed in their own thoughts. Kirsty nodded and fell asleep with her head against Madison's shoulder.

"You stay awake," Norris said as he caught Madison's eyes. "I don't want you shooting back to your other world."

"I'm not tired at all," Madison said. "Would you like me to take both reins?"

Norris shook his head and the pair lapsed back into silence.

The valley ended where the two cliffs circled in and joined. The front wagon stopped and Sean walked back to them.

"It's not magic but I have no idea how this works," he said and held a remote control in his hand. He aimed it at the cliff and pressed a yellow button. The cliff face slid back to reveal a concrete tunnel lit with ceiling lights.

Norris stared but Madison merely grinned.

"It's just a door," she said. "Sean's remote activates it."

"If you say so," Hamish said. "I may be thick as a post but I have no idea what you're talking about."

Madison laughed. "It's just a fancy sort of lock that uses that thing in Sean's hand to unlock it. A little motor like the one in our washing machine back in Buckoway then starts up and opens the door."

"For sure, I knew that all along," Sean said. "Anyway follow our wagon inside then we can shut the door behind us."

The wagon teams moved inside and Sean used his remote to shut the door. Madison stared ahead. The lights went for about twenty metres before they stopped.

"What's there, Sean?" she asked.

"Nothing unusual," Sean gave her a grin. "When we reach the darkness, another row of lights come on and these ones go off. " He shrugged. "Perfectly natural, isn't it?"

"You're being sarcastic, Sean," Madison said

"And why is there a wind blowing in here?" Norris asked.

"I guess a fan is sucking in fresh air in from an outside vent," Madison said. "It was probably switched on with the lights."

"But we're safe from the Muds?" Kirsty was suddenly awake.

"Aye lassie. We go right through under this range of hills. I guess they're too steep to climb for there are never any Muds on the river side," Sean said. "It takes about twenty minutes for the oxen to go through. "

*

They came out into a broad valley with a river of brown water in the centre. There was no bridge but their road led down to a group of wooden buildings and a jetty built along the shoreline. Tied to this was a low boat that reminded Madison of the canal boats she had once seen on her trip to England. It had with a long cabin and windows that ran the entire length of the craft. There was even brightly coloured red paintwork and name *Gentle Lady* painted on the bow in curly letters.

Hamish pulled his wagon in beside one building and came back to the others. "Welcome to Station Five," he said.

"Why Station Five?" Madison asked

"I've no idea," Hamish said in a casual voice. "We stay the night in the dormitory and go home in the morning," he said. "The oxen can be released in the field behind these buildings. There's always plenty of grass at this time of the year and they prefer to sleep outside rather than in the barn."

"Where is everyone?" Kirsty asked.

"There's only us and the newcomers in stretchers aboard the barge," Hamish said. "We never see the crew."

"Never?" Madison asked.

Hamish pulled on his beard again as he often did when he was thinking. "Not on my trips, Madison. One of the other wagon masters may have. I never bothered to ask."

Madison frowned. Perhaps this was part of the *You should remember* conditioning. Hamish was usually quite interested in everything around himself.

"Probably," she said. "It doesn't really matter."

*

After caring for the oxen they walked into a long wooden building. At one end was a kitchen and living area while the rest contained one dormitory with bunk space for twenty. In many ways it was a smaller version of their accommodation back in Buckoway with modern facilities such as electricity and bathroom facilities. Again Hamish or Sean answered questions she asked with a shrug or noncommittal reply.

"Okay, I'll look around myself," Madison snapped. "Anybody want to come for a walk around with me?"

"I will," Kirsty said after Norris look reluctant to get out of the soft armchair he had deposited himself into.

"So what's wrong, Madison?" Kirsty asked when they walked out into the sunshine.

"I think Hamish and Sean are conditioned not to notice anything different . I need to find out what's here."

Next to the dormitory block was a blacksmith's forge that looked like a museum piece. Everything inside was set out neatly on wooden pegs or shelves. Ashes in the forge itself showed recent use and a broken wagon wheel nearby confirmed this.

'This is where they repaired the wagon wheel," Kirsty said. "It's similar to the one back at the stables."

"Almost," Madison replied and pointed to the forge. It wasn't powered by coal or charcoal for beneath the iron chamber were two gas cylinders. Other items pointed to modern technology such an electric drill and soldering iron.

The pair walked outside and Madison pointed to back of the dormitory roof that faced the direct sunlight.

"Why is it made of glass?" Kirsty asked

82

"That's where our electricity comes from, Kirsty. Those are solar panels. I bet there are storage batteries somewhere."

She pointed to a cord that led from the panels to a small adjacent building. The door was locked but Madison could hear a humming inside and the sudden rumble as an electric motor started up.

Kirsty looked alarmed until Madison reassured her that it was probably a pump house. "It probably pumps water up from the river, through a filter and into that water tank," she said and pointed to a fresh looking concrete tank.

"Oh Madison," Kirsty said. "I wish I knew everything you do."

"Don't worry, these are just things we have in Buckoway but on a smaller scale. Come on, we'll see what's in the other buildings then visit the barge itself."

"If you say so."

Madison frowned. "Why, what's wrong, Kirsty?"

"The idea of mindless bodies scares me."

Madison was about to laugh when she saw Kirsty's frightened face.

"I was scared when I woke up in the wagon, too. You were all with me but I couldn't talk to you. It wasn't too bad, though. You were all breathing and just looked as if you were asleep. You weren't like corpses."

Kirsty nodded. "I know but..."

"Okay," Madison said. "We'll wait until later. Hamish said he was going to check the newcomers out. I can go with him and you can remain on the jetty."

"No, I'll come but I would like to have Hamish with us."

Madison smiled and tucked an arm around her friend's shoulders. "Thanks. You're a real pal," she said. "Let's look in the next building. I'd say it's the barn."

It was a combined barn and stables with food bunkers and room to house a dozen oxen. Again, it was really just a smaller version of the stables in Buckoway. The last building looked like an office. Madison grimaced when she examined the locked door. It looked ordinary but the old fashioned keyhole had no hole to insert a key. It was just wood. The hinges on the far side were fake, too. Beside the brass doorknob was a metal box. This was an electronic door that slid back when someone used a swipe card. Madison walked around the small building and peeped in the one window. Inside was a drawn curtain but in the gap between them she saw a dark blue panel. It was metal. There must be some sort of electronic equipment or computer inside.

Ten minutes later, Hamish ambled out and asked if they'd like to see inside the barge. They walked up a small gangplank near the bow, ducked their heads under the low door that lifted vertically and stepped down inside. The interior was modern without even pretence at having an old fashioned look. It was constructed in a synthetic material with a row of recessed lights in the low ceiling. To her right Madison saw stainless frames with stretchers clamped into them. They filled the whole space with no room to walk between. The stretcher closest to the door contained a girl probably in her late teens. Long hair filled the pillow beneath her head. She looked quite peaceful with her chest moving slightly as she breathed. She was dressed in blouse; sweater and kilt just like herself.

"Poor kid," Kirsty said. "What's her name?"

Madison saw a card tied to the frame and turned it over. It had handwriting on it written in the old fashioned curly style everyone used at Buckoway. If she didn't know better she would think the words were written with a fountain pen, again of the sort in vogue at Buckoway.

Wendy Pratt, Aged 18.3 Personality Category 5, Health excellent. Possible use; Breeding and academic work. Altered memory. Alpha condition.

She snorted at the word *breeding*. It was an affront for the girl to be treated like an animal. The other newcomers she could reach had similar cards with only the personality category changing. They were all Caucasian, female and aged in their late teens.

"What did my card say?" she asked Hamish.

"Much the same, Lass. They always write *breeding* for the females so don't take offence. You know nobody is forced to become a mother."

Madison sucked on her lip but made no comment. "What's this personality category?"

"Well basically it goes from a one, being very quiet and shy to being outspoken and a possible problem. That's an eight, Categories three to six are preferred."

"And what was I?"

"I can't rightly remember, Madison."

"Hamish!"

"Okay you were a seven"

"Meaning?"

Hamish handed Madison a notebook he had in his hand. "Read it yourself."

Has an independent personality. A possible leader but could be resent authority and become stubborn. There was more written along the same lines.

"Okay," Madison retorted, "but how do they know?"

Hamish shrugged. "I've no idea but it's pretty accurate. We used it as one of the criteria when we selected you as wagonmistress." He grinned. "We mainly used our gut feeling after we got to know you, though."

"Thanks Hamish," she said.

"What was that all about?" Kirsty interrupted.

"It appears they knew all about us before we came," Madison replied. "I don't like it at all."

Kirsty nodded. "They look well cared for, though."

"I guess," Madison replied and continued across the barge. To her left in the centre was a small doorway that led through to a cabin with seats around the sides. She glanced up and saw the windshield with a view of the jetty and river outside. Beneath the windshield was a pilot's seat, a steering wheel, what looked like hand throttles, a console and television monitor. Under this was an aqua coloured panel.

"I bet that's the engine," she muttered and wriggled into the seat. She turned to see Kirsty watching her.

"What do you notice?' Madison asked.

Kirsty screwed her nose up. "The seat looks comfortable but it's huge."

"Exactly," Madison replied. "Look, my feet can barely reach those pedals on the floor."

"So?"

"This was designed for someone much bigger than me or even the men for that matter."

Kirsty bent down and looked out the window. "Yeah. It would be difficult to see the oxen team outside. It's too low down."

"I don't think they use an oxen team, Kirsty. It's self propelled."

Kirsty shrugged as if she didn't understand. "Okay but what are all these glass thingies and handles for?"

"Let's try it out," Madison whispered.

She reached forward and pressed an end button with her thumb. The monitor lit up and Kirsty gasped as words began to cross the screen. It was, though, in a meaningless alphabet.

"Oh damn," Madison said and pressed the next button.

The console lit up with three dials like a speedometer or fuel gauges showed.

She studied the console and pressed a third button beneath the first one and gasped in delight as the words changed to English.

Warning. Please start the engine and untie the mooring lines before proceeding.

"That's telling me," Madison grumbled. "But how do I start the engine?"

The words on the monitor changed into a list of instructions.

"My God, It's voice activated," she gasped.

"Madison," Kirsty whispered. "Be careful."

"Sure, sure," Madison muttered and pressed three buttons as directed in the instructions. There was a rumble as the engine that was behind the panel as she had guessed, purred into life.

"Hell, Madison," Hamish yelled from behind them "What're you doing?"

"Just testing,"

"Yeah so why is everything shaking like its come alive?"

"It's a machine, Hamish just like a refrigerator at home."

Hamish came and stood behind the pair. "With all those dancing lights and red words that tell you to untie the mooring lines?"

Madison glanced down. The red warning was flashing.

"This is a test," Madison said. "We don't wish to move."

"Now who are you talking to?" Hamish muttered.

Madison grinned as the words *Testing Procedures* came on screen followed by a huge list that scrolled up with fifty-seven instructions. "The boat," she said.

"Oh hell, Madison," Kirsty moaned. "You just told us it wasn't alive but you're talking to it."

"I'll try just one more thing," Madison said "What cargo do we have aboard"

There are twenty life forms yet to be activated. They are duplicates of human females from the planet Earth 2, continent North America in the habitat of San Francisco. They have been delivered by this craft to Station Five where they are due to be transferred to the settlement of Buckoway by local contractors using oxen. Please note that this is a Class C settlement that does not have motorized transportation. Again the screen scrolled down with more information much of which was meaningless to Madison.

"Okay, when will you go back?" Madison asked.

Terminology unknown. Please rephrase.

"Madison!" Kirsty gasped.

"How do I shut down?" Madison asked.

Immediately the screens went blank and the engine stopped.

"This scares me," Kirsty said. "I'll rather deal with stubborn oxen than this thingie."

"It is a bit frightening," Madison admitted. "I've seen enough. Let's go back outside."

"So what have you found out?" Hamish asked.

"This barge doesn't need oxen to pull it back up river. Somebody comes here and drives it back but we still don't know who they are."

"Fair enough but no more experiments, Lass. We don't want to hurt those twenty young people in our care now do we?"

86

Madison nodded. "Sorry, I should have thought of them." She smiled and climbed out of the pilot's seat.

*

CHAPTER TEN

Madison awoke and heard the shower going. Damn she was back home again on Earth. She still found the jumps back and forth quite disconcerting. Norris came in with a towel wrapped around his waste and grinned at her.

"So how are we getting on in the other place?" he asked.

"There are problems." She sat at up in bed and gave him a brief description of the day's events.

"You acted recklessly," he said. "Just be careful. It appears your two halves are linked somehow. If you were killed there it would probably be fatal for you here, too."

"Yeah, I guess Colonel Davis' great experiment proved that."

"Did you see any star patterns?"

Madison grinned and reached for a notebook on the dresser. "With everything happening I almost forgot. It was a beautiful cloudless night and stars were everywhere." She screwed her nose up. "I don't know much about astronomy but saw a couple of patterns where Hamish said the north was." She sketched them in her notebook.

"And are you going to call Colonel Davis on that hot line he gave you?"

Madison glanced at the clock. It was just after six thirty. "Yeah why not wake the old sod up."

She found her cellphoneand hit a memory button. It rung eight times before a sleepy voice answered. "This had better be important Sergeant," Brad's voice said.

"Madison here, colonel. How's Wendy Pratt?"

The tone was on immediate alert. "How do you know that name, Madison?" he said.

"Oh I've met her on the other side. Well sort of. She hasn't been activated yet."

"How many arrived?"

"Twenty. They're all girls from San Francisco."

"You know that, too?"

"Yeah!"

"We need to talk."

88

"Isn't that what we're doing now?"

"Face to face, Madison. Can you get to my office at the air force station by eight?"

"I've got work..."

"I'll call them." Davis said and the line went dead.

*

"They are from an exclusive private school in one of those upmarket suburbs above the harbour," Davis said after he welcomed her to his office. "One class was on a biology field trip. Three teachers with them were not stung."

"As we suspected, it's not random," Madison said. "They had Wendy's name and age recorded on a card and the barge they came down the river in is modern. They didn't even pretend to make it old fashioned inside. Also, we met another part of the Mud tribe. These were warriors who almost killed us all."

"You have had an interesting time. You'd better tell me everything."

Madison grinned and told about her day. "Oh yeah, I sketched some stars, too." She handed the colonel the notebook page.

"I'll get some experts onto that." Brad Davis glanced across at her. "There were twenty young women there, you said."

"That's what Hamish said. I never counted them as they were all squeezed in this barge and I could only see the front six."

"Twenty-one were stung in San Francisco."

Madison pouted. "I see, so if one never came across she must be one of those set up to receive transmissions."

Davis nodded. "Now if you can get those twenty names we can find who the missing one is."

"I know six and can get the rest."

"Good."

"So what do I do with the boat, Colonel Davis?"

"Leave it for now. It would be foolish to attempt to go anywhere. You would just play your hand to the aliens. I've got several experts working on your situation so I should have a plan for you soon."

Madison nodded but felt a little let down. Surely she could do more on the other side to help. She sighed. It was funny too. The other world was beginning to feel more like home than here on Earth.

*

"Hi Madison." Kirsty said. "Did Norris behave himself back there?"

Madison woke up and saw the unfamiliar room around them. She was back in the dormitory by the river. "Yeah, he was okay but you weren't?"

"Me. What did I do?"

"Stayed out all night with that new guy you met. I never saw you until supper time."

Kirsty shrugged. "Seems like I'm having more fun there than here. Anyway, did you talk to old Brad Boy?"

"Yeah. There we twenty one girls stung..." Once again she repeated everything that had happened during her day on Earth.

Kirsty listened with interest and grinned when Madison confessed she enjoyed life in Buckoway more than at home.

"Why?"

"The excitement, I guess. Over there I just do mundane things like millions of others around."

"Talking about excitement, let's get going before the men give up on us. They left to start unloading the barge before you woke up"

By the time the pair arrived, Hamish and the others already had the two wagons backed up on the jetty and were lifting Wendy's stretcher onto one.

Madison walked across and watched in silence. She noticed the extreme care Hamish and Sean took and even Norris was caught up in the respect they showed for the newcomers. With each girl, the men undid the restraining straps and slid her stretcher forward on tiny rollers. They wiped her face with a damp facecloth, checked the pulse and carefully brought the stretcher across to the wagon. Norris helped as they manipulated the stretchers into the wagon and tied them together. They covered each girl with a light quilt and strapped her in securely.

"You look after them well," Madison commented after the sixth newcomer was strapped in the wagon."

Hamish glanced up. "If they turn out as good as you three they're worth protecting, aren't they?"

Madison grinned. "Can Kirsty and I help?"

"Sure, we now have access to the next six. You can get all their cards and enter them on the tally sheet. Just be careful you don't muddle them. I usually make a wee comment such as any special features, hair colour and style etc. so I know what name goes with what girl."

The two went inside the barge and saw that Sean had taken the front frames apart so they could walk back to the next six stretchers. As

90

Kirsty read the names and comments Madison wrote them down. As she did this she tried to think of ways to remember the names. It was easy to recall half a dozen names but twenty became difficult, especially when there were several repeated first names.

When ten were loaded, Hamish came up to the pair. "That's your wagon filled. Now if you can get your oxen hitched up and pull it up by the dormitory we'll get the other wagon loaded."

It took them half an hour to round the four oxen up, feed them and lead them to the wagon. By that time Hamish's wagon was filled and the three went and inspected the empty barge.

"Is this barge used for anything else?" Norris asked as Sean strapped the disassembled frames along one wall.

"Not so much now. We used to get loads of supplies and extra food. That was a few years back. We were the first settlers here and there were only about fifty of us and the farms weren't established." He grinned. "I remember when the first load of dairy cows arrived. They had forty of them jammed in the barge."

"Didn't they make a mess?" Kirsty said.

"Nope. They were in the deep sleep, too. You should have heard them moan at the castle when we told them they had to revive forty cows."

"And where did you come from?" Madison asked.

Sean stared down at her. "We woke up in the castle like everyone here except you. Madison."

"But if you were one of the first ones here who ran the machinery to wake you up?"

"The Guardians, " Sean replied.

Madison glanced at Kirsty. This was the first time anybody except the woman in the castle had mentioned the name. "And who are they, Sean?"

Sean stared at her and frowned. "What did I just say?"

"You said the Guardians were here before you. Who are they?"

"I've no idea. Did I say that?"

"You did. Are they the ones who operate this barge?"

"Could be," Sean muttered. "You'd better ask Hamish. He's more into that theology stuff than I am."

"It doesn't matter," Madison said and changed the topic. "Do you think Thinrisodor will keep his word and let us through?"

Sean smiled. "For sure, Madison," he said as if relieved to get onto a topic he understood. "In all my encounters I have never known Muds to go back on their word. At The Trading Post, if a Mud promises to pay you for some goods on the next trip, he will. In many ways they are more trustworthy than humans." He squinted. "Mind you, if he says he'll attack any wagons crossing his land you can guarantee that will happen too. They may be honest but they are still uncivilized by our standards."

"So what happens when the next barge load of newcomers arrive here?" Kirsty asked.

Sean grinned. "You got us a full time job, Madison. Up until Thinrisodor's decision to attack everyone except us, all the wagonmasters shared this trip. There's good pay so everyone wants to do it." He shrugged. "A few like old Alfred, bless his soul, were pretty casual though. We actually complained about one wagonmaster who brought his load of newcomers back covered in bruises. Seems he didn't bother to strap them in. Some of the men have no respect for the Muds either."

"Perhaps that was why Thinrisodor attacked us," Madison said.

"Probably was," Sean said.

"And if those wagonmasters think you're lying when you tell them about Thinrisodor?" Kirsty asked.

"After Alfred and the stable manager's body are dumped outside the town walls, they'll believe us," Sean said.

"Oh hell, will they do that?" Madison asked.

"For sure. That's the way the Mud operate."

*

By midmorning they were at the Buckoway side of the tunnel and the door had opened.

"Oh hell," Madison gasped for she could see Mud warriors lined up along the valley outside.

Sean came back and looked up at them. "We go on," he said. "Just keep behind us. If they wave, wave back otherwise ignore them. Unless someone directly approaches, you avoid eye contact."

He ran back to the front wagon and climbed aboard. A moment later the front wagon moved forward.

"Here goes," Madison said and started their oxen moving. When they were outside, the doors shut behind them. The Mud warriors stood as still as statues as they rode by. Forty minutes later they were on the main road and turned towards Buckoway.

"Sneaky little bastards," Norris called from the rear of the wagon where was peeping out through the canvas

"Why?" Madison called back without turning her head.

"As soon as we go by, the Muds at the back slip off into the trees. I guess they run forward to the front of the line."

Madison used her eyes to glance sideways. Norris was right. She saw several warriors running through the trees. The next unexpected happening was when they arrived at the place where they had to use planks under the wheels. Hamish's wagon just kept going but it wasn't until Madison's oxen were walking across the area that she noticed the change. The ruts had all been filled with gravel. It was as good as the road close to home. Someone, and she assumed it was the Muds, had filled the ruts in. They didn't have to stop, after all.

Five minutes later a warrior stepped out between the two wagons and held up his hand.

"Whoa!" Madison cried. The oxen stopped just before they reached the man. It was Thinrisodor.

He waited while the wagon ahead continued on before he moved to the grass and the warriors still along the roadside disappeared. Thinrisodor's spear was stuck in the ground.

"He wants to talk," Kirsty whispered.

"Yeah. You stay put. I'll climb down."

Madison climbed down off the wagon backwards and turned to face the warrior.

"You promised us free passage, Thinrisodor," she said.

"We Sumatti keep our word. I stopped you for another reason."

Madison looked into his eyes. "If you wish to speak to Hamish, he's in the front wagon."

"It is you I wish to speak to."

Madison waited. Inside, her heart raced and her throat felt dry. But she fought to control her outward emotions and achieved it well. Not even her hands trembled while she stood waiting.

"I see why you are so accurate with your bow, Candy Lady. You have the pride of the Sumatti."

"I recognize that as an honour and thank you," Madison replied. "Now, what message have you got for me."

"No message but a messenger. She is yours if you wish it that way. Like yourself she is brave and uncontaminated."

Before Madison could reply the Sumatti leader held up his left hand and three people appeared. Two Mud warriors pushed a terrified human girl out of the bushes. She was dressed in a business suit that would have been very formal if it wasn't covered in mud and ripped down one side. Her hands were tied in front with flax that also twisted around her slim body. She sort of stumbled until a warrior probed her in the back with a spear. Her head came back and she glanced up for the first time. This was when Madison noticed the girl had oriental features.

The girl saw her, stopped and said something in a high-pitched voice.

"What's she saying?" Kirsty whispered.

Madison frowned for she understood the language a little. She'd studied it for a couple of years back home on Earth while at high school. The stranger spoke Japanese.

"I know a little of your language," she said in hesitant Japanese. "Do you speak English?"

The girl stopped and frowned. It was as if she was trying to remember something in the back of her mind.

"I speak English," Madison said in her own language.

"I don't know the word English but I understand you," the girl said. She blinked back tears and added. "I don't know why."

"I am Madison Evans and with me are Kirsty and Norris."

"I am Risa Hatayama," the girl whispered.

Thinrisodor looked Madison in eye. "So you don't regard her as inferior because she speaks the other village's tongue and her face is tight?" he asked.

"Of course not. Why should I?"

"Many, including some of my own people do. Will you take her?"

"Yes."

Thinrisodor nodded, a warrior cut the flax and stood back.

"Help her aboard," Madison whispered out the side of her mouth.

"Sure, Madison." Norris jumped down to the ground and smiled at Risa.

"Would you like a lift up, Risa?" he asked.

"Please."

Norris grabbed the girl around the waist and lifted. She placed one foot on the front wheel and took Madison's extended hand. A moment later she was beside Kirsty who wriggled over and smiled. Norris climbed aboard and squeezed in behind them while Madison ordered the oxen forward.

She glanced sideways but every Sumatti warrior including Thinrisodor had gone. Hamish's wagon was by the side of the road a couple of hundred metres ahead but, otherwise, the land looked barren and deserted.

"Thank you," Risa whispered. "I was trying to reach a town but the Muds found me."

"Found you?" Kirsty said.

"Two male friends and I were lost for three days on the plains. We woke up this morning to find the Mud warriors around us." Risa stopped and glanced around. "Newcomers," she whispered when she saw the girls on the stretchers. "You still have newcomers?"

"Why yes," Norris said. "Don't you have them?"

"Not any more," Risa said. "We've been alone for six months now. Last winter was bad as our electricity supply failed and we had no way to repair it. Summer's not too bad but we won't have enough food when the cold weather comes." The girl swallowed. "Our referees said we were the only people in this world except for the Mud. There was a big argument and three of us set out to look for somebody..."

"Where are your two friends?" Madison asked.

Risa wiped her eyes. "The Mud killed them with their spears. That chief you were talking to stopped them killing me but we couldn't speak each other's language so I don't know why."

"He recognizes bravery," Norris said.

Risa bit on her lip. "I refused to go on my knees when the chief appeared even though they poked spears in my back."

"That would have done it," Kirsty said.

"I was bound and made to walk for hours. When we stopped I was forced to lie down in the bushes while your wagons went by..." Risa looked across at Madison. "Now, here I am."

"You are safe with us". Madison said. "In a couple of hours we'll be home at Buckoway. That's what we call our town."

"So there is another town?" Risa whispered.

"There certainly is," Madison said.

The Japanese girl attempted to smile but her mouth dropped and she broke down into shuddering uncontrolled tears.

*

"I reckon Thinrisodor has an eye for the fairer sex, don't you reckon, Sean?" Hamish said a few moments later when the two wagons were together again.

"For sure, Hamish. I hear he has more than one wife."

"Shut up, Hamish," Madison hissed. "Can't you see Risa is upset. Her two friends were killed."

Hamish nodded. "I'm sorry, Risa, I was just trying to lighten the air." He reached across between the two drivers' seats and squeezed girl's shoulder. "You are welcome. We had heard there were other towns around but thought they were too far away to ever reach. That's wild territory out there, I know. Here Lassie, take this."

Risa took the massive handkerchief handed to her and nodded. "I should be so happy. We were right and..." She shrugged. "I don't even know why you look different and speak different words or why I even understand them. Everything is so strange but you are all so kind."

"For sure," Sean added. "You should have seen Madison when she first arrived. I don't know who got the biggest fright, her or us."

"Me!" Madison said. "Your fierce beards are enough to scare anyone."

Risa wiped her eyes and this time she did smile.

*

The rest of the trip was almost an anticlimax until Buckoway came into view. Risa went quiet and just stared at the wall, castle and other buildings.

"It's identical to Sakita-mura, that's our village, except that's it's bigger and we don't have all this farmland around," she said.

The guard on the main gate stared at the Japanese girl but made no comment. He was more interested in Hamish's report about the Mud attack and asked for a full written report.

When they were inside the town walls, Risa frowned.

"Is it still the same?" Kirsty asked.

"The roads all go the same way with this ring road inside the wall are but the buildings and signs are different. We have curly roofs." She glanced up. "The castle is identical, though."

Hamish's wagon pulled to the kerb and he came back to them. "It's best if Risa doesn't go near the castle," he said. "Could one of you take her to your dorm?"

Madison glanced at Kirsty "Could you go, please. I think I should stick with the wagon and Norris can hardly show her through the female quarters. "

"Sure," Kirsty said and turned to Risa. "It's only a couple of blocks away if you don't mind a short walk."

"But how can I impose?" Risa said. "Perhaps I should just go and report to the authorities. I need to tell them about our village."

Madison grinned and thought back to how polite the Japanese students were at university in Sacramento "Don't rush things, Risa," she said. "We'll help you but in the meantime I think you should go with Kirsty and relax. I'm sure you're hungry, would like a shower and a change of clothes. You're about our size."

Risa nodded but looked relieved that she wasn't going to be just abandoned by her newly found friends.

"I'll stay with you, Madison," Norris said. "If you go charging into the castle by yourself anything could happen,"

"There's Hamish and Sean."

"Yeah, I know," Norris said. "But I still want to be with you."

Madison smiled. "Thanks Norris. We've had an interesting couple of days, haven't we?"

*

CHAPTER ELEVEN

After all the excitement, the following day on Earth came as an anticlimax for Madison. She woke up, immediately wrote down the twenty newcomers' names and sent them by email to Colonel Davis. He called her on the telephone that evening and said they had followed her information up. The name of one girl who had been stung but was missing from Madison's list had been found.

"By the way, have you heard of a Japanese girl called Risa Hatayama?" Madison asked.

"No but I assume the name is important."

"There's another village near us and we think it is filled with Japanese rather than English speaking people." Madison told the colonel about the events of her day.

"This may fit in with one of the scenarios we've come up with," Davis replied. "As far as I can remember there have been no attacks by our robotic bees in Japan for years but there were some in South America. I'll check it out and get back to you. I may also have information about those star patterns that you drew. We have a computer comparing it with astronomy charts on Earth."

*

Risa sat in the morning sunshine in the dormitory living room and stared at those around her. Hamish and Sean had arrived and sat around with the others. "So you believe the authorities won't do anything to help my village."

"I doubt it," Hamish said.

"So what can I do?"

"We will help you," Madison said. "Our first step is to find out about your village and work out how to get there."

"I have a map," Risa said. "Before we were captured we recorded every important feature that we saw. Shall I get it?"

Hamish grinned at Sean and nodded. Risa slipped away and returned a moment later. "I hid it in my bunk," she said and placed a roll of paper onto the table. "Our village is by a river and..."

"Did anything travel up this river?"

Risa frowned. "What do you mean, Madison?"

"Boats, canoes or things like that?"

"Only at night," the girl replied.

"Isn't a boat on the river at night unusual, Lass?" Hamish asked.

"I guess they didn't want us to see it but we heard them. It was usually after midnight when we heard this noise like a refrigerator going up or down the river. Something was there for after it went by we could hear waves lapping on the shore."

"But you never saw anything?" Hamish asked.

Risa glanced up. "Once we did when a group of us were coming home from a party. When we heard the noise we climbed up the steps on the inside of the town wall and looked out. There was a full moon and we saw a boat low in the water. There were no lights but after it went by the waves hit the beach below the village."

"How often did it come by?" Sean asked.

"Not very often. Once a month, I guess. It wasn't regular at all." Risa unrolled her paper and showed them a beautifully drawn map dominated by the river like a large letter "S down the left side of the page. Japanese characters named various parts of the map.

"And this?" Hamish pointed to a curved line down the centre.

"That's the road we found and began to follow. I think it's the same road you drove your wagons along but this would be further north."

"And this?" Kirsty pointed to a shaded section.

"A range of hills between the plains and the river further south. When the river turned east into that valley we followed the road west across the plains. We'd heard rumours from the local Mud tribe of a town in this direction." Risa smiled. "I guess they were right."

"Oh my God," Madison said. "Aren't they the hills the tunnel goes through to where we picked up the newcomers from *Gentle Lady*?"

"Aye it is and Risa's village would be twenty kilometres upstream from there," Hamish said.

"About an hour's journey in the barge," Madison muttered to herself.

*

After their discussion Hamish and Sean said they had a job to do at the stable so would have to leave.

"Do you need help?" Madison asked.

"No, Lass. It's just administrative stuff. Rest up for now and enjoy your day off."

Risa agreed to take a low profile that day but she was obviously worried about her future. One unusual thing Madison noticed as they showed her around the town was that nobody made any comment about the Japanese girl's oriental features or different accent. Perhaps the locals were conditioned to ignore any cultural differences. And of course she was probably regarded as one of Buckoway's new citizens. Madison never saw Wendy Pratt or any other newcomers but heard they had settled into a dormitory a couple of blocks away.

So the day drifted into evening and finally night. Madison felt unusually tired so excused herself and went to bed early. Another day was over and the new one on Earth was about to begin.

*

The morning was hot and clear but it felt wrong. Madison opened her eyes and found herself still in the narrow dormitory bunk and not the double bed she shared with Norris.

"Oh hell," she muttered and flung the blankets aside.

"I know you always wake at some ungodly hour but you don't need to feel we have to get up, too," Kirsty muttered from the bunk below her.

Madison stared around. Across from her, Yasmin was snoring peacefully and below her Risa was also asleep.

"Damn!" Madison hissed.

Kirsty's voice turned serious. "What is it Madison?" she asked.

"I didn't go back," Madison whispered. "This is the first time I've woken up in the same world as when I went to sleep. I expected to be in Sacramento."

"Well, Norris is only next door..."

"Shut up, Kirsty. This has never happened before and to be frank, I'm scared."

Kirsty glanced up. "So go back to sleep."

Madison shook her head. "No, I don't think that will make any difference." She jumped down to the floor and reached for her clothes. "Damn skirt," she muttered. "Why can't we have decent clothes for the hot weather?"

She dressed and sucked on her lip as she glanced at Kirsty. "I'm going for a walk in the park by the wall. I need to think."

"I'll come." Kirsty grabbed her clothes and also dressed.

"You always have a morning shower," Madison protested.

"So? My best friend has a problem. That's more important than a shower." She grinned. "Anyway, after looking after the oxen I'm always covered in stinky sweat anyway."

"I guess."

The street was deserted as the pair walked along. No reason for Madison's waking up still in Buckoway was found so their conversation turned to other matters. There was plenty to discuss from the Mud chief to the Japanese girl suddenly thrust in their care. They walked downhill to the ring road inside the wall and were about to cross when an oxen team and wagon appeared.

"Isn't that Hamish and Sean?" Kirsty said. "I thought they said we could have another day off today as there were no trips planned."

"They did," Madison replied. She waved and the wagon pulled into the kerb beside them.

"A top of the morn' to yah." Hamish grinned down at them. "And why are you lassies wandering around the streets on your day off?"

"Madison's had..." Kirsty began but stopped when she was poked in the back. "We couldn't sleep," she muttered.

"Of more interest to us is why you're here with all the oxen hitched and already working?" Madison asked.

"Our other job, Madison," Sean said

"I never knew you had another job."

"Aye. It's one we don't advertise."

"I see." Madison pouted. "And you can't even tell us."

"Why not?" Hamish said. "We take the deceased up to the morgue for disposal."

"What?" Kirsty gasped.

"People do die, Lass," Hamish said. "Our job is to remove the remains while the citizens are asleep."

"Oh hell. Who have you got?" Madison asked.

"Alfred and John's bodies were found outside the main gate an hour ago." He shrugged. "We knew that would happen."

"Can I come with you?" Madison blurted out.

"I don't know..."

"I want to see what happens. I have been to funerals before, you know." She grabbed her friend's arm. "If you don't want to come I'll understand, Kirsty," she said and turned back to the wagonmaster. "Well?"

Hamish shrugged and slid across his seat. Madison climbed up and grinned when Kirsty shoved her from behind and wriggled up beside her.

"You aren't leaving me behind," the girl whispered even though her face looked pale.

The wagon continued around the ring road until they were in a part of town Madison hadn't visited before. They turned uphill and a few minutes later arrived at the wall that circled the castle. Hamish turned right instead of the expected left where the main gate was and followed the road around to a small entrance at the rear. He put two fingers in his mouth, gave an almighty whistle and the twin doors opened.

"Still want to come?" he asked.

Both girls nodded.

The oxen moved through the passageway that was so narrow, Madison was sure the wagon wheels would get jammed. The wheels didn't, though and they were soon in a different courtyard from the one they'd taken the newcomers into. Hamish circled around and stopped by another indiscreet looking door.

Sean jumped down and glanced at Madison. "Want to help?" he asked. "We'll pay you overtime."

"Shall we?" she asked Kirsty.

Her friend nodded. "We came this far and I could use the money. Do you know there are some new shoes at the market?"

"Oh Kirsty," Madison laughed and jumped down onto the cobblestones.

The corpses were covered with a sheet and lay on similar stretchers to those used for newcomers. The girls took one stretcher and followed the men who carried the other one inside to the castle cellar. A blast of hot air hit the pair when they walked in.

"We'll do this part, thanks," Hamish said and pointed to a long conveyor belt on top of a steel table. "We put them on there."

The girls watched as the men lifted the bodies off the stretchers and placed them one behind the other on the belt.

"Let 'em go, Frankton!" Hamish yelled to man Madison noticed in a small control room above them.

"Hell, look!" Kirsty said and grabbed Madison's hand.

She turned and saw that the conveyer belt ended at a gigantic furnace. A steel door at the front was open so she could see flames roaring inside. At the same time the conveyor belt began moving the bodies toward it. The bodies were being cremated there and then!

Madison could only stand dumbfounded as the first one reached the end of the belt and tipped into a chute. It slid through the door and disappeared into the flames. The second body followed and the door clanged shut.

"What about the funeral service?" she gasped

Hamish turned and wiped perspiration off his forehead, "It's the second time you mentioned that word," he said. "What's a funeral?"

Madison on her lips and stared at the closed furnace door. "A ceremony for friends and loved ones to say good-bye to the person who died. It's usually held in a church and..."

"Church?" Hamish asked in a kind voice. "I don't know that one either I'm afraid, Lass."

*

Madison glanced up with her eyes wide in horror. She stood with her lips quivering for a moment before she burst into tears "Oh hell, I hate this world that I'm stuck in," she cried, wiped her hands down her skirt and ran out into the courtyard.

"What did I say?" Hamish asked Kirsty. "I've never seen her quite so upset." He looked dismayed himself.

"It's more than just seeing you dispose of the bodies, I think," Kirsty whispered. "She never woke up in her other world last night." She ran after her friend and left the two men staring at each other.

"Could it be this place isn't quite the utopia they want us to believe?" Sean whispered.

"Aye Sean and it takes one wee lassie to point it out to us." Hamish tugged on his beard. "But you know, I reckon her heart's in the right place."

The wagon caught up to the two girls half way along the ring road. Hamish pulled in beside the pair.

"Climb aboard," he said. "I'm taking you home for breakfast."

"It's okay," Madison said. "Don't blame yourself, Hamish. I was the one who wanted to see what happened."

"Aye you did but I reckon you still need some breakfast. My Noelene cooks up a nice pot of porridge and the coffee will be hot."

"Come on," Kirsty whispered. "Hamish is trying to understand, you know."

Madison nodded. "Of course he is." She turned and smiled at the two men. "Sometimes remembering the old world is more trouble than it's worth."

"For sure," Sean said. "We don't rightly understand your concerns Madison but we do know what love and friendship means. It's not that those two men are forgotten. Their families will always have them in their thoughts. We have a saying; *Immortality is in your loved one's mind*. I think that could apply here."

Madison nodded and followed by Kirsty, climbed up onto the wagon. "I need to get back to Risa."

Hamish glanced across at her with a look of empathy. "Like I tried to stress yesterday, we are the only ones who can help her," he said. "We've learnt things about this place and you have taught us more."

"Meaning?" Madison whispered.

"At the best, the authorities will ignore our new friend and at the worse they will arrest her and take her to the castle."

"What for?" Madison hissed

"They'll remove memories of her other village from her mind and substitute the *Alpha Condition.*"

"That's what Wendy Pratt had on her card. What is it?"

"The memory Kirsty and the rest of us have of being brought here from an orphanage in the city."

"But what about the village of Sakita-mura?"

"She won't remember it any more than we remember our real childhood."

"But they need help. We can't just let them starve." It was Kelly who spoke up this time.

"I know," Hamish said. "I think the time has come for us to band together and do something before it is too late. What is happening at Risa's village may very well happen to us, sometime in the future. We can ignore her plight at our own peril."

*

In Sacramento when Madison wouldn't awaken, a desperate Norris called an ambulance and she was rushed to hospital where she was examined by a young intern and put on emergency oxygen.

"Can you name Miss Evan's general practitioner and her medical health insurance company?" the receptionist asked Norris in a detached voice.

"I only know she is one of Doctor Joel Mitchell's patients, He's a consultant at..."

"I know Doctor Mitchell," the woman retorted as her fingers flashed across the computer keyboard. She waited a moment while the page loaded and reached for the telephone.

"Doctor Mitchell's surgery. This is Accident and Emergency at Sutter General Hospital. One of Doctor Mitchell's patients has arrived here for treatment with severe breathing problems. She is on oxygen but may need more acute services ... Yes, I shall wait." She glanced up at Norris. "His nurse is contacting him... Yes Doctor Mitchell..." The receptionist repeated everything she'd told the nurse. "Yes, a doctor is with her now... You will?" The woman sounded surprised. "Yes, we shall admit her and do what we can until you arrive. Thank you, Doctor Mitchell." She hung up and turned to Norris. "I don't know why your young friend is such a high priority patient but Doctor Mitchell said he'd be here within the next half hour. You will still need to provide me with details about her."

"Of course," Norris replied. He filled in a document handed to him and sat in a waiting room chair just as Kirsty rushed in.

"I just heard that Madison's been brought here. What's wrong?" She stood there catching her breath as if she'd run half way across the city.

"She never woke up this morning then about an hour ago her condition became worse, Her pulse slowed and her face turned a ghastly white. That was when I called for an ambulance."

"And how is she now?"

"They're going to admit her and Doctor Mitchell is coming over."

"Oh hell," Kirsty gasped and sat in a chair beside Norris. "It sounds bad."

Norris just stared at the floor and nodded.

An hour later Doctor Mitchell walked into the waiting room where Norris and Kirsty still waiting.

"She is breathing without the need for a respirator and appears to be in REM sleep as her eyes are moving beneath the lids. However, there is no sign of her waking so we have put her on an intravenous drip."

"When will she wake up, Doctor Mitchell?" Kirsty asked.

"I'm sorry but her condition is unknown. She is asleep rather than in a coma but I'm reluctant to try to wake her with any sort of stimulant."

"So she's active and awake in her other existence?" Kirsty asked.

"I believe so. I am arranging to have her transferred to the East Pacific Research Institute."

"Why?" Norris asked. "Aren't the facilities here as good as any in the city?"

"Of course but we want to take a full body and brain wave scan and the EPRI has advanced equipment that hasn't even been commercially released."

Kirsty frowned. "Last time you tried something experimental on her she almost died."

The doctor nodded. "That was military electronic interception apparatus not medical diagnostic equipment. Nothing we use will physically harm her. It will receive and record data such as her brain patterns, heartbeat, and will look for foreign objects in her blood stream but will not attempt to alter or extract more than a blood sample." He glanced at the pair. "Madison has you both on record as next-of-kin so with either or both your permissions we can proceed."

"Can you promise as her doctor that these tests are to help her recover and not just to help Colonel Davis in his attempts to trace this alternative existence?" Kirsty said.

"I can promise you that my immediate concern is Madison's health. Colonel Davis will not even be told where she is without your permission."

Kirsty glanced at Norris who nodded.

"Okay, but we want to know about everything that happens to her and the results of the tests even if the information is negative."

"Thank you." The doctor replied. "I have no proof but I think her immune system has discovered a foreign object in her bloodstream and is fighting it."

"What about her crushed spine," Norris asked.

"That's the one piece of good news. As far as we can tell, her spinal cord has repaired itself completely. When she wakes up she should be able to walk without even a limp."

"So let's pray she does wake up," Kirsty whispered.

*

CHAPTER TWELVE

Her dream was weird and consisted of confused images. She lay on a hospital bed with her friends around her but in some strange way they seemed to change. Kirsty's modern tank top and shorts changed to a blouse and tartan skirt while Norris's long shorts suddenly changed into old-fashioned trousers and shirt. Other people came and went. Doctor Mitchell took her pulse and a Japanese girl slept in the bunk across from her.

Madison shook her head and woke up to find a worried Kirsty bending over her. For the second time she had not returned to Earth.

"Oh Madison," Kirsty said. "You were moaning and flinging your arms around something awful. Are you okay?"

"I think so." Madison sat up and saw only Kirsty's bedside lamp on in the darkened room. "What time is it?"

Kirsty glanced at the wall clock. "Four-fifteen. You never wake this early." She handed Madison a warm damp face cloth. "I was going to wipe your face. You're covered in perspiration." She frowned. "You told me you never dream."

Madison smiled and wiped her face. The warmth made her feel more alert. "I think I was half awake back on Earth but couldn't quite make it. I was in a hospital bed and you and Norris were with me. Both of you wore different clothes and your hair was shorter just like your otherselves. You both looked worried as if I was ill then I saw Risa in the bunk here and woke up."

"How do you feel?"

"Normal now," Madison said. "In my dream I was all confused." She stared at Kirsty. "I think I was really in a hospital on Earth but couldn't wake up there."

"Why?"

"That's it Kirsty. I don't know. Here I am fine but something has happened to me on Earth. For some reason I can't get back."

"So do you want to try to get back to sleep?"

Madison shook her head. "No, I'll get up. It's going to be a big day anyway. I'll pack everything up and perhaps cook some biscuits to take with us. You go back to sleep, though and thanks."

*

When the oxen pulled two wagons through the farms outside Buckoway, dawn made the eastern sky red. Dairy farms were an oasis of activity as farmers using modern milking machines, milked their cows ready for the tanker wagon that arrived at six to take milk back to the town's bottling plant. Every farmer waved for they recognized the wagons. The silhouettes of two women were clearly visible in the front wagon. The farmers knew it was Madison Evans and her sidekick Kirsty Bell. Their reputation had spread and the town gossip now called them the *Maidens of Granite*. They alone had stood on their wagon like granite to fire arrow after arrow at the invading Muds. Only their deadly accurate bowmanship had cowered the enemy.

Madison and Kirsty waved at a farmer as they moved past. Behind them Norris sat leaning against the sideboard talking to Risa. To Madison, their wagon made them appear like gypsies, another term unknown by her friends. It was set up as a living quarters with the bunks folded away along the sides behind boxes of clothes and food. Two wooden barrels tied to the sides held water and a dozen bales of hay were arranged like seats. These would be used to feed the oxen in the days ahead. Their journey to take Risa home was going to be a long one so they brought supplies for weeks on the road.

The second wagon with Hamish and Sean in the drivers' seat was packed with food and supplies that Risa said were in short supply at Sakita-mura. Bags of potatoes, rice, flour and salt sat beside crates of fresh vegetables and fruit. Other wooden containers held clothes and building supplies that Hamish and Sean had bought, bartered for or perhaps even stole in the town. There was even a small armoury of modern bows and hundreds of arrows that were brand new, still wrapped in greaseproof paper and stamped with the border guard seal.

"It's only six-thirty," Kirsty said. "We certainly got away early."

"Yes," Madison replied. "Normally this would be my wake up time so perhaps only having one life has its advantage."

Kirsty turned and studied her friend. "It will work out," she whispered. "I know it will, just like I know our journey to help Risa's village will be a success."

Madison smiled. "Your optimism could become contagious," she said. "We are going into the unknown, though."

"When we arrived, everything was unknown," Norris cut in from behind her. He caught Madison's eyes when she glanced back. "And much of it still is."

"Sure," Madison said.

She lapsed into silenced except for giving a few curt commands to Olive, Twinkle, Thelma and Florence. The oxen appeared content as they strolled forward along the dusty road and her orders to increase speed up a little were ignored.

*

An hour later the Mud warriors appeared and lined the roadside. Again, the wagons continued on until Thinrisodor stepped into the middle of the road and waited.

"Good morning, Thinrisodor," Madison called down as her wagon pulled to a halt.

"So you take the lead now. Madison?" he replied.

"I have the safe passage, don't I?"

"True, but men don't usually like to step aside for women."

Madison just smiled and waited.

"I have news and perhaps someone who can help you," the Mud chief said. "However, your reputation must be proved."

"Oh hell," Kirsty whispered but clamped her mouth shut when Madison glowered at her.

"What do I have to prove to you?"

"Not me but my companion." he lifted a finger and another warrior appeared. This new man stood beside, not behind Thinrisodor and appeared to have the bearing of a leader. Like Thinrisodor, his spear faced the ground.

"This is Cannad, leader of the Sneednim people."

"They are the ones around our village," Risa whispered from behind Madison's ear. There was a tremor in her voice.

Madison turned her eyes to the new warrior and bowed her head. "I am honoured," she said.

"He doesn't speak Buckoway," Thinrisodor said. "Only Sakita-mura."

Madison hid a frown as she worked out what the man meant. Of course, this new chief spoke Japanese but no English. "Welcome him in your language," she hissed to Risa without turning her head.

Risa nodded and moved up to the drivers' seat. She stood bowed at the warrior and spoke a few words of Japanese.

He said one word in reply and stood expressionless by Thinrisodor.

"Okay, " Madison said. "What's the test?"

"See that red rag?"

Half way up a grass hillside to their left, a tiny red rag was pinned to the ground.

Madison nodded.

"Your reputation is that you can hit a running warrior with an arrow at a hundred paces. This is further away than that but does not move. Can you hit it with an arrow from here?"

"Possibly," Madison said.

The other chief spoke in Japanese and Risa paled. "You will only have three arrows and have to hit it at least once." she said when Madison indicated she had not grasped the rapidly spoken words.

"So we do it together," Kirsty said. She already had two bows in her hand and handed one to Madison.

"You do it from your wagon," Thinrisodor said.

"I'll do it," Madison said and stood up.

However Kirsty also stood while Norris tapped Risa on the shoulder and signalled her back behind the seat. "Show no sign of fear," he whispered.

The two bow-women placed their left legs behind the seat, their right one on it and lifted their bows. Madison caught Kirsty's eyes and gave a brief nod. Simultaneously they pulled their bowstrings back, lined up and released their weapons. The arrows curled up into the air almost too high but arched back in a curve and dropped in a small cloud of dust. When it cleared the rag was not punctured once but twice by two quivering arrows.

"We did it?" Kirsty gasped.

Madison turned to Cannad, nodded and sat down.

"The punctured rag will give you free access through Sneednim lands," Thinrisodor said. "However, there are other tribes in the area who will not respect this treaty."

"Thank you," Madison said. "We are honoured to called your friends." She glanced at Risa. "Can you translate, please."

"Now the news," Thinrisodor continued. "The fastest way to Risa's village is by the boat that travels against the current and wind."

"The *Gentle Lady?*" Madison frowned. "There are no newcomers coming so we don't expect it to be at Station Five?"

"There is always a boat there," Thinrisodor replied. "The strangers bring one down river and take the other one back. Take this boat and travel upstream to Risa's village. The strangers come from half a day's journey further up and only travel by darkness. Travel by day and you will not see them."

"That's good news," Madison said.

"Don't go ashore on the right bank as you go upstream. Regard anyone on that side, our peoples or strangers as unworthy. Don't be fooled for they may feign friendliness. There are powers there we do not understand."

"Thank you. I have a gift for you both," Madison said. "In Hamish's wagon are two barrels of milk, powdered milk. We heard your babies are sometimes short. You can have one each as our way of thanking you."

Risa took Madison's cue and repeated her words in Japanese.

The two chiefs spoke in their own tongue before they turned back to Madison. "Thank you. Remember to fly the pierced rag on your wagon or the boat. If you need help, replace it with the other one." He handed her two rags. Both rags had two holes through them but one was coloured blue.

"Only use the blue if you are in danger," Thinrisodor said and stepped back.

Madison nodded, climbed down and walked back to where Hamish and Sean sat in the other wagon.

"All solved, Lass?" Hamish said. "We saw your arrows fly."

"Yes," Madison said and wondered if she should introduce Cannad who stood beside her. Hamish caught her eye and gave a tiny shake of his head. "We are giving both chiefs a barrel of powdered milk for their children," she said. "Will you get them, please?"

" Sean?" Hamish said without turning his head.

Sean jumped down the far side and walked to the rear of their wagon where two Mud warriors stood. The barrels were heavy but the warriors held them in their arms and disappeared.

By the time Sean returned to the front there wasn't a Mud warrior in sight. "Disciplined aren't they?" he said as he climbed back up beside Hamish.

"So get going," Hamish said to Madison. "We can talk in the safety of the tunnel."

"Right." Madison walked back with her head held high, climbed aboard and nodded to Kirsty and Norris who had slipped forward to take the reins. "Go," she said and sat down beside Risa.

*

By mid afternoon the two wagons were through the tunnel and headed towards Station Five.

"The *Gentle Lady* is there," Kelly cried in excitement and pointed to the jetty where the barge floated.

They moved closer and Madison poked Kirsty in the side. "Look at the boat again," she said. "What do you see?""

"The *Gentle Lady* looks no different. The river level is lower so it's ... Oh I see..."

"What is it?" Norris cut in.

"Look at the name, Norris," Kirsty said.

Norris squinted in the bright sunlight. The name on the front of the barge read *Gentle Warrior*. It was a different boat.

They arrived and walked into the dormitory block. It appeared no different until they walked into the kitchen. The food supply had been restocked. The main other change was in the barn where the food bunkers had been refilled and the whole building had been cleaned out.

"It looks as if they stocked up for our visit," Hamish said.

"But we weren't due to come here," Madison replied.

"Unless there is another load of newcomers coming," Kirsty said. She turned to Hamish. "How much notice do you get when you're asked to come and pick them up?"

"And who tells you?" Madison asked

"One of the officials from the castle calls in," Hamish said. "They usually tell us two days ahead but sometimes they want us to go the next morning."

"So they could call in tonight and ask you to come here in the morning?" Madison said.

"No they know we're out of Buckoway and know the Mud will only let our wagons through," Hamish said. "We have to tell a referee whenever we expect to be away overnight." He grinned. "I told them we were going to The Trading Post to build a new market stall and would be away several days,"

"We've done that before so it's not unusual." Sean added. "It also gave us a reason to stock up the wagons."

"Including the bows and arrows?" Madison said.

Hamish almost blushed. "Yeah, well they sort of got lost in a transhipment from the factory that builds them."

Madison only glowered at him. "Okay," she said. "Let's go and examine the new boat."

Gentle Warrior was identical to *Gentle Lady* except it had no stretcher frames aboard, just one big empty space.

"Okay, what now?" Norris asked.

"It's two thirty," Hamish said. "It gives us about four and a half hours of daylight. I think that if we left now we'd be cutting it too fine. Risa's map is not very accurate at this end so..." He glanced at Madison.

She nodded. "I agree we don't want to be stuck on the river but what if someone arrives here during the night?"

"Perhaps we could cover all possibilities," Sean said.

"How?" Madison asked.

"We could take the wagons back to the tunnel and stay there over night. Once inside, we'll be safe from spying eyes or hostile Muds. We could back the wagons in and be ready to come out at first light."

Everyone agreed so after using the facilities in the dormitory, washing down and feeding the oxen they cleaned everything so no sign of their visit was evident. By six they had retreated into the tunnel. The oxen were settled and appeared to be quite content to sit and munch the hay given to them.

The humans moved into Madison's wagon that was closest to the entrance and set it up for the night. As a precaution, Hamish arranged for a night watch over Station Five. "We need to do it in pairs," he said. "I think we should all take part except you, Madison."

Madison frowned. "Why not?"

"Your other life," Hamish replied. "You may go back or have another dream. We don't want to wake you up after you've gone to sleep."

"So I take the first shift before I go to asleep."

"Okay, but just for a couple of hours," Hamish said. "If anything does happen come back and shut the tunnel door. Nobody can get in."

"Except the people who built the tunnel," Norris said. "What's the bet it's the same ones who bring the newcomers down river?"

*

It appeared that the tunnel was designed to have guards for they found a small stairway just inside the main door. It led up to a small door that opened out to a parapet above the door. This was cut in the cliff face and couldn't be reached from the ground below.

"It's like the town wall at Buckoway," Kirsty said.

"Yeah, probably built by the same people," Norris said.

The view of the river and Station Five from this lookout was perfect. If anything came along the river it would be seen. As well, the jetty and barge were in full view. The first unexpected thing was when Madison and Norris had just begun their watch. As it became dark, a row of lights came on along the jetty and streets of Station Five."

"Who did that?' Norris asked in a nervous voice.

"A light meter switches it on the same as it is done with the streets in Buckoway," Madison said.

113

Norris grinned. "So nobody's down there?"

"I doubt it."

"But why would they have lights when there's nobody to use them?"

"Probably so they can see it when their boat arrives at night. Remember, Risa said the boat travels without lights. If Station Five wasn't lit up they might go right past."

"Yeah or perhaps want to keep the Muds out of town."

"Could be. I'm sure the Muds wouldn't want to go in a lit up town. Back home they keep lights on in shops at night for safety."

"Helps us now, doesn't it?' Norris said. "Nobody can go near Station Five without us seeing them."

"True," Madison whispered. She sat down on a seat and gazed out. Apart from the lights of the tiny station all except the river was dark. It looked like a wide silver line cutting across the valley ahead. The temperature was warm and a few moths fluttered around. Overhead, stars shone in moonless sky. Back on Earth she had spent many summer nights outdoors at campgrounds and outdoor parties. She turned to Norris beside her. He was different here. Back home in a similar situation he'd be all over her by now. Somehow, here he was gentler and almost shy. She chuckled.

"What is it?" Norris asked.

"Oh nothing," Madison replied. " I just... oh no, I can see two of you, Norris."

"What is it?" Norris reached across to grab her.

However Madison didn't reply because she was sound asleep.

*

CHAPTER THIRTEEN

Norris's concerned voice cut through Madison's subconscious mind. The smell of pines had gone and was replaced by that antiseptic scent of a hospital.

"Can you hear me?" Norris said.

"Of course I can," Madison said. She opened her eyes and found him staring at her from behind a green surgical mask.

"Oh my God," Norris gasped. "It worked."

A gloved hand touched Norris's shoulder and pushed him gently aside. Doctor Joel Mitchell shone a beam of light into her eyes and held a hand out. "How many fingers do I have showing, Madison?" he asked.

"Two."

There was a gasp of relief around the room and Madison realized there were people everywhere. She wriggled up from under the blankets and looked around. "Kirsty," she said. "Why the tears?"

"Your heart stopped, Madison. I thought you had died."

Madison frowned. Sure her heart was racing but otherwise she felt fine, her head was clear and she felt fit and ready for another day. She turned and saw Colonel Brad Davis amongst the masked nurses. Behind her, a gigantic machine thumped and two wall monitors beeped. A needle protruded from a vein in her arm and was connected to a plastic tube filled with the almost black liquid that must be blood. She turned and noticed a second bed beside her. Another patient lay there, a girl unknown to her who also had a tube and needle in her arm.

"Okay, I'm back on Earth but what's happening?" Madison asked.

"It's somewhat complicated," Doctor Mitchell replied. "Just relax and..."

Madison glanced up at the colonel. "And what have you got to do with this, Colonel Davis?"

"Oh Madison," Kirsty laughed. "You are all right."

"And why not?"

Joel Mitchell glanced at Brad Davis who nodded and began to speak in his slow voice.

"We managed to catch one of those alien bees and..."

Jonathan Friedovitz stared at the bank of screens in the research laboratory and whistled.

"Well Doctor Friedovitz," Davis snapped. "What do all your top secret machines tell us?"

"This flying machine is artificial but is not metallic at all."

"Of course it's metallic. It's as hard as steel."

"The hard shell is like that of a beetle but is made of living tissue. It's a biological being, not a machine. Have a look."

Friedovitz pressed a button and a magnified view of the thing being examined showed as a holographic three-dimensional image on the table. The scientist ran his fingers over a small plastic ball on the console and the vision rotated around. It had six legs, sockets that could be eyes and two gigantic antennae, one at each end of the body.

"The front one is the sting," the scientist said. "That's a much more efficient way to get an accurate penetration of a victim's skin."

"And the other?"

"A sensory organ. It receives high and low powered frequency transmissions, probably both visual and sound."

"So it's alive?"

"Not really."

Davis almost snorted. "You can't have it both ways, Doctor."

"It is alive but was artificially created. There are no reproductive organs, a mouth or digestive system. Again, I'll show you."

The holograph became transparent so the bee's interior came into view. There was a heart, brain and some other vital organs. At the front was a sac of dull yellow liquid while at the rear was another sac of clear liquid.

"We've tested them both. The front sac holds the liquid to be injected in the victim while the rear one contains nutrients to feed the creature."

"And when that runs out?"

"It dies. It's an artificially created life-form made for the sole purpose of attacking humans and injecting the liquid into their bloodstream." Jonathan pointed a small jagged point the front of the creature with a pen he had in his hand. "I believe that when the victim's skin is pierced the tip of the front antenna breaks off, travels to the victim's brain, intercepts memory patterns and takes DNA samples. This is the slither of metal you picked up earlier."

"Do you know how?"

116

"There are millions of circuits there powered by a microscopic battery. The technology used is far in excess of anything we know."

"So they now have a copy of the human's thoughts and DNA. What now?"

"The chemical injected alters the victim's blood type and forms an entirely new one. For want of a better name, we call it Type F1. This works like ordinary blood except for one thing. As well as the red and white corpuscles there are new transparent ones..."

"Why doesn't the body reject them?"

"We don't know. Perhaps the slither in the brain transmits a signal so the body thinks the invader is natural blood. These corpuscles are miniature radio transmitters. The whole body transmits signals out, millions of them to tell everything about the body. Every thought, warning, emotion and condition is transmitted out to that satellite above the Equator."

"And from there?"

Friedovitz shrugged. "That's not my department. You'll need to talk to the NASA guys about that."

"What else have you found out?"

"For the ordinary patient this Type F1 blood becomes gradually diluted so after a month the victim's own blood type replaces it. At the same time the slither in the brain dissolves and the person becomes uncontaminated. I'd say, no more information about them is needed and they return back to their old selves except for one thing."

"Their immune system?"

"Yes, this is enhanced so any diseases or physical disabilities are cured."

"Like Madison Evan's paralysis?"

"Exactly. It's almost as if the invader wants to award the victim for violating him or her."

"So why is the girl lying in a coma right now?"

"We found that twenty-first victim in that San Francisco attack. She's a high school girl called Jenny Hannett. She agreed to let us give her a brain scan and take a blood sample." Doctor Friedovitz tapped his keyboard and another monitor lit up that showed a wavy line of coloured bubbles. "That's Type F1 blood." He typed on his keyboard again and a second line appeared beneath the first. It showed a slightly different pattern. "This is Jenny's blood. We call it Type F2. We believe it is different in two ways."

"I'm interested," Davis whispered as his eyes studied the screen.

"We believe it receives as well as transmits information and that it reproduces itself."

"Meaning?"

"Jenny Hannett doesn't revert back to her old blood type but keeps this blood permanently, or at least for several years. Long range testing can only prove this."

"So this girl is under their control?"

The scientist nodded. "We believe something is entered into their brain waves such as a code. When it is activated the victim can receive directions into her subconscious."

"What for?"

"As far as we know it is to find other humans of the type they want, in Jenny's case more English speaking intelligent humans of her own age that more bees can attack to steal DNA and memories from."

"And from what Madison Evans told us, new humans are created on this other world."

"Yes."

"So what went wrong with Madison?"

"She was stung twice and received both blood types. Our original theory was probably right. It by-passed the master computer or whatever it is and created an exclusive loop between her two physical bodies."

"So what is wrong with her now?"

"F1 and F2 blood types are not compatible. It's as if she has leukaemia. They are fighting each other. If nothing is done she will die and within the next forty-eight hours."

"Hell. And her otherself?"

"She should be fine. I would imagine the new clones made have the ordinary blood of the donor."

"And can you keep Madison alive?"

"Yes but only if Jenny Hannett agrees," the scientist replied.

*

Madison sucked on her lip as she thought about Davis's words. "And that's Jenny in the other bed?" she asked.

"Yes. She agreed to participate."

Madison stared at the other girl. "Is she going to be okay?"

"Probably better than when the procedure took place. It was you we were gambling with. If we had done nothing you would probably be dead by now so it was worth the risk. Both Norris and Kirsty as your nominated next-of-kin agreed."

Madison turned and reached out for her two friends. "I love you both." She squeezed their hands and turned back to Doctor Mitchell. "What was the procedure?"

"Similar to that given to unborn babies with rare blood disorders. If we just replaced your blood with ordinary human blood we believe you would have suffered brain damage even if you survived."

"So how did Jenny fit in?"

"She gave you her blood and had her own replaced by donors' blood. Your contaminated blood is being held in our machine. It wasn't as simple as that but that is basically what happened."

"So why is Jenny unconscious?"

"She was awake earlier but was given a mild sedative. We also dissolved the slither in her brain so she should be free of any alien violations now. We will still need to keep an close watch on her."

"Good," Madison replied. "And myself?"

"Again it is only a theory but we believe you will continue to have contact with you otherself permanently."

"So every time I go asleep I'll wake up in my other body."

"Until, we find out more information, yes," Joel Mitchell said.

Madison flopped back on her pillow. "If I'm asleep when Jenny wakes up, tell her thanks and I'll speak to her when I wake up."

She shut her eyes and fell asleep.

*

"She's fine," Joel Mitchell said when he saw Kirsty and Norris's worried expressions. "This is her normal sleep pattern. No doubt she'll be back in her other world soon."

"But how does the time work out?" Kirsty asked. "She hasn't been awake all day like she usually is."

"I don't think physical time applies. If she's only asleep five minutes here she may have been away twelve or more hours there. After all she really is two people but has the ability to communicate with her otherself. That is something you can't do but your clone is alive and doing things on this other world right now."

"Why do you say clone, Doctor Mitchell?"

"Just a term. I could say identical twin, I guess. As time goes by you will become more different as the two of you adjust to the different environments you live in."

"Yeah," Kirsty whispered, "Scary, isn't it?"

*

"Madison!" Norris cried out.

Madison opened her eyes and found herself on the parapet above the tunnel. "How long was I asleep, Norris?" she asked.

"A couple of minutes. I was just going to go and get help from the others when you woke up again. Are you all right?"

"I went back, Norris but everything is fine now."

"Would you like to talk about it?"

Madison smiled. "I've always been fine here. The complications were with my oldself back on Earth. I'll tell everyone about it later."

At ten-thirty there was a cough and Hamish appeared with Risa. "We'll take over the watch now," he said. "Go and get some sleep."

"I'm wide awake," Madison briefly described her trip back to Earth. "Poor old Norris can hardly keep wake, though."

Norris grinned. "I guess I am tired," he said.

"I'll stay with Madison," Risa said. "Both you men go. Someone can replace us for the next shift."

Hamish looked at Madison. "Are you sure?"

"Well, I don't think I'll sleep anyway so I might as well be here as tossing and turning in the wagon."

"Okay but wake me if anything happens," Hamish said.

"We will," Madison replied.

After the men left Risa turned to Madison. "So there is another me on this Earth you speak of?" she asked.

"Yes. Next time I go back I'll ask Colonel Davis to see if he can find you."

"It doesn't matter," the Japanese girl replied. "I've been in Sakitamura for eight years now so we won't have much in common."

"Eight years? How do you know?"

"Every year have what we call an Arrival's Celebration to celebrate the day we left the crowded city and orphanage." She screwed her nose up. "Of course I now know there never was a city."

"So when did your village begin to have the hard times?"

"When no newcomers arrived. That was about three years ago. We haven't got the good soil for farmland like around Buckoway. It's either stony or swamp."

"Perhaps that is why Buckoway was set up away from the river. From what Hamish said our town is younger than yours."

"True. Many of our villagers were there years before I came."

"So why were you abandoned?"

"Because we're intelligent creatures who can think for ourselves. Nobody, no matter how advanced they are, can treat us like puppets and

120

continue to pull the strings." Risa scowled. "We were cut off because we began to question our existence and drove the Emperors out."

"The Emperors?"

"The people in the castle who wake the newcomers."

Madison gasped. "That's right. We have referees but above them are some others called Guardians."

"That will be them," Risa said. "There were only eight of them at Sakita-mura. We had a huge meeting and one night overwhelmed them, gave them a oxen train of supplies and told them to leave."

"What happened to them?'"

"Rumours were that a flying machine landed and took them away. We found the oxen wandering around but the wagons and Emperors had gone. They never came back but neither did any more supplies arrive."

"Couldn't you trade with the Mud?"

"We do but they really have nothing to trade. I think they originally got stuff from these Emperors, too."

"Of course," Madison said. "It all fits in." She gazed out into the darkness deep in thought.

Just before midnight, Hamish and Sean appeared and insisted on take over the watch. "If you're still awake at two, Madison, bring Kirsty back with you. Oh yes, we found a light switch at the bottom of the stairs and turned the lights off. You might need this." He handed Madison a small torch. "Just in case there is somebody out there, don't turn it on until you shut the door."

"Okay." Madison said. "Come on, Risa."

The pair found Kirsty asleep in the wagon and crawled into their bunks. Risa fell asleep and though she expected to stay awake, Madison did too.

*

It was dark outside but a dim light lit the adjacent corridor.

"Madison are you awake?" said an unknown voice.

"Yes but who's that?"

"Jenny Hannett. When they told me that bee sting had poisoned my blood I was scared silly, Madison."

"I was told you saved my life, Jenny. Thank you."

"That's okay." The girl hesitated for a moment. "Can I turn my light on?"

"Sure. I'm awake."

The light across the room came on and Madison studied the other patient. She was a slim dark haired girl who looked younger than her eighteen years.

"So all my friends have been copied on this other world you visit?" Jenny asked.

"Yes but they're quite safe."

"But there's no copy of myself."

"No."

"I'm glad," the girl said.

"Tell me about yourself, Jenny. I hear you're from San Francisco."

"Yeah... "

The girl began talking and the pair chatted away as if they'd been friends for years. Madison grinned. Jenny was like a younger Kirsty even down to her laughter and sense of humour. It was only when a night nurse came in and said they should settle down that they switched off the light and Madison waited to return to the wagon in the tunnel.

*

"Well, you're back into your usual routine," Kirsty said. "It's exactly six-thirty."

Madison glanced outside. The wagon was on the jetty at Station Five and the men were transferring supplies aboard the barge.

Hamish saw her and grinned. "I hope you can get this thing started," he said. "We thought the sooner we could get going, the better."

Madison climbed down off the wagon and accepted a piece of toast and coffee mug Risa handed to her. "Thanks," she said. "I'm becoming a liability aren't I?"

"Only if you can't get this boat going," Kirsty said as she lugged a carton off the wagon. "We've already loaded everything from Hamish's wagon."

The gear from both wagons fitted into *Gentle Warrior* with room to spare. Afterwards Hamish and Sean moved the wagons into the barn and released the oxen into the backfield where there was lush grass to eat and several shady trees for the animals to seek shade under. It was going to be a hot day.

"Well Madison," Hamish said. "Get this contraption going and we'll be on our way."

"Sure." Madison replied with more confidence than she felt. While the other girls gathered around to watch she reached for a button on the console and pressed it. As in the other boat, the console lit up.

122

Warning. Please start the engine and untie the mooring lines before proceeding.

Madison asked for the starting procedures and the engine started. "Well, this was as far as we went last time." She glanced across to Kirsty. "Tell the men we're ready."

Kirsty licked her dry lips and yelled out a window she'd opened. "You guys had better get aboard or you'll be walking."

The three men waved and clamoured aboard. Hamish pulled in the last rope and shut the side door.

"Move away from the jetty at low speed," Madison said as she clasped the steering wheel with clammy hands.

The idling motor sounded louder and the boat shuddered.

"Oh hell," Kirsty gasped. "We're moving."

The boat was already facing up stream so Madison steered out into the middle of the river

Words appeared on the monitor. *Please state destination and optimum cruising speed.*

"Oh damn," Madison gasped

Oh damn is an unknown destination. Do you wish to add it to the database?

"No," Madison was almost panicking.

"Try my village," Risa suggested.

Madison moved the steering wheel down in a clockwise movement and the *Gentle Warrior* moved towards the middle of the river. It was caught the faster current off shore and began to drift sideways.

"We're going too slow, Lass," Hamish said. "You need to increase speed or the current will carry us back into the trees on shore." The jetty had gone but a row of willow trees was far too close.

"I know," Madison gasped.

I know is an unknown destination. Do you wish to add it to the database?

"Our destination is Sakita-mura. Use normal optimum cruising speed." Madison spoke through clenched teeth and was too nervous to take her eyes off the scene ahead...

There was a roar from the motor beside her, the bow lifted and two spouts of water shot into the air from the stern. The boat moved so quickly that the passengers were flung everywhere. Risa landed on top of Kirsty on the side sofa, Hamish managed to grab the door handle to prevent himself from falling while Norris crashed into Sean on the floor.

"Look!" Risa gasped after she staggered up.

Madison risked a glance at the monitor. It showed a map of the river that was almost identical to Risa's original one. At the top of the screen Sakita-mura was marked while at the bottom a yellow blob moved forward.

"That's us," Risa said.

123

Words appeared beneath the map. *Destination is 21.37 kilometres ahead, cruising speed 34.7 km/hr. ETA 0803 hours, 0847 True Time.*

"What's true time?" Madison asked.

Altered ETA taking in account river conditions and the need to navigate the rapids.

The rapids! Madison swallowed and glanced at her friends. They looked as nervous as she felt.

*

CHAPTER FOURTEEN

The last time Madison had been overwhelmed by a vehicle was when a group of friends had hired a truck to shift furniture across town. She remembered the feeling of trying to squeeze the massive truck through city traffic.

Now she felt the same. The boat around her felt gigantic, the controls were unfamiliar and she had to cope with conditions she had never experienced before. But it was up to her! None of her friends had the slightest idea how to operate modern machinery with the monitors, audio input and modern terminology. What they lacked in knowledge, though, they more than made up for in their support. Norris found a hatch in the ceiling and hauled himself up to sit on the roof so only his legs showed. From there he called out about the conditions. Risa crouched on the couch to look out the right hand side while Hamish and Sean kept an eye on everything in general. Kirsty stood behind Madison and worked out what the various controls showed and read out the sentences that appeared on the monitor.

Once they got used to the curt comments it helped. "The dial on the left tells how fast the river is flowing outside and beside it something called RPM has to stay between the yellow and red lines," Kirsty said.

"That's the engine speed," Madison said. "If the current goes faster we give the engine more power to keep the same speed. Understand?"

Kirsty screwed her nose up. "Sort of. It's like when the wheels in our wagon start to slip in the mud. The oxen have to pull twice as hard to move the wagon."

"That's it," Madison said. "Do you want to have a turn driving?"

Kirsty paled. "No way! At least oxen will stop if something goes wrong."

The monitor began to wail like a siren and Kirsty jumped in fright.

Hamish's voice echoed up the craft. "Move right, Madison," he shouted. "Norris has seen a log dead ahead."

"Oh hell." Madison swung the steering wheel over and *Gentle Warrior* behaved in anything but a gentle way. The boat swung right so violently, a wave surged up over the bow and Norris almost fell back inside.

The siren wailed again as Madison swung back. The boat shuddered and she saw an uprooted tree sail by on her port side.

"I got it!" Kirsty screamed in excitement.

"What!"

"That monitor thingie. It showed a picture of the log. The black lines on each side are the shoreline and the things coming down are solid things such as logs or rocks."

"Rocks don't move," Risa cut in.

"No but we move towards them," Kirsty said. "That makes it appear as if they are coming towards us."

"Like a video game," Madison muttered.

The other girls stared at her. "You've driven a boat like this in your other world?" Risa asked.

"Not a real one. It was a game where you pretended to drive a racing car. I loved playing these games when I was a kid."

"What's a racing car?" Risa asked.

"A fast wagon with an engine to drive itself like this boat."

"What a mess they must make," Kirsty said.

"Why?"

"Look at all that water shooting out those pipes at the back. Think of what it would do to our roads as it went along."

"Oh Kirsty, a car doesn't shoot out water. The engine turns the wheels."

"And you use that thingie instead of reins to make it turn corners?" Kirsty said and nodded at the steering wheel.

"That's about it."

Risa joined Kirsty and the pair soon worked out what was coming even before Madison could see anything out the windshield. For fifteen minutes the *Gentle Warrior* travelled upstream with Madison gaining confidence all the time. That was until they went around a long curve. The river became narrow and the water more swift. To the right the shoreline trees disappeared and a massive grey cliff rose out of the water.

The boat banged on the waves and water splashed up everywhere.

Hamish retreated inside and appeared beside Madison with his hair and shirt drenched. "Damn wave just about knocked me over," he muttered.

"Help the girls," Madison yelled above the banging roaring noises around. "Tell me whether to go left or right to avoid hitting anything."

"Right," Hamish said. "Oops, I meant okay."

"Go faster," Risa screamed. The dial is down into the yellow area."

"Oh hell, words are coming on the screen," Kirsty howled.

"Read them!" Madison yelled.

Kirsty repeated the words as they appeared.

Warning! Turbo boost needs to be activated to navigate the rapids safely. Do you wish to use the turbo boost? Warning, you are too close to the port bank. Danger, the water is too shallow on port side. You must...."

"Oh hell," Madison muttered. Luckily the noise drowned her words for the computer did not respond.

"Rocks ahead!" Norris screamed. He had taken Risa's place by the right hand windows.

"Start turbo and navigate a safe course!" Madison screamed.

Do you wish to switch from manual to automatic control?

Madison caught terrified eyes Kirsty's eyes just as a gigantic wave hit them. For seconds they were below a wall of white and green water. The boat trembled and rose. All Madison could see was the cliff top and sky above. They shuddered and the engine screamed.

"It's in the red!" Risa screamed.

"Switch to automatic," Madison called out in an enforced calm voice.

Everything happened!

Another motor switched in with the howl of a jet fighter, the monitor cut off the map and was replaced by a series of numbers, the steering wheel moved without Madison's grip and they increased speed. The boat twisted and turned, slowed for a second before the turbo boost howled again and they rocketed over the top of an incoming wave.

Everyone just clung on and stared out the windscreen. Madison wiped one hand on her blouse and realized her clothes were wringing wet ... from perspiration not the river water.

In fact, except for the wet floor where Norris had had the hatch open, the interior of the *Gentle Warrior* was dry. It was obviously designed to go through these conditions.

"You're going well," Norris yelled in Madison's ear. "I'm proud of you."

"It's not me," she shouted back. "The boat is controlling itself."

"Tell us about it later, Lass" Hamish's calm voice filled the cabin. "I reckon we're through the worst part."

They were! The river became wider and the mountainous waves and crashing surf came directly at them rather than every-which-way of a few seconds before. Madison swallowed. There was no way she could have navigated the rapids manually.

But their troubles were not over.

Words appeared on the screen that Kirsty read out.

Approaching craft. Upstream traffic has right of way but we will need to deviate off the programmed course to avoid a collision Do you wish...

"Take the necessary action!" Madison snapped.

She saw it!

Another boat just like their own was heading straight towards them. She could see the red and black bow, the windscreen and even a person's face inside. The person had his mouth open in alarm. Both boats turned towards the closest shore, they went left and the other craft towards the cliffs on their right. How they missed each other Madison never knew ... but they did. Waves stirred up by both boats hit in the middle of the river and exploded up like an inverted waterfall. The other craft disappeared.

The *Gentle Warrior* was in a tunnel of water but Madison saw blue sky ahead. She was tossed sideways into one of the others as the boat turned yet again. Sunlight shone through the windscreen. They were safe!

Sean gripped Madison's' shoulder and caught her eyes. "That was the *Gentle Lady*. I saw the name on the back."

"Oh hell."

"Strange people, too," Hamish said.

"You saw them?" Kirsty gasped.

"A glimpse. They wore silver clothes, shiny silver clothes." Hamish grinned. "I'm sure they were more terrified of us than we were of them."

"Oh hell, what now?" Madison asked.

"They won't be turning around for a while," Sean said. "I doubt if they will have any chance of catching up to us before we reach Risa's village,"

"We'll be safe there," Risa added. "Our walls are as big as those in Buckoway and the town guard is very efficient."

"But you use bows and arrows?" Madison asked."

"A little. Most guards use swords,"

"Samurai swords?' Madison asked.

"How did you know?" Risa asked.

"Just a guess. You have no guns or cannons, though?"

Risa shook her head. "I don't know of those things," she said. "Are they important?"

"If those people in the *Gentle Lady* have them or more advanced weapons we could be in trouble," Madison replied. "The town walls will not protect us."

"So we use stealth and outmanoeuvre them," Hamish said. "Perhaps now is the time to ask Thinrisodor for help."

"How?" Kirsty snapped.

"Change that soaked red flag outside for the blue one."

128

"I think we might need to," Madison replied. "I don't think those Guardians, Emperors or whatever they call themselves aboard the *Gentle Lady* will ignore us any longer."

"Madison," Risa interrupted in excitement. "Look!"

The river had become wider and the cliffs on the shore became sloping hills covered in evergreen trees while the closest bank was covered in tussock and course grass.

"What is it, Risa?" Madison asked.

"That hill ahead. I know it. See how the edges curve up like an emperor's palace? I think the river curves around it and our village is on the other side."

"Like that big 'S' on the map you drew," Kirsty said.

"Yes, the river does wriggle. We never realized there were those rapids, though." Risa smiled. "We should come to where the river flows beside a road soon."

The road appeared ten minutes later, Madison switched back to manual control and slowed their craft down. "I doubt if the boat is programmed to stop at Sakita-mura," she said. "Is there a jetty, Risa?"

"Oh yes. Our jetty is like the one at Station Five. We have some fishing boats so it's been kept in good condition." She screwed her nose up. "They just have little sails and paddles but we catch quite a few fish to help feed my people."

Risa's eyes sparkled as she recognized more and more of the local features. A few farm animals appeared but they looked in poor condition compared with those at Buckoway. Then along the road came a wagon pulled by oxen. The two drivers just stopped and stared as the *Gentle Warrior* chugged by.

They continued on around another curve to the right and there it was! A village was perched on the hill to their left and it did look like Buckoway right down to the square shaped castle on the hill.

Madison slowed the boat down almost to a walking pace and turned towards shore. As she did so she could see people running up the roads and from the jetty. Everyone was heading for the town gate.

"Well, Lassie," Hamish said to Risa. "You'd better show yourself. I'd say your friends out there think they're about to be invaded."

"You're right," Risa said, "Having two boats go past in one day must be worrying. What should I do?"

"Stand up in that top hatch so they see you. Wave and yell like crazy. We don't want to showered with a thousand arrows now do we?"

"I'll put the blue flag up, too," Risa said. "Someone from the Sneednim tribe will be watching. They always are."

Norris opened the hatch and helped Risa up while Madison tried to think of a suitable command to issue to the computer. After getting them all this far safely she didn't want to go crashing into the jetty.

*

When *Gentle Warrior* slid into shore, Norris jumped out of the hatch, slid off the roof onto the jetty and grabbed a mooring line Hamish tossed him from the opened door. Within minutes three mooring lines held the boat secure and Madison gave the order to shut the engine down. For a second she just sat in the seat with her hands shaking.

"You did it, Madison," Kirsty said. "Aren't you proud?"

"No, relieved would be a better word." Madison glanced around to see the cabin empty. "Where are the others?"

"Risa is standing on the roof waving and the men have just secured the mooring lines."

Madison stood up. "So shall we join them?" she whispered and walked towards the door.

It was a hot cloudless day but quiet, too quiet. Except for the men who gazed up at the village, the jetty was deserted.

"They shut the main gate." Hamish looked up at the girl sitting on the roof. "Try shouting your name out and a few 'We're friends' in your own language, Risa." he said.

"They're afraid," Risa replied.

"So convince them."

"I'll try."

She stood up, waved both hands and screamed out a string of Japanese words. Two faces appeared in the parapet above the gate and disappeared a second later,

"You caught their attention," Hamish said. "Come on down. That's all you can do."

"Yes," Risa whispered

"So if they don't come to us we go to them," Madison said. "Come on Risa. I'll need you with me." She turned to Kirsty and Norris beside her. "I think just the two of us should go. We don't want to appear threatening,"

"But... "

"Norris, this is Risa's home. They're hardly likely to harm us are they?"

Norris shrugged and stepped back while Risa slid off the roof and walked up beside Madison.

"I'm ready," she said.

130

The pair walked to the end of the jetty and onto a gravel road that led about two hundred metres up a hill to the walls of Sakita-mura. They were about half way there when there was a rustle in an adjacent clump of bushes and a Mud warrior stepped onto the road.

"Just stand still," Madison whispered out the side of her mouth for the warrior had his spear raised.

"Why does the Lady-With-The-Bow need our help?" he asked in rapid Japanese.

Madison worked out what he said and touched Risa on the arm to tell her it was okay. Of course, the blue rag was flying from the roof of their boat.

"I am who you seek," Madison fumbled over the Japanese words. "My friend Risa speaks better than me, Can I talk through her?"

The warrior switched his eyes to Risa for the first time, nodded and lowered his spear.

"Tell him we are afraid... no not afraid, concerned that the people in the other boat may turn around and come back. They are ... what shall we say... enemy of both our peoples. We are here to bring food to Risa's village and have no wish to upset the Sneednim tribe," Madison said in English.

Risa spoke rapidly. The warrior was silent for as moment before he replied. The conversation was so fast that Madison failed to understand it.

"The *Gentle Lady* turned around before it reached Station Five and is heading back up through the rapids right now," Risa said. "Do you want the crew slain?"

"No," Madison said. "Tell him I want the boat stopped and the crew captured. His warriors should be very careful. The crew may have weapons that spurt fire and can kill from well beyond arrow range."

Risa translated and the man gave one nod.

Madison spoke in a serious tone. "The crew should not be hurt as I need to speak to them."

Risa nodded and again spoke in Japanese.

"It shall be done," the warrior said in halting English. He stared unblinking at Madison for a second and was gone.

"I didn't expect this," Risa gasped but was attracted by something else.

Madison swung around and saw that the main gate of Sakita-mura had risen and a line on men in long ceremonial robes had walked out. "Who are they?" she asked.

"Governor Natiko Kobayashi and the ten councillors who run our village," Risa whispered. "After the Emperors were driven out these men were elected like your referees. They are good and fair but very traditional."

"There are no guards with them," Madison said. "I guess they waited until our Mud warrior left."

"Yes," Risa said in a nervous voice.

"What's wrong?"

"I left Sakita-mura without permission. My two friends were killed and they might blame me."

"But you found us, we have supplies and are here to help," Madison said. "I'll talk to them first and explain everything."

"But your Japanese is..." Risa whispered.

"I'll manage. Stay silent unless I touch your arm. Okay?"

Risa nodded but appeared pale. It seemed she was more afraid of her own people than of the Mud warrior they'd just spoken to.

*

CHAPTER FIFTEEN

Gentle Lady stopped by the shoreline just before the corner that would put it in view of those in Sakita-mura. The side door opened and three silver clad people jumped onto the sand. One grabbed a mooring line and tied it around a willow tree trunk.

"I still don't like it, Undul" the second-in-line said in a language that to Madison would have sounded like a high-pitched whistle. "It's against the directives for this planet."

"So we attack a fortified town ship with their bows and arrows, Fyddal," the leader said. He pulled a silver ray pistol from his pocket, slipped the safety control off and glanced back at the others. "It will be over in fifteen minutes. One amicir discharge will render the entire population unconscious, we walk in, take the ones responsible for stealing *Gentle Warrior* and depart. Nobody else will be hurt or even remember it happened." He turned and called back at the boat. "We'll be no more than an hour."

"Make sure you are," someone called back.

"How will we recognize them, Undul?" the person at the rear asked. There was a slight tremor in the female's voice.

"They come from Buckoway so look different, Drety. You should know that. We've been carting so many of their hulks to Station Five over the last few months. They're classified as Caucasians not Orientals. They are distinguished by round eyes, the females have prominent mammary glands and the males grow more facial hair."

"They look different in the in elastic condition," Drety whispered.

"Ugly creatures," Urdul muttered. "And they're meant to be our salvation."

Fyddal glowered, "If the Inner Council heard that comment, Urdul..."

"They aren't here, are they?" Urdul retorted. "This damn planet," he whispered to nobody in particular and led the other two into the trees.

They crept forward through thick undergrowth until they came to a stream that flowed into the river from a small ravine.

"This is it," Undul took a marble like ball from his pocket and shook it. It rolled out into a page with a detailed map of the area. "Perfect. This stream circles around the back of the village. I think one shell will do it." He grinned. "It will be nice to be more than transportation flunkies for a change."

Undul placed his ray pistol back in his pocket so he could use both hands to climb down the small bank. The foliage hid the others. He reached the bottom and glanced back. Nobody followed.

"Hurry up," he called.

There wasn't a sound.

He turned and a silver arm flopped down in front of his face. "What the... !" he retorted as Fyddal slid down the bank beside him and Drety gave a soft moan further up the bank. Undul looked up just as a grey arm reached out and seized his neck. Pressure was applied and he collapsed on top of his companion.

On board *Gentle Lady* the five remaining crew never even managed to shut the door. Five darts no bigger than a pin hit them, fast acting poison flooded their veins and they collapsed to the floor. Mud warriors jumped aboard, bound and gagged the crew with flax and disappeared back into the trees.

*

Risa need not have worried for when the group of councillors moved closer there was a look of compassion in their eyes.

"Risa?" Governor Natiko Kobayashi said when the two groups met each other. "The guards on the tower said it was you waving from the boat but I had to see for myself. Your friends' bodies were brought home and we thought you suffered the same fate."

"I got help, Governor Kobayashi," Risa whispered and gazed at the ground.

Natiko turned so his eyes rested on Madison and he spoke in English. "So Risa reached your village Madison Evans? Welcome to Sakita-mura."

It was Risa who gasped. "You know her and speak the language?" she said in Japanese and suddenly her cheeks burned when she realized to whom she was speaking.

Natiko Kobayashi smiled. "Yes, it is some inherited trait from a past life. A few of us understand other tongues but how or why, we do not know. Rumours of your friend come to us from the Sneednim. They call her Candy Lady, Maiden of the Granite, the first wagonmistress and friend of the Mud."

"I am honoured," Madison said.

"You must be weary. Bring up your friends and come inside. Refreshments await you. Don't worry, our people will guard your boat."

He nodded and a line of guards marched out of the gate. They looked similar to the guards at Buckoway but carried swords instead of bows and arrows. When they reached the jetty they stopped and waited.

Madison couldn't help comparing them with the Sneednim warriors.

"You look amused, Madison," Kobayashi said.

Like Risa earlier, Madison flushed. "I compared your noble guards with the Sneednim warriors, Governor Kobayashi. You are both proud people and that is good. I did not mean to offend you, and apologize."

"No apology is necessary. The Sneednim and ourselves are becoming friends but it takes time when cultures cross."

"It does," Madison said. "I'll call the others." She turned and beckoned to Kirsty who was standing impatiently at the end of the jetty mere metres from the local guards. "It's okay. Tell everyone to come, Kirsty," she shouted.

"Okay!" Kirsty's voice came back. "I'll get 'em." She turned and ran back to the *Gentle Warrior*.

When the others arrived, brief introductions were made and Kobayashi led them towards the gate. Just as they were about to walk in Madison felt a tap on her cheek. She turned and saw the same warrior that they had talked to earlier.

"Come," he said in Japanese and beckoned her.

Risa saw what happened and whispered. "I think it's important so go. I'll give your apologies to Governor Kobayashi."

Madison nodded and stepped sideways into a clump of trees. She heard rustling and saw that Kirsty was with her.

"I'm coming too," Kirsty grumbled. "I'm sick of just watching you do everything."

Madison felt relieved and squeezed her friend's arm. "Come on," she said. "That warrior looks impatient."

*

The two followed the warrior along the riverbank until they came to a bend. The beach ran out and they had to climb up through grass and low willow trees. They reached the crest of a knob and could see the rest of the river,

"Oh damn!" Kirsty gasped.

The *Gentle Lady* was tied to a willow trunk and tugging against the mooring line in the current.

"It's safe. All there. All yours," The warrior again spoke in Japanese. He almost smiled before he disappeared into the trees.

"Well, let's go," Madison said and grinned when Kirsty looked hesitant. "You're the one who was sick of just watching."

"Yeah, I was wasn't I?"

They slid down the bank to another small beach and approached the boat with their senses on full alert. However, again everything was silent with only a cloud of sandflies being a nuisance. Kirsty flapped her hands to create a breeze in her face and reached the mooring rope. Madison joined her and they pulled the boat towards them.

The side door was raised so while Kirsty held the rope, Madison scrambled aboard. She turned, reached for Kirsty's hand and hauled her aboard,

They turned and jumped in alarm. Tussled on the couch and floor of the front cabin were eight people all bound together with platted flax.

"Our aliens," Kirsty gasped.

Madison just stared. They were human but different. It appeared that five were male and three, females but this was really a guess. Everyone wore a silver one-piece uniform that reminded Madison of safety gear fire fighters or racing drivers wore on Earth. Their heads were uncovered to show tanned skin, not unlike their own. Their facial features could easily pass for someone like at home with a long nose, thin lips and ordinary ears. All the eyes were shut so it was impossible to see the colour but the eyebrows were almost non-existent. They all had close cut hair about a centimetre high with the colours ranging from black to blonde and one a reddish colour. No males had a beard or any sign of facial hair. The females were slightly shorter than the males and had a hint of breasts under the tight fitting garments.

"That's why the pilot seat is so big," Kirsty said.

"What do you mean?"

"Look at that guy on the couch."

One alien stretched from one end to the other out of the couch opposite the pilot's chair.

"I lay on it once and only reached only three quarters of the way along," Kirsty said. "Those guys are as skinny as a rake, never had to shave in their lives but are two and a half metres tall."

"You're right," Madison said. "Oh hell!"

"What now?"

"Look at that?" Madison reached across and took a pistol out of one of the alien's pocket. It was the first gun she'd seen in this world.

"What is it?" Kirsty asked

"A gun like we have on Earth. It's highly dangerous so don't touch the trigger."

"The what?"

Madison felt annoyed at the stupid question until she stopped to think. Of course Kirsty wouldn't know what a trigger was. It was something that had been wiped from her memory in this world.

"See that little curled piece of metal underneath?"

Kirsty nodded

"Inside is another piece of metal. If you pull on it with your finger it will shoot a bullet, that's like a tiny arrow out the front. It goes so fast that if anything gets in the way it will go right through them not just stick in like an arrow or spear."

"I think you asked about these before," Kirsty whispered.

"When we first arrived at Buckoway I wondered why the guards only had bows."

"Well, they've all got them," Kirsty retorted and pulled one out of a female's pocket.

"We need to search them," Madison said. "But be extremely careful with anything you don't understand."

They rummaged through the aliens' pockets and found eight of the strange guns, as well as eight objects that looked like cell phones on Earth and strange balls of a marble-like material. Kirsty shook one and again jumped in fright. The one in her hand shot out into a flat rectangular shape. It hardened in an instant and words appeared like they would on a sheet of paper.

"Their language again," Madison muttered. "I wonder if it will convert to English like the boat's monitor."

"Leave it," Kirsty warned. "That's what you told me."

"Okay," Madison said and placed the balls and communication devices in a box lying on the floor.

"Throw them overboard," Kirsty cried, "If they are so dangerous we don't want them here. Isn't that why these people never gave them to us in the first place?"

"But..."

"You listen to me, Madison Evans," Kirsty said with anger in her voice. "I don't understand about these things and I doubt if even you do. If we start playing around with them we could kill ourselves and everyone else. And what if one of these creatures wakes up? We don't know how strong they are. They could snap those flax ropes holding them, grab one of the weapons before we even turn around and kill us." Kirsty pouted. "I'm scared, Madison and I'm not too proud to admit it."

"The guns are dangerous, I admit but these balls are merely writing tablets to use instead of paper..."

"You're guessing. They might be sending a signal to their castle and listening to everything we say. Even now another boat may we heading down river to attack us."

Madison nodded. "We'll do it," she said.

She gathered one gun up and opened a window on the side away from the bank. With infinite care she reached down and let it go. It dropped the remaining metre hit the water with a tiny splash and disappeared. Good, it didn't float.

"Now the others," Kirsty said.

Within a minute all the guns and other devices disappeared beneath the waves. The water was quite swift and murky so the chance of the aliens finding the weapons was minimal. It was a gamble, of course but far better than leaving the stuff on board or hiding it ashore.

"What about those badges?" Kirsty said. Every alien had a metal badge the size of a button attached to his or her collar.

"Yeah, they could be another communications device," Madison said. She reached for one but couldn't remove it. It was sealed to the silver material without any sign of thread. She couldn't even detach it with a small knife she found by the pilot's seat.

"So take their whole clothes off and toss them overboard, too," Kirsty said. "They seem to unzip."

Before Madison could object she grabbed the zipper on one alien's clothes and pulled. It did unzip right down the man's front and across to his right leg.

"Oh damn!" Madison gasped and seized Kirsty's arm

Kirsty stopped and saw what Madison was staring at. The alien had no undergarments at all. There was just bare skin, completely hairless but the girls were staring at something else.

"What is it?" Kirsty asked.

The alien had no sexual organs. Where the male organs would normally be was just a tiny penis smaller than an index finger poking out. There were no other male organs at all.

"Zip it up," Madison gasped.

"What about the females?" Kirsty asked.

"Perhaps there are no males or females."

"I'm going to look."

"Kirsty!"

However Kirsty had already walked over to an alien they thought was a female and unzipped the silver garment. Except for having no hair on her body the alien woman looked normal.

"But she's got hardly any boobs," Kirsty snorted. "Looks like a girl who hasn't reached puberty. I bet this thingie doesn't have periods."

"She'd be as old as we are," Madison said as she pulled the zipper up again.

"So they have no sexual organs. No wonder they need us."

"And encourage pregnancies back at Buckoway," Madison whispered. "Without us they'd cease to exist."

"Unless they make copies of themselves just like they make newcomers," Kirsty said.

"Clones, a whole civilization that reproduces by cloning."

"Yeah, a scary isn't it?"

The two stared at each other in distaste until Kirsty glanced at the male on the couch and began to giggle. "What a waste of a hulky body?"

"Kirsty!" Madison cried and slapped her friend on the shoulder.

"So what now?' Kirsty asked. "Shall we walk back?"

"No," Madison replied. "We can't risk leaving these aliens. We'll start *Gentle Lady* up and drive it to the jetty."

⚓

Norris sat at the long table in the reception room but was worried. Everything had worked out except that after almost an hour Madison and Kirsty were still missing. He was about to ask Risa if she could ask their hosts to go and look for the girls when she poked him in the arm.

"Look out the window, Norris," she whispered.

The view outside showed the upstream bend. There in the middle of the river and chugging slowly towards them was the *Gentle Warrior*. Norris frowned and turned. No, he was wrong, their boat was still tied to the jetty. It must be the *Gentle Lady*.

"Norris. Who's that waving from the top hatch?" Risa said.

"Kirsty!" Norris exclaimed and gave Hamish, sitting on the other side of him, a poke.

"I know lad," Hamish replied. "Those lassies just can't keep their noses clean, can they?"

"That's for sure," Sean added from along the table and reached for a glass of wine.

*

The guards loaded the prisoners from *Gentle Lady* onto an oxen wagon and delivered them up to the castle where they were put in an unused dungeon. Doctors checked the aliens and found they were under the influence of an antiseptic drug and probably wouldn't awaken until morning. The prisoners were then segregated into cells where the girls changed the women from their silver garments into ordinary clothes.

Norris, Hamish and Sean were told about the males and managed to change them into ordinary clothes without the doctors seeing their strange anatomy. Afterwards the silver garments were checked out. They appeared to made of an unknown fibre but no transmission devices were found. However, Madison suggested that they should be put somewhere remote from the prisoners themselves.

"The aliens could have some internal transmission device," she said. "We can't do anything about that, though."

"So what do we do now?" Hamish asked when they left the castle.

"Unload our boat and check the other one out. It's loaded with boxes and not newcomers, thank goodness."

Risa stood back. She said nothing but looked as if she wanted to talk.

"What is it Risa?" Kirsty asked.

"I know you're all busy but I was wondering if you'd like to visit my apartment."

Madison smiled. "Of course we'd love to," She turned to Hamish. "You can arrange for the *Gentle Warrior* to be unloaded can't you?"

"No need Lass," Hamish said. "There must be a hundred villagers doing it right now."

"And the other boat?"

"It's being guarded but nobody has gone aboard. I said it was better to wait until you have a look or we get information about it from the aliens when they wake up. I must say that the local guards are pretty efficient. They've already sent patrols in both directions to watch the river. If any other boats come along the river we'll get a fair warning. They have a system of flags to pass messages from hilltop to hilltop. I also think the Mud have agreed to help them watch out for any potential enemy." Hamish grinned. "I'll go and check to see how it's going if you like."

"Thanks Hamish." Madison turned to Risa. "Okay, let's go and visit your apartment."

Risa almost looked shy. "There are the guest quarters where the men will be put up. I just thought you girls might like to stay with me."

"We'd love to," Kirsty replied. "It'll be just like at Buckoway." She turned to Madison. "That's right isn't it?"

Risa led them along the circle road and up a side road to a row of apartment buildings almost identical to those at Buckoway. Inside, though, Risa's apartment reflected her culture and personality with beautiful screen prints hanging on the wall and several origami birds suspended from the ceiling.

"I shared it with Isashi," Risa said in a sad voice. "He was one of the men killed when the Muds captured us."

"I'm sorry, Risa," Madison said. "It must be hard."

"I think of him when I'm alone," the Japanese girl said. "That's partly why I'd like you both to stay with me." She glanced up. "Selfish aren't I?"

"No, you are brave and generous, Risa," Madison said.

"We saw the respect the councillors have towards you," Kirsty added. "Everyone is so proud of you."

"Yes," Risa whispered. "I thought they might blame me for Isashi and Takeru's deaths but nobody did."

"So how will you remember them, Risa," Madison asked.

"The Garden of Remembrance," Risa said. "We have roses there. Every rose has the name of a departed one beneath it. I shall ask for a roses for Isashi and Takeru tomorrow."

Madison glanced at Kirsty and thought back to the cremations at Buckoway. In some ways Sakita-mura was more civilized than their hometown.

*

CHAPTER SIXTEEN

SCAR VI was the sixth top-secret satellite in the Satellite Communications and Recovery program that originally started in the 1980s to intercept and, if necessary, disable or destroy Soviet satellites. With the Cold War over the latest model switched its attention to the few rogue states that put objects in orbit above Earth. It was now called in to intercept the golf ball sized alien craft in the stationary orbit over the Equator. This highly manoeuvrable satellite was under control of General Alan Finlay of the Canadian Armed Forces and he was at the moment at the North Shield Radio Telescope station.

The trace on Bee1 as they called the alien satellite had been difficult as it was constructed by no known metal and had some sort of cloaking device around it. Modern computers had used fluctuations in the stars behind to finally trace the craft after it had been lost several times.

"SCAR VI is two hundred kilometres above Bee1 and matching its orbit, Sir. Digital photographs are being transmitted now."

"Thank you Doctor Tharlow." The general watched as the picture built up on the monitor that filled the end of the control room.

The result was disappointing with just a black blob showing. Even magnified views showed nothing more.

"Our computers detect that it is spinning and constantly changing shape, Sir," Tharlow said. "The change is less than a thousandth of a millimetre but there is a definite rhythm indicating that it has been artificially created."

"Can we bring SCAR VI in closer?" Finlay asked.

"We can go right up and grab it, Sir. However, that isn't recommended as SCAR could be destroyed if the alien has a defence shield around it."

"How close?"

"Fifty kilometres, Sir and even that is risky."

"Take it in and continue the digital photographs."

"Shall do, Sir."

Nothing spectacular happened until SCAR VI was fifty-two kilometres above the alien vessel. At this point the monitor changed to static and a series of warning lights lit up.

" We have lost control of SCAR VI, Sir. It is accelerating towards Bee 1. Contact will be in three seconds ... Oh my God!"

Tharlow, Finlay and everyone else in the room stared in frozen fascination at the monitor. A new picture that came on one line at a time was replacing the static. Stars showed against a black background. A planet came into view, a beautiful one with blue oceans beneath a white polar cap. Several continents coloured green and brown appeared but their shapes were completely different from Earth. White clouds circled around in several areas. Computer lights danced and a dozen printers began spitting out information.

"Explain this." Finlay barked.

"One moment, Sir. We shall get a computer hypothesis."

When the monitor picture was competed it was stored in memory and a second picture began to form. It showed the same planet but from a slightly different angle.

Tharlow switched his attention to a smaller monitor and reached for a sheet of paper being printed out. He read the information frowned and glanced up at the general.

"The computer hypothesis, Sir," He held the sheet up.

"Tell me," Finlay whispered.

"The photograph is of a totally unknown planet that is the second in orbit around an unknown star. It is almost exactly the same size as Earth, has a similar orbit around the star, which in itself is almost identical to our sun. It also has a twenty-four hour day and is covered by eighty percent ocean between four land masses that stretch through both hemispheres."

"Is it real or a photograph sent to SCAR VI by the alien?"

Doctor Tharlow gulped. "The computer suggests that there was no Bee 1. It was a black hole. SCAR VI was sucked into it and spat out the other end above this planet. The second picture that we have just received confirms that SCAR VI is in orbit around this planet."

"And the black hole, Doctor?"

"Our backup satellite, SCAR V reports that it has not moved. It is still in a stationary orbit above the Equator."

"Is there any estimation about where this planet and star is?"

"No Sir but it is not in our galaxy or even a known constellation."

"Get the damn computer to guess."

Thorn hit some keyboard keys and his personal computer blinked out a number.

"Minus one light year Sir."

"And what does that mean, Doctor?"

"The computer cannot make an estimation and has substituted a negative number to explain the information it has received. I would say SCAR VI has travelled through a dimension where time and distance has no equivalence to our own."

"A parallel universe?"

"No Sir. It's out there somewhere. That black hole has cut through the so-called time barrier. Physical distance has no meaning but once through the other side SCAR VI would be less than half the distance our moon is away from us?"

"How do you work that out?"

"Those pictures coming in now take 1.356 seconds to reach us. A radar transmission from Earth to the Moon and return takes 2.58 seconds so it is as if that planet is half the distance of the moon away."

"So we now have SCAR VI orbiting this planet and it is still in communication with us?"

"That's correct, Sir. That is why the transmissions from those people stung by the alien bees are so fast. It takes no longer than an intercontinental telephone conversation that goes through an Earth satellite."

General Alan Finlay smiled. "It's been a successful day, Doctor Tharlow. Far better than even my wildest dreams."

*

Madison stared out the window at the rain as it moved across Sacramento. She was back into the routine of awaking back in her other world but with all the happenings in the new world her time on Earth came as a sort of anticlimax. She sighed and returned to her programming duties. Ten minutes later she heard a cough and saw Colonel Brad Davis standing by her desk.

"Hi Colonel," she said. "So you got my email?"

"So you've met the aliens?"

"Sort of. They were still unconscious when I went to bed. Those poisonous darts the Mud used certainly delivered a punch."

"And you said you thought that second boat contained electronic equipment? Where were they taking it?"

"I've no idea. Perhaps they were going to upgrade things at the Buckoway castle or they may have been heading to another destination. I'll try and find out tomorrow."

"And have a look at the sky tomorrow night."

144

Madison's eyes lit up. "Why, do you want some more star patterns. I thought they were of no value?"

"No we don't need them now."

"You don't?"

The colonel grinned slightly. "A little after sunset you should see a shooting star moving across the sky to your south."

Madison frowned. "How do you know that?"

"It's one of our satellites that we have orbiting the planet. At this very moment it is trying to pinpoint where exactly those villages you're in are situated and where other humans or aliens are concentrated."

"Is this a joke or are you being sarcastic, Colonel?" Madison said.

"The secrecy pledge you made..."

"Yeah I know, I can't tell a sole but you came here to tell me something important, didn't you?"

Colonel Davis nodded and told Madison about the black hole and SCAR VI. "So we want you to get as much information as possible from those aliens you caught. They may be natives of the planet but we are more inclined to think they came from somewhere else. Those Muds are probably the only indigenous peoples."

"And what do your superiors think about these aliens being sexless?"

"There are several theories from natural evolution over millions of years to a natural or artificial catastrophe on their home planet."

"Such as?"

"Long term radiation after a nuclear holocaust could render all animal life sterile without actually killing them off."

Madison screwed her nose up. "That could fit in but why are there the separate villages with different cultures in them, no religions and that strange situation of just disposing of the dead?"

"They tried separating cultures here on Earth, you know. Think of South Africa up to the late 1980s or even the Germans or Japanese in World War II?"

"And the lack of religion?"

"A reaction against oppressive religions. Again, I could name many situations on Earth right now caused by religious conflict."

"So they could be trying too hard to create a perfect society?"

"Ask them tomorrow?"

"Sure, and they're just going to come out and tell me everything." Madison said. "I'm not naive, Colonel Davis."

"That's why I'm offering you a new position."

Madison frowned. "I've just started here, I get a great salary and..."

"It's with this company. We were the ones who recommended that you should be placed on the short list here. There were something like twenty people with your qualifications or better who applied."

"Thanks," Madison retorted with sarcasm in her voice. "And I thought I got the job on my own merits."

"You did. Even we couldn't get you beyond the short list. You won the position in that interview, I believe."

"Okay, so what's the new position anyway?"

"Manager of Personnel Resources"

Madison laughed. "What's that ... all the hiring and firing?"

"More like fitting the staff into the right places and getting them to do things they don't even realize they can do."

"Like zapping back and forth to other planets?"

The colonel remained serious. "No, getting people to tell you things without them feeling they've betrayed friends, family or society."

Madison leaned back in her chair and folded her arms. "Oh, I see. And my first little exercise will be to squeeze information out of our aliens in Sakita-mura?"

"That could help?"

"So it's a trumped up job to keep me under your thumb?"

"Not at all. If you look in your latest company newsletter you will see it advertised in the Situations Vacant. This company has a policy of offering positions to staff before they are advertised to the general market." The colonel shrugged. "The Japanese have a majority shareholding and insisted on doing it their way."

Madison grinned. "You know, I am beginning to like the Japanese culture more and more. What did you say the salary was?"

"I didn't," Davis said but wrote some numbers on a piece of paper and slipped it across to Madison.

"Oh damn," Madison gasped when she read the digits.

"There's a training course that needs to be completed..."

"And it starts today, no doubt."

"Actually it does," Colonel Davis replied. "Topic One is a crash course on how to make possibly hostile or frightened personnel learn to trust you. This is followed..."

"And you're practicing all the methods on me?"

Colonel Brad Davis merely smiled and left the room.

*

The guards officer stood and bowed his head when Madison, Kirsty and Risa walked into the main reception area of the castle. The furnishings and fittings looked new but again the architecture was similar to the castle at Buckoway. Madison suspected that the aliens had shifted everything out when they abandoned Sakita-mura.

"Thank you for coming," the officer said in Japanese. "I am Captain Koti Wantana and would like your assistance."

Risa translated and replied, listened to his comments and turned to the other two. "The aliens either don't speak Japanese or pretend they don't. All except one are refusing to say anything and won't even reply to questions in your Buckoway language."

"But one will talk," Madison said.

Risa spoke again to Captain Wantana.

"Yes. She said a few words in our language but appears to speak fluent English. She appears scared of us. That is why Captain Wantana would like you to speak to her." She grimaced. "He thinks that if you approach her alone, Madison you might find out something."

Madison nodded and thought back to the two hours of training that she'd had just that afternoon back on Earth. "Has she been allowed to refresh, had food and been reassured her friends are not harmed?" she asked.

Risa spoke to the captain who shook his head.

"Well," Madison said. "I want her taken out of the dingy dungeon into a comfortable room. There she needs to be given a good breakfast and told her silver clothes be will be returned soon."

"Why? "Risa asked after talking to the captain.

"How would you like to wake up by yourself and know somebody has taken everything including your clothes from you?"

"It is unusual," the captain said after hearing the translation of Madison's words.

"That's what I want Captain Wantana," Madison said in Japanese. "Please try it my way."

The officer looked surprised when Madison spoke his language and gave a slight nod. "There are unused rooms upstairs," he said. "We shall transfer her to one. If you want her to be refreshed and have a meal perhaps you could return in an hour."

"Thank you." Madison replied again in Japanese.

When the three were out in the courtyard Risa stared at Madison. "You are so brave," she whispered. "I couldn't speak to the captain like you did."

"That's Madison," Kirsty said proudly. "She won't let anyone boss her around."

"It's not that," Madison said. "If we can make even one of the aliens our friend rather than a potential enemy it must help. After all, if they wanted to harm us they could have done it a thousand times in the last few months."

"But our village?" Risa said.

"They abandoned you, yes but did they actually hurt anybody here?"

"I guess not," Risa said. "It was the Mud tribes that we had to protect ourselves from."

"So I'll go and speak to this alien woman. If she appears co-operative I think we should all then try to befriend her."

Kirsty grinned and Risa nodded

"It sounds a good idea," the Japanese girl said.

*

Madison walked in the room prepared to meet an aloof and openly hostile adversary. That was after all the first thing she had been told to expect only a few hours earlier.

'*Don't expect the opposition to have your values,*' the lecturer had said. '*If you expect the worse case scenario everything that happens will be an improvement.*'

The woman stood and turned. In that fraction of a second Madison realized several things different from her original view of the unconscious figure lying on the boat's floor. The woman's hazel coloured eyes looked scared, her tongue ran over pale lips and her hands shook. She was a head higher than Madison was but looked amazingly ordinary in the blouse and tartan skirt. Her hair was close cut or perhaps it never needed to be cut at all.

"Hello," Madison said. "My name is Madison Evans. Do you understand my language?"

"Yes. We all speak English on this planet."

"Good," Madison said. "I'm sorry you had to spend the night in that horrible cell. As soon as I heard I asked for you to be given a proper room. Were you given breakfast?"

The woman frowned. "What do you want to know?" she said. Her voice would have been determined if there wasn't a slight quiver in it.

Madison glanced up. "Sit down and relax ... err..."

"Drety. My name is Drety."

"Hi Drety, That's a very English sounding name. I knew a Betty at school once."

Drety frowned. "How can you remember school friends?" she stopped and shut her mouth.

148

"And why shouldn't I?" Madison said in a slow voice.

Drety's face went chalk white. "But that's impossible."

Madison raised an eyebrow. "Is that what they told you?"

Drety hesitated. "You will need to talk to Superior Officer Undul," she said. "I am not permitted to discuss our reasons for being on Quargis."

Quargis! Madison had never heard that name before. *If someone tells you information that is new or useful don't admit it is so.* The lecturer had stressed that, too.

She shrugged. "It doesn't matter. We know why you are here anyway," she said in a casual voice. "God, we got a fright when we saw the *Gentle Lady* heading straight for us in the rapids. I had no idea that there were automatic controls."

"You were the one piloting Gentle *Warrior*, weren't you?"

"I was. It was similar to driving a car on Earth."

"You do know about Earth, then?"

"My one," Madison replied and stared at the woman.

"But how did you know there was more than one?" Drety clamped her mouth shut again but her eyelids blinked as if she'd said too much

Don't be too ambitious. Stop before they begin a cover up and you become confused.

Madison shrugged and switched the conversation to neutral things but found out several more interesting things. It appeared that most of the crew were like Drety, volunteer cadets who came to help on the planet but a few were professional Guardians. This Superior Officer Undul and another man called Fyddal were the only Guardians on the *Gentle Lady*. Fyddal was quite a pleasant sort but Drety appeared to be scared of Undul.

"Why did you swing your boat around and chase us back?" she slipped into the conversation.

"Undul's orders."

"But you were not meant to come here to Sakita-mura were you?"

"It's a cut-off village," Drety whispered. "We only support ongoing places like Buckoway. Undul wanted to capture and take you home." She shrugged. "He's ambitious and impulsive."

"And breaks rules if necessary?"

Drety nodded. "He outranked us all."

"I'm not blaming you," Madison said in a soft voice. She stood and walked towards the door.

" Madison?" Drety called out.

Madison turned. "Yes?"

"It's probably Buckoway that will be selected."

Madison frowned. "Selected for what, Drety?"

"Of the villages set up on Quargis most have ended up like Sakita-mura and have been abandoned to fend for themselves."

Madison walked back and sat down. "And have they survived?"

"No, most were overwhelmed by local Mud tribes. We doubt if Sakita-mura will last past the next winter."

"Go on," Madison said.

"Buckoway is the only culture still supported and given newcomers. We were bringing in new equipment for your town when we met you in the rapids."

"And what nationality are the people in the other cut off villages?"

"They are from Earth 2 or Earth 3."

Madison frowned. This was becoming confusing. "So where do we and the residents of Sakita-mura come from?"

Drety frowned. "I thought you knew. You're from Earth 2. There are four earths in the known constellations." She shrugged. "That's not counting planets such as this one that have been colonized from the other earths."

"So what do your people call Earth, Drety?"

"A planet where humans have evolved. Our Earth has all but died, there's Earth 2 where you come from, Earth 3 where some other cultures come from and Earth 4, of course."

"Why, of course?"

"We have been told Earth 4 isn't suitable even to visit." Drety shrugged. "It's probably a primitive place."

"So your Earth is more advanced than ours?"

"It was?" Drety whispered. "That was before the long winter that we are still not out of."

"The long winter?"

"International wars between races and religions. Atomic warfare devastated the planet and radioactive clouds kept out sunlight for several months and made us survivors what we are." Drety bit on her lip. "You've changed my clothes so know."

"Know what, Drety?"

"Survivors of the last war became freaks of nature who can not reproduce. We are trying to create a new world of humans who can live in harmony and peace. We wish to hurt nobody so took only copies of humans from Earth 2 and 3. The original humans are left to continue their lives without knowing they have been copied."

"Until now," Madison let slip out. She glanced up. "So how does this affect us?"

150

"At the moment Buckoway seems to be the culture most likely to be selected."

"For what?"

"To be absorbed."

"Absorbed?"

"When there is a big enough population brought in as newcomers or born naturally we will transfer our minds and personalities into your bodies. After that we will be human again, be able to reproduce and live ordinary lives."

"And what happens to us when our minds are replaced."

"We were told it didn't matter because you are all still alive on your original planet."

"So you'll kill us," Madison hissed.

"Your present minds will cease to function, yes but your physical bodies will remain alive"

"With your mind in mine or Kirsty's body?" Madison hissed.

"We will be able to select who we want to have as our host body, yes. Any conflict of choice will be balloted for."

Madison felt ill inside. Her eyes flashed in anger. "You aren't human. You're creatures bent on genocide. No human would even consider doing the despicable thing your race is considering." Her voice dropped to a whisper. "I for one shall do everything within my power to stop your vile ambitions."

She turned and stormed out of the room.

*

CHAPTER SEVENTEEN

"Did you have any success?" Captain Wantana asked Madison when she walked out of the room.

"Yes," she said in English with the anger she felt still in her tone. "It appears that people like yourselves are the lucky ones." She turned to Risa who stood beside the captain. "Tell Captain Wantana, I'm sorry I broke one of the basic rules of interviewing prisoners. My emotions clouded my judgement."

"Come," Koti Wantana beckoned Madison into his office. He introduced another officer sitting there and turned to Madison.

"They found out a little from the other aliens but would like to hear what you found out first," Risa translated.

Madison nodded and through Risa told the Japanese officers everything including information about her life on Earth and the information about the black hole and the possibility that an Earth probe was orbiting Quargis.

"So you are the breakthrough," Wantana said. "Without your abilities we could only guess for the reasons that we are here." He smiled slightly. "Mind you, our theories were close to reality."

"And what did you find out Captain Wantana?" Madison asked.

"Two important things that tied in well with your information. The boat *Gentle Lady* is filled with equipment and weapons that was destined for the aliens in your town, Guardians don't you call them?" Risa nodded for Madison and Koti continued. "One of these weapons was going to be used against us yesterday. It's called an Amicir and is fired from a machine to loop an arrow over the city. This pops like a balloon and gas drops down to put everybody asleep. They were then going to come in and find all non Sakita-mura peoples."

Madison nodded. For someone with no knowledge of modern weapons his description was quite accurate.

"We dropped the ones we found in the river," Madison said. "Are there more?"

"My men have unloaded the *Gentle Lady* and everything is lined up along the jetty for you to inspect. Your Hamish said you might know what the equipment is used for."

152

"And what will you do with Drety and the others?"

"I think it will be wise to keep them apart for a few days. We will wait until after you've left and let them go. If they have no boat it will take them a day to reach their base."

"The Mud may not let them through."

"And who never bothered to try to communicate with the indigenous people and told us they were mere animals?" Koti asked.

"True," Madison replied. "But aren't ones like Drety victims, too? "

"What do you suggest then?"

"I agree they should be kept here for several days or perhaps even a week. If we take one of the boats and the supplies we think shouldn't be destroyed they could have the other one. They can then go home in safety."

Koti Wantana sat and doodled on a piece of paper for a moment before he looked up. "There are two remaining problems. The food supplies you brought to Sakita-mura are appreciated but cannot last all winter. We cannot survive on our own. Secondly, how are you going to fight the aliens with their superior technology? One of those Amicir arrows sent over Buckoway will render you all helpless. They will come in, put you on a newcomers' machine and your minds will be sucked from you. Next time I see you, it may be Drety in your body."

Madison nodded. "I don't know," she admitted. "We need to talk with Hamish and make plans."

"Yes," the captain replied. "I'm sure that between us we can decide what is best for both our communities."

"And perhaps even include the aliens and Mud." Madison whispered. She stood up. "Thank you Captain Wantana. I'll go and examine that gear on the jetty."

*

If she was back on earth Madison would not have found the equipment sitting on the jetty unusual but here on the planet she now knew was called Quargis, it was totally out of place. Everything was in black plastic boxes with interior compartments of polystyrene that electronic gear was delivered in at home. There were computers and monitors and keyboards

"Oh hell," Madison said as she pulled one out of its container. The keyboard had English alphabet and numbers and all the packaging was in English.

"So they decided our culture was the best," Norris said. "Everything here is in our language."

Madison glowered. "I guess they will retain our basic memory of the English language when they take us over," she muttered.

"Madison!" Kirsty cut in. "It's not like you to be so bitter."

"I'm not bitter, just mad."

"So what's the difference? Both emotions will cloud your judgement and in the long run will hurt nobody except ourselves."

Madison nodded. "You're right of course. Let's look in that next container."

This one held twenty handguns, again not unlike those used on earth. There appeared to be ammunition, though. She lifted one out if the box and held it up. Oh hell, the writing on the handle was also in English. *Ray Pistol Model 3. Not to be used by other than trained personnel. To operate release the safety button and select power level.*

"Stand back," Madison said to Kirsty and Norris who were on each side of her.

She found the safety lever and found it clicked up to show the numbers 1, 2 and 3. She moved it to 1, aimed it across the river at the top of a tall fir tree and squeezed the trigger. A white beam hissed out and the top of the tree disappeared in a cloud of smoke.

Kirsty screamed, Norris swore and Hamish just stood tugging on this beard. Across the river, the top third of the tree had gone! There was just smoking wood!

"I see why a bow and arrow wouldn't be much use against this thing," Hamish said.

"I must have been on high instead of low power," Madison said. "I'll try again."

"Oh damn," Kirsty retorted. "Do you have to?"

Madison switched the lever to 3 and aimed at something closer, a log floating by in the middle of the river. Another beam hissed out and water near the log splashed up.

"Missed it," Norris said.

"But I know the 1 is high power and 3 is low," Madison said and clicked the safety lever on. "My guess is the Guardians at Buckoway were being reinforced."

They continued to search but except for being electronic, Madison didn't really understand what the other equipment they found was for. This was until they came to two crates the size of single bed.

When they pulled the plastic aside it was Hamish who grunted. "More of the machines they use to wake up newcomers," he said. "We lie the newcomers on that platform, the glass bit comes over them and all those lights go on. These must be a advanced models. The ones at Buckoway don't have as many dials and screens."

"Look at the side of it," Kirsty said. "Doesn't it look as if is meant to connect with something?"

Madison saw a row of clamps and several lose wires with plugs at the end. "The other machine!" she exclaimed and began to pull the polystyrene out off the second crate.

The others helped and soon they had two of the machines beside each other. They looked identical but when moved closer together, Madison saw that the clamps linked and the wires from the first one plugged into the second.

"This is definitely different," Hamish said.

"Yeah," Madison whispered. "We lie on one side and someone like Drety goes on the other and her brain waves are transferred into our body." She stared at the others. "This should be destroyed here and now!"

"No," Hamish said and placed his hand on Madison's shoulder. "I have a better idea."

"What!"

"We make it unusable but still deliver it to the castle. If we just throw it away our Guardians will just get another one, won't they?'

"But when they see a broken one they'll know we're on to them," Kirsty said.

"Could you break bits off inside and make sure it won't operate, Madison?" Sean asked. "If you can made it appear to be in mint condition so much the better."

Madison glanced around at her friends. "I'm sorry," she whispered. "I'm letting my emotions take over again, aren't I?"

"Just a wee bit, Lass," Hamish said. "We are all under a fair bit of stress, you know."

Madison nodded and smiled at Sean. "If we can open the casing there should be tiny circuits inside. They probably look like little black or clear buttons. There may also be tiny strips or wires imbedded in glass type stuff. With their advanced technology they may be so small we can hardly see them."

At the side of each machine was an elongated tube that looked sealed but Hamish took a pocketknife from his pocket and plied off the end of one. He slid a black cylinder about thirty centimetres long out. It looked like black glass but on closer examination was pitted with circular dots of a slightly lighter colour that spiralled around it.

"This would be it," Madison said. "Those are circuits and I'd say the middle part is a battery." Using two pieces of polystyrene in case the cylinder was live, she turned the it over and pointed to a piece of flat glass. "Photo sensitive cells. It's solar powered but probably also plugs into the power grid as well. This is quite ingenious."

The others stared at her with serious expressions until Norris poked Kirsty in the side. "Have you the slightest idea what she's muttering on about?" he whispered.

"Of course," Kirsty said. "This little thingie packs a wallop like that gun thingie Madison fired a few minutes ago. The energy from the little thingie goes into the big thingie and fries our brains." She glanced at Madison. "I'm right, aren't I?"

Madison just had to laugh. "That's just about spot on, Kirsty."

"So this tube is like the engine on the boat?" Hamish asked.

"Yes."

"And without it the machine won't work."

Madison said. "I'll need to examine the rest of it but I'd say this is the main circuit board that operates the machine."

"Just like I said," Kirsty said. "I'm not just a dumb blonde, you know."

"No, Kirsty," Madison said and hugged her friend. "You're anything but."

*

Amongst the other equipment were more of the transparent balls that shook out to become like paper pages. Madison found a plastic pencil attached to them that could be used to write words on the sheet. When she shook one again it zipped back into a ball shape. The cellphone type devices they found had the familiar zero through nine digits on them as well as other keyboard symbols common back on Earth. Other gear was totally new but looked like electronic and medical gear.

"So what do we destroy and what do we keep?" Hamish said.

"I think the balls are just modern writing devices to replace paper but these..." She picked up a cellphone. "...are communications devices that may be traced. Don't destroy them but ask the guards to keep them somewhere secure here at Sakita-mura. "

"And the weapons?"

Madison pouted. "We'll take the ray pistols but those other bigger weapons may be more dangerous. I would get the guards to bury them well away from the village where nobody can find them. Don't try to disassemble them as they could explode like a fireball."

"I'll tell them," Risa said.

156

"And the things you don't know about?"

"Handle them with care and store them in a secure part of the village. They may be helpful to us in the future." She glanced up at Risa. "Got that?"

"Sure," the girl replied and went to talk to one of the Sakita-mura guards watching on.

Madison continued to examine the gear but glanced up when she realized someone different was standing beside her. It was Captain Wantana.

"One of the aliens wishes to speak to you, Madison," he said. "I think it's important."

"Drety?"

"No. It's one of the males. His name is Fyddal."

"I'll come." Madison turned to Hamish. "You can finish sorting through this stuff can't you?"

"Sure Lass. What do we do with the stuff we want to keep?"

"Put it on the *Gentle Warrior*. The best way back home is to go back up to Station Five and take our wagons."

"My thoughts, too," Hamish said. "I think we should go soon before more aliens come looking for their lost companions."

*

The dungeon cell was cold and dark with only one light dangling from the ceiling.

"Tap on the door when you want to come out," the jailer said and the door clanked shut.

Madison looked up. Except for being tall, the alien man looked quite ordinary in his normal clothes. Like Drety, he seemed nervous.

"I'm Madison. I was told you wished to talk to me."

"Is Drety okay?' he asked.

Madison frowned. "Yes, of course she is. She's probably better off than you are. I asked them to shift her upstairs to a proper room."

"Why?"

"I wanted to speak to her and didn't think a dungeon was an appropriate place." She looked into the man's eyes. "Why are you concerned about her?"

"We are good friends and I wouldn't like her to be hurt."

"And that is why you asked to see me?" Madison walked across to a chair and sat down.

Fyddal coughed as if he was embarrassed. "Drety and I wish to defect," he blurted out. "Is that the word?"

"If you mean to come over to our side if there was a fight, I guess it is."

"That's what we want to do."

Madison remained serious. "I see. May I ask why you want to give up a sophisticated life for our quite primitive one?"

"We don't agree with what our people are doing."

"And?"

Fyddal frowned. "What do you mean?"

"That's not the only reason, is it?"

"Drety and I are attracted to each other like humans were before the wars. All emotional contact between the genders is now banned."

Madison stance softened a little. "But you people should have no feelings that way. After all..." she stopped.

"We don't change in our minds," Fyddal whispered. "Nobody can regulate how we feel inside."

"So when you take our bodies over you can become sexually active again, can't you?"

"I suppose so," the alien replied.

"Isn't that the whole idea of bringing our minds here and placing them in cloned copies of the original person?"

"It doesn't work," Fyddal whispered. "It's just the next step of an experiment to stop us from becoming extinct."

"The next step?"

"We tried transferring our minds straight into imported bodies but nobody survived. Apparently the DNA of the new body still retained memories of the formerself. After a few weeks antibodies built up and within six months everyone in a cloned body died by this rejection process. That was why these colonies were established."

"To find the species most suitable to use."

"Partly. The leaders also wanted the most advanced and adaptable society. The theory was that if they all spoke the same language and were from the same ethnic background, inherited conflicts would disappear."

"And you wouldn't have wars that ruined your old planet."

"Yes."

"So why won't it work?"

"There is no way to completely eliminate the memories of the host body. It can be erased from the conscious memory but at some time the hidden memories maintained in the host's DNA will surface and the host and the new brain waves will fight."

"And what happens?"

"The mind fights itself and causes psychiatric conditions such as schizophrenia, and psychosis. Within a few weeks the mind seizes up completely and the person dies."

"How do you know this?"

"I'm know a scientist who has been brought to Quargis to try to solve the problem. One village from your Earth has already been wiped out."

"What were they?"

"Humans like you."

"I guessed that," Madison said with creeping anger in her voice. "What nationality and language did they speak."

"Oh, I see. We chose the most peaceful people from Earth 2, ones with their own language and who hadn't fought in wars for hundreds of years."

"And who were they?"

"They came from Sweden. Do you know them?"

Madison almost nodded but just stopped in time. "Why should I?" she asked instead.

"We know about the Alpha and Beta transfusions in your body and that you have knowledge of both your new life here and your old one on Earth 2."

Madison fought her inner turmoil but managed to keep her face unchanged. "Oh yes, and how am I meant to go back and forth between my two selves?"

Fyddal hesitated. "Perhaps you can't," he said. "Unfortunately that won't help you. The Leaders believe you have this ability and want to find out how it works."

"So?"

"If you return to Buckoway, you will be arrested and taken to the castle. If you end up there you won't survive the tests they want to perform on you." He stared at Madison. "If you are linked as I believe you are, your mind in your other body won't survive either. Both of your minds will have seizure and die."

Madison paled. This had almost happened already so she had no reason to doubt Fyddal.

"So you tell me all this out of sympathy for me, a stranger whom you've never met before?"

"No, out of my love for Drety. She belongs to a group opposed to all cloning. They're called *Mindsouls* who are classified as terrorists and outlawed back on Earth 1."

"So why was she allowed to come to this planet?"

"All surviving humans have to serve two years of civil service. It's really military service but that term isn't used any more. Drety was lucky she was here when the mass arrests took place. The *Mindsouls* at home have nearly all been arrested and been treated."

"Killed?"

"Oh no, we don't kill them. We just reform their brain waves so they forget they were members." He shrugged. "They do the same for criminals of serious crimes, too."

"But you said this didn't work?"

Fyddal's eyebrows dropped. "It doesn't. They all die within a year. It would be more humane to kill them outright."

"And your humans are a thousand years more advanced than ours?"

"So you do remember?" Fyddal asked

Madison glowered but didn't reply.

"We're on your side," Fyddal whispered. "If you let us come with you we can be a great help."

"Just Drety and yourself?"

"Superior Officer Undul is ruthless and cannot be trusted. I have not spoken to the others but doubt if they would help you. They all like the idea of new bodies and haven't been told of the likely side affects."

"Orders from above, no doubt,' Madison muttered,

"Yes."

"And Drety will support everything you told me?"

"She may be too nervous to confide in you but she does know everything I told you. Speak to her if you like."

"Oh I will, Fyddal." Madison whispered. "I shall get back to you." She stood, tapped on the door and waited while the jailer undid the old fashioned lock.

*

CHAPTER EIGHTEEN

Fyddal stood up and wipe the perspiration from his eyes. "That should do it," he said and glanced down at his spectators.

"So what exactly have you done, Lad?" Hamish tugged on his beard as he studied the open engine box in *Gentle Lady*.

Feudal held up a small metal card. "This is the autopilot that the computer uses to guide the boat through the rapids. Without it my colleagues will have to use their own skills." He gave a slight grin. "I doubt if they will attempt it."

Hamish turned to Madison. "And this wee card of tin foil controls the whole boat?"

"I'm no electronics engineer but that printed circuit certainly is one of the major components in the boat's control." Madison glanced at the two men. The tall thin Fydall looked the complete opposite to the bulky Hamish. Fyddal was dressed again in his immaculate silver body suit while Hamish still managed to look scruffy even though his clothes were fresh and clean.

Madison had decided to trust the two aliens and was cautiously supported by the others. On Hamish's insistence the pair had still been kept apart and Fydall was grilled on how they could proceed. The alien man's suggestion that they should return to Station Five in *Gentle Warrior* and take the now mainly disabled equipment back to Buckoway was similar to Madison and her friends' ideas. There were only two boats designed to navigate the rapids and they had them both. This was when Fydall offered to sabotage the boat left at Sakita-mura.

Madison glanced at the sky as she had got used to doing in this world. The sun was on its descent so it would be close to three p.m.. "I think we should go," she said.

The three stepped out onto the jetty to where the Sakita-mura guards had completed loading *Gentle Warrior* and stood in a line along the jetty side. Norris, Sean and Risa waited by the gangplank but Kirsty was conspicuous by her absence.

Ten minutes later five people walked out of the village gate. The smiling blonde girl in blouse and tartan skirt only reached Drety's shoulders as they walked out. Looking smaller still were the two guards and Governor

Kobayashi. Kirsty waved and said something to the alien girl. Drety looked up and broke into a smile when she saw Fydall on the jetty.

The governor walked up to Madison and took both her hands. "Our thoughts are with you, Madison," he said. "We shall await a message of your success at Buckoway."

"Thank you. Now we know the reason for being here, our two villages can support each other. I hope you will still consider our suggestion that you move your people to Buckoway. We have space and fertile lands for your farm animals."

"That is the future," the governor said. "There are obstacles to be solved before the light of peace shines across our lands." He looked serious. "Look after Risa. I would have preferred her to stay with us but, though young she is an adult and can make her own decisions in life."

Madison hid a smile. By standards back home on Earth the governor could barely be called middle aged but here he was one of the elders. "We shall look after her, Governor Kobayashi. She will be your first ambassador in the free Buckoway, that I am sure."

The governor bowed his head, stepped back and watched as Madison walked into *Gentle Warrior*. She turned and waved, the door swung down and a faint rumble indicated that the engine had started. A guard undid the last mooring line and water spurted out of the rear exhaust pipes as the red and black boat glided away from shore.

*

Madison was quite relieved to be sitting on the side couch while Fyddal drove *Gentle Warrior* into the rapids. He spoke in brisk English to the computer and the boat twisted and bounced in a wall of white water. Kirsty clung on and managed a nervous grin at her friend while the men and Drety sat out of sight in the main cabin.

"Why are you using the English mode?" Madison shouted above the roar.

"The home language used is not my own," Fyddal replied. "Like Earth 2 there are hundreds of languages on our Earth. I come from a small country with our own language. I actually understand your English better than the language used by The Leaders." He grinned. "English is the official language of this planet now."

He held the steering wheel casually and let it turn back and forth under the autopilot but kept his eyes on the churning water outside. "We found the English language difficult to grasp but once learned it offered far greater potential than the other main Earth or Earth 2 languages. By being

162

off planet it also prevented a major argument about which of three main home languages was the best to use in the future. When millions spoke the languages it was different but it seemed stupid to have twenty or more languages for about a hundred thousand people."

"That few?" Madison asked.

Fyddal glanced sideways and caught her eyes. "I'm afraid so. About a million survived the long winter but the two older generations have almost all gone in the natural cycle of life. " He shrugged. "Of course it's not natural any longer. Every death is one less with no children born to replace the deceased."

"So clones like us are the last chance for your once great civilization to survive?"

"It is the most successful of many programmes attempted. A few others were tried like storing brain waves in a master computer while the bugs in the present system is sorted. They even tried making robotic bodies to transfer people's minds into." He shrugged. "Didn't work though."

"Why not?' Madison said.

"Either the mind waves rejected the robotic body or visa versa. Nobody in a robotic body survived so the programme was discontinued."

"So instead of stealing people from our Earth why didn't your leaders approach our leaders?"

"Experience, I guess. Why should your United Nations help us? The members can't even get on together can they? There would just be panic and war."

"Yeah I guess but what about those other earths you know about."

"They all have fragmented societies that are more entrenched than on your planet. Let's say Earth 2 was the best of a bad bunch."

"Some of us try," Madison whispered.

"Just like Drety and me," Fyddal replied.

The pair lapsed into silence as their boat headed directly towards a wall of water that slashed over a rock. At the last second one of the rear water spouts cut out, the other increased power and the *Gentle Warrior* made a sharp turn. It bounced in the torrent of water before the autopilot switched engines and they swung back into the middle of the river with the obstacle behind them.

"We'd never have done that manually," Madison shouted.

She gripped the couch edge and stared back though the mist. Just before another wave blocked the view something caught her eye. There was a sort of slither in the sky. She turned but saw that Fyddal had his eyes on the white water ahead.

"The bastards have broken the third protocol." An angry Drety knelt on the couch beside her so she could see out the side window.

"What's wrong, Drety?"

"That's a drone following us. Under the third protocol it was agreed that no aircraft would be used on Quargis."

"You mean a pilotless aeroplane?"

Drety turned to Madison. "You know about them?"

"We have millions of aeroplanes on Earth and the air force uses drones." She glanced out but could only see waves and mist behind them. "What can it do?"

"Probably this version will just relay back a live visual of us. Their equipment will scan us with heat seeking equipment to tell how many of us are here. They can also differential between our species so will know six of us aboard are Earth 2 humans as well as Fyddal and myself."

Madison paled. "Can they do anything else?"

"An electronic impulse can burn out all the controls on the boat or a higher charge can kill everything aboard."

Madison stared out and thought she saw the flash of a wing above the waves. "But it hasn't done it yet?" she muttered. "Why?"

"They probably don't know the situation here. We could have you all tied up and be going back to find lost crewmembers. There are other scenarios."

"And after they realize you are helping us?"

"They'll probably wait until we reach Station 5 then send a disabling ray down."

"I know I shouldn't ask but what does it do?"

"Incapacitates us. We are still conscious but become paralysed. They can then come and see who we are without any fear of any counter attack. Drety and I would be classified as traitors and you would be seized for experiments. Afterwards, all of us would undergo mind alterations and end up like docile vegetables."

"Is this breaking a protocol serious?" Kirsty who had come up to join them asked.

Drety nodded. "A protocol can only be broken by direct command from our home planet. The drones and other equipment are stored here but are electronically incapacitated. A local commander cannot just use them on his or her own initiative."

"So someone on your home planet authorized this. But why?"

"To get you, Madison. Until you arrived, nobody here realized they were clones of somebody else from another planet."

Madison felt a tap on the shoulder and turned to see Sean. "Hamish wants you down the back," he said.

"Okay, I'll come."

The gear had been strapped in containers along each side of the boat so there was a passageway down the middle. Hamish and Risa stood gazing out the stern windows. The valley walls and a patch of sky could be seen between the water spouting out the twin exhausts.

"There's a giant bird out there Lass," Hamish said. "It is directly above us and following every move we make." He gripped Madison's arm and pointed with his other hand. "Look there it is."

The drone was quite unlike anything Madison had seen on Earth. It appeared to have silver feathers, wings that flapped, eyes and a beak. However, on closer inspection she could see that the beak was really an antennae and the eyes were like camera lens."

"It's a machine, Hamish!"

"But it's above the water like a bird, not on it."

Drety arrived and studied at the pilotless aeroplane. "This is a new model I've never seen before. I don't like it."

"So use your bow skills and shoot it down before it harms us," Hamish said.

"My arrows would be useless."

"I know Madison but use your same skill with those ray pistols."

"They'll work," Drety said. "The ray pistol can home in on any target. You just set the beam wide."

"Okay," Madison replied in a grim voice. "You will need to show me what to do."

*

Even with a safety harness, a lifejacket and Norris holding her legs, Madison received quite a shock when she flung open the top hatch and wriggled out. Water hit her face and left her spluttering. The boat turned left and she was almost hurled out. She flung her hands out and managed to grip on the ledge. She clipped a flapping piece of the harness to a handhold and reached up to remove hair from her eyes ... just as another wave hit her. Water splashed everywhere and Norris uttered an oath as he too became saturated.

"You okay?" he screamed.

"Getting there," Madison replied. She was so wet now it didn't really matter if more water hit her. She unclipped the harness from the ladder below and re-clipped it on another handhold. Now with both hands free she could concentrate on her job ... Where was the drone?

She felt rather than saw a shadow above and turned her head back. Oh God, it was directly above her.

"Quick Norris," she screamed. "Hand me the ray pistol."

She reached down and felt it placed in her hand. Now came the tricky part. She leaned back so the harness held her and bought both hands up with the weapon held in a vice grip. Now her left arm was fully extended just as it would be when she held a bow. She shut her left eye, switched so her right eye was closed and moved the pistol so the back sight lined up with the tiny glass cross at the front. One finger rested on the trigger; all the other controls had been pre-set by Drety so she was ready.

Damn! The Gentle Warrior swerved left and the drone had disappeared.

"It's out the side," Norris shouted. "Move to the right."

She did but again the boat twisted and she was slammed sideways by a wave that crashed over the roof. She gasped, spat out a mouthful of water and shook her head. The drone followed the boat but in doing so it's left wing dipped. For a moment it was fully exposed like a gigantic glider caught in an updraft.

Madison bit on her bottom lip and held her breath as the alien aeroplane continued to turn. She squeezed the trigger. A yellow bean hissed out, there was a bang and Madison saw the drone's right wing disintegrate in a cloud of smoke. Before she could squeeze the trigger a second time the aeroplane disappeared and another wave smashed over her.

Two hands came up, unclasped the clips and she was lifted back inside. Someone shut the hatch and Norris pulled her in a massive hug.

"You did it!" he yelled.

There was a sort of muffled crunching sound outside that was followed by a crack and a ball of fire erupted to their left.

"It flew into the cliff and exploded," Kirsty yelled.

Madison glanced around. As well as Norris and herself, Kirsty, Drety and Risa were also saturated. Water ran across the floor and the nearby gear was wet.

Only Hamish and Sean stood there, bone dry and grinning like two school boys who'd just watched their favourite rugby player score a try.

"Drenched wench," Hamish laughed.

"That's for sure," Sean added. "Nerves of ice though. I wish Thinrisodor was here to see her."

"Look at the drone!" Drety shouted in a more serious voice.

Everyone turned to where the downed craft was already out of sight behind them. However, a ball of orange flames and black smoke spiralled up above the cliff.

"That's more than just the drone crashing," the alien girl said. "There were explosives aboard. If Madison hadn't shot it down we'd be that exploding fireball right now."

"You're right Lass," Hamish said. "I think your friends know who we are and, come hell or high water want to stop us."

"But they won't," Kirsty cut in. "Their days of controlling our lives are over, you just wait and see."

"That was too close," Madison muttered and turned to Drety. "I don't think you and Fyddal can go back now even if you wanted to."

Drety nodded. "I think we made the right choice," she said. "I'll go and tell Fyddal we're all safe. He must be getting lonely up there in the pilot's seat all by himself."

*

Station Five looked like home. After they tied up, Kirsty and Risa ran out the back of the barn to check on the oxen. Madison and the others made a thorough check of the buildings but it appeared that nobody had visited. Drety and Fyddal were fascinated by the oxen wagons and helped round them up and hitch them to the wagons. Hamish and Madison drove the teams down to the jetty and everyone loaded the equipment from the boat.

Fyddal s disappeared aboard and came out with a box of bits and pieces. "Vital components," he said. "*Gentle Warrior* won't be going anywhere without us." He glanced down at Hamish. "Have you a good spot where we can hide this stuff?"

"Aye Lad, I have. Just follow me..."

The three men, together with Risa and Drety wandered into the barn.

Madison glanced at Kirsty beside her. "You know, I think we've made a couple of friends. They're so much like us I wonder..." She sort of stared out over the river to where the afternoon shadows stretched out over the water.

"Well go on," Kirsty said.

"I just wondered if we have a common ancestry, that's all."

"Yeah, I know. Even using the term Earth to describe their planet. They're tall but isn't every human generation taller than the one before it?"

"How did you know that?" Madison asked.

167

Kirsty grinned. "Oh hell, I don't know. I guess some of the memories from my otherself were dragged out the back of my mind. You'd better tell her about it when you see her over night."

"Oh Kirsty," Madison laughed. "You're no different. I don't even realize there are two of you."

"Or that right now there's another Madison across the galaxy fast asleep. There's two of you too, you know."

" I suppose there is," Madison whispered. "I didn't really think of it that way."

*

As darkness descended over the lonely river valley, the two oxen teams headed up to the tunnel where they decided to spend the night. They arrived and were just settling the animals down when Thinrisodor appeared beside the innermost wagon.

"Hi Thinrisodor," Kirsty said. "How did you get here?"

The warrior almost smiled. "Once we realized no magic keeps the mountain door shut we worked out how to open it."

"Without a remote?" Madison asked.

Thinrisodor shrugged. "We cut some wires and pushed it open. My people will let no strangers in." He glanced up to where the two aliens stood back. "These long shadows are not the ones who tried to melt your boat with the mechanical bird?"

"You know about that?" Risa cut in.

"We have eyes in many places."

"These are friends who were in the boat with us." Madison fixed the Mud warrior with a serious look. "What else do you know, Thinrisodor?"

"More long shadows are coming down the inner trail where Risa was caught. They have wagons without oxen and will be here before dawn. You should not stay."

"Motor vehicles," Madison whispered.

"Another protocol broken," Drety added.

Hamish looked at the pair and raised his eyebrows then merely grunted after Madison explained. "You mean our oxen teams will be of no value if we all get these things?"

"There aren't many here," Drety said. "Half a dozen in use and another ten in storage."

"But they've never been used outside the base," Fyddal said.

"Do you want them stopped?" Thinrisodor asked.

"Stopped but nobody is to be hurt," Madison said. "I have a feeling more longshadows will follow if they are killed and next time they'll be prepared."

"With their fire sticks?"

Madison nodded.

"And the wagons that go without oxen?"

"If necessary, destroy them but try to stop them first."

"It shall be done." Thinrisodor turned but Madison stepped in front of him.

"Everyone here is my friend and your friend. If we travel through the darkness to reach Buckoway, will we be safe?"

"Our people will guide and protect you, Maiden of Granite."

"I may be asleep in the wagon and not be able to be awoken," Madison said. "Even if I'm asleep I want my friends protected."

"Your shell will be protected as will be your friends," Thinrisodor nodded and was gone.

"Oh hell, is there anything he doesn't know?" Kirsty asked.

"Probably not," Madison replied.

*

CHAPTER NINETEEN

Kirsty sat in the driver's seat of the wagon beside Madison and peered through the gloom. Only Olive, Twinkle, Thelma and Florence, their docile oxen seemed unworried about late hour. Drety sat behind the drivers while Norris maintained a watch out the back. On Hamish's insistence, the two aliens travelled in different wagons and Risa also offered to travel in the front wagon.

They were a half an hour out from the tunnel and not far from the area where they'd first met Thinrisodor. Kirsty nodded but forced her eyes open, it was so easy to doze off with the rhythmic sway of the wagon, squeaks of leather on wood and the rumble of the wheels on the gravel below.

"Oh my God, there it is," Madison said.

Kirsty glanced up. Above the silhouette of trees on each side of the road was a strip of star-studded sky. Across this a line of light curved like a meteorite.

"The thingie from your world, Madison?"

"I think so. Colonel Davis said I might see it."

"So it's up there and we're down here. How can it help us?"

"I don't know," Madison admitted. "But it's like a friend somehow, something tangible that joins our two worlds."

"Yeah, but from what you've told me your world isn't much better than Drety's."

"We're trying to make it better and our technology does a lot of good, you know."

"That's what we tried," Drety said. "The idea here on Quargis was to keep the good things but not the bad." She shrugged. "Like everything else it was a great theory."

"It still might work," Kirsty said.

"Of course it might," Madison said." I..." She stopped mid-sentence and flopped sideways.

*

Drety reached forward and grabbed Madison before she toppled off the wagon. "What's wrong with her?" she asked in alarm.

170

"Gone home," Kirsty said. "Normally she would have been asleep an hour ago. It seems that she can't be awake in both places at the same time. If she wakes up there she must be asleep here." Kirsty grabbed both reins and called out. "Whoa girls!"

The oxen obeyed and their wagon halted.

"Madison's asleep. I need a hand to lift her into the stretcher we made up," Kirsty shouted back at Norris who wondered why they'd stopped.

"I'll do it," Drety said. She reached over, lifted Madison in her arms, swung around and gently laid her on the stretcher. "Shall I strap her in?" she asked.

"Yes. The road gets a little rough ahead. Pull a blanket over her, too."

"Right." Drety finished then slid over to the drivers' seat. "Can I take the reins for this side?"

Kirsty glanced over, grinned and handed Madison's reins across. "Are you okay, Norris," she shouted.

"Fine. There's nothing around."

∗

Offworld Prime Clav Vihin, the senior Earth 1 officer on Quargis, sat in the front of six vehicles and glowered at the tiny monitor built into the dashboard. The screen was lit up with dozens of dots ranging in colour from brown to a dull red. He turned to the officer behind him who monitored a similar, though larger screen.

"Explain this Underofficer Triobu," he grumbled. At the same time he cast a glower at the vehicle's driver, Sergeant Bebop Sreke who was fighting to maintain control as their six-wheel drive transporter crawled though the rough trail.

"The road is surrounded by over two thousand Mud, Offworld Prime," he said. "Only our force fields are keeping them at bay."

"And where are the Earth 2 newcomers?"

"The old equipment fitted to this six wheeler cannot tell the difference between the humanoid races on this planet. The newcomers and Mud as well as our kind all appear the same when read by the infrared visual beams."

"Typical," Vihin snorted. "So how do we find them?"

"See those slightly redder dots on screen Prime?'" Kint Triobu said.

"I do."

"I adjusted the readout to find other animals. There are eight of them in a pattern."

"So?"

"I believe the newcomers and defectors are travelling in two wagons and those are the eight oxen pulling them. Notice that there are four humanoids clustered together behind each four dark red dots."

Vihin smiled for the first time. "Good work, Underofficer Triobu. You might just fit into this desolate planet after all."

"Thank you, Prime."

"How far ahead are they?"

"Three kilometres, Prime. Even at our slow speed we can catch them up within half an hour."

"At their present speed, when would they reach Buckoway?"

"A little over three hours, Prime."

"Good. We'll keep pace with them for two hours. By that time they'll be tired and also looking forward to arriving home. Also, we'll be out of these damn hills and travelling through farmland."

"And the Mud along both sides of the road, Prime?"

"Ignore them."

"I would treat them with respect, Prime Vihin," the driver said. "They are not the dumb half humans we originally thought."

"Possibly," Vihin muttered. "Meanwhile slow down, Sergeant Sreke. We don't want the newcomers to know they're being followed."

"They already know," Sreke whispered to himself. He changed down to a crawler gear so they moved ahead at a mere walking pace.

*

Five other transporters behind them also slowed while in the nearby bushes Thinrisodor watched. Something prevented his warriors from getting close to these wagons that had engines like the boats. Even their poison darts merely bounced off an invisible jelly. He muttered a few words to the warriors beside him and broke into a slow trot through the trees. He knew that without their help his friends in the wagons never stood a chance.

*

"Kirsty," Norris came up to the front of the wagon and spoke to her. "Can you get a message to Hamish in front?"

"Yes, I think its Risa at the back watching us. What do you want me to do?"

172

"Give them the signal to stop."

"Why?"

"Thinrisodor is beckoning us. He looks exhausted."

"Thinrisodor exhausted. You must be kidding?"

"Just signal Risa will you? It's important."

"Okay," Kirsty muttered. She picked up her torch and flicked the beam on and off twice. One beam flashed back and the front wagon pulled off to the right beside a row of high trees. Kirsty pulled their oxen in behind and also stopped just as Thinrisodor appeared outside beside Norris and moved forward. His actions suggested something was wrong.

He glanced down at Madison and turned to Kirsty. "Madison is in the deep sleep until dawn?"

"Yes. What's wrong Thinrisodor?" Kirsty asked.

"Six wagons that travel without oxen are three bends behind us. They've been there for an hour but we cannot get inside their invisible jelly. An attack is imminent."

"They've put up a force field," Drety whispered. "Not even our ray pistols will be able to penetrate it."

"So what can we do?" Norris said.

"Leave the wagons now," Thinrisodor said.

"We can't leave Madison." Kirsty pouted. "I will not leave her."

"I will carry her," the Mud warrior said. "Come now. If they know we aren't moving they will attack."

"They will know," Drety said. "They will be using heat seeking gear. Our body heat will register."

"We have a shield of my people. They are constantly moving around in circles to confuse the heat machines. Can you bring those in the front wagon here? We must act quickly."

"Right," Kirsty said. "She turned the torch on for three seconds and followed it with two quick flashes. Two quick flashes showed inside the front wagon. "They're coming," she said.

Four shadows appeared out of the darkness and Risa followed by the men climbed aboard. Hamish looked serious but reached out to squeeze Thinrisodor's hand.

"Thank you my friend," he said. "What do you want us to do?"

"Come," Thinrisodor walked over to Madison and stopped to pick her up.

"No," Fyddal said. "You lead the way. I'll carry her. I have as much strength as anyone here."

Thinrisodor looked at Kirsty.

"It is okay," she whispered.

"You need warm clothes, food and a rope."

"A rope?" Kirsty asked.

"It is dark in the forest. We can show no light but if you are joined by rope nobody will get lost."

Fyddal with Madison in his arms and the rope tied around his waist followed Thinrisodor into the trees. Kirsty came next then the others with Sean again covering the rear. As they began to climb the steep slope, four warriors climbed aboard each wagon, commands were called out and the two oxen teams moved forward.

Two minutes later the lonely spot almost became empty. The dozen warriors that ran across the road turned and dashed back in regular intervals barely raised dust on the road but they made a certain machine a few hundred metres away look as if it had broken out in dancing measles.

*

"What's happening to that God damned screen, Underofficer Triobu?" Offworld Prime Vihin snapped.

"I thought it was the Muds running around, Prime," Kint Triobu said. "I'm not so sure now."

"What is it then."

"Bats, Prime."

"Bats?"

"We've been fooled by them before, Prime. They are warm-blooded as you know and in this world their body temperature is similar to humans. They come out of the caves in the valley at night in search of food. They are the only things that could produce such a regular pattern back and forth across the road. I'd say someone in the rear wagon is tossing fruit out at them."

"Will they hinder us?"

"I doubt it Prime. They are vegetarians and except for attacking farmer's crops are quite harmless. Give them a few moments and they'll go away. Once we're out of the forest they'll head off to the fruit trees or vegetable plots on the farms."

"You'd better be right," Vihin muttered. He glanced up as a map replaced the red dots on the dashboard monitor. "We attack in fifteen minutes, Sergeant Sreke. Radio the transporters behind us."

"Any other orders, Prime?"

"Hand me the microphone." Vihin spoke his crisp orders into the instrument. "On my command, troopers from Transporters Two and Three will attack the wagons. Weapons are to be on stun. I need them all alive."

174

A hushed cheer went through the small convoy. After all these hours it would be nice to be finally doing something.

*

The climb was steep and soil crumbly. Kirsty felt her heart pound and she gasped for breath. After forever, it seemed, she reached a slight dip and could stop for a rest.

"You okay?" Norris asked. He sat down beside her and wiped a dirty handkerchief across his forehead.

Kirsty nodded. "Where are the others?" she finally managed to gasp.

"Hamish is helping Fyddal lift Madison up that steep bit below."

"I have to help," Kirsty said and stood up.

"No," Norris replied and put his hand out to stop her. "Rest a minute. There would be no room for you anyway."

"I guess," Kirsty said and sat down again.

A moment later Hamish appeared out of the darkness below. "She's one heavy lass," he said. He held Madison over a shoulder with one hand and used the other to grab an exposed tree root. "I might need a hand."

Both Kirsty and Norris reached down and grabbed the sleeping girl under the armpits. Someone behind Hamish reached up and between them all they managed to get Madison into the dip. Sean followed Hamish up and Risa appeared, followed by Fyddal and Drety.

"Where's Thinrisodor?" Hamish asked.

"He's above us," Norris said. "He said we're safe for the moment and we're to wait here."

They sipped water from a mug Hamish handed around, stretched tired limbs and waited. Kirsty listened to the distant gurgle of water falling on rocks, the hoot of an owl and far off cry of an animal. By herself she would have been scared but now she was more apprehensive about her sleeping friend than any fear of the forest around.

Minutes slipped by before there was a faint rustle and Thinrisodor appeared. "I found it. Come," he said.

They were off again. In the dense undergrowth the rope became a hindrance so one of the men looped it around his shoulders before they carried on. Fyddal now carried Madison and Kirsty found herself at the rear with Risa.

"We're lucky," the Japanese girl puffed.

Kirsty hauled herself up another small slope before replying. "And why's that?"

"We're all working together when we were once apart."

"What do you mean, Risa?"

"You, me, Drety and Thinrisodor are the people of this world. We are different yet we are working together. If we can continue in this way think what a marvellous world this will be."

"Madison too," Kirsty said. "She's different again."

"And we're all friends. We can be different and still be friends."

"We sure can." Kirsty grinned and reached for the next tree root.

They reached the crest of a ridge where an animal trail wound along through the trees. Thinrisodor followed this for a couple of hundred metres before he headed down a far slope. To their left the rocks parted to reveal a cave entrance.

"Our friends will hide our body temperatures from the enemy heat seekers," Thinrisodor said.

"What friends?" Kirsty asked.

"Bats live in this cave," Thinrisodor said. "They are out gathering food now but will be back an hour before dawn."

"Bats!" Kirsty's face paled.

"A harmless flying animal," Thinrisodor said. "This species eats nothing more than the local farmers' fruit. When they return they will settle on high ledges and ignore us. If we continued to walk through the forest we could be traced. Even my people won't be able to fool the machines for long."

Kirsty gulped as they twisted and turned through narrow passage. It was so dark she had to run her fingers along the wall to navigate. Finally, though, they stopped and a torch came on.

"It is safe to use a light here," Thinrisodor said. "Don't use your torch near the entrance."

Fyddal lay Madison down and placed a backpack under her head. "I agree with Thinrisodor that we'll be safe here. It would be foolish just to stumble on through the trees.

*

Half the troopers formed an outer ring and watched for Muds while the others rushed the wagons. The attack on the two wagons was fast but the result unexpected. A hail of tiny darts ambushed the first troopers and they slumped into the road. The outer ring realized what happened and

176

an organized attack decimated the wagons with ray shots. Those inside slumped unconscious to the floor and troopers rushed aboard.

Bebop Sreke pulled his transporter in beside the stationary front wagon and Offworld Prime Vihin wound down his window. "Very good, Underofficer," he said to the man who saluted outside. "It was a fast and effective assault."

"I'm afraid not, Prime," the underofficer replied.

"You didn't kill them?" Vihin snapped.

"No Prime. Mud warriors drove the wagons. There were no newcomers or traitors aboard."

"What?" Vihin jumped down and rushed over to the front wagon. Three Mud warriors were asleep on the front seat and another five at the back. He swore and almost ran to the second wagon. Another eight Mud warriors were asleep there. "Damn!' He swung around and glowered at the underofficer beside him. It was Kint Triobu. "Kill them all," he ordered.

"I wouldn't Offworld Prime Vihin," Triobu said in a formal but firm voice.

Vihin stopped and glowered at him. "And why not Underofficer?" he whispered

"If those warriors are killed Prime, we will not make it back to base or even Buckoway, if it comes to that. The Mud will overwhelm us by sheer numbers. Sure we could mow them down but more will come. We estimate that close to ten thousand Muds live within a fifty-kilometre radius of Buckoway. The tribes will unite and no modern weapons will stop them all." Triobu held his commanding officer's gaze. "I was on Quargis during the first uprising, Prime."

"So what would you do, Underofficer Triobu, pat them on the back?"

Vihin ignored the sarcasm. "Just leave them, Prime. Drive our patrol up the road and regroup. Perhaps then we could call in the last drone."

"To do what?"

"We issue gas masks to all the troopers and drop a line of Amicir discharges. Everything within walking distance of the road will be rendered unconscious. We then use the more sophisticated search gear on the drone to trace our two traitors. Our blood temperature is slightly lower than newcomer humans and the Mud. Once they are traced the girl we're seeking won't be far away."

Vihin studied Triobu. "If it works I'll recommend your promotion to overofficer. If it doesn't... " He never completed the sentence.

*

At the usual time Madison awoke.

She stared around but could see nothing in the darkness. This was the wrong. It should be morning. A strange smell tickled her nose. It was sort of like hot honey and stronger than the background smell of dust and soil.

"Hi everyone, where are we?" Her voice echoed back at her.

Oh hell. Madison hair rose on the back of her neck in fright. "Kirsty! Norris! Are you here?"

She felt out with her hands and found dry soil to push on. She sat up but everything was pitch black. She listened!

No far away from her, at least one person was breathing. Madison crawled towards the sound until she felt clothing. Her eyes could now see a little. Off in the distance was a lighter grey shaped like a rough oval. She was inside something, probably a cave. She glanced down and realized she had found Kirsty and another person.

"Kirsty," she whispered and shook her friend. There was no response.

Madison moved on found Risa then the others. Everyone, including Drety and Fyddal were in a deep sleep. All had normal pulses but could not be awoken. Her own head ached and she began to feel dizzy. Whatever it was beginning to affect her but what could she do?

She found a torch and turned it on. The beam made her eyes water for a moment but in the light she confirmed that she was in a cave. Everyone from both wagons was there and several backpacks were stacked neatly along the wall. The oval probably led towards an entrance and in the opposite direction the cave walls disappeared beyond the torch's range.

The first backpack contained food and a canister of water but the second was more promising. It held two ray pistols and what looked like scuba diving glasses. She frowned. Why would they be needed here? She examined one more closely. The close fitting nozzle would fit over her nose as well as her eyes. Attached to it was a tube that led to a small cylinder.

"A gas mask," she muttered to herself when she read the label. *Emergency Air Supply* was printed in large English yellow letters along the side of the cylinder. Beneath in smaller writing were instructions in English and the other strange language that she knew was the aliens'.

She tested one and the fresh slightly scented air made her feel better. Good. She strapped it on and took slow breaths. Yes, it worked well. She searched all the packs but found only one other gas mask.

"Okay girl," she said to herself. "Who shall I try to wake up?"

178

One of the aliens would be helpful but there was still a chance that they couldn't be trusted. Kirsty would be the best company or even Norris but in the end Madison decided to try to awaken Hamish. He probably had the best knowledge of what was the reason for their present predicament.

She walked across to the ginger bearded man, strapped the gas mask on and turned a valve. A moment later Hamish's eyes opened and he stared at her.

"My God, it's Madison but why are you wearing sunglasses?"

"It's a gas mask, Hamish. You have one, too. Now just relax and take slow breaths..."

After several moments of coughing and spluttering and with the help of water to sip Hamish became his old self again. He listened to Madison's explanation of what happened and told her how they'd evacuated the wagons and carried her to this bat cave.

"I don't think Thinrisodor's here," she said.

"No Lass, he slipped away before the gas came. It was all sudden like. We heard that drone come over just like the one we shot down from the boat. There was a swish, the smell of honey and the walls spun. The next thing I knew was when you woke me." He glanced around. "How are the others?"

"Unconscious but breathing."

"And there are only two of these air masks?"

"Yes. They were in Fyddal's pack. I decided it was safer to awaken you."

"Aye Lass, a wise precaution. I think they're trustworthy but we can't be a hundred percent sure, now can we?"

He stood up and frowned.

"What is it?" Madison asked.

"Get those ray gun things. I think that drone is coming back."

Oh hell it was. The faint sound of a jet engine came from beyond the entrance.

The pair walked around the corner and saw daylight shine in a further bend.

"Slowly, Lass," Hamish whispered. "We don't know who's out there."

They crept forward into morning sunlight. Madison could see fir trees across the valley and a strip of blue sky. The silver drone was flying directly towards them at a slow speed like a crop duster Madison had seen once on Earth.

"It's searching for us," Hamish whispered. "Keep down."

*

CHAPTER TWENTY

The pair watched as the drone flew over the hilltop. However, it had barely moved out of sight when there was a change in the engine noise and they saw it swing back into view over the valley below. It kept coming across in front of them.

"It's found us, " Madison said.

Hamish looked worried and nodded. "You shot the last one down from the moving boat, Lass," he said. "This should be easy."

"But we may give our position away."

"It appears that's already happened, Madison. Every time it flies over it comes closer."

"Okay." Madison set the ray pistol to full power, raised both hands up and aimed. Like the first time she concentrated on an area in front of the drone, held her breath and squeezed the trigger.

Again a white beam hissed out. She held the trigger back and waited. A second passed and she was about to release the trigger when the drone blew apart with a crack like distant thunder. One wing dropped off while the fuselage became a ball of flames. There was a secondary explosion and debris plummeted into the forest.

"Now the trucks," Madison whispered.

"The what?"

"The mechanical wagons. No doubt destruction of the drone has given us time but the odds are that the aliens have a pretty good idea where we are." There was grim determination in her voice. "Are you coming?"

"What about the others?"

Madison nodded. "Of course they'll need protection if anybody arrives. You stay and I'll go."

"No Lass, we'll leave a note where it will be found and I'll come with you."

Madison gave a slight smile. "You're right Hamish. I guess I'm far too impulsive."

"And why not?" Hamish replied. "We could also have a look and see what other weapons there are that could come in handy."

"Or hide them."

"And why would you say that."

180

"So they can't be used against our friends."

Hamish nodded and led Madison back inside. They found four ray pistols and tucked one in Kirsty, Risa and Norris's pocket. Madison kept the last one for herself. The only other modern weapon they found was in Fyddal's pack. It looked like a small rocket attached to a pipe about twenty centimetres long. Written instructions were written on the pipe section.

"We'll take this, Madison said when she realized the instructions had an English version that she could read.

"Right but we'd better go."

*

Once outside again, Hamish pointed uphill to the ridge above the road. "That's where we came in.," he said.

When Madison reached the top she gasped, flung herself down under a shrub and peeped out. Immediately below them was a line of military trucks. They were camouflaged and rode on six massive wheels. At the front of each vehicle was a cab above an engine while the rear was enclosed with windows along the side. In some ways they looked like the *Gentle Warrior* on wheels. A line of aliens stood along the near side of the road dressed in similar clothes to Drety's except that they were a dull brown colour. Every one wore a gas mask and carried a ray pistol.

"Didn't take them long," Hamish whispered as he squeezed in beside Madison.

For the first time she felt doubtful and glanced at Hamish. "We have no hope of hitting them all before they shoot back. One shell and this whole ridge will go up and us with it."

"So try Fyddal's firecracker. He must have had a reason for carting it up here."

"Did he mention it?"

"Not a word. Mind you, we did leave in quite a rush."

"Okay, I'll see what the instructions say. "

Hamish watched as Madison squinted to read the words in the dull light. She nodded to herself and pressed the side. A panel slid back to reveal a row of buttons showing the ten digits and a hash key

She looked up. "Can you do it while I read the instructions?"

"Sure but keep half an eye on those aliens. I reckon they'll be coming soon. There's a head guy talking to them."

Madison read the instructions out loud. "Firing Procedure. Select the required result. It goes from one to five a little like the ray guns. Now let me see..." She grimaced and glanced at Hamish. Hit the following sequence

23367 then the hash key at the end. That's like two lines crossing another two lines."

Hamish nodded. After he hit the hash key a small green screen lit up with alien words.

"It's armed." Madison said. "Next thing is to aim it." She read the writing and glanced down at the road. "It's about two hundred metres below us wouldn't you say?"

"Aye Lass."

"Press 7843 and the hash key."

Hamish pressed the keys

"Now, how far is it from the front vehicle to the rear one?"

"About eighty metres."

"Good. Press 800 then the hash. How wide would the valley be?"

"Try sixty metres."

"Do we want ... " She continued on until Hamish had everything programmed in. "Now we're set," she whispered. "Make sure there aren't any tree boughs above us and sit it on the ground pointing straight up."

"You'd better hurry, Lass. Those aliens are beginning to move towards us."

"Press one for total destruct, two for stun and three for air warm, whatever that means. Four cancels the whole program."

"They've got some machine out with a spinning saucer on the top of it. I don't like it one bit, Madison."

"Which number?" Madison's voice quivered.

"It's them or us, Lass."

Madison nodded, bit on her bottom lip and pressed the *one* digit.

Whoosh!

The rocket blasted off in a cloud of compressed air that enveloped the pair. It looped up in a streak, the compressed air turned to orange flames and black smoke that curled up and arched over the valley.

Shouts came from below and the aliens dived for cover or attempted to aim ray pistols. Four rays cut through the air but they were too late. A high-pitched scream shook the hillside as the rocket headed straight down. It hit the ground right in the middle of the convoy and for two seconds nothing happened before, in complete silence, a white cloud spun out along the valley. It looked like a ground fog on a winter's day. Once formed it became denser until it looked like solid concrete, not gas. Still there was not one sound.

Hamish placed his hand on Madison shoulder while they both stared transfixed at the scene below.

"Oh damn," Madison gasped.

182

The solid 'concrete' changed again to look like white jelly. It vibrated and began dripping off itself like hot butter. As it melted away the solid white appearance became transparent so the pair could see inside.

There was nothing there!

Finally the sound came like a gigantic gulp. Wind rose around them and Madison had to grab a branch to stop herself from being sucked off the ridge. For perhaps ten seconds the wind blew before it stopped as quickly as it had started.

Below Madison and Hamish the valley had no vehicles, no aliens, not even a gravel road, trees or grass. The entire area was filled with orange lava. Only the edges hissed where it touched grass and trees.

"Perhaps we should have used the stun button," Hamish said

"It destroyed everything, Hamish," Madison gasped. "Even the air. That wind was air pouring in the vacuum created." She felt a cold shiver in her body. "I didn't realize..."

"But they knew," Hamish said. "I have no doubt what-so-ever that they would have done the same to destroy us. I reckon only one thing stopped them."

"What?"

"They wanted you alive. That was why they used that sleep spell in the first place."

"Let's go back to the cave," Madison said. "I don't want to look at the valley any more."

*

When they reached the cave mouth, Kirsty was very much awake and waiting for them. "I'm mad at you Madison Evans," she grumbled with her hands placed on her hips. "And why are you both wearing those stupid glass thingies?"

Madison was taken back. She took off her gas mask and sniffed the air. All she could smell was the scent of fir trees. "What have I done, Kirsty?"

"We lugged you up this Goddamn mountain, look after you while you're off visiting this Earth of yours but when you wake up do you wait for me?" Kirsty threw her hands out wide. "Oh no, you have to tear off on your own..."

" I was with her," Hamish cut in.

"Yeah! Yeah! You with a wife and all back at Buckoway."

"Kirsty," Madison shouted. "What are you insinuating?"

Kirsty gulped and her anger turned to embarrassment. "You are my best friend Madison. Why didn't you wake me up?"

"She didn't want you to get hurt, Lassie," Hamish said.

"Well it's a funny way to show it. We always share everything ... well we did up to now."

"I wanted to wake you but there were only two gas masks. I thought I might need Hamish if the aliens were close. Two women wouldn't be strong enough if we were attacked."

"And were you?" Kirsty snapped.

"Yes," Hamish said.

Kirsty swung around with her mouth open. "You were attacked?"

Hamish broke into a grin. "Tell me, Kirsty, is anybody else awake in the cave?"

"Well, no..."

"And did you notice anything different when you woke up?"

"I had this terrible headache, still got it actually and I could smell burnt toast. No it was more like..."

"Burnt honey," Madison said.

"Yes, that's it."

"Here, put on my gas mask and breathe in slowly," Madison said. "It's okay for you can still talk while you're wearing it." She helped Kirsty place the mask on and turned the valve on. "Is that better?"

"Much," Kirsty muttered, "But what happened?"

"We had a gas bomb dropped on us," Hamish said. "Everyone went to sleep. Somehow, though, Madison wasn't affected and she woke up at her usual time to find us all asleep. If she hadn't awoken, we'd all be prisoners of the aliens by now."

"Oh hell." Kirsty gasped and looked at her friend. "Is that true?"

Madison nodded.

"And where are they?"

"Who?"

"The aliens?"

"Dead," Madison whispered.

Kirsty bit on her bottom lip. "How?"

Hamish glanced at Madison. "Shall we take another brief walk up to the ridge?"

"Yes, I want to show my friend how much I care for her and everyone in this cave."

A more subdued Kirsty, still breathing through the gas mask followed the other two up to the ridge. She gazed out at the lava in the valley below. "So that was the burnt honey?" she gasped.

184

"No," Madison replied. "This came later. It was caused by Fyddal's rocket, actually."

"Oh hell, you'd better explain."

Between them Madison and Hamish told Kirsty everything. She listened in almost stunned silence until they finished.

"Oh Madison, what must you think of me blowing off like that."

"Proud."

"Proud?"

"Yes, proud that you are my friend and you care about me so much you're even prepared to share the dangers with me."

Kirsty's lip quivered. She turned to Hamish. "I'm sorry for making that nasty remark, Hamish. I just thought I was left out and wanted to... oh hell, I don't know what I wanted." She turned away and burst into tears.

"No offence taken, Lassie," Hamish said. He glanced over to Madison. "I think I'll slip back to the cave and see if the others are waking up."

"Sure," Madison said and tucked an arm around Kirsty's shoulder.

"Were the oxen killed when you melted the road?" Kirsty whispered.

"No they're further down the valley. I think they'll all be asleep, too but as far as I know nothing else has happened to them."

"Good," Kirsty sniffed. "Who wants those horrible engine thingies when we have our oxen teams?"

"I don't think anyone would." Madison grinned. "Come on, Kirsty, let's go back. I reckon we'll have lots to do today."

"And we do it together, right?"

"Right!"

The two women slid down the hillside and headed back to the cave together. Already the sun had dried the damp grass. It was going to be a hot day.

*

At six thirty that morning, the same time as when Madison woke up in the cave, the situation in one of her friend's apartment was bizarre. Yasmin never liked staying alone and, with Madison and Kirsty away, had asked Wade to stay with her. Yasmin was a shy girl but really had ulterior motives. After all, mating between consenting adults was the norm in the town.

She jerked awake to the blast of a voice vibrating through the room.

185

Citizens of Buckoway, a great crisis has arisen in our town. You will remember the following instructions. If you are in bed when you hear this, relax and go back to sleep. If you are moving around your apartment, stop whatever you are doing and return to your beds. There you will go to sleep. All citizens hearing this outside their homes will move to the closest safe place, sit down and go to sleep. No citizens will awaken until a siren is sounded throughout our town.

Yasmin frowned at what she heard. She did not, however, go back to sleep but instead poked Wade in the ribs.

"Did you hear the voice, Wade?" she asked.

Wade turned. "Damn thing woke me up. Who was shouting out?"

"It came out of a wall vent," Yasmin said. She was worried. "But what did it mean?"

Wade frowned. "I think everything Madison has told us is true. Think back to the time we couldn't move our hands off our head just after we arrived from the city."

"Yes, but it only worked once. When she told us to touch our noses it didn't work."

"And she looked relieved," Wade said. "I think she told us something to cancel any hypnotic suggestions made to us."

Yasmin stared at Wade. "So you mean that all over Buckoway everyone except us will be asleep right now?"

"All except the people who made the announcement."

"Who are they?" Yasmin whispered nervously.

"The Guardians in the castle," Wade replied.

Wade stared at her and slid out of bed. They both dressed and crept out into the corridor. It was silent, empty and still gloomy in the early morning daylight.

"It's not even seven," Yasmin said. "Nobody gets up this early."

"Many do," Wade said. "Those on guard duties have to be at the wall by seven. They would normally be roaring around and arguing over someone being too long in the bathrooms."

"You're right." Yasmin gasped. She reached for a light switch but Wade grabbed her arm.

"Leave the light off," he said. "If a Guardian sees a light go on they'll realize somebody is awake."

"So what do we do?"

"Check to see if everyone in the apartment is asleep then I'll check outside. You wait here."

"No," Yasmin said. "We stay together. If the whole town is asleep we have to get out."

Wade nodded. "I guess but we'll have to be very careful. If the Guardians have machines that can speak in every building they might also have things to see us."

"Like what?"

"Powerful binoculars attached to buildings. We need to stay away from the roads."

Wade was right. High above every street and the main roads of Buckoway, video cameras sent pictures back to a control room in the heart of the castle. None though, picked up the two friends as they sneaked out into a small backyard behind their apartment. The small service lane was filled with rubbish bins, an occasional cart and several rats that scurried away from them. The lane crossed a small drain that headed downhill to the ring road. Thick shrubs overhung the drain on each side like a tunnel.

"Come on," Wade said and took Yasmin's hand. "We'll follow this down."

He helped Yasmin down to the rocks below. After the long dry summer there was a mere trickle of water so she didn't even get her feet wet. As she waited for Wade to join her, the girl listened to the sounds, or rather lack of them. Buckoway was hushed, no wagons rumbled by, no voices came from the adjacent buildings and there was no shout from the town crier calling out the time. It was scary.

Wade slid in beside her. "Okay," he whispered. "Keep under the overhanging bushes. If we go down the middle, someone looking out an apartment window may see us."

"Nobody is awake, Wade," Yasmin replied. "There may be spying machine eyes watching, though."

*

"They lied," Fyddal whispered as he stared down at the lava filled valley. The liquid was cooler now and the edges had changed from orange to brown. "No weapons of mass destruction are allowed on Quargis. We were told all the maximum settings were disabled."

"I'm sorry, Fyddal. I never knew this would happen," Madison said. "We only wanted to stop the soldiers before they found us."

"And even without the drone they would have traced us," Drety said.

"How many of our kind were down there, Madison?" Fyddal asked.

"Fifteen to twenty, I guess. They were lined right along the roadside and had some tracking gear. If we hadn't fired I'm sure they would have traced us within a few moments."

Fyddal nodded. "I'm not blaming you Madison. If it wasn't for your quick actions I'm certain we'd have been caught by now."

"And I hope you appreciate that," Kirsty snapped.

"We do, Kirsty," Drety said. "Some of our friends would have been down there, that's all. The Earth community on this planet isn't that big, you know."

"Yeah, everything's screwed up isn't it?" Kirsty muttered.

"But we're safe," Risa said. "Please let us not fight. We need to remain friends."

"And we shall," Madison said. She walked over and tucked her arms around the aliens. "I'm glad you two are with us," she said. "We are the citizens of this planet and will only survive if we help each other." She smiled at Risa. "Wasn't that what you told me earlier?"

"Something like that," Risa said.

"Right," Fyddal said. "What do we do now?"

"The problem is how much do the Guardians in Buckoway know?" Hamish said. "We'll need to assume they know about these transporters and will be waiting for Madison to arrive home."

"How many of my kind are there in Buckoway?" Fyddal asked.

"I'm not sure," Hamish said. "They seldom come out of the castle. Only three or four, I'd say."

"There are eight that I know of," Sean said. "I made a note whenever I met a new one. There could me more but I doubt it."

Hamish looked up at Fyddal. "Would they know you and your good lady, Lad?"

"By the old rules, no for photographs and television were banned along with motor vehicles but now so many of the protocols have been broken they could easily have digital visuals of both of us."

"Pity," Hamish said. "We need to capture the Guardians before they harm us. The longer we wait, the greater the chance will be that reinforcements will be brought in. I just though that having Fyddal and Drety with us when we arrive at the castle could just give us that edge. We'll get the wagons and head on towards Buckoway. When Thinrisodor shows up we'll ask his advice," Hamish said.

"And how do you know he'll show up?" Kirsty added.

"He will," Hamish said, "That's perhaps the only certainty we have at the moment."

*

CHAPTER TWENTY-ONE

When Yasmin and Wade reached the circle road inside the wall they crawled up the side of a concrete culvert and peeped out. The only thing visible was a wagon across the road. Four oxen stood placidly chewing their cuds and the two men sat slumped over in the driver's seat. The rest of the road was empty.

"What shall we do?" Yasmin asked.

"See those shrubs on the other side. From there we can make our way along to the main gate. If the guards are asleep we can just walk out. Better still, why don't we take that wagon?"

"Don't be stupid," Yasmin retorted. "There is no way we could even get the oxen moving let alone drive them out the gate."

Wade grinned. "You're right but I still think we can walk out the gate."

"And how do we get across the road?"

"Run like hell," Wade said.

"Well, okay..."

"Come on," Wade said and went to climb the small fence by a footpath.

He straddled the fence when a loudspeaker howled. '*I suggest that the citizen continues to climb the fence and afterwards sits on the footpath and goes to sleep,*' the pair heard.

"Oh hell," Wade cursed and began to climb back.

'*I suggest that the citizen stops, holds his arms out wide and waits for a Guardian patrol.*' the loudspeaker blared out.

"Damn you, buster," Wade grumbled and dived down the drain side of the fence just as a rock came flying through the air.

It missed Wade but landed just below Yasmin's foot. It wasn't a stone but a round metal object that hissed. A cloud of smoke began to pour from the top of it.

"Hold your breath," Wade shouted.

Yasmin reacted. She not only held her breath but also kicked the metal stone. It rolled over and splashed into a puddle of water in the drain. For a second the object bubbled before there was a hiss and it stopped.

Fumes reached Yasmin. Her skin stung and eyes watered but she kept her mouth clamped shut and found Wad had gripped her hand. He pulled her along behind a small wall beneath the fence. She had to breathe and broke into spluttering coughs as the fumes affected her.

"I love you Yasmin," Wade whispered.

"Thanks," she spluttered, "But why the tender moment now?"

"You kicked that gas thing into the water. Only a few fumes got out."

Yasmin continued to cough and splutter, accepted a handkerchief from Wade and wiped her burning eyes and the tears running down her cheeks. His own eyes were red but he had not suffered as much as she had.

"Okay," she whispered a few moments later. "What now?"

"We go back down into the drain. Be careful that you head doesn't show above the concrete. We might not be so lucky if they throw another gas stone at us."

They reached the bottom safely and searched around.

"So we go under the road," Yasmin said.

The drain ran into a small culvert about eighty centimetres in diameter. The water was only a few centimetres deep but sludge and slime covered the lower half of the pipe.

Yasmin knelt down and looked inside. "I can see the other end," she said. "It's a long way."

"Any obstacles?" Wade asked.

"Only this stinking mud." She turned and grinned up at Wade. "Madison would be in her element here. She wouldn't think twice about crawling through it."

"And you?" Wade whispered.

"Oh what the hell," the girl said and slid into the drain.

She wriggled forward into the culvert and found she could bring her knees forward into a crawling position.

"I'm right behind you, Yasmin," Wade called in a soft voice.

God the place stunk! Yasmin spluttered again. Probably some of those gas fumes still hung around. She wiped a damp hand across her face and the cold water made her feel a little better. Ahead, was the distant circle of the far end but it looked a kilometre away. She crawled forward and ignored the mud that clutched her blouse and skirt. Drips from above rolled down her neck and soon her shoes were squelching in mud.

She continued on. Her knees felt raw and was sure something sharp cut across her arm. With every metre, the air smelt fresher and the distant exit became larger until she could see beyond it. Outside, there appeared to be leaves and pale light. It could even be the sky. Water and mud splashed in her face and she knew her hair was plastered with the stuff.

"Wade," she called back. "I don't think you'll like the look of me when we reach the other end."

"Beautiful girls don't stop being beautiful just because they're covered in mud," Wade's voice echoed back. "You're doing better than me anyway."

Yasmin stopped and managed to glance back. Wade's shoulders almost filled the space. He was so large he had to slide rather than crawl along. He glanced up and she saw his white teeth behind a smile.

"We're over half way," she said and continued to crawl forward.

Sunlight! Sunlight shone in on Yasmin as she crawled the last few metres to the exit. Grass, wonderful dry grass grew beside the culvert. She stopped and listened. After all this effort it would be stupid to walk out and have another gas stone hurled at them.

"What's there?" Wade whispered.

"Sunshine and grass."

"I know that but what else?"

"I'll look."

Yasmin crawled two steps forward until her head was out. Oh God, there was a steep drop down a hillside. The water tricked down over mossy rocks in a miniature waterfall. She moved further out, twisted her head and gasped.

"Well?" Wade hissed.

"I can see the wall towering above us, Wade. We're outside the town wall." She almost screamed in delight. "I can see farms and the road through the valley."

She slid out onto tall grass beside thick shrubbery. Wade followed and wriggled up beside her. She was splattered with mud down her front but he was covered in the stuff. Hardly a square centimetre of his clothes or body was clean.

"How about a sloppy kiss," he chuckled and grabbed her in his arms.

"We did it," Yasmin whispered and kissed him on muddy lips. "No damn Guardians are going to stop us now, are they?"

"They wouldn't dare," Wade chuckled. "Come on, we'll follow the wall along away from the main gate. If I remember correctly there's a corner ahead and an area of trees. When we get there we'll rest and decide what to do next."

*

It took almost half an hour of climbing through thick undergrowth beside the now tacky but still hot lava before Madison and her friends could move back onto the road. Except for Madison herself and surprisingly Kirsty, everyone appeared exhausted.

"There they are," Kirsty laughed and grabbed Madison's arm.

In the middle of the road were the two oxen teams and wagons. The oxen looked up saw the humans and, as one, rose to their feet.

"Poor things," Kirsty cried. "I'll get them some food and water." She ran ahead and within a few moments every ox had a basin of water and pile of oats beside it.

"Where does she get the energy?" Hamish said.

"Sheer adrenaline," Madison replied. "What do you want to bet that once we start moving the wagons she'll be asleep within half an hour."

"Half a crown, lassie," Hamish said and held his hand out.

Madison grinned and shook it. "You're on but the clock doesn't begin until the wagons start moving."

"Aye Lass, that's a fair deal."

Everyone went and helped Kirsty give the animals a rub down. Afterwards they gathered in Madison's wagon to share a meal and discuss what to do if they didn't met Thinrisodor. Their plan was somewhat vague but they agreed that Madison, Drety and Fyddal would hide inside the wagons when they went though the main gate. It was very rare for the guards to search a wagon when it carried supplies for the castle.

"Right," Hamish said. "Of course when we meet Thinrisodor he may have updated news if anything has happened in Buckoway."

"Kirsty," Madison said in almost a sly voice. "You don't mind if Hamish joins us on our wagon. He wants to keep an eye out behind us. Norris said he'd go up on the front wagon with Sean."

Kirsty shrugged. "Sure," she said. "You can help drive if you wish, Hamish."

The ginger bearded man caught Madison's eye. "No Lass, you help Madison there. I'll be okay at the back."

"Want to make it a whole crown?" Madison whispered out the side of her mouth when Kirsty gave an almighty yawn as she climbed aboard.

"No, Lass. A half will do. I don't want to run you short."

Twenty-five minutes later Madison hissed back at Hamish. "Get up here, quickly," she said in an urgent voice.

"What is it Lass?" Hamish whispered as he moved through the wagon.

"Look!" Madison said and smirked across to where Kirsty was sound asleep with her head leaned against the side of the wagon. "Half a crown I believe it was."

Hamish broke into a broad smile, dug into his pocket, brought out a large silver coin and placed it in her extended palm. "Now don't go spending it all on wine, young men and song, will yah?"

Madison laughed. "I've heard that expression before but I'm sure it went slightly different, somehow."

"Possibly. Who wants to pay for music these days?"

*

When they reached the outer farms around Buckoway, Sean pulled the front wagon to the side of the road and waited while Madison came in behind him. He climbed down and walked back to the wagonmistress and Kirsty who woke up when the motion of their wagon stopped.

"I don't like it, Madison," Sean said.

Madison glanced around the fields where the sun shone and animals grazed. Cows mooed in a nearby field.

"What is it, Sean" she asked.

"This is Grant Domney's farm. He has one of the largest and most well looked after dairy farms in Buckoway."

"So?"

"He's not here and the cows haven't been milked."

Hamish joined them and looked at Madison. "Sean's right, Lass and where's Thinrisodor? I was sure he'd turn up before we left the valley forest."

"What do you suggest?" Madison asked.

However before she could answer Risa climbed out the back of the front wagon and ran up to them. "Norris has sent me back," she said in a rush of words. "Someone is up ahead. He said to be careful for they don't look like ordinary farmers."

Madison frowned and nodded at Kirsty. Both girls reached for their bows while Hamish and Sean stepped back to the side of the road. "Get those in the front wagon out," Hamish ordered.

A moment later Drety, Fyddal and slipped out the rear of the wagon. The two aliens joined Hamish in a small dip beside a roadside hedge while Norris came over to Madison and Kirsty.

"They aren't aliens or Muds," he said.

"So who are they?" Kirsty asked.

"Locals."

"So what's the problem?" Madison added.

"Their behaviour. They're sneaking along that hedge, not walking on the road. If they hadn't crossed an open gateway in a gap I would have missed them. They look more scared of us than we are of them."

Madison nodded. "Tell Hamish and to circle around behind the hedge. We'll go along the road."

"Is that wise?" Norris asked.

"Probably not," Madison retorted. She turned. "Coming, Kirsty?"

The other girl nodded. Together the pair walked out on the road with their bows held on full alert."

"Oh damn," Norris gasped. He pulled a ray pistol from his pocket, saw it was set on stun and ran after the two women.

*

When Hamish dived through a gap in the hedge he jumped in fright. There squatting on the ground was Thinrisodor with his spear held ready for action.

"Oh hell," Hamish whispered. "Don't do that!"

Thinrisodor lowered his spear and grimaced. "I wondered why the cows were not milked," he said. "Then I saw your friends coming. They're scared and I wanted to find out why."

"My friends?"

"Your smelly friends," Thinrisodor said in a monotone. "I've never seen newcomers look so filthy."

*

Madison and Kirsty with their bows held ready, almost marched up the road. If they were nervous it didn't show for they gave the impression to anyone watching that they were bow mistresses of the Buckoway Guards, determined and not about to be intimidated by anybody. Only the young man who followed with a strange weapon in his hand looked fidgety and nervous.

The road was empty, the sun shone and the cows mooed.

Fifty metres in front of their wagons Madison stopped and turned. Near her was the gap in the hedge where an old wooden gate stood closed.

"You have ten seconds to show yourselves," Madison cried out, her voice cold and determined.

Kirsty bit on her lip and dug Madison on the arm. Something moved beyond the hedge.

194

"Six... seven, " Madison called out and a pulled her bow string back.

"My God it's Madison," a high-pitched female voice screamed. "We're coming Madison."

"Put that goddamn bow down," a male voice called out. "We've been shot at too often this morning."

Madison frowned and turned to Kirsty. The voices were familiar. Her frown relaxed when two mud covered people appeared at the gate.

"Oh my God, Yasmin and Wade. What are you doing way out here and why are you covered in mud?"

"We had to warn you," Yasmin gasped. "You must not go any closer to Buckoway."

*

Grant Domney's farm was the closest and best temporary place to go. The two wagons were driven into a barn, the oxen unhitched and let go in an empty field. The friends found a small kitchen and living area attached to the barn and gathered around to hear Yasmin and Wade's story.

"They're anticipating your arrival with the new equipment," Fyddal said.

"But why put everyone asleep at this time?" Madison asked.

"There could be a number of reasons," Fyddal continued. "They may know about the destruction of the convey or it could be something they were going to do anyway."

"And if that was the case, what would they do next?" Madison asked.

"There is a code for every newcomer. They'd could call your kind up to the castle in batches and begin transferring themselves into your bodies. They're probably expecting the convey to arrive." Fyddal shrugged. "I guess more of our people will be brought in over land or even by air. After the equipment is installed every citizen of Buckoway could be absorbed within a couple of days."

"Killed is the word," Kirsty snorted.

"Okay, what would happen to all the bodies left after they've taken the new ones over?" Madison asked

"They'd be incinerated." Hamish cut in. "The crematorium under the castle is far too large for natural deaths in the town. I asked about it once and was told it was built in anticipation of a much bigger population or another fight with Thinrisodor's people."

"My people make good scapegoats," the Mud chief muttered.

"There is one urgent problem," Drety said. "The equipment in the castle can be adapted to transfer minds. If the news of the convoy's destruction has reached them, those in the castle may not wait."

"What do you mean?" Madison asked.

"They could transfer into newcomer's bodies and you would not know."

"If that happened can it be reversed."

"If the memories taken are kept on in the computer they could. Also if their old bodies were not incinerated they could be reactivated." Drety said. "I wouldn't count on that though. The plan is for our kind to keep the new bodies we are placed in. There would be no reason to keep the newcomers' minds or our useless bodies, for that matter."

"So we couldn't trust a newcomer in Buckoway because they might be an alien?" Hamish said.

"There would only be a few," Drety said. "But yes you will have to be careful."

"And you two," Norris said. "Are you still prepared to help us?"

Fyddal glanced at Drety who nodded. "We can't go back. Sure, we'd love new active bodies but not at the price of killing all of you. We will help you and once peace is restored we may find a new way to become whole again."

"What else can we do to prove that we are sincere?" Drety whispered. "If our roles were reversed I wouldn't trust us either."

"So," Madison said. "Let's go and free Buckoway."

*

There was some disagreement over what should be done. Norris and Kirsty suggested it would be too dangerous for Madison to go into Buckoway but she insisted everyone else was in as great a danger as she was.

"Anyway if I'm killed here, I can just carry on with my other life on Earth."

"But you could die in both places Lass?" Hamish said.

"I guess," Madison admitted. "But I'm coming with you to Buckoway and that's that!"

A slight cough made everybody look up. A Mud warrior stood at the door beside Sean who had been keeping guard. Thinrisodor stood and walked over. The new man spoke in urgent whispers to the chief who listened and replied. The warrior nodded and disappeared as quickly as he came.

"What's wrong?" Madison asked.

"Perhaps something right," Thinrisodor said. "We have stopped another wagon with no oxen on the road north of here." He flicked his eyes across at Fyddal and Drety. "Old habits don't always change quickly. We are used to trusting nobody."

"What is it?" Drety appeared pale.

"My commands only stretch to the Sumatti. This northern road goes through Sneednim lands."

"Tell us, Thinrisodor," Madison said.

"There was one wagon, larger than the ones we found. The five crew were all killed."

Drety nodded but reached out for Fyddal's hand.

"And this transporter?" Hamish said.

"It is waiting. Our visitor was a Sneednim warrior. He said Cannad still respects the punctured flag. Everyone who travels with the *Maidens of Granite* will not be harmed if they want to go and remove this wagon."

"How far away is it?" Madison asked.

"The fastest way is over the northern hills. It is a forty minute walk but there is no trail for your oxen."

*

"Nobody told us the forty minutes was by a warrior running downhill." Kirsty muttered almost an hour later as she wiped her face and stared up at another steep slope through the fir trees. There was no trail at all and without Thinrisodor's guidance they would have been hopelessly lost.

"I shall go now," Thinrisodor said. He pointed up the slope Kirsty had just complained about. "That ridge is the boundary of our lands. From there it is downhill to the road below. Keep the punctured flag in sight."

"Thank you Thinrisodor," Madison said. "Where shall we see you?"

"At Buckoway. I will go now," the chief said and was gone.

"Is it my imagination or is he becoming more talkative?" Hamish said.

"Yeah, a real old gossip," Kirsty said. "He even said goodbye. Usually he just disappears."

"So Risa," Madison said. "You can be a help again."

Risa frowned. "Me! Why?"

"Don't the Sneednim only speak Japanese? If we meet any of them you do the talking."

"Of course." Risa smiled at her friends.

With a new burst of enthusiasm, the group made their way up to the ridge and stared over into a new valley. It looked similar to the one they had travelled on with a narrow mud road along the middle. Sitting all alone on the road was a massive tractor unit. The trailer carried a huge tube that to Madison looked like a missile.

"What is it?" she asked.

"The construction unit," Fyddal said. "There were rumours that they were finding the boats and wagons to take newcomers to Buckoway too slow."

Madison frowned. "What does it do?"

"It builds the newcomers bodies from the DNA information programmed in. One of these was used to build all of you. Up until now only the brainwaves were stored in Buckoway. It confirms that they have decided to make Buckoway the main centre."

"And abandon all the other villages like my own?" Risa said.

The alien pair nodded.

"So if it's destroyed no newcomers could be built?" Norris asked.

"No. There are at least three units and others could be landed if necessary."

"From where?" Madison asked.

"The citizens of our Earth will soon be evacuated from the surface onto three orbiting space cities. If the decision is made to make Quargis the new homeworld they can come through a black hole and be orbiting here almost instantaneously. In interspace travel, time has no meaning." Drety said

Again it was only Madison who really understood what Fyddal and Drety were talking about. "But there aren't enough newcomers here to supply your people with bodies," she whispered.

"True," Fyddal said. "Thousands more will be needed." He stared at the transporter. "This could be a new construction unit to increase the production line."

"We are not machines," Madison snapped. "Don't talk of us like that."

Fyddal flushed. "Sorry, Madison," he said. "I didn't mean it that way."

"So let's get down there," Hamish cut in. "You can have all your philosophical arguments later."

*

CHAPTER TWENTY TWO

Madison sat behind the steering wheel of the gigantic eighteen-wheeled vehicle and stared at the controls. They looked similar to those on the *Gentle Warrior* except for four foot pedals. "Do you know how to drive these?" She glanced across at Fyddal in the cab beside her.

He shook his head. "I've never driven land vehicles, only boats."

"But you know how the controls operate?"

"More or less."

"Okay," Madison said. "First of all why do they have four foot pedals?"

Fyddal explained how the vehicle operated. It had the usual accelerator and brakes. The extra foot controls worked like a clutch and semiautomatic gearbox to change into a crawler mode. The hand controls never had an autopilot but there was a small monitor that showed a map of the area and suggested routes to a destination.

When Madison reached up to the sun visor she noticed a card not unlike a credit card or driver's license on Earth attached to it. She took the card down and examined it.

There was a photo of an alien woman with the name *Overofficer Israr Mannil* written beneath it, what looked like a circular barcode and further writing in the alien's language.

"What's this?" she asked Fyddal.

"Identification and driver's license. It probably belonged to the driver."

"I see," Madison said. She slipped the card into her pocket and climbed down to the ground just as Hamish walked around the front of the vehicle.

"There are no alien bodies, Madison," he said. "Not even remains."

"Okay. Does this mean anything?"

Hamish tugged on his beard. "I'm not sure of the local Mud tribe's customs. Perhaps their silver uniforms fascinated them. Usually, the Mud just abandoned bodies of those they kill."

Drety and the others appeared. "The cylinder loaded aboard is definitely a construction unit but it is quite different from those back at our base," Drety said.

"How?"

"It's all self contained and ready to go. There are even solar panels to provide electricity. If we had someone's DNA we could switch it on right now and it would begin creating a body."

Kirsty stared at Madison. "You stick a piece of skin in one end and your whole body is created out the other. Isn't that right, Drety?"

"Not quite," the alien girl said. "The DNA of newcomers have all been received by our satellite station as electronic data."

"And is it capable of transferring minds from one physical body to another?" Madison asked.

"Oh yes," Drety said. "I guess that's why it's being taken to Buckoway."

Madison scowled. "We'll unhitch the trailer unit and blow the whole thing up," she said.

"Hold on Lassie," Hamish said. "Let's not rush into things. We may be able to turn this to our advantage."

Madison stared at him and relaxed a little. "Okay, Hamish, what have you got in mind this time?"

"I reckon we should sit down, have some food our alien friends have so kindly left for us and weigh up all the alternatives we have at our disposal."

Norris chuckled. "He's beginning to talk like you, Madison," he said.

"That's for sure," Kirsty added in a perfect imitation of Sean's accent.

*

With Madison at the wheel, the giant tractor unit drove through the silent farmlands and up to the raised main gate of Buckoway.

"Well here goes," Madison whispered. She kicked the right hand pedal to engage low gear and glance in the rear vision mirror. The cylinder behind blocked any view but she was more interested in seeing that it was straight as the transporter edged forward between the narrow walls. She hoped that there would be room for the massive vehicle to clear the wall before she had to turn onto the ring road. To be wedged in the gateway could ruin their plans. They were beyond the overhanging parapet adjacent to a guardhouse when movement caught her eye.

"Kirsty, Risa. Someone's there!" she hissed

The two girls were crouched out of sight behind the front seats with ray pistols set on stun and ready to fire.

200

"You'll do fine," Kirsty whispered back.

Four aliens in silver uniform stood around the front of the vehicle. One man had his hand in a stop signal while the other three stood by with ray guns drawn but facing the ground.

The leader walked up and stared in complete surprise at the driver. He reached for his ray pistol and gasped. "Madison Evans! But how?"

"Relax sergeant. I am in that traitor's body, that is true but won't we all be transferred over soon." Madison held out the driver's license. "My name is Overofficer Israr Mannil. Check your data file if you wish."

The sergeant nodded at his troopers who stood back but raised their weapons. "Check who is in charge of this transporter, Dellen," he said.

The trooper took a ball from his pocket and shook it into a notebook page. He tapped one side and read the writing that appeared beside a photograph. "Overofficer Israr Mannil is the name here, sergeant but there is no report of her transformation into Madison Evan's body."

"Of course not," Madison snapped. "Haven't you heard the latest directives?"

"And what are they, Overofficer Mannil?"

"A small group of traitors allied to Evans has managed to intercept our command signals. Do you really want them to know I'm in her body?" She opened her hand casually to the other front seat passengers. "Ask my underofficers if you don't believe me."

The sergeant caught Drety's stern look and hesitated. "That will not be necessary, Ma'am. We expected the convoy to arrive first, that's all," he said.

"It was destroyed sergeant. The traitors with Mud warriors intercepted it. We were lucky to catch the two oxen wagons and capture the woman whose body I now occupy."

"And the others from the wagons, Overofficer?"

"They are unconscious and in the back. Two resisted and were wounded so will need repairs before they can be used." Madison looked grim and stared at the sergeant. "Aren't you taking a risk being here in your military uniforms?"

"Buckoway is asleep, Overofficer. We received the orders from headquarters..."

"Right," Madison retorted. "Now perhaps you could help guide this transporter onto the ring road. There isn't a lot of room."

"Of course, Overofficer Mannil."

The four aliens placed their ray guns away, moved back across the road and guided the transporter forward. Madison's expression remained stern but relief flowed through her body as she drove slowly forward across the ring road, turned right and began to straighten the vehicle. The construction unit followed and cleared the town walls by centimetres until the whole vehicle was on the ring road.

Just as the four aliens moved across to speak to Madison, rays shot out from small holes in the cylinder and they collapsed onto the road. A door at the rear opened. Hamish, Norris, Wade and Sean ran out. Within seconds the aliens were dragged back inside the cylinder and the men shut the door.

"Four down, four to go," Kirsty whispered in Madison's ear. "I knew you could do it."

"Yeah. When they checked my story out, I thought it was all over. One guard was ready to fire, you know."

"Before he fired I would have," Risa whispered. "I had him in my sights."

*

The road that headed up to the castle was steep and narrow so Madison was content to let the transporter crawl up at a walking pace. Hamish had joined the other girls behind the front seat and gave Madison instructions when they reached the castle wall. "The back entrance we used will be too narrow for this transporter," he said. "Our wagons can barely fit through."

"The main entrance isn't much bigger. We might have to stop and see what happens." She turned towards the main entrance and stopped when it came into sight. "What the hell," she muttered and searched around for a horn. On her second attempt a loudspeaker sounded above them and everyone jumped in fright.

"Well they know we're here," Madison said when Hamish muttered an oath.

"They do," Fyddal said in a calmer voice. "Look next to the gate?"

The wall to the right of the narrow entrance slid aside to reveal a wide entrance.

"The stone wall's a fake" Kirsty muttered.

"Yeah, like most things about the castle," Madison retorted.

She gripped the steering wheel and drove the transporter through this new entrance. When they were through, the gate slid back to become a stone wall again but another gigantic door slid open next the main entrance of the castle itself to reveal a long down ramp.

"Can you see anybody?" Hamish muttered

"Nobody," Fyddal replied.

202

"They want us to drive inside," Madison said.

"Don't do it," Kirsty said.

"Why?"

"It's too easy. They may have realized something happened at the main gate. Once we drive down that ramp there is no way we can get out again. Swing around the courtyard and face the way we came in."

Madison glanced at Fyddal,

"Kirsty's right," he said. "It would be logical for them to come out and greet us. After all, the towns asleep and they control it."

"When you stop, slip over the back, Madison," Drety said. "I'll take your place in the driver's seat. Next time we mightn't be able to convince them you're that overofficer."

"Then what?" Madison asked.

"We wait," Drety said. "If they're waiting inside and see the transporter just sitting out here in the courtyard, won't they become curious?"

"Or suspicious," Hamish said.

Drety flushed. "It was only a suggestion," she said.

"We'll do it," Madison added. She turned to Hamish. "When we stop I want you to sneak out the passenger door. Get back to the cylinder and tell the others what's happening. If four come out stun them all."

"And if they don't all come out?" Hamish said.

"It's Drety's turn to do the bluffing."

*

Madison swung the transporter around the courtyard in a tight circle, stopped so the cab faced the new gate and turned the engine off, Hamish slipped out and walked back to the cylinder. Five minutes ticked by before a speaker in the cab burst into a staccato of alien language. Fyddal nodded at Drety who reached for a button on the dashboard, pressed it and replied in the same language. The voice came back and there was a brief exchange of conversation.

"They asked why we never drove inside. I said I was going to back the transporter in but needed them to guide me." Drety frowned. "The person talking sounded nervous rather than angry."

"So what did they say?"

"They said I was meant to drive straight in, not back in but I said my orders were to back in so I could drive out to pick up the gear from your wagons that were stuck in mud on the road."

"Good thinking, Drety," Madison said.

"Psst," Kirsty interrupted. "They're coming out."

Four people dressed in ordinary Buckoway clothes walked out the castle's main door and headed across the playground."

"I know one," Madison whispered. "It's the receptionist I talked to when I first arrived here. I don't think I've seen her in town since then. Start the engine, Drety "

"But I can't drive," Drety spluttered.

"You won't need to but if you don't start the engine they may become suspicious. Fyddal why don't you lean out and give them a wave."

"Good idea."

The end was almost an anticlimax. When the four saw Fyddal waving they seemed to relax and walked across the courtyard towards them; right into a hail of stun rays fired from the cylinder. The four collapsed onto the stones. The men and Yasmin jumped out the back. Yasmin ran towards them while the men fanned out. Two went in the main door and two ran down the ramp where the transporter was meant to go.

"It's no fun in that big empty cylinder with the unconscious guards." Yasmin said. "Can I come into the cab?"

"Sure," Drety said.

Yasmin climbed the small ladder and crawled in behind the front seat. "It's getting a bit too nervy for me," she said and grinned at Madison and Kirsty beside her. "Why's Drety driving?"

"Oh, Madison didn't want to take the transporter down the ramp so I said I'd whip it back for her."

"But I thought... " Yasmin noticed the grinning faces and laughed. "Okay, joke's on me. So everything's okay?"

"We think so," Madison said. "Sean was pretty certain there we only eight aliens in Buckoway."

*

Hamish and the others returned to say they found nobody else awake. "There are half a dozen newcomers asleep in the reception area but nobody is in the cellar or the top floors of the castle." He stared at Madison. "You were right, you know."

"How?"

"Remember the very first day here and you realized something was wrong with the place?"

Madison nodded. "I also took exception to the word remember ... remember."

Hamish grinned. "Anyway, we haven't searched everywhere but it appears everything here except floor one and the crematorium in the cellar is of alien design with all sorts of monitors and equipment. You, Fyddal and Drety will have to sort that lot out."

"Yeah," Norris said. "That crematorium is only a tiny section of the cellar. The part we were meant to drive into is huge." He shrugged. "Bigger than the area of the castle above it."

"I think it's designed to take several of these cylinders but at the moment it is just a huge open space with wires all through the roof rafters," Sean added.

"So I can drive the transporter down the ramp and have plenty of turning room?" Madison asked.

"For sure," Sean said. "It's bigger than this courtyard,"

Madison grinned at Drety. "Do you want to drive the transporter inside?"

The alien girl shook her head and slid across to the middle seat. Madison climbed over and started the engine. She still found the entrance ramp narrow but there was ample clearance on the sides and above for their vehicle.

"It was designed to take this cylinder," Kirsty said from the far passenger seat. "Everything has been planned for it from the very beginning."

"I'd say so," Madison said.

The area they entered looked like an underground car park on Earth except that the roof was higher. Rows of electric lights cast a dull glow over the concrete floor and pillars. As Hamish had said, the ceiling was a mass of steel frames with wires everywhere. Again, this reminded Madison of similar buildings on Earth. She had once looked through a half constructed laboratory block at university that looked the same. A builder explained that by having a huge open space supported by just a few beams, internal walls could be added later and it was easy to change them around without affecting the building's strength. She had returned a couple of months later to find offices and lecture theatres everywhere with no sign of the bleak concrete and the steel superstructure.

She drove around to a convenient spot, stopped. And heard the outside door close with a faint rumble.

"There's another priority," Fyddal said when everyone gathered by the transporter. "The first guards we stunned will be waking soon. We need to find a place to keep them secure."

"And we need to wake everyone up too." Madison said.

"We can help there," Drety said. "There must be a broadcasting studio somewhere in this building."

"And those rocks that let off sleeping gas need to be cut off," Wade said. "They might be activated automatically when everyone begins moving around."

Yasmin coughed. "I need to go home first," she whispered.

"And why's that?" Wade asked.

"You need to come too, Wade, " Yasmin said. "Don't you think a shower and clean clothes would help? I feel as stinky as you look."

*

An hour later the citizens of Buckoway awoke to find it was not early morning but a hot summer's day with the sun high in the sky. They did not realize but Madison had carefully worded the instructions over the loudspeakers so nobody would panic but regard the missing hours as a slight inconvenience. Also incorporated in the broadcast was the final *you must remember* suggestion that cancelled all acceptability to any other post hypnotic suggestions. Only the eight aliens found their freedom curtailed when they awoke to find themselves in an old fashioned but secure cell that Hamish found in the castle's guardhouse.

As well as the loudspeaker-broadcasting unit, Fyddal and Drety found that electronic surveillance cameras around the city were linked to sixteen monitors. From this control room every street in the town as well as much of the farmland around could be brought into view.

"What do you want done with this room, Madison?" Fyddal asked.

Madison glanced around at her friends who all nodded. "Do the same as we did with the inside of the cylinder," she said. "Melt it down."

Fyddal nodded and everyone moved out into the corridor. Four people set their ray pistol to a second level and fired into the room. Rays shot out and the equipment, grew red, and began to melt. The result was similar to the valley attack except that the walls, windows and ceiling remained intact. Within seconds everything in the console room was reduced to flowing streams of smoking lava. The molten lava would be hot for hours but the covert electronic monitoring devices would no longer encroach on the lives of Buckoway citizens

CHAPTER TWENTY THREE

High above Earth's equator the minute black hole expanded and a two-metre diameter sphere spun out. It did not go into orbit as the observers from the top secret California satellite tracking station predicted but instead approached the atmosphere in an entry orbit that computers predicted would bring it down over North America.

More, though, was to come. Within minutes the black hole expanded again and another alien craft arrived. This one was different. It was shaped like an oversized space shuttle with delta wings, pointed nose and high tail. Digital visuals showed a streamlined windscreen and octagonal windows along the craft's side.

Scientists stared in awe, as the new alien ship appeared to follow the smaller one. Just before the sphere entered the Earth's atmosphere the larger craft moved in behind. A burst of yellow light cut from the larger craft and the smaller one glowed for a second before it disintegrated.

Rocket engines in the larger craft fired as if it was attempting to leave the atmosphere but its downward journey became more pronounced.

"It's fired rockets a to avoid burning up in our atmosphere," one scientist muttered as the scene unfolded on a monitor in front of him.

For forty minutes hundreds of the Earth's scientists could only watch as the space vehicle plummeted down over the Pacific Ocean. The vision looked like a meteorite that entered United States airspace at a speed that would have melted any Earth made space vehicles. At thirty thousand metres the alien ship's engines fired again and it slowed and stopped dropping. Now, what looked like steam came out of vents in the wings and the craft began to fly like a conventional aeroplane directly towards central California. It was three a.m. local time.

Even before F16 Falcons scrambled from two air force bases the control tower at Edwards Air Force Base received an incoming call on an emergency frequency.

"This is incoming space craft New *Dawn* requesting an emergency landing at your Edwards Air Force Base space port. Please acknowledge," said a clipped English voice.

The senior officer in the control tower tapped the air control operator on the shoulder and reached for his microphone. "Edwards Air

Force Base Control Tower," he said in a terse voice. "Who are you and what is the emergency, *New Dawn*?"

*

Norris awoke, switched on the bedside lamp and answered the telephone. His watch said four twenty.

"Colonel Brad Davis speaking. I need to speak to Madison."

Norris frowned. "Norris Moore here. She's asleep Colonel Davis," he said in a cold voice. The caller could at least apologize for waking him up or say please. "You know she is never awake until six -thirty."

The colonel's voice softened a little. "There has been an emergency, Norris. When she wakes up tell her there will be immediate transportation waiting for her."

"Okay. Is there any other message?"

"Just tell her to be dressed and waiting. I will explain everything when I arrive."

By dawn, police and army vehicles closed off the street in front of Madison's apartment. Madison awoke, listened to Norris's explanation and stared out the window.

"Oh God, it must be important. Look Norris?"

An air force helicopter hovered above the empty road and the district shape of Brad Davis could be seen gazing out the cockpit window.

"He looks frustrated," Norris said.

"Yeah," Madison said. "Offer him a coffee and tell him I'm having a shower before I go flying off in that dumb helicopter of his."

"But..."

"He can wait ten minutes, Norris. If he doesn't like that it's just too bad." She flung the blankets aside and headed for the bathroom with her thoughts more on the happenings at Buckoway than back on Earth.

*

When Madison emerged from the bathroom twenty moments later she smiled at Brad Davis and ignored his scowl "I hope Norris offered you some breakfast," she said.

"Something's happened," Davis retorted. "I'll tell you about it in the chopper."

"So why is my attendance so important, Colonel Davis?"

"Your friends have arrived here in person and won't come outside a force field until they talk to you."

"My friends? What friends?"

"Aliens," Davis hissed. "Their space craft made an emergency landing at Edwards Air Force Base."

Madison frowned. "You aren't kidding are you?"

"Not if we're talking about two metre tall people with short hair and metallic space suits."

"Oh hell," Madison gasped. She turned to Norris. "I'd better go," she said and scrambled aboard the helicopter.

A few moments later they landed at a military airfield where a Learjet waited on the tarmac. As soon as Madison and Davis were aboard, the executive jet took off and headed south.

*

As they flew in over Edwards Air Force Base Madison knew where the alien craft was, not by its appearance but by the mass of vehicles that surrounded it. Even two helicopters hovered immediately above the craft. Fire trucks, ambulances, jeeps and even two tanks surrounded a slightly blacken silver vehicle that reminded her of a space shuttle. The delta winged craft sat on a dozen or more tyres with a side door swung up and a ramp lowered to the ground.

"Yeah, that's one of the alien craft all right," she said.

"You've seen one like it?" Brad asked.

"No but it looks similar to those barges I told you about. That door is identical to the one on *Gentle Warrior*." She turned to the colonel. "These aliens are probably hostile. Their actions on Quargis are anything but friendly."

The colonel gave a slight smile. "They shot down another spacecraft that they said contained thousands of those bees. Apparently they never intended to come here but chased this other craft through the black hole and got too close to our gravitational pull. It seems they have not been damaged and only need fuel to be able to return home."

"Distilled water?" Madison asked.

"How did you know that?"

"A guess,"

Davis frowned. "Is there something that you haven't told me, Madison?" he asked.

"I'm having a busy time on the other side. I was going to tell you everything but when you decided to almost drag me out of my apartment I decided to wait and see what was happening here." She frowned. "I must admit it doesn't add up. I knew thousands of bees were going to be released on Earth but can't understand why would they destroyed the sphere bringing them here."

"Honour before Humanity."

"Who said that?"

"The alien we were talking to. It seems he doesn't agree with the methods used to restore humanity to their worlds. Can you make sense of what they are saying?"

Madison nodded. "Yes," she whispered. "Perhaps these people could be friends after all."

*

Their helicopter landed beyond the outer perimeter of vehicles and an air force officer approached, saluted the colonel and brought them up to date.

"They will only allow you in Ma'am," he said to Madison. "We have spoken to two men who appear unarmed but I wouldn't trust them."

"Thank you lieutenant," Madison said and followed the man through a gap between two tanks.

"You walk up to that yellow pole they've stuck in the ground and wait for further instructions."

Madison nodded. She felt strange. Her heart raced and she mentally reached for her bow. That was stupid, as she never used bows and arrows on Earth. The alien ship stood silent and empty while behind her, the spectators seemed to hold their breath as she reached and touched the yellow pole.

"Madison Evans, sometimes known as Maiden of Granite?" The voice came from an embedded speaker in the pole.

"I'm Madison Evans, yes."

"Can you name something unique in the other world, Madison?"

Madison coughed and stared ahead at the still empty concrete area around the space ship. "How about the Buckoway Castle with a crematorium in its cellar or Thinrisodor, the Sumatti warrior?"

"You don't call them Muds, Madison?"

"They are proud people and that is a derogatory term. In no way are they inferior to us."

The speaker became silent and Madison waited until she saw an alien appear at the door. The crowd behind gave an audible gasp at the man's height and metallic blue one-piece uniform. She frowned. This was a different colour than the silver ones Drety and the others used.

210

The man walked up and stopped a metre in front of her. "My name is Knoge Jelta and I am from the planet Pynoto. Have heard of it?"

"No."

"Sometimes it is called Earth 4"

Madison thought back. Wasn't that one that the one Drety described as backward planet? "You've colonized it I suppose?" she said.

"A small colony that decided to become independent from home rule."

"Hence the blue uniform?"

"True. If you would like to step forward and come inside..."

"I would prefer to remain on the tarmac, thank you."

Knoge nodded. "You will not be harmed but if that is your wish, so be it. However, you will still need to step forward to come inside the force field."

Madison turned to see a marine sergeant right behind her. "I'll be fine, sergeant," she said. "I'm going to walk forward but I doubt if you'll allow you to follow."

"As you say, Ma'am. I shall remain here."

Knoge walked back to the space ship and for a moment disappeared. He appeared a moment later with three white canes. He shook them and three camp chairs unfolded. "Take a seat, Madison," he said. "I guess you want an explanation?"

Madison smiled and sat down. "Many," she said.

"We are on your side, if that simplistic term can be used as an explanation. You are cautious and sceptical and have not learned to trust our species."

" I believe I can trust Drety and Fyddal but they proved their trust."

Knoge studied her. "We found out about this planet by tracing back the path of your satellite that is orbiting Quargis. When we saw the remote craft transporting thousands of those so-called mechanical bees through the black hole between the two worlds we followed and destroyed it. Is that enough proof?"

"It is only your word I'm afraid."

"We do not need human bodies Madison nor do any of our species. All they need is patience and not a quick fix, if I can use one of your clichés?"

"Go on. I'm listening."

Knoge smiled. "I would like you to meet Ajiei Lojir, my partner. " He turned and called out. "Ajiei, come out and meet Madison."

A woman stepped out the door. Like the other aliens she was tall, wore the close fitting metallic uniform and had a mere fuzz of hair.

Madison stood up, swallowed and stared. "Oh hell," she gasped.

This alien woman in a very advanced stage of pregnancy with an enormous swollen stomach and well formed breasts.

"Our first," Ajiei whispered. "It took five years of trying but ... " She flushed. "I'm proof that our species can become fertile again without stealing DNA from this planet."

Madison turned to Knoge. "And are you the father?"

Knoge nodded. "The natural way used by our common ancestors for millions of years."

Madison turned to the woman. "Oh Ajiei, I'm sorry to have stared at you. It's wonderful. It's just that I've seen your people on Quargis. They have no developed sexual organs at all."

"Neither had we," Knoge said.

"But how?"

"On Pynoto our scientists took a different approach. It's a complicated procedure but we found a method to trigger our puberty."

"So why doesn't everyone use it?"

"It involves sticking to a herbal diet to introduce hormones into our bodies and also we have had to have a course of regular injections over several months to neutralize the chemicals in our system that stopped puberty"

"So it's not the quick fix you mentioned earlier."

"Exactly."

Madison nodded and accepted an invitation to sit down again. "I'm sure you never made an emergency landing so why did you need to meet me?"

"I told Knoge you would be an intelligent and astute woman," Ajiei said. "He originally picked your friend Kirsty."

"What do you mean?" Madison asked with suspicion in her voice.

"We needed a way to get into Quargis. It is classified as a quarantine planet and is surrounded by a series of force fields that our space ships cannot penetrate. We needed somebody who could infiltrate that world but remain conscious of their present one."

"So I was selected and stung twice on purpose. It was not by chance?"

Both aliens nodded but remained silent.

"And the aliens who sent the bees?"

"They know about you now but, as far as we know, think it was a equipment failure that caused your condition."

"I should be as angry as hell," Madison retorted. "I suppose, though, that if I wasn't selected I would have still been stung and be like Kirsty and my other friends with no knowledge of my otherself."

"We could not stop the stinging so, yes, that is right," Knoge said.

Madison nodded. "Then I guess I should thank you." She turned her eyes up and looked at one and then the other. "What do you want me to do?"

Knoge glanced at Ajiei and broke into a smile. "You've already started. We can help you in your battle to free Buckoway and Sakita-mura."

"How? You can't keep landing here at Edwards Air Force Base to have a chat."

"No but in Buckoway Castle there is communications equipment that you can use to keep in contact with us. We will give you new codes to program in to set up a secure channel between Quargis and Pynoto."

"Through another black hole?"

"Yes."

"But why should I help you? Sure you've solved your peoples' reproduction problems but how do I know your ultimate aim is as honourable? As far as I know you might want to kill us all off. I could be just a pawn in a master plan of conquest." She stopped and frowned. "Anyway, how do you know as much as you do about me?"

"We have intercepted the transmissions between your two bodies and have electronically reproduced your senses," Ajiei said. "If we had wished we could have killed one or both of your conscious bodies with a flick of a switch."

"And you still can?" Madison retorted. Anger rose inside her.

"No," Knoge said. "Our superiors made us invoke the code of ethics, I guess you'd call it."

"What's that?"

"Once it was established that you were two independent human beings capable of all the higher emotions, a fail safe program was activated. Even if we wanted to, we could not reverse the process to alter either of your personalities," Knoge added. "This is where we differ from the rest of our species. The practice of creating newcomers and then using their bodies is immoral and an abhorrence to our beliefs."

"Well, that's something," Madison muttered. "So how can you help my friends at Buckoway?"

"We can provide scientific and practical advice about how to overwhelm the main base on Quargis. We have already stopped any more bees from coming to this planet," Knoge said.

"And your ultimate aim?"

"To restore peace and a functioning civilization where humans are born, live their natural lives and are followed by their children and grandchildren," Ajiei said.

"Like us here on Earth if we don't ruin our own future?"

"Yes," Ajiei said. Her hazel eyes looked compassionate. "We have to trust you, Madison. I hope you can trust our kind even if it is just Drety and Fyddal. Think of them and how you'd like their lives to become. We can help but cannot do everything."

Madison smiled. "Okay," she said. "What say we go inside and you can tell me what to do." She stood, waved at Colonel Davis outside the force field and walked inside the alien spacecraft.

*

An hour later Madison came out the door and walked over to the impatient Colonel Davis. "A present for you, Brad," she said and handed him a marble ball.

"What is it?"

"Don't worry it won't hurt you. Give it a shake."

In spite of his military training the colonel shook the ball. An electronic page rolled out and stiffened.

"Write on it with any instrument and it'll be converted into a word processor copy, press the top right hand corner and an English language keyboard shows. Touch the ..." She continued with instructions before adding. "Oh yes, they won't need any water after all but advise the helicopters hovering above to move aside."

"Why?" Davis snapped.

"The helicopters will move aside voluntarily or a tractor beam will shift them out of the way."

Davis stared at Madison for a second before he spoke in his radio, the helicopters moved away but the vehicles and infantry remained around the alien craft.

The fuselage door shut and an engine rumbled.

"What the..." Davis roared but, like everyone else on the tarmac that day, he could do nothing except stare.

New Dawn sort of trembled for a moment before it rolled forward. Two blue beams shot from its nose and a tank and fire truck in front were nudged aside. Slowly at first, it taxied along the access way to the main runway. It turned and waited.

When the runway was clear, orange flame shot from vents in the wings and it rocketed forward so fast there was a sonic boom before it reached the edge of the runway. Seconds later it was a mere vapour trail that arched into the sky.

"Thanks, Madison," the colonel said sarcastically. "You will now be debriefed on everything that was said inside that craft."

"There's no need, Colonel Davis," Madison replied. "Press the top left corner of the little ball I gave you and you will have a complete video of everything that was said. Most of it is for my otherself and doesn't affect us here in California. Now, could you give me a lift back to Sacramento, please?"

Davis was so busy trying to read Madison's mood that he never noticed the small communications device shaped like a ballpoint pen that was clipped in her blouse pocket.

*

CHAPTER TWENTY FOUR

Even though Buckoway appeared normal, rumours raged like a summer grass fire. Nobody could explain why three quarters of a day had disappeared from everyone's lives and many people found items affected by time needed attention. Dairy farmers were busy milking and caring for distressed animals, morning markets found supplies had not arrived and many routine jobs had been bypassed.

Workers at the castle arrived to find the gates shut and a sign that redirected them to other government buildings in the town. Inside the cellblock, the eight aliens complained about being held in cells and demanded that they were released in the care of Guardians.

One alien was a sullen male named Turg Ceeler who refused the breakfast brought to him and threatened to prosecute his jailers for the infringement of his personal rights.

"I demand to see the highest ranking Guardian officer at once," he grumbled after his earlier shouting had been ignored.

Sean, who had the job of dealing with this individual, walked to the cell door and unlocked a steel padlock. "You can accompany me," he said.

"Good," Ceeler said. "Who is the senior officer present?"

"The Guardian has been disbanded in Buckoway."

"You can't to this..." The alien clenched his fist in frustrated fury with one hand and reached for his left earlobe with the other.

"The communications device in your ear ring has been removed as has the implant under your left armpit," Sean said. "We are establishing a civilian police force but in the meantime the Border Guard will begin overseeing civilian order in Buckoway. Madison Evans wishes to speak to you."

"Who?"

"You know Madison, I believe."

"Of course," Ceeler muttered "She's a..." He caught Sean's eyes and clamped his mouth shut. "I will not speak to this woman."

"Aye, I agree she's a hero, that's for sure." Sean's eyebrows lowered and his mouth became tight. "You have a choice Overofficer Turg Ceeler and former senior officer of the Buckoway Guardian Outpost. You can either walk out of here and up to an interview room to speak to Miss Evans or we will send Thinrisodor down to interview you." Sean raised his eyebrows. "I assume you've also heard of Thinrisodor?"

Ceeler paled.

"Aye, I believe the Mud systems of persuasion are somewhat crude but effective."

"I'll talk to Madison Evans."

Sean smiled but the expression never reached his eyes. "Thank you. Madison told me you'd be prepared to co-operate with us but I have less confidence in your humanity."

"This is but one small outpost," Ceeler hissed. "If you think..."

Sean was a head and shoulders shorter than Ceeler but was as strong as the oxen he drove. He swung around, seized the alien by the throat and stared into the surprised man's eyes. "We know about your orders to take our bodies and kill every newcomer in Buckoway, former Overofficer Ceeler," he said in a whisper. "If you make one wrong move I shall personally tussle you up, throw you in my wagon and deliver you to Thinrisodor. You are damn lucky Madison shows more remorse than I do." With one mighty heave he hurled the alien across the cell.

*

Ceeler was obstinate but made his lies so plausible that if Madison had had no prior knowledge of the situation she may have even believed him. After an hour she glanced across the table.

"Your apartment in this castle and the rest of this building is confiscated by the Buckoway Border Guard, Turg," she said. "Your personal belongings and those of your companion Margaret, to use her English name, have been transferred to Apartment 93 in the new Sunshine Court complex. You are free to go."

Ceeler blinked half a dozen times before he spoke. "I'm what?" he spluttered.

"We do not prosecute citizens for crimes they have not committed," Madison said. "As far as we know you have done nothing wrong in our town. The Guardians are no more but you are entitled to the rights of any Buckoway citizen."

"What's the condition?" Ceeler asked in a more restrained voice than his earlier bravado.

"If you obey our laws there are none. If you wish to leave Buckoway and make your way back to your base to be with your own kind, you may."

"How?"

Madison shrugged. "Take a wagon, I guess. It was your Guardians who decided not to introduce motorized transport into our society."

"But I'd never get through the Mud lines."

Madison's eyes turned as hard as Sean's did earlier that morning. "Stay and become a useful citizen in our society, Turg Ceeler or leave." She stopped. "Sean will be watching you, of course. Any attempt to...." She smiled. "... But I think he told you what could happen, didn't he?" She stood up and walked out of the room.

*

"Have you heard of an antwire?" Madison asked Drety.

Drety frowned. "Pardon?"

"Antwire!"

Drety glanced at Fyddal. "No I don't think so."

"It's a long range visual and sound communication device your people use."

It was Fyddal who laughed. "Of course. You mean..." He said an unpronounceable word in an alien language that sounded vaguely like antwire.

"I guess," Madison said. "I was told that if we had a... what do you call it..."

"Antwire will do," Fyddal said with a laugh.

"Yeah, well, I was told that if there was an antwire in the castle I could program it to communicate with anybody I wanted."

Drety stared at Madison? "Who told you that?"

Madison remained mysterious. "I guess I'll pronounce this wrong too but have either of you heard of Pynoto?"

"That's the original name for Earth 4," Drety said. "But how did you know that?"

" I was talking to someone from there last night. I think they might be able to help you."

"But that's impossible. That's a closed planet not suitable for habitation. There's been no contact with it for years."

"From here and your home planet, maybe but not from my Earth..."

"By antwire?" Fyddal asked. He used Madison's pronunciation.

"No, in real life. They were just like you two except for one basic difference." Madison grinned at the pair.

"Okay, what are you holding back, Madison?" It was Kirsty who cut into the conversation.

218

"A space ship from Pynoto landed near to where my otherself lives. I met a guy called Knoge and his partner Ajiei. They found my Earth after they traced that satellite that came though the black hole from there. Then they chased and destroyed one of your drones that was going to deliver thousands of those bees to Earth."

"That's good," Drety said in an unconvincing voice.

"But you aren't entirely happy?" Madison said.

Drety flushed. "Of course I am but..." She glanced away. "I'm being selfish I know but we thought that if some DNA could be transferred straight into us we could perhaps gain our fertility without having to kill a newcomer."

"If the newcomer's bodies were created but they weren't awoken in the first place we wouldn't have to kill them to get a new body," Fyddal added. "Is that immoral?"

"But didn't one of you say that wouldn't work?" Madison asked.

"It hasn't up to now." Drety sighed. "I guess we were just dreaming."

"Ajiei is a lot like you, Drety," Madison whispered. "Same height and complexion. She could have been you except for one thing."

"And that is?"

"She is pregnant." Madison said.

The two aliens stared at her in disbelief then at each other before Fyddal replied. "They must have been a different species," he said. "I know Earth 4 has indigenous people like the Mud here."

"No these two were once like both of you but their scientists discovered a way to bring on puberty in adults of your age. Both males and females can become fertile again."

Drety looked excited but Fyddal remained sceptical. "Exactly like us?" he said.

"Yes. It takes patience and time," Madison said and gave the pair all the details she had learned. "Now if we can find one of these antwire thingies..." She grinned at Kirsty... " I can program in the code they gave me and you can talk to them."

"Oh hell," Drety whispered. "If that's true there would be no need to steal DNA from fertile humans. This whole program could be made redundant."

"So let's see if we can find an antwire," Fyddal added. He tucked an arm around Drety and kissed her on the cheek.

*

Floor two of Buckoway Castle was an apartment block with several self-contained apartments, a large recreation centre and several offices. The top floor, though, was entirely different. One tower was set up as a small hospital and equipment to awaken newcomers but the other end was of more interest. Even Drety and Fyddal looked quite overwhelmed at the mass of electronic equipment, computers and monitors while Kirsty, Norris and the others just stared.

"I asked Hamish to shut most things down," Madison said. "We shut off the surveillance and remote ray guns around the town."

"That looks like the main antwire equipment," Fyddal said and walked into a small room that could have been a television control room on Earth.

Kirsty, Norris, Risa, Drety and Madison crowded in beside Fyddal.

"That's the communication console," Fyddal said.

This looked a little like a computer keyboard with the keys marked in the alien language. Several, though, had English letters and numbers taped on them.

"We only need the numbers," Madison said. "Can you start it, Fyddal?"

"Sure!' Fyddal rubbed his hand over a disk and a monitor above them lit up. "Okay, Madison but be careful. We don't want to contact our home base."

Madison nodded and typed in more than a dozen digits.

"How did you remember all those?" Kirsty gasped.

"My telephone number in Sacramento plus my date of birth," Madison said and pressed one final key,

Alien words appeared.

"Oh hell," Drety gasped. "It has accepted your code and is telling you this is an interplanetary connection that is being re-routed though our black hole."

The words faded and were replaced by a spiral of orange dots that changed to yellow.

"When they're all yellow we're though," Fyddal said. "See that glowing thing like an eye just above the monitor?"

Madison nodded.

"That's the visual input. You face that if you want eye contact with the person at the other end."

"And speech?"

"You just talk. If they understand English it goes right through otherwise you can set the language that you want your voice to come out as.

If they speak another language you can change it to English from this end if you wish."

When all the dots were yellow the screen reloaded and a face appeared.

"Hi Ajiei. Madison here from Quargis. Do I look the same?"

The alien girl on screen grinned. "Your face is thinner and you have more of a tan. I guess your Earth body doesn't get as much exercise as you do there."

Madison flushed. "I didn't realize..." She glanced sideways and saw Drety sucking on her lip. "Can you see my friends around me, Ajiei."

"Sure, three of your kind and two of mine." She glanced around. "Hi guys, pleased to see you all. Madison told Knoge and me all about you."

"Where are you?" Madison asked.

"Still on *New Dawn*. There's a traffic hold up and we're in a waiting orbit. Knoge's piloting us in. We should be home in about an hour of your time."

"Madison..." Drety whispered.

Madison grinned. "Ajiei can you move out a little so we can see more than your face?"

Ajiei turned her eyes at Drety and smiled. "I think Madison's been gossiping about me," she said. She reached forward and the vision moved out to show her standing in her tight uniform and very rotund body. "I still have a few weeks to go."

"It is true," Drety gasped. She grabbed Fyddal hand and burst into tears.

"Did Madison tell you it takes a few months but our success rate is over ninety five percent for people our age," Ajiei said in a compassionate voice.

Drety nodded through her tears. "I'll do anything," she sobbed. "I don't know how to thank you."

"Yeah thanks." Fyddal also fought back his emotions.

"Thank Madison. Without her, none of us would have been able to be in contact with each other." Ajiei glanced up beyond the screen. "But I must go. Private black hole conversations have a short time limit." Her eyes switched to Madison. "While we were talking I've sent more data though. You can play it any time and get back if you have any questions."

"Right," Madison said. "I think I have most things sorted out. Say hi to Knoge..."

Without any other warning the screen flickered and was replaced by alien words.

"Our time's up," Fyddal said. He read the writing as it moved across the screen. "Except for an emergency we're only allowed one contact a day."

"I have one more number," Madison said. She reached for the keyboard and typed in another fourteen-digit number. The same spiral of orange dots turned to yellow before a face appeared.

"Oh my God, it is you, Madison," said Kirsty from the monitor. "What have you done to your hair?"

"Oh hell," the Kirsty behind Madison gasped. "Is that me?"

"Kirsty meet Kirsty," Madison grabbed the blonde woman beside her so she was in front of the video-input camera.

"Oh damn," the Kirsty on the screen gasped.

The two Kirstys just stared at each other for a second before one of them, and Madison wasn't really quite sure which one it was, muttered. "It's like looking in a mirror."

"Norris," Madison whispered. "Come and meet your otherself."

The two Norrises looked shy and awkward but managed a few words before the Kirsty on Earth grabbed something and the vision spun around to show the apartment.

"Come and look at sleeping beauty," she yelled.

It was Madison's turn to be embarrassed. There on the screen for everyone to see was herself fast asleep in bed with the blankets tossed aside.

"You are fatter there," Norris said from behind her.

"Norris!" Madison screamed but it was the one on Earth who answered.

"You're beautiful in both places, Madison," he said.

Again, after a few more words, their call was cut off and the same writing came up with the same conditions. Madison turned around and found both Kirsty and Norris looking at the orange spiral, wide eyed in amazement.

"Ajiei and Knoge set it up so we can talk to both worlds," Madison said. "I just wanted to show you that everything I'd told you was true."

"Do we always get around with hardly any clothes on, on your Earth?" Kirsty asked.

Madison laughed. "No, it's the middle of the night there. You were both wearing shortie pyjamas."

"You too," Norris said with a grin. "It didn't hide much."

Madison felt her cheeks burn. "Oh shut up Norris," she muttered.

*

The new Sunshine Court complex consisted of six high-rise blocks designed to accommodate hundreds of newcomers from that Evans woman's home planet. With the new installations in the Buckoway Castle and thousands of newcomers produced, these apartments were constructed to accommodate them until their bodies were required by the citizens in the final evacuation of Turg Ceeler's dying home world. After the transfer into newcomers' bodies they would simply take over the apartments. This had the advantage that newcomers still to be used would notice no difference in the physical appearance of their neighbours. Keeping the entire population asleep was not practical as the newcomers' physical condition began to decay if they were dormant for more than twenty-four hours.

In Apartment 93, Ceeler glowered at the empty flask of highly alcoholic konghun and flung it across the room.

"Stop it," shouted the alien woman in the room with him. "Thank your lucky stars you're not sitting in a castle cell right now."

"Damn the woman," Ceeler muttered and walked over their still unpacked bags and flung clothing everywhere.

"If you want more drink, there is none. Why don't you take a pacifier pill instead? It will calm your nerves."

"Damn my nerves, Margaret. If you hadn't been fooled that day Madison Evans walked into the castle..." He laughed sarcastically. "Fancy thinking she was one of us. One glance at her short developed body should have warned you."

"Don't blame me, Turg. You're the one who told me that some of us had already transferred into newcomers' bodies."

"Yeah Margaret, I know. The damage one newcomer could do because some fool didn't activate the fail-safe injection surveillance monitors."

Margaret frowned. "You said it was sabotaged."

"Well, I had to say something, didn't I? You'd be the last one who'd want to be transferred to that low oxygen planet where you can't go outside without breathing apparatus." Ceeler shrugged. "Anyway, if they want to run themselves, so be it. Damned if I'm going to let them use our latest technology, though. Are you still wearing your rings?"

Margaret held her right hand out to show two ornate almost ugly rings on her thumb and index finger "I wish I'd taken them off," she whispered.

"Give them to me."

Margaret still hesitated. "You might need the technology. We have to live here, you know."

"Electricity and water supplies will not be destroyed. The town will be no different from what the citizens are used to."

"But we will lose contact..."

"Better that than the transfer I just mentioned."

"Well okay," Margaret said. She slipped the two rings off and handed them to her partner.

Ceeler held the larger ring and placed the smaller one on top of it. He grunted in satisfaction as they clicked together. "Don't worry. It'll implode. Nothing outside the castle walls will be affected."

"I hope so," Margaret whispered.

She watched as Turg twisted the rings back and forth in a predetermined pattern.

*

On the hill overlooking Buckoway, the castle that had ruled the skyline since the town was built began to glow. The grey stones turned pink and sort of hissed. Steam rose from the cemented cracks and glass windows shattered. The stones became soft like melted chocolate and began to drop. The pink became red and the chocolate turned to lava.

Spectators not running away downhill would have seen a spectacular site. The castle turned golden before it shivered and slid in on itself. Red lava and hissing steam flowed to the castle wall. The wall crackled and shook but remained solid and contained the liquid within. But now there was no castle. Just a circle of three-metre deep lava began to cool and solidify into a gigantic oval of smooth black marble.

*

CHAPTER TWENTY FIVE

"All the aliens have been arrested and thrown in the Border Guards' jail," Hamish told his friends whom, like hundreds of Buckoway citizens, had gathered around the castle wall to examine the destruction within.

"Drety and Fyddal, too?" Kirsty asked in alarm.

Hamish turned to the blonde girl. "They aren't aliens, Lass. They're us." He grinned. "Look behind you."

Both Kirsty and Madison turned around and glanced over the crowd. There, four rows back Drety and Fyddal towered above the rest of the heads. Drety now wore the traditional blouse and tartan skirt and Fyddal the slightly old fashioned clothes the local men wore.

Madison smiled at the pair but turned back and became serious. "It's all my fault," she muttered. "I should never have let Turg Ceeler go."

"You didn't, Madison," Hamish said. "You know the decision was really made by the Border Guards Command Council. You were merely doing what they asked."

Madison sighed. "I know but it was really on our recommendation. Why would he destroy everything?"

"Power," Hamish said. "Or lack of it. Ceeler remained out of sight but I have no doubt that he really controlled everything that was happening in Buckoway. Drety and Fyddal will know more about the hierarchy on this world but I think he would have been one of the most senior officers here."

"Yeah," Madison said. "It doesn't help us now, though, does it? We've lost our communication, the transporter and all the things to help improve life."

"No," Hamish replied. "We are exactly where we were. Everything is working. We have electricity, water, housing and food. We still have our farms..."

"Actually, we're actually better off," Norris added.

Madison frowned. "And how's that?"

Norris grinned. "We have taken control of our own lives. Also, as well as Drety and Fyddal, who else do we have here that we never knew before?"

Madison glanced around. There, a few metres away stood a quiet spectator who, though perhaps not as striking as their tall friends further back, still had different features than the rest of the crowd.

"Risa!" Madison said.

"That's right."

"And Thinrisodor is also a friend," Kirsty said. "I reckon we've done really well."

"And we've stopped everyone here losing their identity. Without us, how many of those in this crowd might be transformed aliens?" Hamish said.

"Not to mention the thousands of new ones they were going to bring in," Kirsty added.

"Okay," Madison said. "You've got sound arguments. I guess I'm just feeling sorry for myself. But we need to think ahead now and decide what to do." She reached out and tucked her arms around her friends. "If everything went exactly as one wanted, it would be a boring life, wouldn't it?"

"That's for sure," Sean said from behind her. "Anyway, I reckon driving a wagon team is much better than pushing buttons that dumb transporter machine. Sure the oxen are slow but they're friends too, you know."

Madison turned and smiled. "They are, Sean," she said. "There are some things in our lives it would be foolish to change."

*

At dawn after Madison awoke to report no real changes back on Earth, the others told her the wagon train was loaded and they were ready to head out. Even though it was not yet seven, crowds of Buckoway citizens lined the ring road to wave good bye to the four wagons that headed for the gate. Madison drove the front wagon with Risa sharing the drivers' seat. The tiny flag with her arrow hole through it blew above the canvas cover. A proud Kirsty with Drety beside her took command of the second wagon that was one of two hired from other wagonmasters reluctant to travel through Mud territory. Sean and Norris drove the third wagon while Hamish and Fyddal came up the rear. The wagon train's destination was Sakita-mura with supplies for Risa's people. Their plan was to travel to Station Five and take *Gentle Warrior* upstream but they had equipment for several days if it was necessary.

An alternate plan to travel onto the alien's main base had been discussed but everyone decided they needed to look after Risa's people first and to prepare Buckoway for any possible alien attacks. The Buckoway Border Guard now had several ray pistols but nothing to defend themselves against a sophisticated attack by the enemy. Madison was worried but decided that any comments she made would only demoralize the local citizens.

Now as Olive, Twinkle, Thelma and Florence plodded on though the farms, Madison felt more relaxed. It was another fine day and except for the dairy farmers who waved from their cowsheds, the road was empty.

"No sign of Thinrisodor or his people," Risa said as she shaded her eyes from the rising sun.

"No," Madison said. "Once we are past the last farm he won't be far away." She smiled at her companion. "How are you feeling?"

Risa stared out over the oxen to where the first hills appeared ahead. "Guilty," she replied.

Madison glanced up. "Guilty, Risa. Why?"

The Japanese girl shrugged. "When we found the castle destroyed I somehow felt relieved. That giant transporter would have been wonderful to use now but I like our more simple life. Then I saw the disappointment in your face and thought I was being mean."

"You always think of others, don't you Risa?"

"Do I?"

"And never complain. Kirsty moans away and Norris makes his caustic comments at times but you are like the Rock of Gibraltar."

"The what?"

Madison laughed. "It's an expression about a fortress rock back home on Earth that hasn't been conquered for hundreds of years. It means you are trustworthy and can always be relied upon."

"All of us in this wagon train are," Risa whispered. "Even Drety and Fyddal who probably have the most to lose." She reached across to a small bag and brought out a couple of apples. "Like one?" she asked.

Madison nodded, reached in for an apple and crunched into it while the oxen ambled forward, seemingly without a care in the world.

*

Their journey continued throughout the morning with only the valley where the enemy had been destroyed, different. Here the lava had solidified into a smooth surface of marble similar to the ruins of Buckoway Castle. Madison was pleased to be through it and back on the original dirt road. Dust rose but the ground remained hard. They made steady progress and stopped for a break and food at the junction where the trail turned towards the tunnel and Station 5.

Hamish came up to Madison. "I thought we would have met Thinrisodor by now," he said. "There are no sign of any Mud."

"You know them. They could be a few metres away and we'd not see them," Madison said.

"They aren't near," Hamish replied. "No matter how careful they are, insects and birds are always disturbed. The cicadas have never stopped chirping, no birds or ducks have taken to the air, and there are no footprints of crushed grass. No Madison, I think they've left this area."

"But why?"

Hamish shrugged. "This is Sumatti country. They would not leave without a reason."

"Perhaps they've been caught by the aliens," Kirsty said. "You know one of those gas bombs could have been dropped, put them all to sleep and they were carted off in a transporter."

"I don't think so," Fyddal said. "There are no tyre marks or damaged plants. Wherever they've gone it was by their own choice."

Madison nodded. "No other tribes seem to be around. Nor are there any aliens. The whole countryside is empty."

"That's what I'm worried about," Hamish said. "It's too quiet."

"So what do suggest?" Madison asked.

"Get to the tunnel and use the lookout at the far end to observe Station Five."

*

Madison never had time to act on Hamish's advice. Just as they were about to leave something chirped in her pocket. If she was home on Earth she would have known it was her cell phone.

"You've got one of those writing balls haven't you?" Risa asked.

"Of course," Madison replied and took the glass ball out of her pocket. It was definitely where the chirping came from. She shook it; the paper appeared and hardened. However, this time it looked more like a flat computer monitor than paper. It still chirped from a tiny speaker at the top. "Okay," Madison muttered and touched the speaker.

The images of the aliens Madison had met on Earth appeared on the screen.

"Knoge and Ajiei," Madison gasped.

Knoge nodded. "We have been trying to find your frequency for hours." He looked concerned. "Has anything happened since we talked?"

228

"Lots. The Buckoway Castle has been destroyed..." Madison gave a quick explanation of what had happened.

"So that's why we had trouble contacting you," Knoge said. "Are you still in Buckoway?"

"No, we're heading for Sakita-mura with our Oxen wagons. Remember I told you that was Risa's village."

"And the *Gentle Warrior*?"

"We haven't reached it yet."

Ajiei looked relieved. "You are not to go there. We believe if you go in the tunnel you will activate a self self-destruct mechanism to collapse it and kill you all."

Madison nodded. "Why?" she asked.

"We've intercepted orders that you are to be found. You were lucky that all the communications to Buckoway were cut but if we found you, so can the Quargis main base."

"So what do I do?"

"When we've finished talking, destroy this monitor and any other communications equipment you still have then head back to Buckoway. It's as safe as anywhere at the moment."

"I can't abandoned Risa's people," Madison said.

Knoge nodded. "Then go there by road. Are you safe from the Mud tribes?"

"I think so."

"Good. They are your best friends at the moment. Remember, you can still be traced by your unique DNA."

"So I'm endangering my friends?"

Ajiei stared at Madison but shook her head. "If they trace you they'll also be able to trace them. Our advice is to stay together and seek help from that chief you told us about."

" Thinrisodor?"

"Yes."

"Then what?"

"We're working on it. If all else fails we'll contact your otherself on Earth."

"Okay," Madison said. She cursed when the screen faded and the appearance turned to that of a notebook page. She turned to everyone gathered around her. "So we take the road right through to Risa's village," she said. "Has anybody any other suggestions?"

"Keep the flag flying," Hamish said. "We'll soon be in the Sneednim lands. I'd keep the ray pistols, too. I don't know anything about their communications devices but I doubt if the guns can be traced." He glanced up at Fyddal.

"Only if they're fired," Fyddal said. "There's no communication equipment embedded in them but the chemical residual from their rays can be traced."

"So they must know that Buckoway Castle and their convoy has gone?" Kirsty said.

"Oh yes, they'll know," Drety said.

"So keep the ray pistols," Hamish said. "We need to press on as fast as we can." He turned to Madison. "I've been on this road a few times so I'll lead if you wish."

"Okay," Madison said. She took her communications ball and handed it to Norris. "See how far you can throw it into the forest. Perhaps if they try to trace it here, they'll leave us alone."

Norris grinned. "Sure, Madison," he said.

He shook the instrument back into its ball shape and hurled it down the valley into a thick wooded area.

Kirsty produced another communication ball and handed it to Norris. "Throw this in another direction," she whispered. "Somewhere where there are lots of thistles."

*

An hour after leaving the turnoff they moved out of the hills onto a vast plain stretched to the horizon that Madison had never crossed before. The road became just a rut in the course grass and at times disappeared altogether.

"We seem to go on and on and get nowhere," Madison muttered. "I hope Hamish knows where to go."

"It's worse when you're walking," Risa said.

They chattered for a while and lapsed into silence while the oxen plodded on behind the front wagon. Risa fell asleep but Madison knew that if she did the same she would wake up on Earth. She reached for another apple and a satchel of water.

Still they plodded on through the afternoon. About three, Fyddal jumped from the front wagon and waited for them to pull up.

"Hamish said the oxen need a rest and some water," he said. "We're going to stop in a few moments."

"That's a good idea," Madison said. They were still on the featureless plains that reminded her of a vacation she'd had crossing the

Canadian prairies on Earth. Even in a car it had become a monotonous journey.

After half an hour's rest and a picnic lunch they started off again. Later Risa pointed to a row of hills that appeared ahead. "Those are near to home," she said. "We should be there soon."

The grass turned into a gravel road but there was still no sign of anyone or anything. Their wagon train was an oasis of movement in the vast empty land.

Or was it?

"It's not windy?" Risa muttered almost to herself as she stared out across the grasslands.

Madison glanced at their limp flag propped up above the canvas. "Not a breath," she said. "Why?"

"Then why is there a line of dust off to the left of the hills?"

Madison swung around and squinted in the afternoon light. The line of blue sky that touched the grasslands was now a blur of brown.

"Oh hell," Madison whispered. She reached for her whistle and gave it a long blast. The front wagon stopped and Hamish's head appeared around the side.

"You saw it too," he yelled.

"What is it?" Madison called back.

"We found our Mud." Hamish jumped down and came back just as Kirsty arrived from the wagon behind.

"Thinrisodor or the Sneednim?" the blonde girl asked.

"By the look of that cloud, I'd say they've joined forces. There could be even more tribes but they're going away, not coming towards us," Hamish said.

"Okay," Madison said. "What have I missed?"

"The Mud are great environmentalists," Hamish said. "But in sheer numbers even their nimble feet leave signs. Look at the grass, Madison and you'll see crushed grass and an occasional footprint."

He was right. When she looked closely, Madison could see where dozens, perhaps hundreds of warriors had walked through the area. Footprints had been brushed away but flattened grass and wavy lines showed where bushes had been dragged along. It was well done but Madison's eyes were now becoming more sophisticated.

She turned to Risa. "Where is that cloud in relation to Sakita-mura?"

Risa pointed to the original hill she'd mentioned earlier. "That's home. They appear to be passing it to the west but the valley curves around to follow the river."

"Do you know what's straight ahead of that cloud?" Drety said.

Hamish nodded and stroked his beard. "Tell us Lass," he said.

"Our home base. It's quite a long way, probably fifty kilometres but the river heads west beyond Risa's village in a huge curve. The main military base and headquarters where I came from is beside the river."

"Where the *Gentle Warrior* and *Gentle Lady* came from?" Hamish asked.

"And more. The incoming spacecraft land there. It's a massive airfield with three, kilometre long runways." Fyddal turned to Madison. "Do you understand what I'm talking about?"

"Yes. It sounds like airports on my Earth."

Except for Sean, who had stayed to guard the rear, their other friends had walked up to join the conversation.

"Even if we headed home there could be problems," Hamish said.

"Like what?" Kirsty asked.

"More Mud may be following. I was here for the last uprising. At that time twenty or thirty tribes combined and almost overran Buckoway." He frowned. "Of course it all fits in..."

"What?" Madison asked.

"We thought it was just luck and the weather that stopped them succeeding but thinking back, Drety and Fyddal's people must have used their weapons to drive them off. Some of those sleep bombs would have been used. Compared with some Mud tribes the Sumatti and Sneednim are quite sophisticated. Other more remote tribes are quite superstitious and may have thought the gods were angry with them."

"How did it end?" Norris asked.

"That's it. We were under siege and our supplies had all but run out. We awoke one morning to find they'd all gone. They'd slipped away during the night. It wasn't long after that when we began trading with them and realized they were not just savage beasts."

"Okay, but how does that help us now?" Madison asked.

"We go on with our flag flying and our maidens standing up showing their bows." Hamish squinted at Madison and Kirsty. "Do you think you can do it?"

Both nodded.

"And if the new tribes don't recognize our symbols of peace?" Norris asked.

Hamish tugged on his beard again. "As much as I detest them we may need to use our new ray guns to defend ourselves."

*

The new arrangement showed the tiny wagon train in full state of preparedness. Hamish drove the front wagon with Madison standing in full view holding her bow and the punctured flag flying just above her head. Behind the seat, though, Drety lay across the gap with her ray gun ready. Norris drove wagon two with Kirsty in full view, Norris was by himself in wagon three while Sean drove the last wagon and Risa hid at the back to watch their rear.

Ten minutes later the empty countryside filled. Hundreds of Mud warriors stepped out of the grass across the road in front of the wagon train.

"Cylyfy," Hamish muttered. "Look into their eyes, Madison, hold your bow out and be grim. Got it!"

"Yes."

This new tribe was different. They were all male and wore red smocks that reached from a left shoulder down to each warrior's knees. Every one carried a square shaped metal shield and a weapon that looked like a crossbow. All had short-cropped curly hair and no facial hair. A few wore shell shaped earrings in a left ear.

"The leaders have the earrings," Hamish said without taking his eyes off the road ahead. "Bigger the rings, the more important the person. Find the one with the biggest rings and stare him out. Don't move your lips, though. That is a sign of weakness."

" Got it." Madison said through her teeth.

*

A gigantic warrior stood to the side of the oxen that approached. His earring was as large as a plate so Madison held her bow and focused on the man's eyes. My God, they were blue! She held his gaze and tried to remain unblinking as the Cylyfy chief stared back.

The line of Mud across the road parted as the oxen plodded by. Madison was adjacent to the chief and she still stared, her lips fixed in grim determination and her bow held up with one arm. Hell, her arm ached in that position.

The wagon moved on past the chief. Madison turned slightly so she still held his gaze. Seconds went by and the second wagon was by the warrior. Of course Kirsty would have no idea what to do but the chief still watched her.

"Keep it up," Hamish whispered. "They know who you are."

Suddenly the Cylyfy chief changed his stance. He raised his shield up high glanced towards the sky and shouted two words in English. "Maiden Granite!"

Every warrior along the road repeated the words. Hundreds of Cylyfy warriors stood three or more deep along the roadside with raised shields and shouted, "Maiden Granite! Maiden Granite!" over and over as the wagon train moved by.

Madison glanced at the sea of faces and moved her eyes. Brief seconds of contact were met with men looking back. Every eye was blue, every expression serious, but Madison realized the people below her appeared proud and friendly. She wanted to smile but dared not break the pattern so continued to link gazes as they drove forward.

Finally, they reached the end of the crowd and moved onto the empty road ahead. Madison lowered her bow and almost collapsed into the seat. "I couldn't have lasted much longer," she gasped as the cheers behind were replaced with silence.

"Aye, but you did," Hamish said. "They're the most fierce tribe I know. It speaks well of Thinrisodor to know he has them in his trust."

"But why are they here," Madison asked.

"I'd say the alien base is about to be attacked," Hamish replied with a shrug.

*

CHAPTER TWENTY-SIX

Risa sat in the front wagon with Madison for the last stage of the journey to Sakita-mura. The sun was low in the sky and the road shaded by the hills by the time they reached a wide valley and saw the river they'd travelled down. They came to some of the small farms but met nobody. The Japanese girl searched around when her village came into sight.

"It's all wrong," she gasped "There should be people on the road, boats in the river and chimney smoke."

"They wouldn't be expecting a wagon train," Madison said. "Perhaps they're just being cautious."

"There's not even the flag at the town gate," Risa said. "Everyday we have a flag flying. It's a tradition the governor insisted upon. Also there should be farmers and their wagons around. Workers bring wagons out here to load up with peat from near the river. It's used as fuel in the winter."

"Would you like me to ask Hamish to go ahead and check it out, Risa?"

"No. If anybody is there they would have seen us."

"Okay. We'll all go in together and stop just out of bow shot range from the wall. Don't worry, there could be a simple explanation for this."

"I hope so," Risa whispered. She smiled but her eyes looked afraid.

*

There were no boats at the jetty and the road up to the town wall was empty. The wagon train pulled to a halt by the main gate that was shut but not locked. Risa pushed it open a fraction.

She glanced around. "Shall I keep going?" she asked.

Madison glanced at Hamish who nodded.

The circle road inside was not empty for parked a few metres away was a trailer unit exactly like the one they'd captured and taken to Buckoway.

Risa's lips trembled. "They're here," she gasped.

"No I don't think so," Madison said. "Only the trailer's here, not the truck that pulls it."

"Be careful," Hamish warned. "I don't like this."

They walked forward and found the first villagers. Two border guards lay on the grass behind the trailer. Risa gasped and fought to stop the tears swelling in her eyes.

"They've killed everyone," she whispered.

Madison frowned. "No, I don't think so," she said. "Why would the guards be here on the grass and not lying on the road or on the parapet itself?"

She walked up to the guards, knelt down and turned one over. He was breathing!

"Risa," she called. "He's asleep, not dead."

Risa rushed up. Her chin quivered but she wiped her eyes and managed a smile.

"There're more here," Hamish called out from further up the road.

Four more villagers lay in a neat row on the grass fast asleep.

Madison stared at Risa. "I think they've done the same thing here as in Buckoway and used a posthypnotic suggestion to put everyone asleep."

"But we haven't had aliens here for months," Risa said. "When they abandoned us they took everything with them."

"But probably left enough behind so they could come back if it was necessary," Hamish said.

"But where are they?" Risa asked.

"Taken the truck and gone, I'd say," Hamish said.

"But why?" Risa asked.

"If the Mud are surrounding their alien base they may have been called back to help there."

The trio walked a little further into the village where they found two people asleep in the first apartment and one in the second. It appeared that everyone had picked a safe place to lie down and fall asleep. Villagers on the footpath were close to walls or on park benches. There was a wagon with the oxen sitting patiently down chewing their cuds while the wagon drivers were asleep inside it.

"That proves one thing," Madison said.

"What?" Risa asked.

"They never used a sleep bomb over Sakita-mura or the oxen would be asleep too."

*

By early afternoon the visitors had searched through most areas but had found no aliens. Villagers were everywhere but remained asleep.

While Hamish organized bringing the wagontrains inside and finding a stable to house and feed the oxen, Madison, Drety and Risa walked up to search the castle.

As Risa said it was completely clear of alien equipment and now served as the government centre for the village. After half an hour of searching around Madison was about to declare that the building housed nothing unusual when a thought hit her.

"Where's the cellar entrance, Risa?" she asked.

"Cellar? I know of no cellar."

"This is almost identical to Buckoway Castle except it has no cellar," Madison said. "Doesn't that strike you as being unusual?"

"There's no staircase down," Drety said. "Perhaps there's an outside door."

"Let's look," Madison said.

The three walked out into the courtyard and around the side. A small alleyway between the castle and outer wall led through to a second smaller courtyard.

"This is like the one where Hamish brought bodies to the crematorium in Buckoway. Look there's even the second gate in the wall." Madison nodded at the small closed gate on their right. "Now the entrance was across the courtyard."

"It's just a blank wall," Risa said with disappointment in her voice.

Drety, though, appeared more excited. "This wall is newer than the rest of the building. There are no water stains or moss growing on it."

"Oh hell, you're right," Madison said.

The wall in front looked exactly like the other ones around except that it was too clean. On this shady side of the castle the other walls had dark patches under window frames where water had trickled down. Also many of the stones had moss growing from cracks and even an occasional weed grew through broken pieces of stone.

The wall in front was clean. It towered up to windows in what must have been the second floor where the older stained stones showed. The entire section was one blank wall without windows or ornate pillars on the corners like the other ones. There was no sign of an entrance.

"I think we'll get Hamish to look at this," Madison said. "He'll find a way to get through it."

"I'll do it," Drety said and pulled her ray pistol out. She set it to a middle setting and aimed it at the wall. "Get back," she warned and squeezed the trigger.

A yellow beam shot out and a section of wall the size of a dinner plate melted in a hiss of smoke. Drety moved the beam down until an area the size of a door had melted. Hot lava flowed across the courtyard.

"Oh my God," Madison gasped. "The cellar is there!"

A smell of musty air encircled her and in the gloom she could see a floor about two metres below her. Drety had cut through the top half of an interior wall.

"It'll take a few moments to be cool enough to touch," Drety said. She grinned when Risa walked over and squeezed her arm. "I think we'll find a whole control centre inside."

∗

The trio walked back down to the circle road where the wagons were lined up near the trailer. The oxen had been taken away and the gate shut again. Kirsty, who had been sitting by a wagon rushed up to them.

"Well, what did you find?" she asked.

"Nothing really," Madison replied.

"Don't lie," Kirsty snapped. "I can tell by your mannerism."

"We found a secret room beneath the castle," Madison said.

"Is that all?" Kirsty replied. "We found that this trailer contains another of those thingies to transfer newcomers' minds. Hamish reckons they decided to take the minds from Risa's peoples after they found out we'd destroyed their machines in Buckoway."

"He's probably right." Madison said. "And where is everyone else?"

"Searching around the stables. After all the oxen were fed I thought I'd come back here and wait for you."

∗

"Well, there are no aliens around and everyone else appears to be safe but asleep," Hamish said a few moments later after everyone had gathered around the wagons. "Is there anything else before we go and look in the castle cellar?"

"Someone should stay on the wall," Sean said.

"Why?" Madison asked.

"The Mud have returned," Sean replied. "They're not in sight but are definitely out there."

"Do you know what tribe?" Madison asked.

"I'm not sure," Sean said. "The two I saw were women."

238

Madison frowned. "The only Mud women I've seen were at the trading post. What does this mean?"

Hamish explained. "If the men go into battle the Mud women are often used as a rear guard. They don't usually fight but can, if called upon." He grinned at Madison. "I've learned to never underestimate the women of any species."

"That's for sure," Sean added and winked at Kirsty before she could even say a word. "Anyway, I'll stay here on the gate parapet. I reckon it might be prudent to raise Madison's flag there, too."

While Norris stayed with Sean, the others headed up to Sakita-mura Castle.

"We should have brought a torch," Hamish said as he gazed in the hole they'd made. However, as soon as he slid inside and his feet touched the floor, lights flooded on to show a small storage room with shelves and what looked like cleaning equipment. A steel door, again similar to those in the castle at Buckoway stood closed at the far side.

After they were all inside Hamish walked forward and the door slid open. They stepped out into the main cellar where ceiling lights came on. To their left was a furnace and conveyor belt but it looked dusty and unused. Other equipment was stacked along walls in tidy piles while at the end was what they were looking for. In a small alcove a control room with the now familiar monitors, computers and other equipment was set up. It appeared more compact than the Buckoway Castle console but appeared to be brand new. Indeed some equipment was still covered in white plastic wrapping.

"All set up if they needed to return," Madison said. She glanced to where a trashcan was filled with plastic wrapping. "They must have come here to use the village loudspeakers."

"Can you get it working?" Risa asked.

"I think so."

It took Madison, Drety and Fyddal longer than they expected to start up the computers but finally Madison announced she was ready to go.

"Now hear this," she said in a microphone. Her voice boomed out from a speaker in the cellar. Kirsty and Hamish went outside and came back a few moments later to say her voice could be heard everywhere.

"Okay," Madison said and switched on the microphone. "You must remember to wake up after I count to three." She added a few more instructions, glanced at the others and counted to three.

Nothing happened. Again Kirsty and some of the others went back into the street but Sakita-mura remained as quiet as a ghost town. Nobody woke up.

"Oh hell," Madison muttered. "They could have used any words."

Risa stared at her. "But you were talking in English," she said. "Wouldn't the instructions be in my language?"

"Oh hell. Of course," Madison said. "You do it, Risa and don't forget to add that bit about this hypnotic suggestion being cancelled from this time on."

"I will," Risa whispered. She slipped into the seat where Madison had been and pressed the microphone button.

*

Risa's Japanese reached every corner of Sakita-mura. Above the gate Sean grinned at Norris when they heard her voice echo through the streets.

"Logical," Sean said. "I didn't think anybody would understand Madison."

Risa's instructions continued on for several sentences before she paused and said the first three Japanese numbers. "Ichi, ni, san!"

"Glory be," Sean muttered and grabbed Norris on the arm.

Below them the two guards sleeping on the grass across the road sat up and shook their heads. They glanced around, obviously saw the wagons up the road and jumped to their feet. One glanced up, saw them, shouted in Japanese and reached for a sword still stuck conveniently in his belt.

All over Sakita-mura, citizens awoke, staggered to their feet and stared around. Some were disorientated, others scared. Some appeared angry while still others just kept doing whatever they were doing when they'd been put to sleep. Border guards blew whistles and the wagonmaster up the road shouted at his oxen. People rushed into streets and everyone talked to friends and companions.

"I reckon we'd better get Risa back here to explain," Sean said as the Japanese guards continued to shout up at them in angry tones. "Those chaps look a might unfriendly."

"Hi," Norris shouted down at the guards. "Do you know Risa or Madison?"

One of the guards stopped in the middle of a sentence and stared at the pair. "Risa?" he shouted then added a few words in his own language and pointed at the wagons.

"Yes, Risa!" Norris shouted back. He gestured at the wagons then at Sean and himself. "Our wagons," he said. "We've brought you supplies."

240

The two border guards looked at each other and chatted away before the first guard stared up and them again, broke into a grin and beckoned them to come down. He said something to the second guard and they both put their swords back in their belts.

"Come on," Norris said. "Let's go and meet our hosts."

*

Madison and the others barely had time to climb out of the cellar when they found themselves surrounded by guards. An officer at the rear came forward and was so busy examining the hole in the wall that he never noticed who they were.

"Hello Captain Wantana," Madison said in Japanese. "You can thank Risa here for waking Sakita-mura up."

Koti Wantana swung around. "Madison and Risa?" he replied in the same language. "When the Mud army arrived I suspected you might be near."

"Mud army, Captain Wantana?" Madison asked. "Were they here?"

"They still are. Thousands of them arrived yesterday and just sat around outside our wall. Attempts to communicate with them were unsuccessful."

"And when did the transporter arrive?"

This time the captain looked perplexed. "Transporter? Do you mean an oxen wagon or one of the boats?"

"So you haven't been down to the main gate since you woke up?"

"No. My men heard sounds back here and we found the hole in the wall." Koti frowned. "I admit I did fall asleep in my office upstairs but how did you know?"

"Everyone in Sakita-mura was asleep. Ask your guards."

Wantana swung around and his embarrassed men confessed that they had been asleep too.

The officer turned back to glare at Madison. "Can you explain, please."

"Risa will," Madison said. "My speech is not that good." She grinned at Risa and switched to English. "You don't mind, do you?"

"What do I tell him first?"

"About the hypnotic spell and the equipment in the cellar and you'd better mention that trailer too."

"Well, Risa?" Wantana asked.

Madison noticed that Risa spoke with confidence and didn't appear overwhelmed by the officer at all. This was quite different from the previous time they were in Sakita-mura.

Koti asked several questions and followed them inside to the console. He made a thorough inspection and asked how the speaker system worked. "So it is your belief that the aliens intended to take over our bodies?" he concluded.

"Yes. They must have discovered they were unsuccessful at Buckoway so you became their second source."

"But why?"

"It was the real reason human DNA was brought here from our Earth. You see their species are all sterile and will cease to exist when the present generations die. Drety and Fyddal are probably the youngest of their race. There are no children."

Koti turned to Drety and Fyddal and studied them. "I think I understand," he said. "I can see that Drety is not..." He almost flushed and turned back to Madison. "Could they have started this process of transferring into our bodies?"

"The equipment down by the gate is self sufficient. However, I don't think they would have had time to start using it. They left in a hurry in the truck that pulled the trailer here." Madison said.

"Perhaps they wanted to get away before the Mud warriors arrived," Risa said.

Koti frowned. "But you don't really know, Madison?"

"No, I'm sorry but I don't. We were more interested in waking everyone up. If you are left asleep too long your body begins to deteriorate through lack of food and water."

"So what day is it?"

Risa told him.

"Bad. Very bad," Wantana whispered.

"What's wrong captain?" Madison said.

"It appears that we've been asleep for two days," he said. "I was in my office and heard a voice calling out. When I woke up I thought I'd just nodded off for a few moments. Now I find two days of my life has gone." He grimaced. "No wonder I feel hungry and thirsty."

Madison could understand his concern. If the aliens were here two days perhaps they had already taken over some of the newcomers' bodies. Her friends and herself would have to be very careful. Anyone could be an alien, even Captain Wantana himself.

*

242

CHAPTER TWENTY-SEVEN

Madison awoke and sighed.

"You sound as if you're not pleased to be here?" Norris said from across their double bed.

"Of course I am," Madison said. "It's just that I wish I had a control over this shooting back and forth. There's so much danger there I feel I am letting them down by going to sleep and not being able to be awoken if something goes wrong. "

"So what happened?" Norris asked.

Madison told him about the events of the previous day.

"So did you find anybody who'd taken over Japanese bodies?" Norris asked.

"No, but they wouldn't show themselves would they?"

"I guess not."

"Anyway, we spent the rest of the afternoon unloading the wagons. It was mainly food and everyone was so appreciative I wish we had more. Afterwards, we went back with Risa to her apartment." She grinned. "They're segregated there so your otherself had to go off with Hamish and the other men."

"I'm glad," Norris said only half in gesture.

"Why?" Madison asked.

"Well, you're you but that Norris isn't me, is he?"

Madison broke into a grin. "I see the jealousy beginning to raise its ugly head."

Norris flushed. "You must admit it's a little like knowing only half of you."

"I tell you everything, I've done when I wake up."

"And my otherself everything when you go back?"

Madison shook her head. "Actually, I don't. I tend to tell Kirsty and lately Risa too rather than Norris. In some ways they're quite old fashioned but in others..."

"Yeah, you told me about all the females getting pregnant."

"I think we've stopped that in Buckoway. It was just the aliens trying to repopulate themselves."

"Let the women all have children then take their bodies over so they don't have to go through the trouble."

Madison frowned. "I never thought of that but that could have been one of their aims. Everything there seems to have a sinister reason behind it." She stopped when she heard a chime. Someone had rung the doorbell. "Oh hell," she whispered and grabbed a dressing gown.

The peephole showed nobody outside so she made sure the security chain was still attached before she unlocked the door. Outside standing by the wall and both dressed in casual Earth clothes were Ajiei and Knoge. The girl looked red faced but relaxed but Knoge appeared quite agitated.

Madison flung the door open. "What are you two doing on Earth?" she gasped.

"We weren't going to come so early in the morning," Knoge gasped. "We don't know what to do?"

"About what?"

"I think junior is coming," Ajiei cut in. "It's only nine months so I wasn't expecting it to happen."

"Nine months," Madison gasped. "Oh my God, that's full term. Come in." She turned. "Norris we need an ambulance. Can you call 911?"

*

By noon, perhaps the very first alien to be born on Earth arrived. In size, weight and condition it was no different from an ordinary baby and the staff never knew they were witnessing an historic event.

"It's a little boy," Ajiei said in between sobs. "He's perfect. Absolutely perfect."

"And why not?" the nurse next to Knoge and Madison said. "With such athletic parents what else would you expect?"

"Nothing," Ajiei sobbed. "I'm just so relieved that's all."

The nurse nodded and glanced at Madison. "We need some information and Knoge doesn't seem to understand. He said they are aliens and don't know about our system.

"Yeah, they're refugees from Iraq who are sponsored by our firm," Madison blurted out.

"Oh the poor things," the nurse said. She turned to Ajiei. "Now you just relax and cuddle your son. I'll get everything sorted out for you." She smiled and left the room.

"So why did you risk coming all the way here with Ajiei so close to giving birth?" Madison asked Knoge.

244

"All historical records at home said the human female gestation was eleven months. We thought there were two months to go."

"And how long is it?" Ajiei asked.

"Let's say you were right on time," Madison said. "Can I hold your son?"

"Yes," Ajiei said and burst into tears again when Madison bent down to pick the tiny baby into her arms.

*

When the pair arrived back at Madison's apartment she found a note on the refrigerator from Norris.

"I'd forgotten. He had to go to work today. He'll be home this evening." She smiled at Knoge. "Can I get you a coffee and something to eat."

"I'd like that," the alien man replied. "I haven't eaten for hours."

He sat down at the table while Madison turned the percolator on and placed some bread in a toaster. "So when did you realize Ajiei 's time had come?" she asked.

"It all happened so quickly. We were driving the rental car along the freeway and Ajiei had this terrible pain." Knoge said. "We hoped you were awake but could think of nothing else to do."

"You did the right thing but where did you come from in the car?"

"We landed at that freighter airport about twenty kilometres away. I think it's called Mathei ."

"What? In your space ship?"

"Sort of." Knoge laughed. "We disguised our craft to look like an Earth transport plane, an old Boeing 767 actually. A charter aeroplane flying in from Canada attracts no attention what-so-ever."

"Smart," Madison said. "But why are you back here?"

"We have communication with Quargis but still can't go there without being traced. We also think if we tried to contact your otherself our message could be intercepted."

"So what has happened that is so important?"

"The leaders of Earth 1 have found a new earth type planet through the random black holes."

"What are random black holes?"

"For years black holes have been sent out through the galaxies in an attempt to find suitable planets. That's how our world, this world and Quargis were found. However for every suitable planet there are thousands that aren't suitable. They've refined the search somewhat but it is still a

245

matter of finding a planetary system then searching within it for a water planet as we call them. Most times there are none. Anyway, it seems they found a suitable water planet a year ago but kept the information classified."

"So why is that important now?"

"After we stopped their bees here on Earth 2 and with all the troubles on Quargis the authorities on Earth 1 decided to cut their loses, evacuate both places and concentrate on this new planet to emigrate to."

"Isn't that good?" Madison asked.

"The officers have left the Quargis base but the ordinary workers were left behind. Some are *Mindsouls...*"

"Mindsouls?"

"They're as little like us. They opposed the transfer of our species' minds into your species' bodies."

"Of course. Drety was one of those. You know the girl I befriended back in Buckoway?"

Knoge nodded. "Anyway, the officers on the base set off an Amicir discharge and took the last spacecraft out."

"So they put everyone to sleep?"

"Yes. When the workers woke up, not only were they alone but all the modern weapons had been taken, too. They were left with a situation not unlike Buckoway. They had electricity and other basic services but nothing more. That's the situation now."

"So they will have to be integrated into our society? I don't see a real problem with that."

"Except for the Mud uprising. Thousands of Mud have surrounded the base. If they attack it will be a massacre."

"Oh hell, I see," Madison replied. "You can't help so you need me to go and get them?"

"I know you're already helping the citizens of Sakita-mura but if you can, it would be appreciated."

"How many are there at the base."

"Forty to fifty, I think."

"And you definitely can't get in?"

"That's the trouble. There are remote defence satellites that would attack us if we arrived above Quargis. We'll ultimately be able to neutralise them but it'll take several weeks. By then it will be too late for those stranded there."

"Okay," Madison said. "There are no promises but I'll see what I can do."

"That's all I can ask. Thank you, Madison."

246

"Meanwhile your whole family can stay with Norris and me. They'll only keep Ajiei in for one more night. Hospital care can become expensive in this country."

"There's no problem. We transferred several thousand of your dollars into an account at the Sacramento downtown branch of Bank of America."

Madison frowned. "From where?"

"Earth 4."

"But how?"

Knoge broke into a smile. "Don't ask." he said. "It's suffice to say that it is completely legal."

Madison, however, wasn't listening. She stared at Knoge as the room began to spin and a cold chill ran up her back. "Knoge," she whispered. "Something's wrong."

She reached out but her eyes glazed over and she collapsed unconscious onto the floor.

*

A few moments earlier, if that time span is appropriate across the infinity of space, as Madison was talking to Knoge her otherself was asleep in Risa's Sakita-mura apartment. The tiny bedroom was shared with Kirsty with Risa in an even smaller room across a hallway. Drety and Fyddal had use of another apartment in the married quarters across the road while the men were all in the male apartment block further away still.

By two a.m. the guards outside the women's apartment block had been on duty for three hours, nothing had happened and most of Sakita-mura's citizens were asleep. They did not notice a dark cloaked Japanese man slip from out of adjacent bushes and use two strips of plastic to unlock a small side door.

Nobumi Hayashi grinned in determination and thought back to his good luck. The former Ginnal Zetill had only four weeks earlier stood at rigid attention at his trial while the judge read out his sentence.

"Underofficer Ginnal Zetill this military tribunal has found you guilty of all the charges against you. You were under direct orders not to harm the indigenous tribesmen under your responsibility. You not only fired at them but also used a maximum setting and vaporized an unknown number of these warriors. Your actions almost single handily caused the local tribe to rise in revolt and call in other tribes for assistance." The judge stopped and stared down at Zetill. "You are hereby stripped of all military rank and associated privileges, sentenced to ten years community labour and will undergo mind treatment to rid your body of impure thoughts."

Zetill paled slightly but his words were firm. "Your Honour I wish to use my rights to volunteer for transformation rather than serve my sentence."

The judge frowned. "That is your right of course Citizen Zetill but the experimental procedures now being tried may lead to insanity or death. You are still prepared to invoke your rights."

"Yes, Your Honour."

"Very well. You shall be held in custody until the time and place of this transformation takes place. At that time your present body will be disposed of and you shall continue the remainder your conscious life in the new body allocated to you."

In the female apartment building, Hayashi laughed and felt his new male organs respond in anticipation. He hated being so short and having hair on his head and face but the sheer thrill of having sexual urges far outweighed these disadvantages. Now he was about to do two things, rid the planet of this traitor who was now in Sakita-mura while at the same time satisfy his new found urges with a fully equipped female. Hayashi chuckled sadistically.

*

Kirsty awoke to find a hand around her throat and face mere centimetres from her eyes.

"Make one sound and I'll choke life out of your feeble body," the man whispered as he squeezed so hard that Kirsty could not breathe. In the dim light she focused on the Japanese face and sadistic smile. The room spun and her feeble attempts to lash out with her arms were easily restrained. The man laughed and relaxed his grip enough so she could suck in air.

"What do you want," Kirsty managed to gasp.

"Your body, slut," the man replied. "You Buckoway girls are more endowed than the locals." He laughed and purposely squeezed her breasts.

"You bastard," Kirsty yelled and received a slap on the face for her efforts.

"First things first," Hayashi cum Zetill snarled. "If you co-operate I may even spare your miserable life. You can watch while I evaporate your sleeping friend there. She needs to be disposed of."

"You leave her!" screamed Kirsty. "She can't wake up you cowardly bastard."

248

Hayashi grinned and tightened his hold on her throat. "Shut up bitch," he snarled. "I am about to use my new body to show you..." He laughed, squeezed her throat tighter, ripped the thin pyjama top apart and stared, fascinated by the girl's heaving breasts.

Kirsty screamed in high-pitched terror as he dragged her from the bed and flung her to the floor. He chucked as the semiconscious girl lay whimpering on the floor with blood tricking from a cut lip. She tried to use her hands to cover her exposed breasts and screamed again as he grabbed her wrist and pulled her towards him

.

*

Kirsty's screams and sobs penetrated Madison's mind. She found herself in the Sakita-mura bedroom with Kirsty's screams vibrating around her.

"Shut up, bitch," a male voice muttered.

Oh my God. There was a man in the room attacking Kirsty.

Even as Madison watched the man stood up, flung Kirsty to the floor and leaped on her. Even in the semidarkness Madison saw in horror that the man was naked with his erect organ already pushing down towards her friend. Kirsty continued to scream in terror but the man merely laughed and used his wiry strength to hold her down.

Madison felt under her pillow, found the tiny ray gun there and in an icy calm pulled it out. She stepped to the floor and moved forward. The rapist was so intent on forcing his unfamiliar body on the squirming girl beneath him the squeak of Madison footstep remained unheard.

She poked the ray gun in the man's right ear and spat. "Stop and very slowly move off my friend."

The man gasped, looked up, saw her and reacted. He flung his arm up in a vain attempt to brush her aside. If Madison had hesitated he would have succeeded but she squeezed the trigger just before he reached her arm.

The weapon was set on stun but at that range the beam of electrical charge that entered Hayashi's body was still too powerful. The man's body jerked back and Kirsty managed to fling him aside with a violent kick.

The screaming man hit the floor, the screams stopped and he lay still and silent. Kirsty sat up shaking and sobbing.

"Madison," she whispered in a trembling voice. "But how..."

Madison bent down beside the man and felt for a pulse. "He's dead." Her own voice had a quiver in it.

"Oh Madison," Kirsty sobbed. "Thank you but how can you be awake in the middle of the night?"

"I heard your screams and came to help." Madison said. "I can't stay, Kirsty. See you at half past six."

She walked over to her bed, smiled at the still distort Kirsty, dropped down on the blanket and fell asleep.

*

"Madison," Knoge whispered. "Are you okay? You had a turn and collapsed on the floor."

Madison looked up at the concerned alien man. "I think so," she said as she struggled to her feet. "There was an emergency and I woke up back in Sakita-mura. Kirsty was being attacked." Her lips trembled. "Knoge, a man was trying to rape Kirsty, I had to do something ... There was no time so I shot the guy in the head. I didn't want to do it, Knoge. It was on stun but still killed him. There was no time."

"Of course there wasn't," Knoge said and listened as Madison told him of her last terrifying minutes. "Relax, the toast is cooked and the coffee's ready. How about that meal you offered me?"

Madison managed a smile. "I guess Kirsty's screams penetrated my subconscious."

Knoge nodded. "So that's why you collapsed? You can't be conscious in your two bodies at the same time?"

"Yeah, it can be a damn nuisance. At times I have trouble trying to work out where I am. This time is a perfect example. One moment I was joking with you and the next Kirsty was screaming across the room. It was sort of half a dream but I knew it was real."

Knoge looked intently at her. "Would you like it fixed?" he asked.

"How can it be changed without destroying one of my bodies? I'm me in both places now. Does that sound schizophrenic?"

"Not at all," Knoge said. "I'm not an expert on this phenomena but have a scientist friend back home who may be able to help. When we return I'll see what I can do."

"Okay," Madison said. She sipped her coffee. "But there is no hurry. You have a family to look after first. You make sure Ajiei and your son are strong and healthy before you even consider going back through that black hole."

"I will." Knoge replied. "It's an historic day for us all, I believe."

"Could be," Madison replied. "But wait and see if I can rescue your colleagues back on Quargis."

*

Madison woke up yet again to find Kirsty sitting on the end of the bed. Even though she had a blackened eye and split lip she was smiling,

"You stopped him in time." Kirsty reached forward to hug Madison. "I have never ever been so terrified in my whole life."

Madison stared across the room but saw nothing except a damp piece of carpet where it had been cleaned. "And where is the corpse?"

"Hamish and the other men came and took it away." Kirsty sat sucking on her lip. "There's something else, I'm afraid."

Madison sighed. "Oh hell, what?"

"We weren't to know."

"Hell, Kirsty tell me!"

"The man who attacked me and you shot was called Nobumi Hayashi. He was a guardsman who was highly respected by the local community."

"But he was like a madman when he attacked you."

"Governor Kobayashi is almost certain it was an alien in Hayashi's body."

"Oh hell," Madison said. "How does he know?"

"They found an alien buried in the local cemetery. The local guards became suspicious by a newly dug grave and exhumed the body. It had no signs of any wounds or reason for death."

"So I killed an innocent victim?"

"Someone who was about to kill us both, Madison. It wasn't this Hayashi you know but a ruthless alien."

" I guess."

"Poor Drety and Fyddal are quite upset. I think they somehow feel responsible for what happened."

"But that's silly."

"They aren't responsible any more than we both are, that's what I'm trying to say."

"I know," Madison sighed. "I'll talk to them both. Something else has also come up and we'll need their help and advice. Perhaps that'll take their mind off this whole thing. We're going to have another long day, I'm afraid."

*

CHAPTER TWENTY-EIGHT

For hours the wagon train advanced through empty but well trodden lands. Everywhere, the course grass was flattened, footprints covered the dusty road and evidence of Mud warriors showed. However, the friends now driving their empty wagons towards the alien base saw no sign of any native warriors.

Drety and Fyddal sat in the front wagon with Madison and stared through the barren landscape.

"I'm not sure but we must be getting close by now," Drety said.

"Why is this road so bad?" Madison asked as their wagon rattled and groaned over the rough surface.

"We rarely travelled overland," Drety replied. "The river was used most of the time. When we did cross these plains we used our transporters that were designed for off road work."

They lapsed into silence and travelled on for another hour before Fyddal tapped Madison on the shoulder. "The Mud," he said and pointed ahead. Black dots like a sea of ants stretched across a low hill ahead. "The base is on the other side. If you look to the left you can just make out the river."

Madison saw a line of silver in the haze. She gulped and hoped that the somewhat tatty flag flying above them still held sway with the diverse tribes ahead. There had been no contact with Thinrisodor or Cannad, the Sneednim chief. Even members of the Cylyfy would be a welcome sight at the moment.

When Mud tribesmen arrived it was with their usual sudden appearance. Even with flattened grass nobody in the leading wagon noticed that they had company until hundreds Mud warriors rose from the grass fifty metres on each side and ran towards them. In unison screams filled the air and Madison felt the hair at the back of her neck arrive.

"Just keep the oxen walking," she hissed at her two companions. "Here I go again."

She stood up. It was difficult to stay still on the vibrating floor but she wedged her feet against the seat frames and kept both hands free, one to hold her bow out and the other the string and arrow. If the Mud attacked they stood no chance...

*

At the rear of the last wagon, Kirsty took a similar stance. However, perspiration ran down her neck and she could not stop her arrow hand trembling.

"I'm so shaky, I couldn't hit the Buckoway Castle at twenty paces," she muttered as the warriors behind stopped the bloodcurdling howls and followed them along the road less than twenty metres away.

"You couldn't miss Lass." Hamish shrugged. "I doubt if it'll make much difference in the long run, though."

"We're stopping!" Sean's voice came back from the driver's seat. "Norris is shouting something from the wagon ahead. Wait a minute..."

He went silent for a couple of seconds. Kirsty could hear Norris's voice but couldn't make out what was said. Hamish made his way forward, spoke to Sean and returned. He looked grim.

"Madison wants you to climb down the outside of the wagon when we stop, walk along and join her. Have you bow ready to fire. Okay?"

"Sure." Kirsty gulped and wiped a damp hand across her blouse. "Damn woman always has to go for the grand slam."

"It's a gamble, Kirsty," Hamish replied. "But think of the alternative."

"Yeah sure," Kirsty whispered. "I hope my otherself has a good life.

The wagon stopped and there was no more time for talk. Kirsty swung herself down like a gymnast, held her bow up and walked along the middle of the road with her head high. On the side she knew her friends watched, across the road were a blur of Mud warriors and in front Madison approached.

Nothing was said but when the Kirsty reached her friend they turned shoulder to shoulder and faced the incoming warriors.

The Mud walked right up to them but the closest four hesitated when both Kirsty and Madison moved their bows up ever so slightly.

Another Mud warrior came through the four. He was dressed similar to Thinrisodor and appeared to be a chief. His eyes bore into Kirsty. She stared back but her mind was spinning. Why was the guy concentrating on her right eye ... Oh hell that was her blackened one. Would that be regarded as a sign of weakness?

"Who dared to attack the Second Maiden?" the chief said in perfect English.

"He is dead," Kirsty replied without moving her eyes from the man. "The Maiden of Granite killed him for daring to attack me."

" A slow death I hope," the chief replied.

"We believe he suffered," Kirsty said and hoped she had made the correct response.

"Good." The chief switched his eyes to Madison.

*

"The people from the stars have no home on this world," the Mud chief said. "It has been torn away stone by stone. Within three winters all evidence of their home shall return to the dust of the plains."

"We have come for those left behind," Madison said.

"Thinrisodor said that would happen," the man replied. "Is it your desire that the outworlders are not returned to the dust of the plains?"

"They are innocent victims just like Fyddal and Drety who travel with us. Not all outworlders are evil."

"Many of us remember their deeds and do not agree with Thinrisodor. I am without opinion but shall abide by both your wishes. Go into the town to where the wide road is empty. Thinrisodor waits with the outworlders. The truce finishes when the sun touches the western hills."

"So be it." Madison replied.

The chief flicked his eyes across to Kirsty and back. "I hope the snake who attacked the Second Maiden wasn't an outworlder."

"No," Madison replied in complete honesty. "He was a newcomer."

The chief nodded and waved a hand. The warriors beside him stepped back and held their spears up high. "Go in peace until the sun sets in the west, Maiden of Granite, Second Maiden."

He stepped away and the tribe disappeared into the grasslands around.

"Oh damn," Kirsty gasped. "I can't take much more of this."

"Go in peace Second Maiden." Madison chuckled. "Perhaps your black eye and swollen lip helped that chief make up his mind to let us through."

"Yeah but I still feel like a pawn in a game of chess."

*

Smoke hung over the shallow valley as the wagon train made its way through thousands of Mud warriors towards the alien base. The tribe walking along the roadside appeared different again from those previously encountered but the warriors moved aside and ignored the oxen and wagons.

"It's gone," Drety gasped and grabbed her partner's arm. "The whole base is gone!"

Madison could see what Drety meant. Stretching out along the valley was a runway with a rectangle of roads to one side. But that was all. Where there had once been buildings, were now row after row of smouldering rubble. Burned out hulks of vehicles, debris, and fallen aerials covered the roads while a row of trees were snapped like matchsticks.

"They used ray guns to pulverize everything," Fyddal said. "Look at those trees."

"But where is everyone?" Madison asked.

"Down by the river," Fyddal replied

At the far end of the runway the river curved in and out again like a gigantic U with the curve at the edge of the base. The jetty and buildings had gone and what would have been a boat was sunk off shore. Further along from this was an open space, perhaps a sports field. It was filled with people who, from this distance, appeared to be just sitting in silence around another group standing in the centre of the field.

Fyddal brought up a pair of binoculars and stared at the scene. "It looks bad," he muttered and handed the instrument onto Madison.

She focused on the scene. The Mud warriors were all sitting cross-legged with their spears beside them. The people standing were all aliens. They stood in a circle in pairs lashed together back to back. Each pair had a long rope linked through their arms to the next pair like one human chain. Only one Mud warrior stood in front of this circle with his spear stuck in the ground. He turned and Madison focused on his face.

"Thinrisodor!" she gasped. "He's waiting for us."

*

They reached the sports field twenty minutes later but the sitting Mud blocked the way. Nothing else had changed. Thinrisodor and the aliens still stood in the centre but the expressions on the prisoners' faces came into focus. Some looked up at them with relief or even surprise but the rest just appeared exhausted. Some bit on their lips or just gazed at the ground while others appeared to be trying to remain standing.

Madison handed her reins to Fyddal. "Just keep the oxen going straight ahead," she said. She stood up but left her bow and arrow out of sight by her feet.

As Olive, Twinkle, Thelma and Florence plodded on, the closest Mud slid back on their bottoms without standing. They reached Thinrisodor and Madison climbed down.

"Why are Drety and Fyddal's people tied together like animals, Thinrisodor?" she asked.

"The cleansing," he replied. "If you had not arrived by sunset each pair would have been pierced by one spear and had their throats cut."

"That's barbaric. I thought better of you, Thinrisodor."

"I am but one of twenty. My sway gave us the daylight hours. If you are not back into Sumatti or Sneednim territory by sunset, I cannot help you. Cannad's people have guaranteed your free passage but this land here is hostile after sunset."

"So we get there," Madison whispered. "Can you untie the prisoners so they can climb aboard?"

Thinrisodor shook his head. "No, but we can lift them aboard your wagons. Don't untie them until you are away from this base."

Madison nodded but never asked why. Thinrisodor raised a finger and fifty or more warriors stood. They lifted each pair of terrified aliens into the wagons until everyone; fifty-two altogether, for Madison had counted them, were aboard.

"Will Sakita-mura be safe?" she asked after she climbed aboard.

"It is Sneednim land," Thinrisodor replied.

"Thank you, Thinrisodor. When we are home in Buckoway you will be a welcomed guest."

The Mud chief nodded and stepped back.

"Go girls!" Madison shouted and shook her reins. The four oxen moved forward back through the sitting crowd, out onto the road and back the way they'd come.

*

Once they were back over the hills and on the plains Madison called a brief halt and made her way through the aliens. They were by now untied and a little colour had returned to anxious faces. Drety and Fyddal knew most of them personally and introduced Madison. Hands were shaken and names forgotten but the gratitude showed in everyone she spoke to. After a quick meal and drink the wagon train started off on its slow journey back while the sun headed far too quickly down the western sky.

Risa swapped places with Drety and sat with Madison in the front wagon. "We won't make it home before dark," she whispered.

"No but we'll have a couple of hours grace."

"How come?"

"If any tribes decide to follow us they will not leave until sunset. Their honour system can be relied on. However, once the time is up we are fair game." Madison frowned. "Of course if they run they could catch up to us within an hour."

"So we need to be home by about eight thirty?"

"Or in Sneednim territory?"

Risa grimaced. "I have no idea where their lands start. Out here on the plains there is no logical demarcation line." She stared at Madison. "Would we make better time if we leave the oxen and walk?"

"No. We'd tire whereas the oxen just keep going. I know they don't go much faster than at a walking pace but this wagon train is our only security if the Mud catch up."

Risa shuddered. "This is what happened the first time when I was caught," she whispered. "I'm scared, Madison. If they catch us, not even your reputation will help."

"I know," Madison replied. "I don't even think Thinrisodor will save us this time."

*

By eight thirty it was dark. Even the sky above was black as cloud cover hid the stars. Nothing showed anywhere and Madison relied on her four faithful oxen to follow the road The beasts' eyes must have been good for the thin strip of bare dirt seemed to unroll beneath them like a roller.

Hamish came up and climbed into the wagon beside Madison. "Would you like me to drop back and guard our rear?" he asked.

Madison shook her head. "Five minutes warning won't really help and you could get lost or attacked. If that happened there is no way we could find you."

Hamish nodded. "I'll take over the driving here, then."

Madison smiled. "Thank you but no. I need to keep alert. If I relax I'll fall asleep and will be of no help until morning."

" And how long can you stay awake?" Hamish asked.

"Three or four hours. I stayed awake until midnight once."

"But not after everything you've done today."

"I guess," Madison said. "Perhaps you could stay here and help Risa if I suddenly fall asleep. That's if your own wagon is okay."

"It is. Sean is there now and a couple of the aliens have worked with oxen. We have plenty of good drivers."

"So don't fret, Madison," Risa cut in. "If you fall asleep we'll look after you."

"I know," Madison whispered. "But I will be a burden rather than an asset."

"You are never be a burden, Madison," Hamish said. "Whatever happens tonight, you never will be."

*

By ten, Madison could barely keep her eyes open. The animals and road were no different and the monotony was gripping her. It was as if they had not moved or the oxen had wandered around in a gigantic circle. Hamish and Risa both talked non-stop and Madison knew they were helping to keep her awake.

Her head nodded and that warm cosy feeling of home engulfed her. But it was home on Earth. She could even feel the sheets tucked around her neck and hear Norris snoring softly beside her. No, she had to stay awake until she was sure they were safe.

A whistle pierced the night air and she jerked awake to find herself still in the driver's seat.

"That's Kirsty's whistle," Hamish said. "I'll drop back and see what she wants."

"Are you still with us, Madison," Risa added.

"Yes but I don't think it will be for long. What did Hamish say?"

"Kirsty blew her warning whistle. He's gone back to se what's wrong."

Hamish returned mere moments later. "Look behind, Madison," he said.

She glanced around the side of the canvas and gasped. In the distance behind them flickering lights stretched across the dark horizon.

"The Mud are on their way and prepared for battle," Hamish said. "The lights are to tell us that."

"How far have we got to go, Risa?" Madison asked.

"Probably half an hour if the oxen have travelled at the same speed as on the journey out."

"They're tired and have slowed," Hamish said. "They need to rest."

"So we won't get back before the Mud reach us?"

Hamish shook his head. "No chance."

"Then we'll stop and put the wagons in a circle. It will be a poor defence but will be better than remaining in a straight line." She looked intently at Hamish and then Risa. " I'll get help," she added.

258

"How, Lass," Hamish replied.

"From Earth," Madison said. She sort of jerked once and fell asleep.

*

CHAPTER TWENTY-NINE

As soon as she awoke Madison was out of bed and across the corridor to where Knoge was asleep in the spare room.

"Wake up, Knoge," she cried. "You're the only one who can help!"

Knoge opened his eyes and blinked in the light Kirsty had switched on.

"The surveillance satellites above Quargis would attack my ship if I tried to orbit the planet," Knoge said after he heard about the wagon train's desperate situation. "We wouldn't get through."

"You have to do something. There's no time!"

Knoge sat up and smiled. "Now, that is something you don't have to worry about, Madison. As long as you stay awake the time we use up here will make no difference to that on Quargis. "

"Of course," Madison muttered. "But what happens when I go back to sleep."

"One of two things."

"Two?"

"Either you'll wake up at your usual time in the morning back there or you'll just wake up here."

"Meaning?"

"That would happen if your otherself was killed."

"Oh hell!" Madison bit on her lip and sat down on a chair behind her. "So you can do nothing?"

"I didn't say that," Knoge replied. "Just give me a moment to think about it. Now, why don't you have a hot shower and get dressed. Then we could have breakfast."

Madison flushed when she realized she was only dressed in flimsy pyjamas. "And we could call the hospital to see how Ajiei and your son are," she said.

"I'd like that," Knoge said.

*

Twenty minutes later, Knoge sat at the breakfast table and sipped his coffee. "What a wonderful breakfast. You're an excellent cook, Madison."

"Kirsty did it," Madison muttered but looked impatient.

"If we can find where your wagon train is on the plains we can set up something in that exact space to protect it."

"How? You said you couldn't go to Quargis."

"Not now but the planet was only discovered thirty years ago. Before that, only the Mud were there."

"So?"

"We go back and visit it about thirty years ago before any surveillance satellites were put into orbit there."

"You can do that?"

"Yes, but it can be dangerous. If we do something wrong, say introduce a hostile bacteria we could alter the whole planet's future and kill your otherselves before you were even created."

"What's your plan, then?"

"We go to the exact place where your wagon train will be and leave something there for you to find."

"After thirty years?" Kirsty said.

"We can seal it in a natural looking item like a rock and make it so only Kirsty or Norris can access it."

"Why not Madison?" Norris asked.

"In black hole travel, the crew lose consciousness and wake up again on the other side. In Madison's case that would jump her forward to the next morning on Quargis and defeat the purpose in going. She has to stay here." Knoge stared at Norris. "However, you or Kirsty will need to come with me."

"I'll go," Kirsty immediately responded. "What do you want me to do?"

"Can we both come?" Norris asked in a more cautious voice while Madison just sat back and felt miserable.

"I have a very important job for you too Madison." Knoge said.

"I'm glad," she replied. "What do I do?"

"Go and bring my family home. Ajiei will need lots of help buying supplies. We have plenty of money but she has no idea where to go or what is needed for our son. Also you can drive us to the airport."

Madison broke into a smile. "It's a deal," she whispered.

*

The 767 flew north from Sacramento and it's image on local radar continued on until it was out of range. However, it never appeared on the northern screen but neither operator realized one aeroplane was missing. Meanwhile it circled straight up and hyperdrive engines launched it into space to rendezvous with a waiting starship. Again, sophisticated equipment hid everything from radar screens on the surface.

"Oh damn," Kirsty gasped as she floated through an airlock between the two spaceships. "Will I be floating the whole way?"

"No," Knoge replied. "Once we've brought the 767 inside we start spinning. An artificial gravity is formed and you will be able to walk around just like at home."

"What happens now?" a more pragmatic Norris asked.

"We use our equipment to trace exactly where Madison's wagon train is on Quargis. This will be entered into our computer so we know where to go. Afterwards, we lie in life pods and go to sleep. There will be a slight feeling of disorientation but it isn't too bad."

Kirsty and Norris watched fascinated at the monitors and equipment while Knoge worked. Fifteen minutes later he pointed to a monitor that showed a planet not unlike Earth.

"Quargis," he said. "Buckoway and the plains the wagon train is on is that long continent you can see at the edge of the darkness. The area is north of the equator. My colleagues chose a temperate zone with weather conditions not unlike California where you come from."

He waved his hand over a ball and the pictured zoomed into the dark zone. Everything looked black until Knoge made more adjustments and the area turned a green colour. "Night vision," he said and focused in closer.

"Oh damn," Kirsty gasped. She could see the wagon train looking like toys on a vast plain.

"And that line of flickering lights would be the Mud closing in?" Norris said.

"Yes. They're about ten kilometres away so your otherself will have an hour or so to get everything set up." Knoge smiled. "Okay. We need to go now. Next time you see this view it will be thirty two years ago but over the same place."

Kirsty caught Norris's eyes. "I'm ready," she whispered.

*

To Kirsty the landing craft they flew to the surface of Quargis in was like a metallic spider. It had no wheels but landed on eight legs. Knoge moved it forward by using the legs to walk wherever he wanted to go and later made the machine squat down. He opened a door and they walked out into a warm afternoon.

Kirsty gazed around. She stood in knee high grass that disappeared in every direction. To the south was a line of low hills while north just showed the sky touch the horizon. She could smell hot grass and a sweet scent of flowers.

"How do you know we're in the exact spot?" she asked Knoge who towered up beside her.

"We are," he replied.

He took an instrument like a cellphonefrom his pocket and pressed a couple of keys. A door at the top of the landing craft slid open and one of the spider legs became a crane. It reached in with claw like hands, brought out a large slab of rock and placed it on the ground. Knoge handed Norris a very ordinary looking spade and said. "Just dig a shallow hole to place it in."

"Sure," Norris said. He dug into the hard ground and managed to scoop out enough soil to hold the artificial stone.

Knoge mixed up some chemicals and poured it into the hole Norris created.

"Concrete," he said when Kirsty asked. "We don't want it rolling away over the next thirty years do we?"

"Like our concrete at home?" Kirsty asked.

"Probably. Chemicals are the same throughout the universe."

The stone was surprisingly heavy but the three managed to lift it onto the concrete, Knoge added several drips of a liquid from a flask and the concrete immediately solidified.

"Shove a bit of dirt around it, Norris. Within a couple of weeks even if Mud warriors come by they'll see nothing except a shiny rock."

"And after thirty years it won't look so shiny," Kirsty said.

"Exactly," Knoge said. "Now we set it to be voice or hand activated by either of you. That's the reason you had to be here. Your otherselves are the only ones who will be able to open the doors. If anyone over the next thirty years touches it they will find it is just an ordinary rock. The chances of anyone even noticing it in this vast plain is pretty remote, anyway."

"What about electronic surveillance?" Norris asked. "Couldn't those satellites trace it once they're in orbit."

"No," Knoge replied. "It will be dormant until one of you activates it. Only a small solar panel will operate to recharge interior batteries." He pointed to a dark marble like slither down the southern side of the rock. "That's the solar panel."

"And the equipment inside?" Kirsty asked.

"It will be ready. All they do is follow the instructions you'll give them and turn it on."

"To save our otherselves from the Mud in thirty-two years," Kirsty whispered. "I wish I could be here."

"You will be sort of," Norris said and turned to Knoge. "Could you leave one of those communication balls, too then Madison and the others could call us up like they did that last time?"

Knoge grinned. "Okay," he said. "I'll get one from out of the landing craft."

*

Back in the Sacramento apartment that afternoon Madison sat holding Brorel, Knoge and Ajiei's newly named baby on her knee. She listened to Kirsty's very lengthy description of everything, Knoge's more precise explanation and Norris's additions.

"There's one problem," she said when they had all finished.

"Oh," Knoge said. "I thought we'd covered everything."

"By the time I wake up there it will be 6.30 in the morning and too late. You said the Mud were only an hour away. Wouldn't they arrive at the wagon train sometime in the middle of the night."

"True," Knoge said. He reached into one of his pockets and brought out a very mean looking hypodermic syringe. "An injection of this will give you a burst of adrenaline that will knock you out cold here but wake you up mere seconds after you nodded off in the wagon."

Madison paled. "Okay," she said. "I wish there was a better way of going back and forth, though."

"I may have one the next time I return here," Knoge said.

"You're coming back?" Kirsty asked.

"Of course." Ajiei laughed. "How else will we be able to show Brorel where he was born?"

"So let's do it," Madison said. She gave the baby a cuddle, handed him back to his mother and held out her arm.

*

"Hi Risa," Madison said.

Risa jumped in fright. "Madison! I thought you'd fallen asleep."

"I had but decided you guys needed my help and care. Do you see a large rock in the middle of our wagon circle?"

264

Risa peered out. "There's no rock there." She stopped and stared again. "There is one! I can't remember seeing it before. Did you make the wagons circle around it on purpose?"

"Well sort of," Madison glanced at Hamish who was staring at the rock while tugging on his beard. "What's wrong, Hamish?"

"That rock. It wasn't there before you woke up then I blinked and there it was. "

"Of course it was there," Risa said. "I saw it."

"When?" Hamish asked.

Risa shrugged. "Before," she said.

Hamish glowered and turned to Madison. "And you're awake? It's tied in, isn't it Lass?"

"Get Kirsty and Norris and I'll explain," Madison said.

*

"Now you place your hand on the rock and say 'This is Kirsty's voice activation.' Okay?" Madison said to her friend a few moments later.

Kirsty frowned. "I feel stupid."

"That's better than being dead," Norris said. "I'll do it, if you like."

"No, I will." Kirsty placed both hands on the moss-covered rock and said the words. There was a slight squeak and the whole side of the rock tipped forward to reveal a set of shelves filled with plastic boxes and a few other items.

 Even Madison looked excited as she took out one box and opened it. Inside was a glass dome on top of a clip. "Right, first we have to put our wagons back in a line then place one of these on the top of each wagon just above the driver's seat," she said to the crowd around. As well as her friends all the aliens had come to see this momentous event. "The fifth one goes at the back of the last wagon and we need to attach the last one to my front oxen somehow."

"I'll do it," Hamish said.

Sean interrupted. "You'd better hurry, Madison. Someone's out there watching us, that's for sure."

Madison grabbed the boxes and handed them out, reached for the remaining things and shut the door. It clicked and object became the rock again that had sat there for thirty-two years.

"One final thing," she said. "We need to turn them all on at the same time. I'll blow Kirsty's whistle when I want it done. Okay?"

"Right get aboard everyone," Hamish shouted. "Let's go!"

*

Three shadowy figures watched while the people in the wagon train swarmed aboard the wagons. Madison yelled a command and her wagon began to move back onto the road. The others followed until the four wagons were in line and facing the direction of Sakita-mura.

A whistle blew, six dull blue lights came on and the oxen began to move forward. The shadowy figures became a dozen then twenty or more. Within moments fifty Mud warriors followed the slow moving wagon train.

It was time! The chief, someone unknown to those on the wagon stood up and held his spear high. "The treaty is over! Our ancestors shall be revenged," he screamed in English. "Glorious honour goes to the warrior who brings down the Maiden of Granite."

Thirty spears curved up into the air and headed for Madison whose blouse almost shone in the dim light.

But none reached her! Every spear bounced off the very air before her and plopped onto the ground. Not only that but the dull blue lights began to brighten. A hiss like that of a trapped snake echoed through the still air.

The Mud stood their ground but their eyes showed sheer terror.

"It is a trick!" the chief shouted. He grabbed another spear from a holster on his back and flung it at Madison. This time, though, the spear didn't bounce away. It just melted into nothingness. A beam shot from the light above the front wagon and the chief screamed in agony as a thousand volts of electricity hit his chest.

He collapsed on the ground, still alive but with burn marks on his chest and under his right foot where the electricity had earthed itself.

The Mud warriors stared at their chief and back at Madison on the wagon. She turned, lifted a bow in her right hand and stood up. That was too much! As one, the Mud warriors turned and ran, all discipline and honour gone. The unconscious chief was left lying on the grass as the sixteen oxen and four wagons trudged on by.

"Hell," Kirsty muttered from the rear wagon as she gazed at the man on the ground. "What was it?"

"Modern technology verses superstitious minds," Norris replied from beside her. "I doubt if any more Mud will annoy us tonight."

"And we were saved by our otherselves," Kirsty whispered. "It makes me feel humble, somehow."

In a tiny hour before dawn, four Sakita-mura guardsmen on horses met the wagon train and escorted it the last couple of kilometres back to the

266

village. Only Madison never noticed. She was fast asleep in the front wagon with her head on Hamish's shoulders.

*

One month made an enormous difference to the citizens of Buckoway. It could now be called an inter-species society with one whole block occupied by the Silvers, as the aliens had become known. With only a few exceptions, the aliens had settled into and had been accepted by the citizens of Buckoway. There was also a small contingent of Japanese citizens who had moved into town. With a permanent peace cemented with the Sumatti and Sneednim tribes the road to Sakita-mura was safe to travel through so the majority of Risa's people stayed in their home village. They fished the river and one of the highlights of the Buckoway Thursday market was the wagon that had arrived at dawn from Sakita-mura with fresh fish and other delicacies to sell.

Mud warriors, women and children wandered through the town especially when the marble concourse that covered the space left by Buckoway Castle became the weekly market place.

Communication through two black holes had been established. However, for security reasons it had been decided to keep knowledge of this access restricted to Madison and her friends. Back in Sacramento even Colonel Brad Davis was ignorant of this connection between the galaxies. On Earth 4, Knoge and Ajiei had confided in a small circle of friends about this human outpost on Quargis and maintained contact. The other aliens had not returned but their satellites still orbited the planet and prevented Knoge's spacecraft from coming. He did say that scientists were working on a way to destroy these satellites and it was only a matter of time before Earth 4 astronauts could visit.

In the meantime, all the information to help the Silvers become fertile again was transmitted to Buckoway and Drety and Fyddal were among the first to participate in the programme.

*

"So how's the diet going?" Madison asked Drety. It was afternoon coffee break in the new fifth floor apartment that Drety and Fyddal had shifted into.

Drety screwed her nose up. "The herbal diet is yuck and whoever said the regular injections are painless is a liar." She smiled. "There is one thing better than when Ajiei went through the procedure, though."

267

"And what's that?"

"The Earth 4 scientists have refined the procedures. It only takes three weeks now."

"Drety, that's wonderful. I noticed all the Silvers at the clinic. How many are taking the treatment?"

"Just about everyone we rescued." Drety grinned. "I think Buckoway is going to have a second baby boom next year."

"Yeah but the newcomers becoming pregnant has dropped right away since they are able to decide what they want for themselves."

Drety laughed. "But there are Mud kids everywhere. Aren't they cute?"

Madison laughed. "Did you know Thinrisodor has fifteen children and he is going to enrol all the older ones at our school?"

"Fifteen? Oh his poor wife."

"Wives, Drety. He has at least five."

Drety flushed. "Of course. There are still a lot of differences between the species aren't there?"

Madison nodded. "There are but who are we to impose our values onto them? That caused hundreds of years of wars on my home planet." She screwed her noise up. "It still is."

"And my peoples are worse," Drety whispered.

"But with luck Quargis will be different. Sure, there are only two Mud tribes that have joined us but with Sakita-mura, Buckoway and the dozen or more Sumatti and Sneednim villages involved, we will soon have a fully functional country in operation."

"And are you going to accept the nomination to run as Buckoway's senator in the new parliament?"

Madison sighed. "I don't know. There are many far more experienced people here than me."

"But everyone wants you, Madison? I reckon all my people and most of the younger newcomers would vote for you."

"I'll see," Madison said. "It's not happening until next year so there's plenty of time." She grinned. "In the meantime I just love being a wagonmistress."

*

268

CHAPTER THIRTY

After Knoge, Ajiei and Brorel went home and Kirsty had stopped talking about her wonderful journey through space, life in Sacramento became an anticlimax. Almost in spit of Colonel Brad Davis, Madison enjoyed her position as Manager of Personnel Resources and found that working with staff complimented her life on Quargis well.

She was at her desk reading a pile of job applications she had to shortlist when there was a knock on the office door. This was unusual as she always expected those working with her to walk straight in.

"Come in," she called and moved all the applications and accompanying paraphernalia into a drawer so her desk looked tidy.

Doctor Joel Mitchell and a tall thin stranger walked in.

"Doctor Mitchell. How are you?" she said and moved her eyes to the stranger. "And a visitor from Pynoto. I am honoured."

Joel smiled. "I told Jawin you'd recognize his species straight away. This is Doctor Jawin Osrol, one of the original scientists who discovered how to transfer minds between bodies."

Madison frowned "Indeed," she whispered "Am I one of your successes or failures, Doctor Osrol?"

The man just stood and smiled slightly.

"Please, sit down both of you," Madison continued in a more relaxed tone. "Can I offer you both a coffee?"

Madison's assistant had coffee and cookies in there on a tray within moments and glanced at their visitors. "I'll hold all calls if you wish, Madison," she said.

"Thanks Carol. Perhaps you could get my ten thirty appointment postponed too, please."

"Will do," the woman said and left the office.

"So what life do you like best?" Jawin asked. "You appear to be well liked and successful on both planets."

Madison hesitated and ran a tongue over dry lips. "This is not a social occasion so could you get to the point of this visit, please," she said.

Joel nodded at the visitor as if to say, 'I told you so' and turned to Madison. "Your friend Knoge contacted Doctor Osrol and explained your predicament. We can alter the chemical structure of your blood and brain cells so you don't have to be asleep in one world in order to operate in the other. "

"I'm used to it," Madison said. "I don't really want to be cut off from my otherself, like Norris, Kirsty and the others are." Her eyes bore into the alien. "I don't want to choose between my two existences. There is a downside of course but..."

"Like the times you needed to stay awake and felt you were a burden to your friends?" Osrol asked.

"There were only a couple of times."

"I can make it so you can move between your two selves anytime you wish, both Madison Evans can be awake or indeed be asleep in the same instant."

"But how?" Madison asked. She sat her coffee on the desk and again stared into the man's eyes.

"Basically, you are two people with two minds, Madison. What you share are your memories, thoughts, emotions and everything else a brain does to make the body it is enclosed in function."

"Okay, I know that but how can I be sitting here studying job applications and driving my wagon train right now?" She opened her hands wide to emphasize her point.

"Well, you wouldn't. Not really."

"So I'd just be like Kirsty here and Kirsty at Buckoway?"

"Wrong again."

"Oh hell, I give up. You explain and I'll listen."

"Let's make a scenario of that time you were being chased by the Mud when you were trying to stay awake before you reached Sakita-mura," Doctor Osrol said. "Under my new system you could say a code and fall asleep while driving the wagon. Let's say ten minutes later the Mud warriors arrive. Hamish would give you a dig in the ribs and you'd wake up like any ordinary human. At the same time you'd already be awake here on Earth having your breakfast."

"Who'd be thinking?" Madison asked.

"Both of you would continue throughout the day until one of your two selves goes to sleep that night, let's say it was you in Quargis. Once asleep, all the memories of the day would be transmitted to your otherself. You could be in this very office and feel a sort of shudder. The day's memories from Quargis would flood into your mind. When you go to sleep that night, you'd wake up in Quargis with both memories intact."

"It sounds complicated," Madison muttered. "Wouldn't I become disorientated? I wouldn't know where I was."

"Built in safety procedures would prevent it. Again, let's hypothesise you were driving home and had to concentrate because some idiot had just cut across in front of you. Your concentration would be on avoiding an accident and your blood pressure would be high. In that case the information just received from your otherself would be held in your subconscious until the emergency is over."

"It's an interesting theory," Madison said. "However, I don't really want to be another experiment for your species, Doctor Osrol. I learned to cope with my present situation. Let's leave it like that, shall we?"

"It's not a theory, Madison. We have five operatives on Earth 1 using this duel body system, as we call it, quite successfully right now."

"You mean spies?"

Osrol nodded. "There are still enormous problems in that society. They've moved from Earth here and Quargis but are trying similar methods on the new planet they've discovered. Also, all the latest evidence shows that Earth 1 will be unable to sustain any life, animal or plant with five years."

"So help them," Madison snapped.

"They are militant and arrogant, Madison. One day, they may seek our help or perhaps, through their own stupidity their race may die out."

"Or they may assimilate another human society."

"Possibly but we also have contact with this new planet and have been able to prevent those electronic bees from operating." Osrol sighed. "It's somewhat of a stalemate at the moment."

"But the system is operating, Madison. It is not just an experiment." Joel Mitchell said. "You will also be able to contact your otherself at any time."

"Okay, so what do I do?"

"Two things," Jawin Osrol said. "There will be another blood transfusion and a brain implant."

"To me here?"

"Both of your bodies require them."

"Well, we can't do it then," Madison said. "Knoge said you still can't reach Quargis because of the surveillance satellites."

Jawin smiled. "If you go down the main road about a hundred metres from the Buckoway main gate you'll see a large bolder. It'll probably be covered in shrubs by now. Inside you will find five litres of your blood and the implant device. All instructions can be transmitted to your Buckoway doctor."

"Another thirty year old landing?"

"Yes."

"So my blood has been sitting there for thirty years. Won't it be a little old?"

"No, it's deep frozen in a refrigerated canister. Its life span would be at least another decade."

"Oh hell, you've thought of everything, haven't you?"

The alien doctor nodded. "It is only one of three options, you know."

"Three?"

"Yes, you can do nothing and remain exactly how you are, be split into two people like your friends or take this new treatment. Would you like to think about it or talk to your friends before you make a decision? There's really no hurry."

Madison nodded. "Yes, I would, thank you. I think it would only be fair to talk to Norris, Kirsty and the others. Their opinion is important to me."

"Good. If you tell Doctor Mitchell of your decision he can contact me. Your reputation is well known on my home planet and I am pleased to have finally met you. Good-bye for now." Doctor Jawin Osrol stood, shook Madison's hand and left the office.

"And what do you really recommend, Joel?" Madison asked when the pair were alone.

"He sounds genuine but contact your alien friends both here and on Quargis for their opinions."

"And if they say it's okay."

"I'd do it, Madison," Joel replied. "That's my advice as a doctor and a friend."

*

"Kirsty." Madison said to her friend back at Buckoway. "How'd you like to come for a walk out the main gate?"

"Now?" the sleepy girl replied. "Just because you wake up every day at six thirty, we don't all have to get up."

"I'll come," Risa said from the other bunk. "It must be important."

"I'm curious, that's all," Madison said.

"Good. Tell me about it when you return," Kirsty muttered. She fluffed up her pillow, rolled over and shut her eyes.

"Meanie," Risa said. "If you didn't drink so much at that party last night you wouldn't have a hangover now."

Kirsty's eyes shot open and she flung herself back over. "You're the one who bought those bottles of rice wine," she yelled.

"You were meant to sip it, not gulp it down like coffee."

"Forget about it," Madison muttered. "I'll go by myself."

She dressed and grabbed a coat for there was rain hitting the windowpanes. However by the time she'd walked out onto the wet footpath both her friends accompanied her. The three splashed through the puddles in silence until they reached the ring road.

"Okay," Kirsty said. "What did you find out from your otherself?"

"There's a canister waiting for me."

Kirsty stared at Risa, shrugged but said nothing. The main gate was open as usual and two border guards grinned as the three attractive women walked by.

"Hi Kirsty," one said. "How's the head?"

Kirsty glowered and ignored him but Risa dug Madison in the ribs. "Wasn't that the guy Kirsty said was just so cool last night?"

"Yeah, until I found he had a partner and two kids," Kirsty retorted. "Men with a family should all be locked up in their apartments and made to look after the kids while their partners go out and enjoy themselves."

Madison grinned and pulled her collar up. It was still quite dark but overhead floodlights lit the wet road up like an orange mirror.

"What're you looking for?" Risa asked.

"An old rock, one that is thirty two years old actually."

"What?" Kirsty gasped. "Not another force field thingie left by your starship?"

"No. Something for me."

Risa stared around, saw something in the bushes and ran ahead. The others followed as she pushed through the undergrowth. Water showered over them as they pushed through and saw a rock poking out of the creeper. This rock was completely covered in moss and even had weeds growing through cracks in the surface.

"This could be it." Madison said and placed her hand on it. "Please check my voice pattern," she said.

Rather than opening like a cupboard this rock split open down the middle like a shellfish. Inside were several layers of insulation and a sealed cylinder.

"What's in it?" Kirsty gasped as Madison lifted the cylinder out.

"My blood," Madison replied. "I've decided to become a vampire."

Kirsty pouted and Risa grinned.

Just as they were about to walk back out onto the road Risa grabbed Madison arm. "Hear that?" she said.

All three stopped walking and listened. Madison could hear the rain hitting branches above and water dripping down. In the distance a cow mooed. All the sounds were natural enough. She frowned and was about to speak when she heard it. A little further up the bank someone was trying to suppress a sob.

"Whoever you are, come out!" Madison called.

The sobbing stopped but she heard some twigs break. Whoever it was, was trying to sneak away to their right. Kirsty sprung forward and dived through the trees. There was a scream and Kirsty's curse, followed by a great deal of crashing and yelling.

"Shall we help?" Risa asked.

"Nah. Kirsty has it well in hand," Madison replied.

They stood and waited. The blonde girl appeared carrying a screaming, kicking, saturated boy of about eight. He appeared terrified.

"The little imp," Kirsty gasped. "He tried to bite me."

She plunked the child down but still held him tightly.

Madison squatted down and faced the boy. "It's okay," she said. "We aren't going to hurt you."

The boy stared at her and stopped struggling to get away from Kirsty. He shook his head and wiped a grubby hand over his face.

"You're all wet," Risa said. "What say we take you back to the guard house where it is dry and warm?"

The boy stared at her and burst into sobs.

"What is it, sweetheart?" Madison said.

The boy stared at her and spoke a rattle of sobbing words in a foreign language.

Kirsty stared at Risa who just shrugged. "It's not my language," she said.

"A Mug lingo?" Kirsty asked.

"No," Madison replied. "It's a language from my Earth. I've heard it before." She understood a little Spanish from high school days. This was different but had similarities. Oh hell, could it be Portuguese?

"He must be from another Earth village like yours, Risa. Remember Drety and Fyddal said there were other towns further down the river from Station Five?"

"But what's he doing here?"

"If he is from a village it would have been abandoned when the aliens pulled out. Perhaps they were trying to find us and were attacked by some of those more wild Mud tribes."

"But how can we find out if we can't speak each other's language," Kirsty asked.

"We'll manage," Madison said. "Now let him go, Kirsty. I doubt if he'll run away."

274

She reached out and took the little boy's hand. He glanced at her with large brown eyes and stood shivering when Kirsty let him go,

"Come on," Madison said. "We'll go home."

She lifted the boy into her arms and walked out onto the road. Kirsty followed. Risa smiled but remained where she was. "Madison," she called. "Do you want your cylinder?'"

Madison turned. "Oh hell, of course, Risa. I forgot about it."

Risa grinned and lifted the cylinder under an arm, noticed the rock was still open so gave it a shove with her foot. It slid shut with a solid clunk.

*

"Sound the general alarm," Madison said to the guard after they walked into the guardhouse with the little boy.

The youth, the same one that gave Kirsty cheek earlier, stared at the drenched child. "You must be joking," he retorted.

"I am a reserve in the Border Guard and outrank you, Corporal. Sound that alarm!"

The corporal stared at Madison 's stern expression and shrugged. "The big bosses are not going to like it," he said but pressed a red button on the wall.

Throughout Buckoway sirens wailed while the town gate slid shut. Within minutes, hundreds of reserves and those just plainly curious converged on the guardhouse and other assembly points. A very irate looking officer, unshaven and still half awake stormed into the room.

"What's the meaning of this?" he roared at the two guardsmen who snapped to attention. "If you think this is a joke I'll have you on double duty and half pay for a month."

"They were under my orders, Captain," Madison said from behind the man. "Regulations state that any foreign or alien beings within the environment of Buckoway mean that the general alarm must be sounded."

The officer swung around and saw the drenched boy shivering by three women in rain gear. "Him!" he snarled.

"No exceptions, Captain Hopkins." Madison read the man's name off his lapel while at the same time she removed the cape off her hair.

Hopkins recognized her at once. He quivered slightly and tried to look responsible. "Of course Miss Evans," he said. "What do you want done?"

"Sent patrols out. He wouldn't be here by himself, now would he?"

"It shall be done, Ma'am."

Hopkins proved to be an efficient officer so within moments three mounted patrols fanned out from Buckoway and a lady from social services arrived to care for the boy.

"So what do we do," Risa said when the activity died down and those not needed left the area.

Madison grinned. "We go home and have breakfast," she said.

*

Colonel Brad Davis walked into the hospital ward and approached the nurse. "Would it be possible to speak to your patient, nurse?" he asked.

The nurse glanced up at the military man in his crisp uniform. "Yes, go through, Colonel. Doctor Mitchell is with her now."

Madison still had a blood transfusion needle in her arm but looked bright and alert. "Hi Colonel Davis," she said. "How did the research go?"

"You were right, Madison. At around the same time as you were stung there was an invasion of bees in one of the upper class suburbs of Rio De Janeiro in Brazil. Over a period of three weeks several hundred people were stung. Most were about your age but there were several families where everyone including children were stung." He stopped and stared at Madison. "How are your Portuguese refugees at Buckoway doing, anyway?"

"Fine. The whole township of Santo Azul is shifting to Buckoway. Actually, they were in far worse condition than the Japanese at Sakita-mura. It'll be a bit crowded for a while but new apartments are being built."

"And that boy?"

"Their wagon train got stuck in the mud and he'd wandered off in the darkness. He saw the Buckoway lights and headed towards them. When he got to the wall he was too frightened to go in."

Davis nodded. "And there has been no more contact with those aliens we met at Edwards Air Force base?"

"None," Madison lied. "I think they stopped the bees and have left us to get on with our lives."

Davis stared at Madison's innocent blue eyes. "Okay, but keep in touch. I'd like a full report on your situation when you are on your feet again."

"Of course Brad," Madison said.

She caught Joel's eyes and winked. Both of them saw the colonel bristle at being called by his forename.

"So are you ready, Madison?" Joel asked a few moments later.

"Already?"

"You've had the transfusion and injections on the other side?"

276

"Sure. I've got a massive bruise on my arm there to prove it." She grinned. "Less sophisticated equipment, I guess."

"In theory you should stay awake but if anything goes wrong we'll do what we can."

Madison nodded. She could have just formed the code in her mind but used the system suggested by the doctor.

She fluttered her eyelids three times, three times again and twice more slowly while she said, "Mind Split There!" She lay back and stared at Joel. "It worked ... I think." she said.

*

Madison awoke and pressed the clock button beside her. The time was three ten in the morning. Kirsty and Risa were both asleep in the room.

"Wake up you lazy slobs," she yelled and turned the lights on.

Kirsty woke straight up and stared at the clock. "Oh hell, it's working. You're awake on the other side, too."

"I think so. I'll check." Madison fluttered her eyelids in a different pattern and gasped. She had split vision just as she'd been told. When she shut her left eye she was in the hospital bed with Doctor Mitchell and with the other eye closed she saw her two Buckoway friends.

*

"It works all right," she said to the doctor. "Talk about split vision." She shut one eye. "I'm glad it doesn't stay this way all the time. I'd go crazy."

Then flutter the next code, Madison."

She did and the vision of herself in Buckoway disappeared.

"How do you feel?" the doctor asked.

"A bit disorientated."

"That's only to be expected. Once you've used to it a while it'll become a natural thing to do. Are you up to the message part?"

"Sure. Why not?"

*

"It's all okay," Madison said. "I only see you guys now. I feel a bit dizzy, though."

"The doctor said you would," Kirsty said. Her eyes looked excited. "That means you can come out to our parties and not be scared of falling asleep."

"Kirsty," Risa scolded. "It's more important than that."

"Oh hell," Madison gasped. "The other works, too. A message has just come through from my otherself."

"And..." Kirsty gasped.

Madison stopped and sort of stared in space for a second.

"Go on," Kirsty almost yelled.

"She asked if you were being a pain and I said you were but I loved you anyway."

"Thanks Madison," Kirsty whispered.

The blonde girl threw the blankets aside and jumped to the floor. She grabbed both Madison and Risa, dragged them to their feet and hugged them close.

"Come on," she yelled. "Let's go and tell the others."

Epilogue

As dawn arrived, the captain of the border guard peered out over the battlements of Buckoway's surrounding wall. Thousands of Mud from both the Sumatti and Sneednim tribes assembled outside. They were gathered as far as any observers could see. The warriors carried no spears but instead helped the women with their babies   while younger men and the older generation waited patiently in the foggy air. Every part of the road that wound down the slight rise was filled with a mass of grey faces.

"We need to shut the town gates," the guard said to the sergeant beside him. "There are too many of them."

Madison who was also standing on the parapet spoke. "No Captain Osborne, we do the opposite."

Peter Osborne turned to Madison. "What do you mean Ma'am?" he asked.

"They are citizens and entitled to vote, Peter. We open the polling booths now instead of waiting until eight. That's what they're here for."

"We expected a few dozen Mud, not hundreds."

"Thousands Captain Osborne," Kirsty who stood beside Madison corrected. "Perhaps tens of thousands."

"We can't fit them in," the man muttered.

"We can and will," Madison said. Her chin stuck out in determination. "Open the polling booths now and I'll arrange for more to be set up.

"Okay, Miss Evans." Osborne turned to his sergeant. "We open the guardhouse booth in ten minutes. Is everyone ready?"

"They are Sir. Apart from the high turnout, it should go as planned."

"And here comes Thinrisodor," Kirsty cut in.

Below them the crowd parted as Thinrisodor walked up the road. He was followed by five women dressed in the now traditional white blouses and tartan skirts and a line of children ranging in age from late teens down to toddlers and babies carried in their mothers' arms.

"Who are they all?" Osborne asked.

"Thinrisodor has five wives and fifteen children." Kirsty's laugh was infectious. "I reckon they're all here."

"He's come to vote," Madison said. "I suggest we get those booths open."

*

After Thinrisodor and his family came out of the guardhouse the multitude of Mud filed in. They dipped their index fingers in special permanent ink and recorded their vote by placing a wet fingerprint on a ballot paper beside the photograph of their selected candidate. The cast votes were deposited in yellow boxes, the voters walked out to assemble around the ring road and proudly held their purple fingers up for all to see. Even babies had a purple finger on their parent's insistence and many ballot papers include a tiny fingerprint beside a larger parent's one.

All day, thousands of tribe members filed through, more ballot papers were printed and litres of ink manufactured. By seven in the evening still hundred still waited to vote so the booths remained open. At close to eleven in the floodlit main gate, the final Mud, a little old lady rumoured to be Thinrisodor's grandmother, walked into the guardhouse and stared at the exhausted attendants.

"I come to vote," she said in broken English. "My right."

"You certainly can, Madam," the polling clerk said. "Now if you will place your little finger in this bottle..."

"Young sir," the elderly lady said. "I know what to do."

She poked her finger in the bottle, grabbed a ballot sheet and plunked it on the table. She gazed down the column of twenty-eight photographs and stuck her finger by a name near the top, grinned and gave the paper to the clerk.

"You could have done it in private," the man said.

"Why?" The old lady murmured and ambled out with her ink stained finger held up for all to see.

*

Midnight slipped by and Madison stared glumly at the first election results posted on the massive notice board at the end of the largest assembly area in town. This was the black marble concourse that covered an area once occupied by the castle. It was now a market area and gathering point.

Hundreds of local citizens gathered under floodlights to watch the results of the first election ever held on the planet Quargis. It was to be called The Senate but in fact was more like a city council in California.

"Why are you so glum?" Kirsty said. "You're winning!"

"Yeah, but it's not what I wanted."

Kirsty chuckled but her next comment was interrupted

280

"Hear yea! Hear yea!" the town crier called. A hush fell over the crowd. "I have the unofficial final results of the election for fifteen senators for the township of Buckoway and the surrounding Sumatti and Surganni territories. The man stopped and unrolled an ancient looking scroll. "Abraham George, PVP, sixty one votes." There was a faint sigh. "Calso Kolberg, representing the Portuguese community, 342 votes..." A cheer went up from one section of the crowd. "Evans Madison, independent, 12 894 votes..."

A roar rose through the crowd and drowned out the rest of the crier's announcement. Dozens of bare breasted Sumatti girls in flowing yellow skirts ignored the chilly evening and broke out in a traditional dance around the embarrassed crier.

"Every Mud must have voted for you, Madison!" Kirsty screamed above the noise.

Madison screwed her nose up. "That's the trouble," she said. "They shouldn't have. That's not what a democracy is all about."

Hamish dug Madison in the ribs. "Aye but it's a start, Lassie."

"But they all voted the way Thinrisodor ordered."

"Possibly but it was you who said we shouldn't enforce our attitudes on the local tribes," Hamish added.

"It was, Madison," Drety said. "It was you who told me not to question about Thinrisodor having five wives. Remember?"

Madison grinned. "I did, didn't I Drety?" she said to her alien friend.

It took over five minutes before the jubilant crowd settled down enough for the town crier to complete his calling of the results. Madison listened intently and turned to Hamish. "Well it appears as if you've been elected too, Senator McLean," she said. "You probably got more newcomer votes than I did. Nine hundred and sixty three, wasn't it?"

Hamish grinned and tugged on his beard. "Doubt it, Senator Evans but we'll be a force to be reckoned with won't we, Lass?"

"And only one of the old stuff shirts got elected," Kirsty screamed. "Only one!"

Madison stared up to where the final results had just appeared on the notice board and smiled at her friend. The only organized party, The Progressive Values Party, who advocated quite stringent morality laws aimed covertly at the local tribes, had only succeeded in winning one seat. "Old Mariana will still manage to grumble away about a decadent society," she said referring to the one successful PVP candidate.

"Yeah, " Kirsty muttered. "Probably want your Mud votes to be declared null and void"

"Wouldn't do her any good," Hamish said.

"And why's that?" Madison asked.

"I heard that over fifty-five percent of the newcomers and an even larger proportion of the aliens also voted for you. Even without those ten thousand odd Mud votes you would have still won with ease."

"Oh hell," Madison muttered. "How can I keep up to everyone's expectations?"

The Japanese girl who stood quietly at the side of the circle of friends stepped forward and took Madison hands. "Just be yourself, Madison," she whispered. "That's all we want."

For the first time, Madison broke into a smile. "Thanks, Risa. I'll remember that."

She glanced around and found herself surrounded by well-wishers who came up to congratulate her. It was a proud time in Buckoway that night and everyone wanted to take part in the celebrations.

*

It was Saturday afternoon back in Sacramento, California. Madison sat in the sunshine on the patio of her apartment and sort of kept fluttering her eyelids.

"Oh hell, I hate it when this happens," Kirsty said as she kicked her shoes off and sat in a cane chair beside her.

"What?" Madison replied. She placed a paperback down and reached for the quarter-filled can of beer from a table beside her.

"You're so absorbed in your otherself you're just about in a trance here. I reckon your beer's even gone flat."

Madison grinned. "I'm sorry Kirsty. There was a hold up. It's after midnight there and I'm still up."

"So?"

"So what?"

"How did that Goddamn election go?"

Madison laughed and told Kirsty the full story. Afterwards she glanced around, and asked where Norris was.

"He's gone off with some of his friends to that basketball match," Kirsty snorted. "He did tell you, you know."

Madison nodded. "Of course. I remember now."

"And how's the other Norris getting on?" Kirsty asked.

"Not like here," Madison replied. "He's got a new girlfriend."

"Oh hell. When did that happen?"

"A few weeks back. Lucina de Brito, one of the Brazilian girls now at Buckoway, grabbed his attention." Madison rolled her eyes. "The Norris here is thrilled."

"Why?"

"He was jealous that his clone would make a pass at me."

"So what happens if some other guy on the other side comes onto you?"

"I won't tell him," Madison said. "After all, I feel more and more like two people all the time now. Sure my two halves share memories and emotions but I can go for days before either half of myself bothers to contact the other and exchange our thoughts."

"Weird," Kirsty said.

" 'Pose. It's better than passing out whenever my otherself wakes up. I guess I'm getting more and more like you and Kirsty over there." Madison grinned. "I like your hair cut short. She still has hers long so you don't even look alike so much now."

"And you? Are you still skinnier there?"

"No, not since I started going to the gym here, I'm fit in both places."

"Yeah. It's embarrassing." Kirsty ran a hand through her blonde hair and stuck her tummy out. "I'm always over weight."

"Oh Kirsty, you aren't." Madison stood up. "Anyway, let's go down to the mall. There's a sale at the Westside Boutique and new tops are half price."

"Are they?" Kirsty screamed. "Oh hell, why didn't you tell me?" She grabbed her shoes and headed for the door. "Well, are you coming?"

Madison laughed and followed her friend outside.

*

The End

www.ingramcontent.com/pod-product-compliance
Lightning Source LLC
Chambersburg PA
CBHW061551170626
46811CB00001B/160